PRAISE FOR

SIX
SECONDS

"Rick Mofina's breakout thriller.
It moves like a tornado."
—JAMES PATTERSON

"*Six Seconds* is a great read. Echoing Ludlum and
Forsythe, author Mofina has penned a big, solid
international thriller that grabs your gut – and your
heart – in the opening scenes and never lets go."
—JEFFERY DEAVER

"Classic virtues but tomorrow's subjects –
everything we need from a great thriller."
—LEE CHILD

"Mofina is one hell of a story-teller!
A great crime writer!"
—HÅKAN NESSER

"A perfect thriller, in every way. Very powerful and
very, very clever: this novel hits the ground running
and stays with you long past the finish line."
—NICK STONE

Rick Mofina is a former reporter and the award-winning author of several acclaimed thrillers. He's interviewed murderers on death row, patrolled with the LAPD and the RCMP and his true crime articles have appeared in the *New York Times*, *Marie Claire*, *Reader's Digest* and *Penthouse*. He's reported from the US, Canada, the Caribbean, Africa, Qatar and Kuwait's border with Iraq. He is based in Ottawa, Canada. For more information visit www.mirabooks.co.uk/rickmofina and for a chance to win free autographed books subscribe to Rick's free newsletter at www.rickmofina.com.

SIX
SECONDS

RICK MOFINA

Published in Great Britain 2009
MIRA Books, Eton House, 18-24 Paradise Road,
Richmond, Surrey, TW9 1SR

© Rick Mofina 2009

ISBN 978 0 7783 0289 6

58-0309

MIRA's policy is to use papers that are natural, renewable and recyclable products and made from wood grown in sustainable forests. The logging and manufacturing processes conform to the legal environmental regulations of the country of origin.

Printed and bound in Spain
by Litografía Rosés S.A., Barcelona

This book is for
Jeff Aghassi, Ann LaFarge, Mildred Marmur,
and
John Rosenberg and Jeannine Rosenberg.
Because no one gets through life without
the help of others.

*It is easy to go down into Hell; night and day,
the gates of dark Death stand wide; but to
climb back again, to retrace one's steps to the
upper air — there's the rub, the task.*

Aeneid
—Virgil

Prologue

The woman in the video is wearing a white shoulder-length hijab, embroidered with delicate beadwork. Her immaculate silk scarf frames her face, accentuating her natural beauty. She gives a tiny nod to the camera.

A soft cue is heard, then she begins.

"I am Samara. I am not a jihadist. I am a widow-mother baptized with the blood of my husband and my child when your governments murdered them."

Her strong, intelligent voice underscores her resolve in accented English, suggesting a mix of the Middle East and East London. Her eyes burn into the camera as it pulls back slowly. She speaks directly to the audience who will soon meet her on every television set in the world.

She lets a moment pass in silence. Her hands are clasped before her on a plain wooden table. Her rings glint from her thumb and wedding finger. The camera eases back, revealing a framed family photograph of a man, a boy and the woman herself. They are smiling. Joy swims in the woman's eyes. For it is a portrait of her from another time. Another life. It stands next to her as headstone to her happiness and witness to her destiny.

To exchange pain.

For the intelligence analysts who will study her message, there is no prepared statement. No grenade launcher on display before her. No AK-47 flanking her.

No chanting from the glorious text.

There are no black-and-gold flags on the walls behind her. No flags of any group. No carpet or fabric. The background is simple with angled mirrors.

Nothing betrays the woman's location, where she is recording her video or who is helping her. She could be in a safe house in the West Bank. Or in Athens. Maybe in Manila, Paris or London. Perhaps Madrid, or Casablanca.

Or in a suburb of the United States.

"Your soldiers invaded my home, tortured my husband and child. They forced them to watch as one by one they defiled me. Then they killed my husband and my son before my eyes. They fled when your bombers delivered death to my city. I carried my dead child through the ruins and to the bank of the river of Eden where I buried him, my husband and my life. But I have been resurrected to seek justice for these crimes.

"And it is for these crimes that I deliver my widow-mother's wrath. For these crimes you will taste death.

"Dying for me does not mean death. Dying for me is a promise kept. For I will have avenged the destruction of my world by bringing death to yours. Death is my reward as I join my husband and my child in paradise. For them, I am the eternal martyr. For them, I am vengeance."

Book One:
"Where is My Son?"

1

Blue Rose Creek, California

Maggie Conlin left her house believing a lie.

She believed life was normal again. She believed that the trouble preying on her family had passed, that Logan, her nine-year-old son, had come to terms with the toll Iraq had taken on them.

But the truth niggled at Maggie as she drove to work.

Their scars—the invisible ones—had not healed.

This morning, when she'd stood with Logan waiting for the school bus, he was uneasy.

"You love Dad, right, Mom?"

"Absolutely. With all my heart."

Logan looked at the ground and kicked a pebble.

"What is it?" she asked.

"I worry that something bad is going to happen. Like you might get a divorce."

Maggie clasped his shoulders. "No one's getting divorced. It's okay to be confused. It hasn't been easy these past few months since Daddy got home. But the worst is over now, right?"

Logan nodded.

"Daddy and I will always be right here, together in this house. Always. Okay?"

"Okay."

"Remember, I'm picking you up after school today for your swim class. So don't get on the bus."

"Okay. Love you, Mom."

Logan hugged her so hard it hurt. Then he ran to his bus, waved and smiled from the window before he vanished.

Maggie reflected on his worries as she drove through Blue Rose Creek, a city of a hundred thousand near Riverside County, on her way to the Liberty Valley Promenade Mall. She parked her Ford Focus and clocked in at Stobel and Chadwick, where she was a senior associate bookseller.

Her morning went fast as she called customers telling them orders had arrived, helped others find titles, suggested gift books and restocked bestsellers. As busy as she was, Maggie could not escape the truth. Her family had been fractured by events no one could control.

Her husband, Jake, was a trucker. In recent years, his rig had kept breaking down, and the bills piled up. It was bad. To help, he took a contract job driving in Iraq. High-paying, but dangerous. Maggie didn't want him to go. But they needed the money.

When he came home a few months ago, he was a changed man. He fell into long, dark moods, grew mistrustful, paranoid and had unexplained outbursts. Something had happened to him in Iraq but he refused to talk about it, refused to get help.

Was it all behind them?

Their debts were cleared, they'd put money in the

bank. Jake had good long-haul driving jobs and seemed to have settled down, leaving Maggie to believe that maybe, just maybe, the worst was over.

"Call for you, Maggie," came the voice over the P.A. system. She took it at the kiosk near the art history books.

"Maggie Conlin. May I help you?"

"It's me."

"Jake? Where are you?"

"Baltimore. Are you working all day today?"

"Yes. When do you expect to get home?"

"I'll be back in California by the weekend. How's Logan?"

"He misses you."

"I miss him, too. Big-time. I'll take care of things when I get home."

"I miss you, too, Jake."

"Listen, I've got to go."

"I love you."

He didn't respond, and in the long-distance silence, Maggie knew that Jake still clung to the untruth that she'd cheated on him while he was in Iraq. Standing there at the kiosk of a suburban bookstore, she ached for the man she fell in love with to return to her. Ached to have their lives back. "I love you and I miss you, Jake."

"I've got to go."

Twice that afternoon, Maggie stole away to the store's restroom, where she sat in a stall, pressing tissue to her eyes.

After work, Maggie made good time with the traffic on her way to Logan's school. The last buses were lumbering off when she arrived.

Maggie signed in at the main office then went to the classroom designated for pickups. Eloise Pearce, the teacher in charge, had two boys and two girls waiting with her. Logan was not among them. Maybe he was in the washroom?

"Mrs. Conlin?" Eloise smiled. "Goodness, why are you here? Logan's gone."

"He's gone? What do you mean, he's gone?"

"He got picked up earlier today."

"No, that's wrong!"

Eloise said Logan's sign-out was done that morning at the main office. Maggie hurried back there and smacked the counter bell loud enough for a secretary and Terry Martens, the vice-principal, to emerge.

"Where is my son? Where is Logan Conlin?"

"Mrs. Conlin." The vice-principal slid the day's sign-out book to Maggie. "Mr. Conlin picked up Logan this morning."

"But Jake's in Baltimore. I spoke to him on the phone a few hours ago."

Terry Martens and the secretary traded glances.

"He was here this morning, Mrs. Conlin," the vice-principal said. "He said something unexpected had come up and you couldn't make it to the school."

"What?"

"Is everything all right?"

Maggie's breathing quickened as she called Jake's cell phone while hurrying to her car. She got several static-filled rings before his voice mail kicked in.

"Jake, please call me and tell me what's going on! Please!"

Each red light took forever as Maggie drove through

traffic. She called her home number, got her machine and left another message for Jake. Wheeling into her neighborhood, Maggie considered calling 911.

And what would I say?

Better to get home. Figure this out. Maybe she'd misunderstood and the guys were at home right now. Was Jake actually in Blue Rose Creek? Why would he tell her he was in Baltimore? Why would he lie?

Turning onto her street, Maggie expected to see Jake's rig parked in its place next to their bungalow.

It wasn't there.

The brakes on her Ford screeched as she roared into her driveway, trotted to the door, jammed her key in the lock.

"Logan!"

No sign of Logan's pack at the door. Maggie went to his room. No sign of Logan or his pack there. She hurried from room to room, searching in vain.

"Jake! Logan!"

She called Jake's cell again.

And she kept calling.

Then she called Logan's teacher, then Logan's friends. No one knew, or had heard anything. She ran next door to Mr. Miller's house, but the retired plumber said he hadn't been home all day. She called Logan's swim coach. She called the yard where Jake got his rig serviced.

No one had heard anything.

Was she crazy? You can't drive from Baltimore to California in half a day. Jake said he was in Baltimore.

She rifled through Jake's desk not knowing what she was looking for. She called the cell-phone company to see if billing could confirm where Jake was when he made the call. It took some choice words before they checked, only to tell her that there was no record of calls being placed on Jake's cell phone for the past two days.

By early evening she phoned police.

The dispatcher tried to calm Maggie. "Ma'am, we'll put out a description of the truck and plate. We'll check for any traffic accidents. That's all we can do for now."

As night fell, Maggie lost track of time and the calls she'd made. Clutching her cordless phone, she jumped to her window each time a vehicle passed her house as Logan's words haunted the darkness that swallowed her.

"...something bad is going to happen..."

2

Haruki Ito was alone, hiking along the river when he stopped dead.

He raised his Nikon to his face, rolled his long lens until the bear in the distance filled his viewfinder. A grizzly sow, stalking trout on the bank of the wild Faust River in the Rocky Mountains.

Photographing the grizzly was a dream come true for Ito, on vacation from his job as a news photographer with *The Yomiuri Shimbun,* one of Tokyo's largest newspapers. As he took a picture then refocused for another, something blurred in his periphery.

He focused and shot it—*a small hand rising from the rushing current.*

Ito hurried along the bank to offer help, struggling through dense forests and over the mist-slicked rocks while glimpsing the hand, then an arm, then a head in the water before the river released its victim into an eddy nearby.

He stepped carefully toward the small, swirling pool.

Then he slipped off his camera gear and made his way into the cold, waist-high water, bracing himself as he reached for the body of a child.

A Caucasian boy. About eight or nine, Ito estimated. Sweatshirt, jeans and sneakers.

He was dead.

Sadness flooded Ito's heart.

As he prepared to lay the boy on the riverbank, the sudden loud thumping of something large bearing down forced Ito to flinch as a canoe crashed into the rocks next to him. It was empty.

Taking stock of the river, he shuddered.

Were there more victims?

Ito ran to the trailhead, and managed to wave down two women—German tourists riding bicycles—and within an hour park wardens had activated a search-and-rescue operation.

The area was known as Faust's Fork, a rugged section of rivers, lakes, forests, glaciers and mountain ranges straddling Banff National Park and Kananaskis Country. It was laced with trails and secluded campsites. Access was by foot or horseback, except for a few day-use riverside points that you could drive to, and a cluster of remote drive-through campsites at the river's edge which were served by an old logging road.

After confirming the boy's death, and facing the possibility of other victims, park officials notified the Royal Canadian Mounted Police, the medical examiner, paramedics, local firefighters, provincial park rangers, conservation officers and other agencies. They established a search zone with gridded sectors.

Rescue boats were deployed up and down the river but were not able to look for survivors in the section where the boy was found. The flow was too wild. Search teams were assembled and scoured the area on foot, horseback and ATVs. All had radios, some had search dogs. A helicopter and a small fixed-wing plane joined the operation along with volunteer search groups, who advised other campers in Faust's Fork.

Some distance upstream in a remote campsite, Daniel Graham stood alone on a small rise that offered a panoramic view of the river, the mountains and the sky.

He gazed upon the bronze urn he was holding, caressed the leaves and doves that were engraved in a fine band around its middle. After several moments, he unscrewed the lid, tilted the urn and offered the remainder of its contents to the wind. Fine, sandlike ashes swirled and danced along the river's surface until there was nothing left.

Graham looked to the snow-crested peaks, as if they held the answer to something that was troubling him. But he never had time to find it. The serenity he'd sought was broken by a helicopter thudding by him less than one hundred feet over the river.

A few moments later, it made a second low-altitude pass in the opposite direction.

Must be a search, Graham figured, as he set the urn aside and looked along the river for any indication of what was happening. Not long after the chopper had subsided, the air crackled with the cross talk of radios as two men in bright orange overalls entered his campsite.

"Sir, we're with search and rescue," the first one said. "There's been a boating accident on the river. We've got people looking for survivors. Please alert us if you see anything."

"How serious?"

The searchers assessed Graham, standing there in his jeans and T-shirt. Late thirties, about six feet tall with a muscular build, and a couple days' stubble covering his strong jaw, accentuating his intense, deep-set eyes.

He produced a leather wallet and opened it for them to study the gold badge with the crown, the wreaths of maple leaves, the words Royal Canadian Mounted Police, the bison's head encircled with the scroll bearing the motto, *Maintiens le Droit*. The photo ID was for Royal Canadian Mounted Police Corporal Daniel Graham.

"You're a Mountie?"

"With Major Crimes out of Calgary. Off duty at the moment. How serious is this accident? Are there fatalities?"

"One for sure. A young male. We don't have confirmed details."

"Have any members arrived yet? Can you raise your dispatcher?"

One of the men reached for his radio, made checks with the dispatcher and Graham was told that members of the local Banff and Canmore RCMP detachments were en route. Others were being called in to help.

"Do you have a scene and an identity on the victim?" Graham asked.

Over the radio a park dispatcher told Graham that the body of a young male, approximately eight to ten years of age, was found about a kilometer downriver from Graham's location. It appeared a canoe had overturned and the wardens suspected there were other victims.

"It's all happening now," the dispatcher said.

"I'll help search as I make my way to where the boy was found. Pass that along," Graham said.

The searchers continued upstream while Graham collected some items and headed to the river, moving as quickly as he could along the harsh terrain. The inter-ruption had distracted him from his purpose for being here. Graham pushed his personal problems aside to deal with the tragedy unfolding before him.

He paused to use his binoculars to scan the rugged banks and the water, concentrating on rocks spearing the surface. They created powerful spouts and rainbow-colored curtains of white water, as the current pounded against them. As he searched, Graham heard the inter-mittent whump of the chopper and the buzz of the small plane overhead.

When he came to a perilous section, he slipped on the wet ledges, banging his knee. But he kept going, picking his way along the craggy formations, which stood as a gateway to a waterfall that dropped two stories. He could hear its roar.

As he steadied himself, Graham thought he'd seen a patch of color amid several large rocks that forced geysers of spray in the middle of the river. He found a secure position and focused his binoculars. The spray obscured his view but he was convinced that through the gushing watery fan, he could see a swatch of pink, low against the rock. He got into a better position and dis-tinguished more details: a small head, an arm, a hand.

It's a child. A girl. Pinned to the rock by the current. Clinging for life.

She was about the width of a football field away from him, concealed by a clear dome of water spray. At any moment she could slip under the water or off the rock and be swept to the falls. She'd never survive the plunge.

There was no time to lose. He didn't have a radio. Or a cell phone. No other searchers were in sight. He had to make a decision.

Standing alongside the roaring river, staring at the tiny pink square, Graham could feel the vibrations of the rushing water in his rib cage. He knew the danger of going into the river. He'd have only one chance to reach her. If he missed, the current would carry him away to a life-and-death struggle to save himself before it took him over the falls and to the rocks below.

After all that had happened, what did he have left in his life?

Graham knew the risk. He would likely die. But so would that child if he didn't try to save her.

He had to go after her.

He hurried back upstream, kicked off his boots, set aside his badge, binoculars—everything that would weigh him down—then slid into the frigid water.

The river swept him along, and adrenaline coursed through him as he maneuvered around the rocks while contending with the current. White flashed before his eyes as his lower leg slammed into a rock. Pain shot through him and he slipped below the surface. Water gurgled in his ears, gushed into his stomach.

He fought his way to the surface, coughing and

spitting water, gulping air while struggling to find his bearings and to line up on the girl. The pink patch, his critical guide, had vanished. Rapids and spray concealed her. He was blinded by the water, only guessing her location.

A hidden rock punched the breath from him; he grabbed it, struggled to lift himself upon it, glimpsing pink downstream just as the river pulled him down, tearing his palm against the razor edge of a rock.

Graham slipped under the surface. In the churning water he saw small legs pressed against the rock ahead. Using all of his strength, he guided himself to it. The pressure welded him to the rock.

He was underwater, couldn't move, couldn't get to the surface.

Alarm rang in his ears. His lungs ached for air. He was not going to make it.

"Keep going, Daniel." He heard his wife's voice. *"You have to keep going."*

It took every ounce of strength he had to battle the water's power and to work his head to the surface, where he gulped mouthfuls of air while holding fast to the rock. After several seconds, his mind cleared and he worked his way around the rock, reaching as far as he could, until he felt small fingers, a hand, the arm of the girl. He continued positioning himself until he came face-to-face with her.

Little eyes, wide with terror, met his.

Her lips were blue.

She was alive, quaking with shock.

She appeared to be five or six years old.

Graham got closer, got his arm around her and peeled

her from the rock. She was bleeding from a head wound. Graham worked their position around the rock to where he had more control, struggling to steady the girl and himself against the rock, praying it was not in vain.

As he held her, her eyes locked on to his.

He moved his mouth to her ear to offer her comfort.

"You're going to be all right," he said. "I'm going to help you. Hang on. Just hang on."

She stared at him and her mouth began to move.

He pressed his ear closer, straining to hear above the river's roar, but he was uncertain what she was saying.

"Don't...daddy...don't...please..."

3

At that moment, some eighteen hundred miles south of the Faust River, Maggie Conlin stood before a newspaper building, reflecting on the five months since Jake had vanished with Logan.

The day after it happened, the county had dispatched a deputy to check Maggie's house for foul play before sending Maggie to Vic Thompson, a grumpy, overworked detective. He said Jake had ten days from the date of Maggie's complaint to give the D.A. an address, a phone number and to begin custody proceedings. If that didn't happen, the county would issue a warrant for Jake's arrest for parental abduction. Maggie gave Thompson all their bank, credit card, phone, computer, school and medical records.

He told her to get an attorney.

Trisha Helm, the cheapest available lawyer Maggie could find, "first visit is free," advised her to start divorce action and claim custody.

"I don't want a divorce. I need to find Jake and talk to him."

In that case, Trisha suggested Maggie hire a private detective and steered her to Lyle Billings, a P.I. at Farrow Investigations.

Maggie gave Billings copies of all their personal records and a check for several hundred dollars. Two weeks later, he told her that Jake had not renewed his license in any U.S. state, Canadian province or territory, nor was Logan registered in any school system.

"Assume he changed their names," Billings said. "Creating a new identity is easier than most people think. It looks like your husband went underground."

The agency needed more money to continue searching.

Maggie couldn't afford it.

There was just enough left in their savings for her to keep things going with the house for another three, maybe four months. Then she'd have to sell. She'd been cutting corners. She still had her bookstore job, but things were getting desperate.

So Maggie held off paying the agency more money. She searched on her own, spending most nights on her computer. She contacted truckers' groups and missing kids organizations, pleaded her case to newsletters and blogs. She scoured news sites for crashes involving rigs and boys Logan's age.

With each new tragedy Maggie's stomach knotted.

Maggie attended support groups. They told her to get the press interested in her struggle to find Jake and Logan. Every few days, then every week, she worked her list: the *Los Angeles Times,* the *Orange County Register,* the *Riverside Press-Enterprise* and nearly every TV and radio station in the southland.

"Oh, yeah, we looked into it," one apple-crunching producer told Maggie after she'd left three messages. "Our sources say that while it's *classified* as a parental abduction, it's more of a civil domestic thing. Sorry."

Every newsperson had stopped taking her calls, except Stacy Kurtz, the *Star-Journal*'s crime reporter.

"I don't think we've got a story yet, but please keep me posted," she said each time Maggie called.

At least Stacy would listen. Maggie had never met her but sometimes her picture ran with her articles. Stacy wore dark-framed glasses, hoop earrings and a smile that her job was slowly hardening. Daily reporting of the latest shooting, fire, drowning, car crash or variant urban tragedy was taking something from her. Some days, she looked older than she was.

"I can't guarantee we'll do a story, but I'll listen to your case as long as you promise to keep me posted on any developments." Stacy's to-the-point manner placed a premium on her time in a business ruled by deadlines.

For Maggie, time was evaporating.

What if she never found Logan? Never saw him again?

Now, here she was standing before the *Star-Journal*, a paper that covered Blue Rose Creek from a forlorn one-story building on a four-lane boulevard.

It sat between Sid's Check Cashing and Fillipo's Menswear, looking more like a 1960s strip-mall castaway than the kick-ass rag it once was. A palm tree drooped above the entrance. Weak breezes tried to stir a tattered U.S. flag atop the roof, where a rattling air conditioner bled rusty water down the building's stucco walls.

To locals, the *Star-Journal* was an eyesore in need of last rites.

To Maggie, it was a last chance to find Logan, for, day by day, her hope faded like the flag over the *Star-Journal*. But she'd come here this morning, all the same, with nothing but a prayer.

"May I help you?" a big woman in a print dress asked from her desk, which was the one closest to the counter. The other desks were nearby, situated in the classic newsroom layout. About a dozen cluttered desks crammed together. Most were unoccupied. At others, grim-faced people concentrated on their computer screens, or telephone conversations.

The off-white walls were papered with maps, front pages, news photos and an assortment of headlines. A police scanner was squawking from one corner where three TVs were locked on news channels. At the far end, in a glass-walled office, a balding man with his tie loosened was arguing with a younger man who had a camera slung over his shoulder.

"I'm here to see Stacy Kurtz," said Maggie.

"Do you have an appointment?"

"No, but—"

"Name?"

"My name is Maggie Conlin."

"Maggie Conlin?" the big woman repeated before shooting a glance at the woman nearby with a phone wedged between her ear and shoulder.

"No, that is absolutely wrong," the woman said into the phone as she typed, glancing at Maggie at the counter. She held up her index finger, going back into her phone call. "No, it is absolutely *not* what your press guy told me at the scene. Good. Tell Detective Wyches-ski to call me on my cell. That's right. Stacy Kurtz at the *Star-Journal*. If he doesn't call, I'll consider his silence as confirmation."

After typing for another moment Stacy Kurtz, who looked little like her picture, approached the counter.

"Stace, this is Maggie Conlin," the big woman said. "She doesn't have an appointment but she wants to talk to you."

Stacy Kurtz extended her hand. "I'm sorry, your name's familiar."

"My husband disappeared with my son several months ago."

"Right. A weird parental abduction, wasn't it? Is there a development?"

"No. My husband—" Maggie twisted the straps of her bag. "Could we talk, privately?"

Stacy appraised Maggie, trying to determine if she was worth her time. She turned toward the glass-walled office where the balding man was still arguing with the younger man. She bit her bottom lip.

"I just need to talk to you," Maggie said. "Please."

"I can give you twenty minutes."

"Thank you."

"Della, tell Perry I'm going to step outside to grab a coffee."

"Got your cell?"

"Yes."

"Is it on?"

"Yessss."

"Charged?"

"Bye, Della."

* * *

A few moments later, half a block away on a park bench, Stacy Kurtz sipped latte from a paper cup and tapped a closed notebook against her lap. As Maggie poured out her anguish, seagulls shrieked overhead.

"So there's really nothing new though, is there, Maggie? I mean not since it all happened, right?"

"No, but I was hoping that now, after all this time, you would do a story."

"Maggie, I don't think so."

"Please. You could publish their pictures and put it on the wire services and then it would go all over and—"

"Maggie, I'm sorry we're not going to do a story."

"I'm begging you. Please. You're my last hope to find—"

The opening guitar riff of "Sweet Home Alabama" played in Stacy's bag and she retrieved her phone. "Sorry, I've got to take this. Hello," she answered. "Okay. On my way now. Be there in two minutes."

"But will you do a story, please?" Maggie held out an envelope for Stacy as they hurried back toward the newspaper.

"What's this?"

"Pictures of Logan and Jake."

"Look—" Stacy pushed the envelope back "—I'm sorry, but I never guaranteed a story."

"Talk to your editor."

"I did and, to be honest, this is not a story for us at this point."

"*At this point?* What's that supposed to mean? That he's only news to you after something terrible happens? Like after he's killed, or dead."

Stacy stopped cold.

They'd reached the *Star-Journal*. She tossed her two-thirds-full latte into the trash can and stared at Maggie, then at the traffic. Dealing with heartbroken people every day was never easy, but Stacy's experience had forged her approach, which was to be truthful, no matter how painful it could be.

"Maggie, I spoke to Detective Vic Thompson. He mentioned something about some incident with your husband and a soccer coach. And that this was all about problems at home. A civil matter, really."

"What? No, that's not true."

"I'm sorry."

Suddenly, the buildings, traffic, the sidewalk, all began to swirl. Maggie steadied herself, placing her hand on a *Star-Journal* newspaper box. She raised her head to the sky in a vain effort to blink back her tears.

"My son is all I have in this world. My husband came back from working overseas a changed man. It's been five months now and no one's been able to find them. I may never see them again."

Stacy's phone rang. She glanced at the number then shut it off without answering.

"I have to go."

"What would you do if you were me?" Maggie said. "I've gone to police, a lawyer, a private detective. All in vain. I have nowhere else to go. No one else to turn to. I have no family, I have no friends. I'm all alone. You were my only hope. My last hope."

"I'm sorry. I'm sure things will work out. I'm so sorry. I really have to go." And with that Stacy disappeared through the doors of the *Star-Journal*.

Maggie stood alone in the street, the flutter and clang of the flagpole sounding a requiem to her defeat. She returned to her car and she met a stranger in her rearview mirror. She blinked at the lines stress had carved into her face. She'd let her hair go. She'd lost weight and couldn't remember the last time she'd smiled.

How did her life come to this? She and Jake had been in love. They'd had a happy life. A good life. She thrust her face into her hands and sobbed until she heard a tapping on the window and she turned to see Stacy Kurtz's face.

Maggie lowered her window.

"Listen." Stacy was searching her notebook. "I'm sorry things ended that way."

Maggie regained a measure of composure as Stacy snapped through pages.

"I'm not sure that this will help, but you never know."

Stacy copied something on a blank page then tore it out.

"Very few people know about this woman. She doesn't ask for money. She doesn't advertise and when I asked to profile her, she refused. She does not want publicity."

Wiping at her tears, Maggie studied the name and telephone number written in blue ink.

"What's this?"

"I have a detective friend who swears this woman helped the LAPD locate a murder suspect, and that she also helped the FBI find a teenager who'd vanished and, I guess, about ten years ago she helped find an abducted toddler in Europe."

"I don't understand. Is she a police officer?"

"No, she senses things, sees them in her mind and feels them."

"Is she a psychic?"

"Something like that. It's up to you whether you go to her or not. I apologize, today's been a bad day at the paper. Please keep me posted. Bye."

After Stacy left, Maggie stared at the name she'd written.

"Madame Fatima."

She clenched the note in her fist as if it were a lifeline.

4

Faust's Fork, near Banff, Alberta, Canada

Graham hung on to the girl.

How long had it been? Half an hour? An hour? He didn't know.

The river's force was draining his strength but he refused to let go.

Where's the chopper? They've got to see us. Come on!

Shouting was futile. The current pummeled him, the pain was electrifying. His body went numb. He was slipping from consciousness.

He thought of Nora, his wife. Her eyes. Her smile.

It gave him strength.

The river was relentless but he refused to let go. His hands were bleeding but he refused to let go, reaching deep for everything drilled into him at the training academy in Regina.

Never give up, never quit, never surrender.

He held on until the air began hammering above them.

A helicopter.

Everything blurred in the prop wash: A rescue tech descended, tethered to a hoist and basket. Graham helped position the girl into it, then watched her rise into the chopper. Then the tech returned for Graham, strapped him into a harness and raised him from the water. Mountains spun as they ascended over the river to a meadow where they put down. The techs pulled off his wet clothes, wrapped him in blankets and they lifted off.

As rescuers worked on the girl, the helicopter charged above a rolling forest valley that cut through the mountains. In minutes they came to a clearing near a trailside hostel where several emergency vehicles waited, including a second helicopter—the red STARS air ambulance out of Calgary. Its rear clamshell doors were open. Its rotors were turning.

"She's not responding," Graham heard the techs shout to the medical crew.

Wearing their flight suits and helmets, the emergency doctor, paramedic and nurse worked quickly, administering CPR, an IV, slipping an oxygen mask over her face, transferring her to a gurney. They packaged her into the medical chopper which thundered off to a trauma hospital in Calgary.

Graham stayed behind on the ground. He was barefoot and enshrouded in blankets as paramedics from Banff treated him for mild hypothermia and cuts to his hands and legs. Other officials watched and waited.

"Let's get you to the hospital in Banff for a better look," a paramedic said.

Graham shook his head, watching the red helicopter disappear in the east.

"I'm fine. I want to stay with the search."

A park warden trotted to his pickup, dug out a set of government-issue orange coveralls—the kind firefighters wore for forest fires—woolen socks and boots, and tossed them to Graham.

"They're dry and should fit," the warden said, nodding to a change room. "When you're ready, I'll drive you to the search center." He shook Graham's hand. "Bruce Dawson."

A few minutes later, with Graham in the passenger seat, Dawson ground through all gears as his truck rumbled along the dirt road that cut southwest through pine forests. On the way, he radioed a request to the searchers to retrieve the Mountie's bag from his campsite, along with his badge, boots and things he'd left by the river, and bring them to the center.

"What's the status?" Graham asked. "Those kids didn't come up here alone."

"Right, we figured on adults, too. We've expanded the perimeter downstream." Dawson kept his eyes on the road, letting several moments pass before he said, "I was listening on the radio after they spotted you in the river with the girl. That's a helluva thing you did."

Graham looked to the mountains without responding.

It was a bumpy thirty-minute ride over backcountry terrain to the warden's station for the Faust region. It sat on a plateau near a ridgeline trail. In its previous life the station had been a cookhouse built from hand-hewn spruce logs by a coal mining company in 1909.

Now it was doubling as the incident command center. Its walls were covered with maps. The main meeting room was jammed with people and a massive table was loaded with computers, GPS tracking gear and more maps. Sat phones and landlines rang, amid ongoing conversations as radios crackled nonstop over the hum of search helicopters.

The station was also equipped with basic plumbing. Graham took a hot shower, changed into his clothes from his retrieved bag. As he joined the others, his chief concern was the girl.

"What's her status?"

"No word yet." Dawson offered him a mug of coffee and a ham sandwich. Graham accepted the coffee, declined the sandwich. "We know they landed at Alberta Children's moments ago. While we're waiting for news, I'll update you on the search."

Referring to the map spread out on the big table, Dawson touched the tip of a sharpened pencil to a point along the river.

"This is where the boy was found. Mounties from Banff and Canmore are at the scene, and the medical examiner's just arrived."

"Do we have an idea who the boy is? Or who he belongs to? Any missing children reports?"

Dawson shook his head. "Not yet. Too many possibilities." His pencil followed the river. "You've got scores of campsites, day-trippers. We're going through the registrations and we've got teams going to each site to account for each visitor. People are mobile. They're on trails, or in Banff doing the tourist thing, or in Calgary, or wherever. It's going to take time."

Graham understood.

"We've gridded the area. We've got people on the

ground, on the water, in the air, we're searching every—"

"Is there a Corporal Graham here?" Across the room, a young woman held up a black telephone receiver.

"That's me," Graham said.

"Call for you!"

Taking it, Graham cupped a hand over one ear.

"Dan, we heard what you did. You okay?"

It was his boss, Inspector Mike Stotter, who headed Major Crimes out of the RCMP's South District in Calgary.

"I'm fine."

"You went above and beyond the call."

"No, I didn't."

"Dan, listen, I'm sorry, but they just pronounced her at the hospital."

"What?"

"They just called us. She didn't make it. I'm sorry."

Her trembling body. Her eyes. Her last words, spoken into his ear.

Graham rubbed his hand over his face.

"Give me this case, Mike."

"It's too soon for you."

"I was coming back from leave this week."

"I've got some cold cases ready for you. Look, this one's likely going to be a wilderness accident, nothing suspicious. We don't need to be there. Fornier's rookies in Banff can have it."

"I need this case, Mike."

"You *need* it?"

"Did the chopper crew or the hospital indicate if she said anything? If she tried to speak before she died?"

"Hang on. Shane was talking to them."

Graham looked at the mountains, feeling something churning in his gut until Stotter came back on the line.

"Nothing, Dan, why?"

"She spoke to me, Mike."

"What'd she say?"

"It wasn't clear. But I've got a feeling that this wasn't an accident. We need to be on this. I want this case, Mike."

A long moment passed.

"Okay. I'll tell Fornier. You're the lead. For now. If it's criminal, it stays with us in Major Crimes. If it's not, you kick it back to Fornier's people. Look, Prell's in Canmore on another matter, I'm sending him to you now, to give you a hand."

"Prell? Who's Prell?"

"Constable Owen Prell. Just joined us in Major Crimes from Medicine Hat."

"Fine, thanks, Mike."

"You sure you're good to take this on. You've got two fatals so far and the river's likely to give you more."

"I'm good."

"Better get yourself to the scene where they found the boy."

5

The boy's face was flawless.

Almost sublime in death.

His eyes were closed. Not a mark on his skin. He had the aura of a sleeping cherub as a breeze lifted strands of his hair, like a mother tenderly coaxing him to wake and play.

His resemblance to the girl was clear. He was older, likely her big brother. His jeans were faded, his blue sweatshirt bore a Canadian Rockies insignia, his sneakers were a popular brand and in good shape. He looked about eight or nine and so small inside the open body bag.

Who is he? What were his favorite things? His dreams? His last thoughts? Graham wondered, kneeling over him on the riverbank with Liz DeYoung, the medical investigator from the Calgary Medical Examiner's Office.

"What do you think?" Graham raised his voice over the river's rush. "Accident, or suspicious?"

"Way too soon to tell." DeYoung was wearing blue

latex gloves and, using the utmost care, she grasped the boy's small shoulders and turned him. The back of his skull had been smashed in like an eggshell, exposing cranial matter. "It appears the major trauma is here."

"From the rocks?"

"Probably. We'll know more after we autopsy him, and the girl, back in Calgary. At this stage, Mother Nature's your suspect."

Graham glimpsed DeYoung's wristwatch and updated his case log using the pen, notebook and clipboard he'd borrowed from the Banff members helping at the scene.

"No life jackets," Graham said.

"Excuse me?"

"The girl didn't have one. He doesn't have one. Did anyone see life jackets?"

"No. But if you've got a reason to be suspicious, would you share it?"

"It's just a feeling."

"A feeling?"

"Forget it. I'm still thawing out. Did you find any ID? Items in his pockets? Clothing tags?"

"No. Except for a little flashlight and a granola bar, nothing. Look, you guys do your thing. Get us some names and a next of kin, so we can request dental records to confirm. You know the drill."

He knew the drill.

"So we're good to move him?" DeYoung had a lot of work ahead of her.

Graham didn't answer. He was staring at the boy, prompting her to look at him with a measure of concern.

"Are you okay?"

DeYoung knew something of Graham's personal

situation and took quick stock of him, blinking at a memory.

"Dan, you know the only time I ever met Nora was last Christmas. We all sat together at the attorney general's banquet. We hit it off. Remember?"

He remembered.

"I'm so sorry. I missed her service. I was at a conference in Australia."

"It's okay."

"How are you doing? Really?"

His gaze shifted from the boy's corpse to the river, as if the answer to everything was out there.

He stood. "You can move him now."

DeYoung closed the bag. Her crew loaded it onto a stretcher, strapped it in three areas, then carried it carefully up the embankment to their van. Graham watched the van inch along the trail, suspension creaking as it tottered to the back road. Then it was gone.

For a moment, he stood alone in the middle of the scene.

It had been cordoned on three sides with yellow tape. He was wearing latex gloves and shoe covers. Nearby, members of the RCMP Forensic Identification Section out of Calgary, in radiant white coveralls, looked surreal against the dark rocks and jade river, working quietly taking pictures, measuring, collecting samples of potential evidence.

All in keeping with a fundamental tenet known to all detectives.

A wilderness death can be a perfect murder. Treat it as suspicious because you don't know the truth until you know the facts.

Graham resumed studying his clipboard, paging through the handwritten statements and notes he'd taken from the people who'd found the boy. Haruki Ito, age forty-four, photographer from Tokyo, was first. He'd flagged the women on bicycles. Ingrid Borland, age fifty-one, a librarian from Frankfurt, and Marlena Zimmer, age thirty-three, a Web editor from Munich. They all seemed to be pretty straight-up tourists.

Nothing unusual regarding their demeanor.

The guy from Tokyo was a seasoned news photographer, having covered some terrible stuff like wars and tsunamis. He was fairly calm, philosophical, Graham thought. It was a different story with the women, who were left shaken by their futile attempt to revive the boy. *"That poor child. That poor, poor child."*

Static crackled from a police radio, pulling Graham's attention to the man approaching. He'd emerged from the tangle of emergency vehicles atop the riverbank where members from the Banff and Canmore general investigations sections were with the witnesses. He stopped at the tape. A wise decision.

"Corporal Graham?"

Graham moved closer to the new arrival. He was in his midthirties. Maybe six feet tall, wearing jeans and a checkered shirt under a black leather bomber jacket.

"Owen Prell. Inspector Stotter sent me."

"Got here pretty quick." Graham shook his hand.

"I was already in Canmore."

"Mike said you joined Major Crimes from Medicine Hat."

"Worked GIS. They just set me up by your desk at the office. I'm looking forward to working with you."

Prell looked back to the patrol cars and uniformed officers. "The other members want to know if you're done with the witnesses. The people would like to go."

"We're almost done with them." Graham flipped his pages. "Get them to surrender their passports. We'll run them through Interpol. Just say it's procedure and we'll return them soon."

"Will do."

As Prell turned, a helicopter throbbed overhead, skimming the river. The RCMP's chopper out of Edmonton. The instant it disappeared, Graham heard his name. The FIS member processing the canoe was waving for him to come and see something.

Something important.

Wedged in the rocks where the canoe crashed was a small metal plate displaying the label *Wolf Ridge Outfitters.* The screw holes aligned with those on the canoe. It was a rental. Number 27.

Rental agencies kept records.

"Prell!"

The constable returned with his radio. An urgent request was made to the telecomms dispatcher to contact Wolf Ridge and cross-reference its rental agreement for Number 27 with the park's permits and wilderness passes.

It took twenty minutes for the information to come back.

The canoe was rented by Ray Tarver, of Washington, D.C.

Park permits showed Ray, Anita, Tommy and Emily Tarver as the visitors registered to drive-in campsite #131.

6

Faust's Fork, near Banff, Alberta, Canada

Campsite #131 was upstream, deep in the backcountry, secluded in a dense stand of spruce and pine, offering sweeping views of the river and the rugged cliffs of the Nine Bear Range.

When Graham arrived with the others, he saw no movement.

A late-model SUV was parked near a large dome tent. It was a typical campsite: propane camping stove, lawn chairs, four life jackets stacked neatly against a spruce tree, food kept a safe distance from the tent, and other items, including shirts and pants, hanging from a clothesline tied between two pine trees. Shouts for the Tarvers were answered by the river's rush and the thud of the search helicopters.

The site was silent.

Lifeless.

Graham declared it a second scene and as Prell and the others taped it off and radioed for a request to run the SUV's Alberta plate, he entered the tent alone.

Inside, he detected the pleasant fragrances of soap and

sunscreen. There was also the sense that something had been interrupted but he couldn't put his finger on it. Time had stopped here. To one side, was a sleeping bag big enough for two adults. Next to its left pillow, a Danielle Steel paperback. Next to the right, a large flashlight.

Across the tent, two smaller sleeping bags, side by side. A SpongeBob comic was splayed open on one, while a pink stuffed bunny sat on the other, arms open, awaiting its owner's return.

Graham picked it up, looked into its button eyes.

Children's clothes in bright colors erupted from small backpacks: sweaters, small pants. The larger bags on the opposite side were also open, clothes spilled from them, but not in a disheveled way.

It was orderly.

Graham searched in vain for a purse or wallet. Campers often hid them or locked them away. After making notes, he stepped outside, where Prell updated him.

"The SUV's a rental from an outlet at Calgary International. Customer's Raymond Tarver, same D.C. address."

"Anything inside?"

"It's locked."

"Get the rental agency to open it for us ASAP. Tell them it's a police emergency. Then we'll get forensics to process it and this site. Nobody tromps around here or touches anything."

Graham nodded upriver.

"What about the people in the neighboring sites?"

"Some of the guys have started a canvas."

"Good, I want statements, time lines, background checks."

"Will do. Corporal, what do you suspect happened to the parents?"

"I don't know." Graham surveyed the site again: the life jackets, the cooler of food kept at a proper distance from the tent, a pail of dirt near the fire ring—*did they cook hot dogs, toast marshmallows and huddle under the stars together? Did they die together?* "These people follow the rules, keep things safe, take no risks. I don't know what happened."

Later that night, after Prell had gone back to Calgary, Graham watched flashlights and headlamps probe the dark river valley as SARS teams continued searching. Graham was alone at his own campsite sitting before a fire, listening to transmissions echoing from the borrowed radio next to him.

As the searchers reported, Graham reviewed his case.

After a mechanic from the rental agency had opened the SUV, Prell found more items, including a wallet, a purse and U.S. passports belonging to the Tarvers. The flames illuminated the faces of Raymond, his wife, Anita, their son, Thomas, and their daughter, Emily, the girl who took her final breaths in Graham's arms.

What went wrong here?

Graham wanted to believe that this was your nice, average American family. But where were Ray and Anita Tarver?

Did they drown their children?

Or drown with them?

What happened?

Had they been having a blissful mountain vacation before a horrible accident? Or was something else at work? Was there stress in the family? What was going on in the lives of the Tarvers before the tragedy?

What about his own life?

The firelight also captured the urn visible through the screen door to his tent.

Graham ran a hand across his face.

It'd been a hell of a day. He'd come up here to one of Nora's favorite spots, to distribute the rest of her ashes. He'd come up to quit the force. He couldn't go on without her because he had nothing left.

Nothing.

Because it was his fault.

Then today happened. And in his darkest moment when he was in the river, certain he would die, he heard her, telling him not to give up.

To keep going.

And then came Emily Tarver's final cryptic words.

How could he walk away from this?

He owed the dead.

The radio sputtered.

"Repeat, Sector 17—"

"We've got something here!"

7

It was nearly 1:30 a.m.

In the quiet, Maggie was losing hope of ever meeting Madame Fatima. As she got ready for bed, she considered all the messages she'd left. All unanswered.

She'd try again tomorrow.

Maggie drew back her bedsheet then froze.

What was that?

She'd heard something. Down the hall. In the study area off the living room. She glanced around, listening for a moment.

Nothing.

She was exhausted, dismissed it and tried to sleep but a million fears assailed her.

Were Jake and Logan dead?

Why hadn't she heard from them? She ached to hold Logan, to talk to Jake.

Just pick up the damn phone and call me, Jake. Let me know you're all right.

Why are you doing this?

Why?

For much of her life, Maggie had been a loner. But tonight she wished she had a friend, someone to talk to. When Maggie was six years old, her mother committed suicide after a drunk driver killed Maggie's older sister, April, as she was riding her bike. Maggie's dad raised her alone until she married Jake. Then her father took up with a younger woman, a drug addict he'd met in rehab.

He moved to Arizona and Maggie hadn't spoken to him in years.

She'd called him to see if he'd heard from Jake, but it had been a short conversation.

No.

Jake had no family either. His parents divorced after he'd left high school. His father died of cancer five years ago. His mother died three years back.

Maggie and Jake had always kept to themselves, happy to have each other. Able to handle any problem together.

Until this.

What really happened to Jake in Iraq?

Maggie knew he'd driven on secret missions and that his convoys often came under fire, but he refused to tell her anything as she worried about his brooding, his nightmares, the outburst.

One day, Jake went with her to the supermarket where they'd bumped into Craig Ullman, Logan's soccer coach. As they talked, something icy flitted across Jake's face. A few nights later in bed, he turned his back to her.

"I know you slept with Ullman when I was over there."

She was stunned.

Not only was Jake wrong, he scared her because it seemed as if he was losing it. Then came the scene at one of Logan's games. Jake had been out of town and arrived late. Logan waved from the field, Maggie waved from her place among the parents in lawn chairs on the sideline.

Jake ignored them, marching up to Craig Ullman.

"I know, asshole," Jake said.

Ullman looked up from his clipboard, bewildered.

"Is something wrong, Jake?"

"You were banging my wife while I was away. *I fucking know it!*"

"What?"

Jake drew back his fist and Maggie grabbed it.

"No, Jake! Stop it! We have to go home. Craig, I am *so sorry.*"

Jake stared at her, at Logan who'd watched it all, along with everybody else. Jake just walked off, drove away, and spent the night in his rig, parked in the driveway of their home, exiled from the people who loved him.

She and Logan endured the humiliation and, in the days that followed, Jake refused to speak of the incident. He went on several long-haul jobs while Maggie called anonymous crisis lines to find a way to fix their lives.

She did all that she could for her family.

Maggie opened her eyes.

There it is again.

The noise.

A bit louder this time.

She got out of bed to check.

She went into the hallway and looked around. Unease rippled through her as she headed for the living room and the study area. Nothing obvious. Yet something *felt* wrong. She went to the bathroom, checked behind the shower curtain.

Nothing.

She went to Logan's room. Nothing. She went back to the living room and this time she went deeper into the study area where she kept her computer and her records on Jake and Logan.

The tiny hairs on the back of her neck stood up.

Her papers had been shuffled, some had spilled onto the floor.

Had someone been in her home?

Maggie looked at the patio door just off the study at the back of the house. It was open by about four inches. She closed it. Locked it.

Did she leave it open?

She'd been careless before when she was lost in her thoughts.

If she did, it would explain her scattered file. It was breezy tonight.

What's that?

A faint trace of something. A lingering scent she couldn't identify.

Maybe it was nothing.

Was she so stressed her mind was playing tricks on her?

This is stupid. She couldn't handle this right now.

No. It was strange, but she could feel a presence.

Maggie jumped as her phone rang.

Who'd be calling at this hour?

Hope fluttered in her stomach then fear clawed at her. "Hello?"

Silence swallowed her answer. The incoming caller was BLOCKED, according to her caller ID.

"Hello? Who's there?"

Nothing. No breathing. No background noise. Only silence.

"Who are you calling, please?"

Through the window Maggie saw a car whisk down the street with only its parking lights on.

What's happening?

She hung up and thrust her face in her trembling hands.

Was she losing her mind?

8

North of the White House, beyond the Capitol and the Washington Monument, Carol Mintz analyzed potential threats to the security of the United States.

The pope's upcoming visit to the U.S. made her even more tense.

Watch for everything. Note anything, her supervisor had advised her.

Sure. No problem. That's what we do here twenty-four-seven. It never stops.

Mintz's keyboard clicked softly as she scrolled through the secret file from the U.S. Embassy in Libya.

A French intelligence source listening to Algerian insurgent operatives had intercepted radio traffic out of Tripoli. The chatter indicated a possible shipment of hostile cargo from Africa was nearing the U.S.

No other information was known.

Mintz, an intelligence specialist, checked her archives, confirming what she'd suspected. This one had first surfaced a few weeks ago with an unsubstantiated report of a freighter steaming from Morocco's Port of

Tangier, the cargo thought to be drugs from Ethiopia. According to the latest information, that ship had navigated the Suez, crossed the Indian Ocean and was now thought to be somewhere in the Pacific Ocean.

Still unsubstantiated.

So why was this flaring up again?

Tripoli advised to stand by for an update.

More information would be good. This was going to be another long day.

Mintz worked in the old naval intelligence base known as the Nebraska Avenue Complex. Her office was among some three-dozen buildings on the thirty-eight-acre site, near the operations center of the Department of Homeland Security, about fourteen miles from where terrorists had slammed a jetliner into the Pentagon.

The DHS's mission was to prevent further strikes.

Mintz's job was to track cases and assess the threat with her counterparts at the CIA, FBI, DIA, NSA, Secret Service and various other agencies.

Her team was responsible for distilling intelligence on incoming ships and planes.

Mintz bit her lip as she glanced at her copy of the morning's *New York Times.* A front page headline indicated foreign intelligence agencies were detecting increased levels of terrorist activity—activity that was aimed at heads of state.

Ain't that the truth.

Earlier in the week they'd helped process a threat through Australian and British security services indicating that two men, suspected to be terrorist operatives, had boarded a 747 on a Hong Kong-to-Sydney flight connecting to San Francisco. U.S. fighters were scrambled.

Rick Mofina

Fingerprints obtained covertly from their drinking cups in-flight by two American agents aboard and scanned in-flight to Washington, had confirmed the subjects' identities and ruled out a threat.

Everyone stood down on that one.

Passengers had never known of the events that had unfolded around them.

Mintz reached for a carrot stick just as her computer flashed with a new report.

The embassy in Amsterdam had issued a classified threat. A jailed passport forger in Istanbul had told Turkish police interrogators that a ship was carrying several concealed containers of explosives that would be detonated when it reached Boston Harbor. Registered to a numbered company in Aruba, the vessel had left Rotterdam and was now approaching U.S. waters.

Mintz grabbed her phone when her computer flashed with an update from the Central Intelligence Agency.

The illicit Rotterdam cargo was a dozen mail-order brides smuggled out of Moscow. No explosives were located. No threat. It was common for criminal sources to inflate their claims to better bargain with prosecutors.

Thank you, Langley, for sharing.

Mintz massaged the knot of tension in the back of her neck as she looked at the National Threat Advisory displayed on the wall behind her.

Today we are yellow—an elevated risk of terrorist attacks.

Her computer flashed with an update on the African freighter.

It was still headed across the Pacific to the U.S. The hostile substance was still suspected to be illicit drugs, possibly hashish or qat, a narcotic leafy substance, from Ethiopia.

Fine, Mintz thought, the data seemed to be going full circle.

Still, she directed it to her other agencies.

Sharing information to connect the dots. Once more, over to you fine people at the Coast Guard, Customs, the DEA and the gang at CT watch, who've probably already handled this one.

Then Mintz noticed that she'd just received a security look-ahead from the Secret Service's Dignitary Protective Division—the guys who were protecting the pope during his U.S. visit in a few weeks' time. Mintz scanned the updates on the papal travel agenda. Future destinations and considerations of interest to all security agencies.

Tapping her finger on her desk, Mintz contemplated some of her recent files.

She decided to share them with Secret Service Intelligence Division.

Mintz appreciated that they were going full tilt over there, given they had the lead to protect the Holy Father.

She was sorry to pile up their workload, but her orders were to share everything.

Even an unconfirmed shipload of drugs from Ethiopia.

And let's hope that's all it is.

9

Calgary, Alberta, Canada

Searchers in Sector 17 found Anita Tarver's corpse entangled in a logjam along a stream that flowed off the Faust River.

Less than twenty-four hours later, her naked body lay on a stainless steel tray in the autopsy room of the Calgary Medical Examiner's Office, a few feet from the bodies of her son and daughter.

As Graham watched Dr. Bryce Collier, the pathologist, and his assistant conduct the procedures, he imagined moments in Anita's life with her children. The birthdays. The Christmases. Getting them ready for school. Their excitement at the big plane trip for a vacation in the mountains. Anita kissing them goodnight under the stars.

Had they known what was coming?

Like most detectives, Graham disliked autopsies. But it was part of the job. In his years as a Mountie he'd seen the aftermath of fires, electrocutions, drownings, stabbings, shootings, hackings, hangings, strangulations, beatings with hammers, bats, hockey sticks, pipes, car-wreck decapitations and lost hikers entombed in ice.

But no matter how many autopsies he'd viewed, he could never adapt to the room's frigid air, the multicolored organs, the overpowering smells of formaldehyde and ammonia. Because they all signified the penultimate defeat.

And now, more than ever, it signified that he was to blame for his wife's death.

When the autopsies on Anita Tarver and her children were completed Graham joined Collier in his office. He liked Collier's tiny Bonsai tree and the calming gurgle of his small feng shui fountain. Objects of optimism. What always gave Graham pause each time he came here was the large print beside Collier's framed degrees and awards: Van Gogh's *Twilight, before the Storm: Montmartre.*

The worst is still to come, Graham thought.

Collier opened a can of diet cola, poured it into his ceramic coffee mug and began making notes in his file.

"I'm attributing cause as consistent with blunt trauma from the rocks and the manner as accidental. Noncriminal."

"Not a doubt in your mind?"

"Unless you know something we don't?"

"Emily tried to tell me something before she died."

"Yes, Stotter mentioned that it was incoherent."

Graham exhaled slowly.

"Isn't that correct, Dan?"

"It is. But we haven't found the father yet and there's every indication he was with them in the park."

"You think daddy did it?"

"I don't know what to think, Bryce."

"I see. Well, unless something concrete tells me otherwise, what we have here is a wilderness accident." Collier sipped from his mug. "We need dental records to make positive identifications. Do you have next of kin for the call?"

Graham consulted his notes. On the park registration form, in the section on who to alert in case of emergency, the Tarvers had listed Jackson Tarver in Beltsville, Maryland.

"Ray Tarver's father. I'll make the call back at my office."

Graham wheeled his unmarked Chevrolet sedan out of the M.E.'s lot and headed east on Memorial Drive which hugged the Bow River across from Calgary's gleaming office towers. After passing the Calgary Zoo, he took the Deerfoot Trail expressway, north to the Southern Alberta District headquarters for the RCMP.

The Stephen A. Duncan building near the airport.

In the Major Crimes section he saw no sign of Corporal Shane Wilcox, the file coordinator, or Prell. Good. Graham was a team player, but he liked working alone. He started a fresh pot of coffee then went to the washroom and studied the mirror.

What the hell was happening?

What was the use of going on? Without Nora, his life no longer held any meaning. Maybe that's why he risked it, in his vain attempt to save the little girl. But who was he really trying to save? What happened to him in the water? He swore to God he'd heard Nora telling him not to give up.

And the girl?

Her dying words haunted him.

Everyone believed it was a tragic accident but he remained uncertain.

Maybe he was losing his mind.

He splashed water on his face then went to his desk. It was neat and, unlike the desks of the other Mounties, it was bereft of framed photos of loved ones. No keepsakes or mementos to hint at his personality. Just a phone, a glass cup holding pens and pencils, a yellow legal notepad and the Tarver file.

That's all he had left in this world.

He opened the folder and prepared to make the call to notify the Tarvers' next of kin. Being the bearer of news that destroyed worlds was also part of the job.

The worst part.

As a traffic cop, Graham had been punched, slapped, and had people collapse in his arms as he stood at their door, cap in hand, to tell them what no one should ever have to hear.

Ever.

At times they'd see his police car pull up, watch through the living-room window as he got out and approached their home. They'd refuse to let him in. *Because they knew.* They knew that as long as they never heard what he was going to tell them, their world would remain intact. If they didn't hear the words then their daughter, their son, sister, brother, mother, father, husband or wife would not be dead.

No one knew how much he feared the day it might happen to him.

Then it did happen.

"We couldn't stop the bleeding. We did all we could for her. I'm so sorry."

After five rings, a woman answered the phone in Maryland.

"I'm calling for Mr. Jackson Tarver."

"One moment please, he's in the yard." Footsteps on a tiled floor, a back door creaked. "Jack! Phone! I think it's that salesman again!" A man far off grumbled something as he approached the phone. Graham squeezed the handset, grateful he was alone in his office.

"Hello."

"Mr. Tarver? Mr. Jackson Tarver?"

"Yes?"

"Sir, Corporal Daniel Graham with the Royal Canadian Mounted Police in Calgary."

"Police?"

"Yes. Sir, I'm sorry to disturb you at home, but it's important that I confirm your relationship to Raymond, Anita, Tommy and Emily Tarver of Washington, D.C."

Silence hung in the air as realization rolled over Tarver and he swallowed hard.

"Anita's my daughter-in-law. Tommy and Emily are my grandchildren." Tarver cleared his throat. "Raymond is my son. Why are you calling?"

When Graham delivered the news, Jackson Tarver dropped his phone.

10

Calgary, Alberta, Canada

Dental records confirmed Anita, Tommy and Emily Tarver as the victims.

Ray Tarver's body had still not been recovered.

The tragedy landed on the front pages of Calgary's newspapers with the headlines RIVER HORROR CLAIMS FOUR AMERICANS and U.S. FAMILY DIES IN MOUNTAINS. The *Calgary Herald* and *Calgary Sun* ran pictures of the Tarvers, the scene and locator maps. Through interviews with shocked U.S. friends of the Tarvers, the papers reported that Ray Tarver was a freelance journalist, Anita was a part-time librarian and that Tommy and Emily were "the sweetest kids."

Not much more in the Web editions of the *Washington Post* and *Washington Times* either, Graham thought before he met Jackson Tarver at the Calgary airport. From the passport and driver's license photos, Graham saw the father and son resemblance, except the elder Tarver had thin white hair parted neatly to one side.

Jackson Tarver was a sixty-seven-year-old retired

high-school English teacher. His handshake was strong for someone whose world had been shattered. He insisted on "taking care of matters right away," so Graham drove him to his hotel where they found a quiet booth in the restaurant. Tarver never touched his coffee. He sat there twisting his wedding band.

"Since your call, I've been praying that this has been some sort of mistake," Tarver said. "I need to see with my own eyes that this has happened. I hope you understand?"

Graham understood. He opened his folder to display sharp color photographs of Anita, Tommy and Emily Tarver, on autopsy trays.

Pain webbed across Jackson's face and he turned away.

After giving him time, Graham took Tarver's forearm to ensure he was registering their conversation.

"Our services people have contacted the U.S. Consulate here. They'll help you with the airline bookings and the funeral-home arrangements and they will assist you in getting them home with you," Graham said. "They'll also help you get the belongings shipped home later when we've finished processing them. Here's some paperwork you'll need."

Graham slid an envelope to Tarver who took several moments to collect himself.

"Do you know how it happened?"

"At this stage, we believe their canoe capsized in the Faust River."

"And they weren't wearing life jackets?"

"No."

"I just don't understand. Ray was so careful. When

things were good, he'd taken Anita and the kids to Yellowstone. He was no stranger to the outdoors. For goodness' sake, he's an Eagle Scout."

"You said, 'when things were good.'" Graham was taking notes.

"Ray used to be a reporter with the Washington, D.C., bureau of World Press Alliance, the wire service."

"What sorts of stories did he do?"

"He covered everything before moving to investigative features."

Graham nodded.

"Then he began clashing with his editors. About a year ago he'd had enough and decided to try making a living freelancing."

"How did that go?"

"It was rough. Anita was worried. He'd quit a well-paying job with benefits."

"So there was stress in the home?"

"Some. Sure, over the money and for Ray quitting World Press."

"So why not try to find another news job?"

"I think Ray always felt he was close to a big story, or a book deal. Until then, he was always borrowing money from us to pay the bills, always struggling, worrying about Anita and the kids. About six months ago, he took out extra life insurance so Anita and the kids would be okay, if anything happened to him."

"Really? How much?"

"I think he said it was two hundred and fifty thousand."

"Means more premiums. How did he pay for this trip?"

"I loaned him the money for this trip. He told me they

really needed to get away. He found a cheap package deal. I figured he was going to pay me back with the money he'd get for some travel features, which usually happened. It just took time."

Graham didn't voice his view that Ray came across as something of a contradiction. Here was a guy who was not a risk taker but had taken a gamble leaving his job. Ray's father must've picked up on what Graham was thinking.

"Is there something you're not telling me, Corporal?"

"I'm just trying to figure things out."

"You said it appears to be an accident, at this stage. Is there something you're not telling me?"

"I've told you all we know. We just need to locate Ray."

"Corporal, it's hard to explain a life here. My son loved his family. For him, reporting was a quasi-religious cause. He worked hard on his articles, they were very good. In fact, I'd like his laptop returned to me as soon as possible. It would mean a great deal to me to read what he'd been working on."

"Laptop? I don't think we found a laptop."

Graham flipped through the inventory sheets from the crime scene guys.

"He never went anywhere without it."

"It's possible we have it in an evidence locker, or the lab is processing it."

"He had it with him when I took them to the airport for this trip."

"I'll look into it."

Graham was certain no laptop was found anywhere

with the Tarvers and spent the rest of the night on the phone to the lab and the guys in Banff getting them to search for it.

In the morning, Graham rose early and drove Jackson Tarver two hours west to Banff, then deep into the Faust region to the site. Jackson Tarver tossed roses into the river where his grandchildren, daughter-in-law and, most likely, his son had died.

That afternoon, Graham accompanied him to the airport and badged his way through to the gate where they watched three casket-shaped containers roll along the luggage conveyor and into the cargo hold of Tarver's plane.

Before he boarded, Tarver took Graham's hand and shook it.

"I heard what you did, how you risked your life trying to save Emily. Thank you."

"No thanks necessary."

"I hope you'll find my son, so that he can come home with his family." Tarver's grip was like that of a man fighting to keep from breaking into pieces. "Please."

"I'll do my best."

Graham stayed at the window watching Tarver's jet roll slowly from the terminal, turbines whining, running lights strobing, until his cell phone rang.

"Graham, it's Fitzwald."

"Fitz, did you find the laptop?"

"No laptop, but I did find something you should see."

Twenty minutes later, Graham was at Fitzwald's desk looking at a sneaker.

"We figure it belongs to Ray Tarver."

Graham was puzzled; he'd seen this sneaker and its mate before.

"I don't get it, Fitz, I've seen the shoes. They were in the tent."

"And this was in the left shoe."

Fitzwald tossed a small, slim leather-bound note-book on the desk before him.

"What do you make of it, Dan?"

Graham fanned the pages filled with notes, handwritten in ink. They were cryptic: something about an *SS Age,* another, *see B. Walker.* Scores of notations just before the last entry: *Meet 'x' and 'y' verify link to Blue Rose Creek.*

"Hard to say if it's important."

"It must mean something because it was hidden under the foot cushion. He valued this more than his passport."

11

Tokyo, Japan

Central Tokyo's skyline glittered against the night sky.

Setsuko Uchida gazed upon it from the balcony of her fortieth-floor apartment in Roppongi Hills, but her thoughts lingered on her vacation in the Rockies.

Had she really traveled halfway around the world?

She sighed, then resumed unpacking in her bedroom, happy to be home. Tomorrow she would have lunch with her daughter, Miki, near the Imperial Gardens and tell her about the magnificent mountains.

With great care, she retrieved the gift box from her suitcase and slowly unwrapped the tissue paper until a small polar bear, and a second, tinier bear, hand-carved in jade, emerged. A mother and her cub. She knew Miki would love them. The two women had grown closer since Setsuko's husband had passed away.

Toshiro.

He smiled from the gold-framed photo on her nightstand. He'd been a senior official at the Ministry of Justice and was a kind man. He died of lung complications which had tormented him years after his exposure to the sarin gas attack on the subway system by the Aum Shinrikyo cult.

Losing her husband had almost destroyed Setsuko, who'd been an economics professor at the University of Tokyo. Eventually, she took early retirement then moved from their home in Chiba to Central Tokyo to be nearer to their daughter, Miki.

Miki was angered by her father's death and had withdrawn from everyone, burying herself in her job. Setsuko had refused to accept Miki's isolation, never letting her be alone for too long, always calling or visiting. In time, Miki opened her heart and allowed Setsuko back into her life, allowed her to be her mother again.

This happened because Setsuko's friends, Mayumi and Yukiko, had always encouraged Setsuko not to give up on Miki. She loved them for it. She also loved them for insisting she join them on their recent adventure to the wilds of Canada, a place Setsuko's husband had dreamed of visiting.

It was a wonderful trip, but it was good to be home.

Setsuko took a break from unpacking.

She went to her desk with her memory cards, switched on her computer and began viewing her travel photographs.

Here they were—the girls—on a mountaintop; in a forest; next to a river; here they were on the Icefields Parkway. Here were elk on the golf course in Banff. A man with a cowboy hat. Setsuko clicked through dozens of images, smiling and giggling, until she stopped at one.

Her smile melted.

Setsuko had taken this one of Mayumi and Yukiko in cowboy hats, laughing, seated at their table in the log-cabin restaurant outside Banff. It was during the last days of their trip.

Something about the image niggled at her.

Something familiar.

Staring at it, she tried to remember.

The people in the background.

She returned to her bags, fished around in the deep side pockets where she'd shoved magazines, maps and newspapers, her fingers probing until she found the copy of the *Calgary Herald* the attendants had offered on the plane.

She remembered glancing at it before dozing off during the flight to Vancouver where they'd caught the return flight to Japan.

She unfolded it at her desk.

There was the headline, U.S. FAMILY DIES IN MOUNTAIN ACCIDENT, and pictures of Ray and Anita Tarver and their two small children, Tommy and Emily. A beautiful family, Setsuko thought, reading the article.

Having done her postgraduate work at the London School of Economics and at Harvard, her English was strong. According to the report, the authorities had located the bodies of the mother and her children, but not that of the father, Ray Tarver, a freelance reporter from Washington, D.C.

The article concluded with the Royal Canadian Mounted Police requesting anyone with information regarding the Tarver family's movements in the park area to contact them, or Crime Stoppers.

Setsuko studied the pictures in the newspaper then the people in the background of the photo she'd taken at the restaurant. The man in the background, sitting at the table behind Setsuko's friends, was Ray Tarver.

Setsuko had no doubt about it.

She checked the dates. The tragedy was discovered one or two days after Setsuko had snapped her photo of her friends in the restaurant.

This might be the last picture taken of Ray Tarver.

It could be of use to the Canadian police. Setsuko reached for her phone and called her daughter, who was working late at her office. After Setsuko explained, Miki said, "Can you send me the news article and your picture now?"

Setsuko scanned the article into her computer then e-mailed it along with her travel picture to her daughter, who was a sergeant in the Criminal Affairs Section for Violent Crime with the Tokyo Metropolitan Police Department. Miki would know what to do, Setsuko thought, rereading the terrible story about that poor young family from the United States.

At her desk at the headquarters of the Keishicho, in the Kasumigaseki part of central Tokyo, Miki Uchida studied the material her mother had sent her. She agreed with her mother. The man in the background was the missing American.

Miki glanced at her boss's office. He'd gone home for the day.

Early the next morning, as soon as he stepped into the office, she told him about the information and how it related to the tragedy in Canada. Sipping coffee from a commuter mug, he looked over her shoulder at the article and pictures enlarged on her computer screen.

"Do the necessary documentation. Then contact the Canadian Embassy and get back to our work."

Sergeant Marc Larose was the Royal Canadian Mounted Police liaison officer for the Canadian Embassy, which was located along Aoyama Dori. After assessing the tip Miki Uchida at Tokyo Metro had sent him, Larose e-mailed a report, along with the information, through a secure network to Canada.

The file pinballed down through the command structure until it finally arrived in the mailbox of Corporal Daniel Graham, who would come to realize it was more than a random picture of Ray Tarver before the tragedy.

The background of Setsuko's photo showed Ray Tarver sitting at a restaurant table facing the camera.

He was behind an open laptop.

12

Near Banff, Alberta, Canada

Fear crept across Carmen Navales's face as she studied the pictures Graham had set before her on the table in the Tree Top Restaurant.

Ray Tarver stared back at the waitress from his passport, his driver's license and the tourist photo Graham had received that morning from Tokyo.

"Think hard," he said. "Do you remember serving this man?"

Carmen caught her bottom lip between her teeth.

Earlier, Graham had noticed her watching him in the booth of the closed section of the restaurant where he'd been interviewing other staff. They weren't much help, practically indifferent, so why was Carmen nervous?

The RCMP knew all about places like the Tree Top.

Young people from around the world worked at the motels, resorts and restaurants in the Rockies, lured by the mountains, the tips and the party life. Sure, at times, things got out of hand with drinking, drugs, thefts, a few assaults. Last month, a chef from Paris stabbed a climber from Italy over a girl from Montreal. The Italian needed twenty stitches.

But Carmen hadn't gotten into trouble out here. She was from Madrid and her visa was about to expire. Nothing to be nervous about.

Carmen was the last staff member Graham needed to interview. None of the others had remembered seeing Ray Tarver. *I was, like, so hung over.* Or, *those tour buses just kept coming. It was all a blur, sorry, man, such a shame with those little kids.*

Their responses eroded Graham's hope that his Tokyo tip would lead somewhere because they still hadn't recovered Ray's body.

Carmen's reticence frustrated him.

He tapped the photos.

"Ms. Navales, this is Raymond Tarver, the father of the family that drowned not too far from here. It was in the news. You must've heard."

"Yes, I know, but I was in British Columbia at that time."

"According to your time cards, you worked a double shift here the day *before* the children were found in the river." Graham tapped the photo from Tokyo. "Ray Tarver was here the day before the tragedy. In this restaurant. In your section. On the day you were working. Now, please think hard."

Carmen steepled her fingers and touched them to her lips.

"What's the problem?" Graham asked.

"I need to extend my visa."

"What's that got to do with this?"

"I need to keep sending money home to help my

sister in Barcelona. Her house burned down. I'm afraid that if my records show I've been involved with police—"

"Hold on. Look, I can't do anything about your visa. But things might go better for you if you cooperate, understand?"

She nodded.

"You served him?"

"Yes."

"And his family?"

"No family, he was sitting with another man."

"Another man?"

Carmen traced her finger on the photo, along a fuzzy shadow behind the head of one of the laughing Japanese women. It bordered the edge and was easy to miss.

"That's his shoulder."

Graham inspected the detail, scolding himself for not seeing it.

"Do you know this other man? Have you ever seen him before?"

Carmen shook her head.

"Describe him."

"He was a white guy, but with a dark tan. Slim build. In his thirties."

"Any facial hair, jewelry, tattoos, that sort of thing?"

"I don't remember. I'm sorry."

"What about clothes. How was he dressed?"

Carmen looked at Graham.

"I think like you. Jeans, polo or golf shirt, a windbreaker jacket, I think."

"Did he pay with a credit card?"

"Cash. And he paid for both. In American cash."

"Do you remember their demeanor? Were they arguing, laughing?"

"They were serious, like it was business."

"Any idea what they talked about?"

"We were crowded, it was loud, I couldn't hear them."

"How long did they stay?"

"About an hour."

"Do you know if they left in separate vehicles?"

Carmen shook her head.

For the next half hour, Graham continued pressing her for details. When he was satisfied he had exhausted her memory, he stood to leave.

"One last thing," Carmen said. "Every now and then, the computer guy would turn his laptop to the stranger so he could read the screen."

Graham didn't know what he had.

Driving back to Calgary, he weighed the new information. The Tree Top was about a forty-five-minute drive from the Tarvers' campsite. The photo put Ray in the restaurant the day before his family was found in the river.

Who was the guy at his table?

And why was Ray showing him his laptop? Was it an arranged meeting? Or spontaneous? Maybe he'd gone there to interview someone for a travel article?

Maybe it was nothing?

But some twenty-four hours later, his family was dead.

Now, Ray was missing and so was his laptop.

The questions gnawed at Graham as he worked alone at his desk.

Since the initial front-page stories, the calls from the public had slowed. Prell and Shane had followed up with a lot of door-knocking. Most of the information was useless, even bizarre. One guy claimed that the Tarvers had been "abducted by alien organ harvesters who will appear at the UN."

Other tips were more down-to-earth, like the local rancher who'd insisted he'd seen a man resembling Ray hitch a ride on a logging rig. Graham had contacted all the lumber and trucking companies in the region.

No one had picked up anybody.

And nothing had surfaced concerning the whereabouts of Ray's missing laptop.

The Banff and Canmore Mounties had put the word out to see if anyone on the street was selling one like Ray's. Graham notified Calgary and Edmonton city police, who circulated information to pawnshops.

Jackson Tarver agreed to release the family's bank, credit and Internet accounts. If someone had stolen Ray's laptop they may be using it, and this information could help track the computer down.

Nothing had surfaced so far.

What was he missing?

Graham's cell phone rang.

"Danny, it's Horst at the site." Static hissed over the search master's satellite phone, mixing with the river's rush and a distant helicopter.

"You find anything?"

"Nothing. Our people have been going full tilt for twenty-four-seven for the past few days. We figure he likely got wedged in the rocks, or a grizz hauled him off. A couple of big sows have been spotted in the search zones. We could find him in the next hour, or the next month, or never. Know what I mean?"

"Right."

"We'll keep it going, but we'll wind it down by the end of the week."

It was early afternoon as Graham ate his lunch, alone, outside at a picnic table.

He chewed on the ham and Swiss he'd made at home, looked at Calgary's office towers and the distant Rockies and tried not to think of his life.

Stay on the case, he told himself.

He was nearly finished his sandwich when the superintendent's assistant, who spent her lunch breaks walking in the neighborhood, approached him.

"There you are. How you keeping, Dan?"

"Day by day, Muriel."

"There's going to be a barbecue with Calgary city vice unit at Lake Sundance this weekend."

"I heard."

"Come join us, if you're up for it." She touched his shoulder.

"Thank you. We'll see."

"Sunday. Around three. Don't bring a thing, dear."

Graham nodded.

But when Muriel left, he decided he was not up to it. He crumpled his lunch bag and tossed it in the trash. Back at his desk, he went at the file again.

At Graham's request, Ray's father had faxed him copies of the insurance policies Ray had taken out on himself and his wife. Each had a two-hundred-fifty-thousand-dollar death benefit. Anita was Ray's beneficiary, Ray was hers. If they both died then Ray's parents became beneficiaries.

Those were big numbers. People had committed

serious crimes for less, but Graham saw no reason to suspect an insurance fraud, unless Ray Tarver emerged from the mountains unharmed to collect a quarter of a million dollars.

Graham returned to the Tokyo photo. He had to be missing something, he thought, staring long and hard at Ray and his laptop, until the light began to fade. With most of day and most of his coworkers gone, Graham began to dread what was coming.

13

Blue Rose Creek, California

After repeated attempts, a woman finally answered Maggie's call to Madame Fatima.

She listened to Maggie's request and told her to call back the next day, which Maggie did.

"Madame says not today. Call tomorrow."

"If I could just come and talk to her, please."

"She has little time to help. Call tomorrow."

"Please, I need to see her. Please. I beg you."

Maggie heard a second voice in the background then a hand covered the mouthpiece muffling a conversation between two people at the other end of the line. Then the woman said, "Madame says you may call back this afternoon, around three."

Maggie thanked her and, with spirits lifted, resumed work at the bookstore.

She restocked shelves and was taking care of orders when a customer jingled her keys to get her attention before thrusting a napkin at her with a title scrawled on it. The woman reeked of cigarettes.

"I need this damn book *right now* for my sister's birthday."

After Maggie's computer search showed it was out of print, the woman left muttering.

"What's the G.D. point of a bookstore!"

Maggie was used to rude customers. Shrugging it off, she glanced at her watch. Nearly three. Her turn to take her afternoon break. She went to the children's section and approached Louisa to cover for her.

"Did you see him, Maggie? He's here again. He was in history and politics, but I lost him on the third floor."

"Who?"

"The creep who pretends he's reading." Louisa stepped up on a toadstool and scanned every aisle she could see from the Enchanted Story Corner.

"Don't be so paranoid. This is a bookstore. I'm going on my break, okay?"

"He stares at us all the time. I'm going to tell Robert to tell the creep to leave."

"I'll be back in fifteen."

Maggie went to the public phone outside the staff room near the coffee shop. As Madame Fatima's line rang, Maggie's heart filled with anticipation. Would this lead her to Logan? She whispered a prayer. How had her life reached the point where she needed a reluctant mystic to help her find her son and husband?

I don't care. I'll do whatever it takes to find them.

Maggie fought her tears as the line was answered and she identified herself.

"Yes, Madame says come tonight."

"Tonight?"

"Yes, Maggie, at seven."

"Oh, thank you, thank you so much."

"There is no certainty she can help you in any way, you understand?"

"I understand."

"You must come alone. Do you agree to come alone?"

"Yes."

"Madame says to bring a personal item of your husband's and one belonging to your son. Something they've touched many times, something metal if possible."

"Yes."

"Here is the address and directions. Do you have a pen?"

"Yes."

Maggie jotted the details on the back of the page Stacy Kurtz had given her, folded it and put it in her pocket and returned to work, never noticing that the man Louisa had called "the creep" had been standing an aisle away in the magazine section.

He'd had a direct line of sight to Maggie.

During her phone call, he'd been reading *The Economist*.

Or so it seemed.

14

Calgary, Alberta, Canada

It was time to face his crime.

As Graham drove south he looked west beyond the skyline to the jagged peaks silhouetted against the setting sun, standing there like a monumental truth.

Hang on, he told himself.

He made good time escaping the fringes of the metropolis and its cookie-cutter suburbs. Some forty minutes south, he exited Highway 2, taking a paved, two-lane rural road that twisted west into the foothills.

His pulse quickened as he mentally counted to what awaited him.

One kilometer, two, three, four, five...

He tightened his grip on the wheel then pulled onto the shoulder and stopped.

He needed to do this. Confront it, even if it pierced him.

He turned off the ignition, got out and walked to the site.

A plain white wooden cross marked the spot where Nora took her last breath.

Where he'd killed her.

A car hurtled by, kicking up a gust that nudged him closer to the roadside memorial for her. Nora had taught the fourth grade. They'd met when he was in Traffic and had come to talk to her class about safety.

Safety.

He pushed away the irony and touched the cross. Caressed its smooth surface. It had been erected by her students who'd adorned it with artificial flowers, pictures, small stuffed toys and printed notes protected in clear plastic sandwich bags.

We love you and we miss you, Mrs. Graham, one said.

We'll be together with the angels, said another.

The epitaphs pulled him back to that night.

They'd gone to a Flames game because they'd needed some time together. And between them, she was the bigger hockey fan. He'd been working a lot of double shifts on a joint-forces operation with Calgary city police. A stress-fest, costing him sleep. He'd yawned throughout the game.

"I can drive if you're too tired," she'd offered as they crawled with the postgame traffic from the parking lot.

"I'm good."

It took longer than usual to get to the expressway.

From there it was fine. It was a clear night. No snow. The roads were dry. The heater was blowing a gentle current of warm air to offset a slight chill. It felt so good being with her. It was tranquil and as they left the city Graham fell quiet.

"You okay there, buddy?" she asked.

He yawned again.

"Yup."

As they got off the highway, heading into the foothills and deeper into the darkness, she gazed up at the constellations, naming them for him.

"Cassiopeia, Cepheus…"

Her soft voice, the hum and warm air relaxed Graham.

"Ursa Minor, Draco, Ursa Major…"

A perfect moment and it lulled him to surrender to his exhaustion.

The last things he remembered—

"DANIEL!"

The car was vibrating, her hand seized his arm.

"DANIEL!"

They'd gone off the road. He'd tried to correct it but overreacted, turning the wheel too sharply. The car rose, then they were airborne, rolling over and over, pavement, grass, metal crunching, glass breaking, dirt, lights and stars, all churning into nothingness.

He's on the ground looking at their overturned car, its headlights pointing in odd directions. He smells gasoline. The rad's hissing. He sees her in her seat with the deployed air bag, head turned all wrong, like a bad joke, like a rag doll.

Someone is screaming.

Screaming her name.

It's him.

Everything blurs.

Emergency radios, sirens and he's on a stretcher moving fast.

So fast.

Something's pounding the air.

It's deafening.

He's flying. Ascending. Glimpsing strobing lights below. A galaxy of suburban lights wheel beneath him.

Next, a powerful antiseptic smell. Starched bed linen against his skin. He's alive but not right. Sore but numb. A tube connects his arm to a bag of liquid on a pole. Faraway, hollow voices echo his name.

"Mr. Graham?"

He's not dreaming.

"I'm Dr. Simpson. You've been airlifted to our hospital. You've been in an accident, Mr. Graham. You've got broken ribs, lacerations and a mild concussion. Nod if you understand."

His head brushes against the pillow.

"Your wife was hurt badly. Her injuries were extreme. I'm very, very sorry."

Graham's heart slams against his chest.

"The paramedics did everything they could but she never regained consciousness. Her neck was broken. Her internal injuries were massive. I'm so sorry."

The earth quakes.

"And the baby."

Baby? What baby? It is a mistake. It is a dream because they don't have a baby.

"She was three weeks along and may not have known she was pregnant."

A blood rush roars in his brain, the universe cracks and darkness coils around him, crushing him with the realization.

HE'D FALLEN ASLEEP AT THE WHEEL AND KILLED HIS WIFE AND THEIR UNBORN CHILD.

Now, all he had to keep him alive was his guilt.

It's why he'd gone to the mountains. To distribute the last of Nora's ashes then use his gun to be with her and their baby.

What else was left?

Standing there alone in the prairie night, the burden of his guilt forced him to his knees. Aching for her, he gripped the cross. "Nora, I am so sorry. Forgive me. Tell me what to do. Please. Tell me what I am supposed to do now?"

He searched the stars for the answer. It was delivered on a gentle breeze, resurrecting what had happened when he'd gone into the river to save the girl.

He'd heard Nora's voice.

"Keep going, Daniel."

This was his answer.

This case would be his redemption because his wife's voice was not the only one guiding him.

"Don't—daddy."

So much was garbled and drowned by the river. He didn't comprehend all of what Emily Tarver was trying to tell him. But now he believed in his gut that the key to unlocking this tragedy was in her dying words…and any break that heaven would allow.

Graham's cell phone rang.

"Corporal Graham, this is Prell. Just spoke with FIS. Just wanted to advise you that they pulled clear latents off the Tarver vehicle and got hits through CPIC. We have a name. Are you ready to copy?"

Graham hurried back to his car.

15

Bonita Hills, California

Maggie battled to keep her hopes in check.

As she threaded her way through the freeway traffic, her stomach tensed.

Would her nightmare ever end?

Would she ever see Logan and Jake again? Where were they?

Each day had passed without news. Nothing from police. Nothing from the courts. Nothing from the support groups, Logan's doctor, Logan's school or the private investigator. Nothing from her amateur Internet searching.

Not a word from Jake or Logan.

Nothing but deepening anguish.

Dammit, why did Jake do this?

Maggie searched the traffic in vain for answers. Whatever it was, maybe Jake just needed time to sort it all out. Maggie consoled herself with that explanation, hoping with all her heart that Madame Fatima would work a miracle tonight.

But who was she?

Maggie had called Stacy Kurtz, who'd pressed her police contacts for more information, urging Maggie to keep what she'd learned confidential.

The woman was known as Madame Fatima Soleil. She'd descended from French gypsies who'd fled persecution in Senegal and roamed Europe in the early 1900s. Her family tree branched into northern Quebec and Louisiana's bayous.

As a young woman working in the cafés of Germany, Poland, Austria and Czechoslovakia reading tea leaves, Fatima had told a Czech police official's wife that her youngest daughter would nearly drown within one year. Some ten months later, the girl was on a school trip in Rome where she was found at the bottom of the hotel pool. She was pulled unconscious from the water and had barely survived.

The girl's mother told her husband, a skeptical, case-hardened detective. But months later when the ten-year-old son of a Russian diplomat was kidnapped for ransom in Prague, he sought Fatima's help.

Fatima met the boy's parents, spent time in the boy's bedroom, then told Czech detectives to search a specific spot near a riverbed in the St. George Forest, an hour northeast of Prague. They found the boy buried alive in a coffin equipped with an air pump. Police traced the pump to the point of purchase, then to his abductors and arrested them at gunpoint.

At her request, Fatima's role was never ever made public. And she'd refused any money. Later in life, her reputation, known only to a few in police circles, accompanied her when she'd moved to California. She'd planned to retire on a small inheritance, but agreed to help California police when they called upon her.

There's the exit for Bonita Hills.

Maggie signaled.

At the first red light, she consulted her directions. She was close to the Serenity Valley Mobile Country Club, where Madame Fatima lived alone in a sixty-by-forty-foot mobile home. She had a tiny, neat-as-a-pin yard with a flower garden beneath a large picture window and a big awning that shaded much of her house. The stone walk invited Maggie to the side porch where she rang the doorbell.

She was greeted by a woman who was less than five feet tall but had a solid frame under her Hawaiian shirt and sweatpants.

"I'm Helga, Fatima's friend." She directed Maggie to a cloth-covered dining table in the paneled living room and kept her voice low. "Please sit down. You should know that she is not well and has very little time left, so you must—"

"Helga!" An unseen voice whisper-wheezed from the dark paneled hallway leading to the rear. "Come get me."

Helga left Maggie who peered down the hall after her, not believing her eyes.

A thin, feeble woman, bent by age and deterioration, emerged from the darkness. One gnarled hand gripped a cane. Her free arm was hooked around Helga's neck. The stronger woman supported her as she inched forward.

Fatima was wearing an emerald muumuu and a green head scarf. Maggie detected the smell of jasmine as

Fatima eased into a chair at the table, the silver cross hanging from the chain around her neck captured the twilight.

Maggie sat across from Fatima thinking that she resembled a concentration-camp inmate. The skin on her face was wrapped tight to her skull behind oversize glasses. Looking beyond them, Maggie met fierce dark eyes as Fatima's ghost of a smile liberated the tips of crooked brown teeth.

"It's finished for me," Fatima said, pulling off her kerchief revealing that her hair had fallen out. Small islands of down were all she had left. "The cancer. Not much longer for me. You are Maggie?"

"Yes."

"Your husband has taken your son away and you wish to find them?"

"Yes, he's a good man but he's mixed up about—"

Fatima's palm stopped her.

"Did you bring me something that belongs to each of them?"

Maggie reached into her bag for Logan's pirate key ring and Jake's penknife which she'd retrieved from the sofa where they were forever losing things. A fond memory flickered in the corner of her mind as she placed them in Fatima's hands.

"My glass please, Helga."

Helga placed a glass with ice chips next to Fatima.

"We shall begin," Fatima said. "Whatever you hear or sense, you must not move or speak, or be afraid. If I ask questions, answer only yes or no. Say nothing more. Do you understand?"

"I understand."

"The window and the candle please." Fatima put some ice chips in her mouth. "The ice cools my throat and stomach."

Helga lit a white candle, placed it in the center of the table, then drew the heavy curtains. Calm filled the room as Fatima extended her arms, resting her hands on the table, her skeletal fingers caressing the key ring in one hand, the penknife in the other.

Helga removed Fatima's glasses for her. Maggie noticed the jasmine smell intensifying. The candle flame quivered in Fatima's eyes while she continued caressing the knife and key ring. A sound akin to soft lowing flowed into the room before Maggie realized its source.

Fatima.

She was humming, creating a surreal aura; candle-light haloed around her round head as she began to sway, her gaze fixated on nothing as if she were searching another dimension, seeing other lives and other worlds.

All the while, Fatima never ceased massaging the knife and key ring, increasing her ardor with each passing moment, drawing energy from them, as if sensing the very thoughts Jake and Logan may have left on them.

Fatima shut her eyes.

Her body began to bounce up and down slightly as she continued humming.

"I see a truck."

Maggie caught her breath.

"A big truck," Fatima said. "Near mountains."

Fatima began bouncing slightly as if she were there in the cab of a rig.

Maggie felt Logan near. Felt his presence. Detected his scent!

"Logan! Honey, it's Mommy! Where are you?"

"Shush." Helga touched Maggie's wrist.

Fatima's humming stopped.

Maggie had trespassed on the moment.

Fatima's work resumed. She continued rubbing the items in her outstretched hands, continued humming and bouncing as if a passenger in a rig.

Fatima's head snapped back.

Maggie gasped.

Fatima's body jolted as if punched by a powerful force. It jerked again, nearly throwing her from the chair. Fatima's hands let the knife and key ring slip to the table as jolt after jolt shook her in her chair.

Maggie's skin tingled.

Fatima's eyes bulged to the point of nearly bursting. Her pupils rolled back in her head, leaving only the whites.

She was motionless.

Each minute melted into the next, devouring time in huge chunks before Helga blew out the candle and drew back the curtains.

Fatima began coughing.

Helga brought her a fresh glass of ice chips and Maggie watched Fatima's jaw work as she crunched them. The older woman's body was depleted as Helga slid her glasses back onto her head then helped replace her head scarf.

"We're done," Helga said. "Thank you, Maggie. You may leave."

"Fatima, did you see my husband and son?"

"I saw nothing that will help."

Maggie's jaw dropped.

"You saw something, didn't you?"

Fatima searched for her cane.

"You have to help me, please, tell me what to do?" Maggie asked.

Helga helped Fatima from the table.

"Please, Maggie." Helga nodded toward the door. "We're done."

"Yes," Fatima whispered, "I must sleep."

"That's it?"

"You must leave," Helga said.

"No! Wait, please, you have to tell me what you saw. You have to help me!"

Fatima extended her shaking hand to Maggie's, then dropped Logan's key ring and Jake's penknife into it. Fatima's eyes held Maggie's for an intense moment.

"No one can help, especially me."

"What are you saying? What does that mean?"

"You should pray."

"Pray for what? I don't understand." Helga was closing the door on her. "Please, you have to help me! You can try again! Please! *I felt Logan with us!* I know you saw something!"

Maggie stepped from Fatima's mobile home and the locks clicked behind her. She leaned against the door, slid to the landing and buried her face in her hands.

16

Calgary, Alberta, Canada

Jesus Rocks filled the police binoculars.

The words strained across Neil Bick's T-shirt, advertising his tattooed physique, earned in Stony Mountain federal prison where he did three years for stealing computers from RVs, cabins and cottages.

He'd also shot at—but missed—the two Winnipeg cops who'd arrested him.

How did this ex-con's fingerprints get on the SUV rented by the Tarver family, Graham wondered, watching through binoculars as Bick walked down a neglected southeast Calgary sidewalk and into a world of trouble.

The Calgary Police Tactical Unit had a perimeter around his ramshackle house. The street had been cleared. Far off, an unseen dog barked.

"All right, take him," the TAC commander whispered over the radio.

Heavily armed police rushed from the cover of shrubs, alleys, porches and parked cars, putting Bick facedown on the street at gunpoint.

"What the fuck?"

They handcuffed him, patted him down and read him his Charter rights.

"What the fuck is this?"

Twenty-five minutes later he was sitting in an interview room with Graham, who'd read his file a third time.

Neil Frederick Bick, age thirty-four, born in Winnipeg, Manitoba. Mother was a hooker murdered by an outlaw biker when Bick was six. He'd been a child of the province. In and out of school. In and out of the military. In and out of jail.

Graham asked Bick if he wanted a lawyer.

"Fuck lawyers. I don't need one because I didn't do nothing. Why are you jamming me, man? I've been livin' straight since I got out. I need a smoke."

The federal building was subject to no-smoking laws but Graham returned his pack. Bick shook one out, lit it and squinted through a cloud.

"Yeah, I remembered that family after I'd read the news. Wild."

"Tell me again how your prints got on their SUV."

"One of my jobs is pumping gas into airport rentals. I filled their tank and cleaned their windshield. I gave them directions to the Trans-Canada. My prints are on a lot of cars, you already know that."

Graham knew it.

He also knew they'd just executed a search warrant on Bick's residence.

"Neil, tell me about the four laptop computers we found in your possession."

"I'm repairing them for people at my church. I studied computer tech at Stony. The church outreach people set me up here in Calgary. New place, new start and all."

Bick tapped ash into the empty soda can Graham had passed him.

Ray Tarver's computer was not among the four they'd found with Bick. None of the models or serial numbers were close. In fact, they all belonged to church members who'd corroborated Bick's account.

And Mounties in Banff had called Graham after they'd showed Bick's photograph to the staff at the Tree Top Restaurant, including Carmen Navales.

"No one can say if Bick's the man who was sitting with Ray Tarver."

By late afternoon, Graham had established Bick's whereabouts for the time surrounding the tragedy. He'd been nowhere near the mountains. A minister came to the Duncan building to confirm that Bick had driven seniors to Dinosaur Provincial Park in a church van on the days in question. He had pictures.

At that point, Graham resumed discussing Bick with his commanding officers. Between making calls and handling other cases in his office, Inspector Stotter had watched most of the questioning from the other side of the room's transparent mirror.

Graham said, "Our guy's not connected to this."

Stotter held Graham in a stare that bordered on concern for a tense moment.

"Kick him loose and go home, Dan. We'll talk in the morning."

Driving from work, Graham had to pass his wife's roadside shrine again.

He had to pass it every day.

The windswept stretch where she'd died was on the

only highway to their home. The white cross jutted from the earth like an accusation but he didn't stop to face it today. Not this time.

Something deep in his stomach turned cold but he kept driving, asking for forgiveness as he passed the site.

Their property was southwest of Calgary on the upper slope of an isolated butte. One of the few modest old ranch homes still standing, it sat on a ridge overlooking a clear stream and the mountains.

Since the day he'd arrived in Alberta, Graham had wanted this acreage, known as Sawtooth Bend. After he'd shown it to Nora, she fell in love with it, too. Six months after they were married they bought the land.

They belonged here.

They'd had dreams for building a big new ranch home and raising children here.

But those dreams had vanished with the ashes he'd released to the wind.

Loneliness greeted him when he opened the door.

He took a hot shower, changed into his jeans and a T-shirt. He wasn't hungry. He poured a glass of apple juice, collapsed in his swivel rocker, turned to the window to watch the sun sink behind the Rockies.

How could he live without her?

How could he go on chained to his guilt?

He glanced at their wedding picture on the mantel, loving how she glowed in her gown. An angel in the sun. He beamed in his red serge. For that moment in time, his dreams had come true.

He was born in a working-class section near Toronto's High Park neighborhood. He grew up wanting to find the right girl and become a cop, just like his old man, a respected Toronto detective. When Graham's dad followed a case to Quebec, he met Marie, a secretary for Montreal homicide. They fell in love and that was that.

The younger Graham grew up in Toronto fluent in English and, thanks to his mother, French. He dreamed of being a Mountie, a federal cop with the most recognized force in the world. His father and mother had tears in their eyes the day his graduating troop marched by them at the RCMP Training Academy in Regina. His first posting was in southern Alberta, where he'd made some key arrests at the Montana border. It led to a detective job with GIS in Calgary. Then he joined the Major Crimes section where he'd excelled at clearing the hardest cases.

But now?

He ran his hand over his face.

Now, his confidence had been shattered. He didn't know if he was on the right track, a fact reflected in the way Stotter had looked at him. Bick was not connected. Graham had no solid evidence to prove the case was anything more than a terrible wilderness accident.

So why the hell was he trying to make it into something more?

Did he believe it was something more?

Was he missing something?

He didn't know. He couldn't think. It was black outside and he went to bed. But night winds rattled the windows and tormented him with questions.

Maybe what happened to the Tarvers was no accident? What about the missing laptop? The stranger at Ray's table? The meaning of "Blue Rose Creek," the last note Ray had written? Earlier, Graham had run the term *Blue Rose Creek* through databases but got nothing concrete.

Then there was the big insurance policy. There was stress in the Tarver home, money problems and the fact that they still hadn't found Ray's body.

Did he flip out, kill his family with plans to emerge and collect the insurance?

Go back.

What if Ray was onto a big story and someone killed him and his family?

How big does a story have to be?

Any way you cut it, a wilderness accident can be a perfect murder.

Mother Nature is your murder weapon.

The wind shook the house. Graham tossed and turned and in his dream state he heard Nora whisper to him as she did when he'd been underwater in the river facing death.

Keep going, Daniel. You have to keep going.

Little Emily Tarver's dying words haunted him.

Don't—daddy.

But the girl's voice was so soft, so small and the river was deafening. These factors raised doubts. Did she actually speak at all? Or did he dream that she did?

Was he dreaming now?

Or was he mining his subconscious as her last breaths played in his memory. He could hear her again. But this time she said more.

He heard her clearly.

An icy chill rocketed up Graham's spine, forcing him to sit up, wide awake.

The time glowed: 2:47 a.m.

He made coffee, sat in his chair and considered his case. Then he went to his computer and by dawn he'd completed a new case status report. He showered, had fresh coffee and scrambled eggs for breakfast then drove back to the office and placed his updated report on his boss's desk.

Graham was convinced he now knew Emily Tarver's dying words.

"Don't hurt my daddy."

After reading Graham's report, Inspector Stotter removed the jacket of his mohair suit, hung it on the wooden hanger, and then hooked it on his coatrack.

"I know you've saved our team many times with solid detective work, Dan."

Graham sat in one of the cushioned visitors' chairs watching Stotter.

"You stood your ground when everyone else thought you were wrong."

Stotter loosened his tie then rolled his sleeves to the elbows.

"But I don't see it here. I don't see a reason to grant your request to go to the U.S. and look into Ray Tarver's history."

"Why not?"

"I think you're using this case as a means of repentance."

"What?"

"I think it's got something to do with why you were in the mountains in the first place and why you jumped in the river after the girl."

"I jumped in to help that girl."

"The result was heroic but the act was suicidal."

Graham averted his stare.

"Danny, you've got to stop beating yourself up for what happened to Nora. You can't go back and undo what happened. It was an accident, which is probably what happened with the Tarver family."

"She spoke to me."

"Who spoke to you?"

"I told you. The little girl, Emily. In the river. Just before she died."

"Dan." He let a long silence pass. "Dan, are you sure you're ready to be back on the job?"

"I swear it happened, Mike."

Stotter looked at him for a long moment, thinking.

"This isn't in your report."

"It was chaotic. I was unclear at first."

"What did she say?"

"'Don't hurt my daddy.'"

"'Don't hurt my daddy'?"

"That's right."

"You're certain?"

"Yes."

"She say anything else?"

"No, just, 'Don't hurt my daddy.' Why would she say something like that? There has to be something else at work."

Stotter looked hard at Graham for a long time then scratched his chin.

"You've attended traffic accidents, Dan. You've seen badly injured people in shock. They fight off people who try to help them. They say all kinds of things that don't make sense when they're in shock. I don't think you have a clear dying declaration here that would warrant a criminal investigation into suspicious deaths. You have no solid evidence."

"We still haven't found Ray Tarver, or his laptop. He met some stranger the day before this happened. The guy was a freelance investigative reporter from Washington, D.C. And there's another thing, the last handwritten entry in his notebook, this Blue Rose Creek."

"All circumstantial. It will not hold up in court."

"But…"

"You know real cases are not like TV crime shows, Hollywood movies or books. There are always loose, inexplicable threads that cannot be tied up neatly at the end, and have no bearing on a criminal act."

"My gut's telling me there's more to this."

"Your gut?"

"Sir, you've got nothing to lose by signing off on a thorough investigation."

"Dan, our budget's tight. We're shorthanded. I need you on other cases."

"We're talking a multiple death case with unsettling circumstances."

Stotter crossed his arms, cognizant of the fact Graham was one of his best, that he needed to keep him on his game and that this case could be crucial to preserving his confidence. After ruminating on the situation, Stotter grabbed Graham's report.

"Give me an hour."

Some forty minutes later, Stotter, holding Graham's rolled report like a baton in his hand, waved him into his office.

"Shut the door. I talked to the superintendent."

"And?"

"Apart from his life insurance—" Stotter had circled part of Graham's report "—Ray Tarver took out a small Canadian travel insurance policy when he booked their trip."

"Right. It doesn't pay much for death."

"In cases where bodies are not recovered the policy has a standard presumption-of-death clause."

"You're going to let me do this, let me go to the U.S. and check his background?"

"Listen to what I'm telling you."

Graham took out his notebook.

"You get in touch with the LO in Washington and give him what he needs to set you up down there. This is how you approach this: You tell people that you're completing paperwork that confirms Ray Tarver was in peril at the time of his presumed death. All efforts to locate him have been exhausted. You're asking a few routine background questions, basically to ensure that he hasn't surfaced, wandering like an amnesia victim, or was acting out of character before the tragedy."

"Right."

"You say that you're tending to an administrative matter while you're in the U.S. following up on other unrelated matters. This will be low-key with no potential for ruffling feathers or causing embarrassment between the force and U.S. law enforcement. Besides, I'm sure some of the guys will be busy with the papal visit. Do you understand what I've told you?"

"Got it."

"You are not authorized to conduct a criminal investigation in the United States. Is that clear, Corporal Graham?"

"Crystalline."

"Register your trip with the travel branch. You have one, maybe two weeks, unless I call you back sooner."

17

Please, God, let it be Logan.

Blurry images of a boy played on the screen before Maggie.

Let it be him. Please.

A few days after Maggie's ordeal with Madame Fatima, a new hope had emerged.

"We believe this is your son," Ned Rimmer said just as the video froze and static snowed on the images.

Rimmer was an LAPD detective—"retired six years now" after a drug dealer's bullet took his left eye. Rimmer wore an eye patch, a ponytail and a sour disposition most days. He was still a detective, just not the kind he'd planned on being.

Rimmer and his wife, Sharmay, an emergency dispatcher with a penchant for dangling earrings, belonged to the Guardian Rescue Society, a national group of law enforcement types who volunteered their money, resources and time, to find children in parental abduction cases who'd slipped through the cracks.

Logan's file was passed to them months ago when

Maggie had first sought help from support groups who'd circulated her plea among their circles.

She'd never heard of the society until today when Sharmay called her at the bookstore, identified herself, then said, "We believe one of our Guardians may have located your son, Logan Conlin."

Stunned into silence, Maggie gripped the phone.

"Hello? Maggie?"

"My God, do you have him? Where is he? Is he okay? I have to see him!"

"We don't have him yet. We'd prefer to discuss details at our Los Angeles office. Please come as soon as it's convenient so we can advance the case."

An hour later, after following Sharmay's directions, Maggie had parked her car on a street that bordered Culver City and West L.A.

The society's L.A. chapter was in a second-story office above the Flying Emerald Dragon takeout restaurant. The aroma of deep-fried chicken and stir-fried vegetables filled it now as Maggie sat before the video monitor.

"Here we go. Fixed it," Rimmer said. "This footage comes to us from our New York chapter from Wayne Kraychinski, retired NYPD detective first grade."

As the Rimmers had explained it, Kraychinski checked Logan's profile with his school sources, as he does with all the cases his chapter takes on.

Kraychinski got a lead in Queens concerning a boy fitting Logan's age and description. According to the history, the boy had recently moved to the community with his father, a trucker, who fit Jake Conlin's general profile.

Kraychinski and some of the other Guardians initiated surveillance.

"We've got a series of sequences recorded over a few weeks," Rimmer said.

The camera shook and a boy about eight to ten years old in a hooded sweatshirt swam into view but not in sharp focus. Maggie couldn't see his face clearly, or his full body and gait. The boy was among a group walking through a schoolyard to a basketball court.

"Now, this is where they reside."

The video jumped to a row of tired-looking two-story detached homes shoehorned into a Queens neighborhood. One house had a rig out front. No trailer. A green Peterbilt. Being married to a trucker, Maggie knew vehicles. Jake drove a Kenworth but he could've sold it or traded it for a Peterbilt.

Next, the boy was in a park with other kids on skateboards.

Again, his back was to the camera. He was wearing a ball cap and was sitting on the grass bordering the skating area. Maggie caught her breath as he turned to offer his profile, but a shadow blocked the image before it disappeared.

Maggie covered her mouth with her hand to stifle a groan.

Is it Logan? She couldn't be certain.

"Now," Rimmer said, "this next sequence, which is the money sequence, was obtained by Kraychinski's friend, Ella Bell. She's a former Customs officer. Ella used a minicamera hidden in her hat to employ a ruse for interaction."

The camera was shaky as it came upon a group of

boys at a park bench in a playground. The audio offered a woman's voice that carried a touch of Long Island. The speaker was unseen as the camera closed in on the group.

"Excuse me, guys, could you help me? I'm lost and could use some help here."

A map was unfolded on the bench.

"I'm looking for the Vander Building. Anybody know where that is?"

The boys huddled around the map and faces bobbed in and out of view. The camera pulled close on a boy about ten with a ball cap.

"This is it," Rimmer said. "Watch."

"Nice hat," the woman said. "You like the Yankees?"

"Yeah."

The cap's brim cast the boy's face in shadow.

"You're not from around here," the woman said. "Where're you from?"

"He's new here from Ohio," another kid answered. "Yo-hi-yo."

"That right?"

The boy's face is clear now, filling the screen as he nods.

"The Vander Building's that way." Another boy pointed. The images blurred for Maggie as her heart sank and tears rolled down her face.

"It's not him."

"Are you sure?" Rimmer asked. "Because sometimes the abducting parent will change the hairstyle and color."

"That boy is not my son!"

"Stop the video, Ned." Sharmay began rubbing Maggie's shoulders. "You're going to be okay, honey."

"I'm sorry I yelled. That's not Logan. I'm sorry. Please thank everybody for me. I'm sorry." Maggie collected her bag and headed to the door.

"We'll keep looking," Sharmay called to her back. "You're going to see him again, I just know it."

Night was falling.

Maggie was losing a battle with her emotions as she hurried to her car.

How could she have been so stupid? How could she let her hopes get so high?

She pulled her keys from her bag and fumbled them. They chimed against the pavement. As she retrieved them, she glanced to the end of the street.

Although it didn't fully register, Maggie glimpsed a man near the end of the block who'd been sitting in his car reading a newspaper.

As Maggie got behind the wheel of her car, he put the paper aside, sat upright then turned his ignition. When she left her parking space, the man behind her pulled out of his.

He stayed several car lengths back in a blue Impala with tinted windows. His lower front bumper was scraped on the driver's side.

Maggie had noticed him as she checked her rearview mirror, but didn't give it much thought as she headed for the freeway. She had other things to contend with.

Traffic was heavy.

The radio news reported that a wreck was choking flow on the San Bernardino Freeway, so she took the 60, her pulse still racing over what had happened with the Guardians. It hammered home the reality that she may never see Logan again.

No. Please. No. She wouldn't survive. Jake, where are you? Please tell me.

Maggie brushed away her tears and focused on the slow-moving streams of red taillights and Sharmay's parting words, replaying like a prayer.

"You're going to see him again, I just know it."

Maggie needed to believe that.

She had to.

By the time she reached her exit some ninety minutes later, her anguish had evolved into exhaustion. As she made her way through Blue Rose Creek, she saw that her tank was nearly dry. She turned into the big twenty-four-hour Chevron that she liked.

It was clean and well lit.

Safe for a woman alone at night.

After filling up and swiping her card at the pump, Maggie stopped dead.

That's weird.

A blue Impala with tinted windows and a bumper damaged on the driver's side was in a far corner of the station's large lot.

Was that the same car she'd seen behind her in Culver City?

Couldn't be. She was being silly. Or tired. Or both. Chalk it up to a bad day, she told herself after she started her car and pulled out of the station.

A moment later, as she waited at an intersection for the light to change, she thought about taking a hot bath to soothe her nerves when she got home. Then in her side mirror, she noticed that a blue Impala had eased into her lane, two cars back from her.

What the heck?

The light turned green and Maggie quickly changed her turn signal indicator and turned right instead of left, keeping her eye on her mirror.

The Impala turned right.

She was being followed!

Stop it, she told herself. You're not being followed. It's probably nothing. Probably a coincidence. To prove it, she turned left at the very next street.

She checked her mirror.

The Impala turned left.

Gooseflesh rose on Maggie's arms as scenarios played in her mind. She pushed on the accelerator. She didn't know this neighborhood and took the next right, glimpsing the Impala behind her, turning right.

Maggie pressed the pedal down farther and began searching the dark houses along the quiet streets, helpless, not knowing what to do, eyes locked on her mirror.

As she came to a stretch where the street coiled, Maggie turned quickly into an empty driveway and her car disappeared into a darkened, empty carport.

She killed her motor, her lights and took her foot off the brake.

She slid down in her seat and peeked from her car to the street, watching the Impala roar by, its taillights disappearing into the night.

Maggie sat up and rested her head on her headrest. She gulped air and took several deep breaths as she sat motionless, wondering what the hell had happened.

Had she been followed? Should she tell police? She imagined how that would go.

Ah, yes, the crazy lady again. How can we help you?

What was it? Carjackers? Teenagers? The imaginings of a distressed woman?

Maggie concentrated on her watch. It calmed her. After fifteen minutes passed, she started her car and drove to her house.

No sign of the Impala.

She sighed.

As she unlocked her door and entered her home, she was numb.

Sleep.

Forget the bath.

Go to sleep.

But she noticed the red light was blinking on her answering machine.

One message.

She pressed Play.

The tape beeped as it cued the message. Maggie recognized that voice.

"This is Helga, Madame Fatima's friend. Madame has instructed me to tell you that she has information about your son. Information you should have."

Book Two:
Blood Revenge

18

Cold Butte, Lone Tree County, Montana

Father Andrew Stone watched the wind-groomed grass undulate across the Great Plains, mile after mile until the earth touched the sky.

Breathtaking in its majesty.

Immortal for its painful history.

So deserving of what was to come.

Soon the pope would arrive here and consecrate this very ground, the Buffalo Breaks, where so many of Stone's ancestors had died.

His heart swelled at a dream come true.

But last-minute concerns were risking cancellation of the papal visit, the first ever to this corner of the country.

Stone wasn't worried.

For if there was one thing he'd learned from an old friend, it was that God's plan was unstoppable.

"Father Stone! We're ready to start!"

Nearly a hundred yards back, the principal of Cold Butte's only school was calling him to the Papal Visit Planning Committee's meeting on the letter from Washington.

Stone had read it.

The Secret Service had alerted the Vatican to the latest security and foreign intelligence—more intercepted chatter about threats and potential attacks. Unrelated to the letter, the *Washington Post* had recently reported that a growing number of influential U.S. church organizations, fearing an attempted assassination, were privately urging the Vatican to cut venues in the papal visit, including the one planned right here in Lone Tree County.

Gripping his copy of the letter and the *Post* story he'd stapled to it, Stone started for the school, certain that the visit would ultimately take place. His faith was anchored by his devotion to God and his blood ties to the land where he was born.

Stone was descended from the Swift Fox, a small Plains tribe nearly wiped out by smallpox in the 1880s. At that time, Sister Beatrice Drapeau, a nun from France, had arrived with Jesuits and stayed to minister to the dying until she died of the illness.

The sick who prayed to her memory survived.

Her story inspired Stone to become a priest. After his divinity studies and ordination he was posted to the Vatican, working among the archives on the church's role in Native American history. There, he befriended a wise cardinal who was taken by Stone's call to God and the nun's legacy.

"Sister Beatrice's sacrifice must not be forgotten." The cardinal raised one finger to Stone before he returned to Lone Tree County. "One day, my brother, I will make a pilgrimage to Montana to honor her."

Years later, to Stone's awe, the cardinal was elected

pope. A few months afterward, Stone's old friend, the new pope, wrote him a personal letter.

"My brother, to remember our Good Sister, I will, as promised, make a pilgrimage to the Great Plains on the next anniversary of her death. You may pass this news to others so that they may join in the celebration."

Stone kept the note private but went online to share the news and the date of the pope's upcoming visit to Montana.

Unlike presidential visits, news of papal visits was often made public in advance because of the scale and preparations involved. But Stone's revelation had long preceded the Vatican's expected official announcement of a multicity papal visit to the United States. This frustrated the U.S. Secret Service because it gave ample lead time to anyone planning an attack.

Now, as Stone entered the school and took his place at the meeting, he braced for a heated debate on any last-ditch effort to cancel the pope's visit to Montana.

"The very thought of canceling at this stage is a preposterous notion," said the reverend from the office of the Bishop for the Diocese of Great Falls-Billings.

"Absolutely," the woman from the governor's office agreed. "We're down to a few short weeks from the event."

"As the letter states, U.S. and foreign intelligence have been picking up chatter about threats and potential attacks," a Secret Service official said through the speakerphone from Washington. "Granted, it's not uncommon, but the volume has markedly increased and gives us concern. Especially since various plots against several world leaders and several other targets have been thwarted in the past sixteen months. The Secret Service is in no way advising the Vatican to cancel any events. Our role is to provide the intelligence for the Vatican to make any decision."

"These groups quoted in the *Post* want a shortened tour and suggested the visit to Lone Tree be dropped," the reverend from the Diocese of Great Falls-Billings said.

"That's got nothing to do with the Secret Service," the agent said.

"We're aware these are challenging times, but to cancel any venue at this stage is contrary to the intent of the Holy Father's pastoral mission to the U.S.," the priest representing the Holy See's Secretariat of State said from Washington. "Each location plays a key role in the pontiff's ecumenical work."

In Montana, the day of celebration would involve a presentation to the pope at the school by the children's choir before he celebrated an open-air Mass in Buffalo Breaks for about one hundred thousand people. There he would bless the site and acknowledge that God allows people to rise above failings to ensure the spirit is not extinguished.

"Has anyone considered the fallout of canceling the first papal visit in the state's history?" the principal asked. "Think of what's been done, accommodating charter groups, arranging motel rooms from Great Falls to Billings, Lewistown, Miles City, even into North Dakota. The cost, the expectations created. Not to mention all the security and background checks everyone has already undergone. And the choir. Goodness, the children have been working so hard for months," the principal said.

As Stone followed the nods that went round the table, he detached himself from the discussion.

"At this stage, the decision is not ours," the Secret Service official said.

"That is correct," the official from the Holy See said. "We must await the Vatican's final decision."

19

Cold Butte, Lone Tree County, Montana

Logan's face turned red.

Everyone stopped to stare at him.

You could have heard a pin drop on the floor of the gym where fifty students from all grades had been assembled into the children's choir that would perform for the pope's upcoming visit.

Sobil Mounce-Bazley, the choir director, tapped her baton on her podium. All voices hushed. Music sheets rustled, someone coughed but no one dared speak. In the silence, Sobil ran a finger down her list until she came to the offender.

Number 27. Alto. Age nine.

"Logan Russell?"

"Yes."

"You were out of time. You threw off the entire group, Mr. Russell."

"I don't care."

Steel-blue eyes peered over bifocals at Logan and held him for an icy moment.

Someone coughed. A snicker was stifled.

"Logan Russell, you will see me after practice."

The spinster Sobil Mounce-Bazley was a legendary music director, having led children's choirs in London and New York until she retired to her brother's ranch near Cold Butte. When word spread of the historic papal visit, she accepted the school's invitation to form and lead the choir that would sing for the Holy Father.

Music had been her life, perfection her standard. But things weren't going well today. Number 27, the lovely alto, was straining her patience.

"You want to tell me what your problem is, Mr. Russell?" she asked Logan after everyone had left.

He didn't answer.

"I'm sure you've heard it said ad nauseam that to sing for the pope is a once-in-a-lifetime oppportunity."

"I miss my mom."

"Where is she?"

"In California. My mom and dad kinda split up and I moved here with my dad and his new girlfriend."

"That might be tough, but it's no excuse for rudeness."

During her time in London and New York, Sobil had directed children who'd had parents murdered, baby brothers or sisters who'd been sold by crack-addicted relatives. Acting out over a divorce was not high on her sympathy scale.

"I won't pry. I'll cut you some slack. Mind your manners. Memorize the songs, practice the tempo. If you don't improve by the end of the week, you're off the team. Is that understood, Mr. Russell?"

It was.

* * *

On the school bus home, Logan leaned his forehead against the window and watched as cloud shadows floated over the eternal empty grassland.

He'd never felt so alone. Tears filled his eyes.

Mr. Russell.

Russell was a lie. His name was Logan Conlin.

He didn't even know who he was anymore.

He didn't understand anything, anymore. Ever since his dad went off to Iraq, nothing seemed right. His dad wouldn't talk about what had happened to him over there. But when he came back, he was weird. Different. He had headaches, lost his temper all the time, argued with Mom all the time. Logan's friend Robbie said that's how it was with his parents before they got divorced.

Logan didn't want his parents to get divorced.

He needed both of them. Together.

Then came the worst moment ever, on the soccer field with Logan's coach, Mr. Ullman. It scared Logan the way Dad wanted to fight him. The look on Mr. Ullman's face—like his dad was a psycho. At night he heard Mom crying in her room. A couple of months later, things seemed better, but Logan still feared his parents were getting a divorce.

Then it happened.

Not with lawyers and courts and papers like Robbie said.

Dad just surprised Logan at school. Just showed up in his rig.

"We've got to go, son."

Dad wouldn't say where they were going, or why. At first it was like the coolest adventure. They just drove and drove. But as they left the city behind, his dad's face got all serious and Logan got scared.

"This will be the hardest thing you'll ever have to face, son. It won't make any sense to you. It doesn't make sense to me. Your mom's in love with another man and wants to have a life with him."

"That's a lie!"

"I wish it was. I'm sorry. I know this is hard, but please listen. There's no other way to say it. Your mom and I are splitting up and you're going to live with me."

"Turn around."

"I can't. There are complicated court orders. Laws, rules we have to follow. A lot of changes I'll tell you about later. But the bottom line is we can never go home again."

Never go home again.

"No! You take me home right now!"

"We can't. There are rules and the law."

"Then let me call her. I want to talk to Mom!"

"Logan, we can't."

He tried to punch his dad but only hit air. Something inside Logan broke in two. Pain shot everywhere. It hurt so bad he couldn't understand why he wasn't bleeding.

Then he felt nothing.

When they pulled into a truck stop near Barstow, Logan snuck to a pay phone on the wall just outside the washroom and tried to call his mom. He couldn't remember her work number, had trouble making a long-distance call. Just as the operator came on, the line died.

His father had disconnected the call, replaced the handset then hauled Logan back to the truck.

"Son, I told you we can't ever call her. We have to

stick to the rules, the laws and the court orders. I'm sorry but that's just how it is."

Logan cried for several hundred miles as the California desert rolled by and he fought to understand what no nine-year-old boy could ever understand.

All he knew was that something he loved had just died.

That something he needed was gone.

And all he could do was cry.

As they reached the outskirts of Las Vegas, his dad told him they were going to meet someone. Then Dad made a call on his new cell phone and they went to a restaurant at one of the big hotels where some woman waved to them.

"Son, this is Samara. Samara, this is my son, Logan."

"Hello, Logan." She had a foreign accent and her hand was cold when he shook it. "Your father's told me so much about you."

Logan didn't give a shit.

Just like he didn't give a shit for the banana split his dad had ordered for him. Like that would make everything okay.

"Son, I never told anyone this but Samara helped me during some pretty horrible times in Iraq. She saved my life. She's a nurse from England and now she's working here in the States—in a part of Montana where they're short of nurses. That's where we're going to live, son. In Montana with Samara."

"No, we're not! We're going home!"

"Son, I know this is a lot to handle and it's complicated."

"I hate you, you fucker!"

The banana split sailed from their table, landing in an explosion of ice cream and glass near the feet of the startled waitress.

Gears clanked and rattled, brakes creaked.

The school bus stopped and the doors opened to Logan's place.

He tensed at the postbox with the name Russell. Sticking out like the lie it was. Dad said they had to change their names, something about court-ordered property law and complex rules.

Logan hated it here.

Dad was on the road driving most of the time, leaving him with Samara. She worked for the county and came to the school more and more for meetings about the big visit. At the start, when they got here, the other kids thought she was Logan's mom.

It made him angry and sometimes he corrected them with his fists.

He got sent to the principal's office a lot when they first got here. His dad and Samara thought putting him in the choir would help him settle down.

Samara kept saying that she thought he had a nice voice.

She never bothered Logan much. She made sure he did his homework and she took care of most of the house stuff. She made him what he liked to eat, like chili.

It was never as good as his mom's.

Besides, she was always busy taking these nursing courses and studying all the time. Always typing on her laptop and talking to friends on her cell phone at all hours. She had a strict rule that Logan was never to touch her phone or laptop, something about patient confidentiality.

He didn't want to touch her stuff. He didn't really like her.

Sometimes, late at night, he heard her talking on the phone in a strange language. From the action movies he'd watched, he guessed it was Arabic, or something. She was from Iraq. He told his dad who explained to him that Samara had friends around the world who worked with relief groups, like the Red Cross. These people did good things and she was just talking to her friends.

Whatever.

Why couldn't Logan talk to his friends in California? He didn't understand it.

Once he secretly tried to e-mail his mother from a friend's computer but he didn't know her e-mail. Then they tried to reach her through the bookstore's Web site but a thing popped up about credit-card security and Logan backed off.

What if what his dad said was true about there being some stupid mean law that he was not supposed to talk to his mom.

He yearned for her today as he got off the bus and walked down the long lane that cut across the flatland to their house, an ugly yellow square thing in the middle of nowhere.

Might as well be on Mars.

Logan saw his dad's red rig parked under the tree where he was working on it.

"How was school?"

Logan shrugged.

"All the kids must be getting excited with the count-down to the big day."

"I think I'm going to be kicked off the choir."

"What makes you say that?"

"The teacher says I'm not concentrating and gave me some extra work to do to prove that she should keep me on."

"Then you'd better do it and focus, son. This is a big deal. Like meeting the president. You don't want to blow it now. Samara worked hard to get you on the choir and you've put in the time."

Logan looked out at the horizon and blinked at his problems.

"Want to tell me what's on your mind, son?"

"Are you going to marry Samara?"

His father wiped his hands on a rag.

"I don't know. We take things day by day, you know that."

"Are you and Mom ever going to get back together?"

"We've been over that a thousand times, Logan."

"How come if this pope thing's such a big deal, I can't call Mom and invite her? She would like to see this. Please."

His dad sat on the truck's step and pulled Logan closer.

"We've been through this. We can't call her, ever, we can't see each other. It's over. It's finished. We might not like it, but that's the way it happened with the court stuff. We just moved on with our lives."

"I tried to call her and e-mail her, Dad."

"What? Dammit, Logan! When?"

"When we first moved here and a few times after."

"I specifically told you never, ever try to call or contact her. Logan—" his dad looked away to soften another lie "—the court ordered us to do everything that we did. We are to have no contact with her, ever."

"But I was really sad and you were gone. I tried to call but I couldn't get through. It's like our phone here won't let me call our old number in California. Same with e-mails."

His dad nodded and told him he had a block arranged with the phone and Internet companies. All part of the court's rules, he said.

"Dad. I don't understand. What happened?" Tears filled Logan's eyes.

"We've talked about this, son. We're just not part of her life anymore. That's why we moved here. You've had friends whose parents got divorced. Well, it's like that. People change. Mom changed. So we had to start over. Start a new life with new names in a new place."

"But how can she just stop loving us? I don't believe she did. I mean, that last day I saw her, she was hugging me. I told her I was worried that you might be getting a divorce. She said it wasn't true, that she loved you and that she loved me."

"Stop it, Logan."

"How can she just not love me anymore? She's my mom. She has to love me. I know she wouldn't just stop loving me. I want to call her, Dad."

His dad put his hands on Logan's shoulders and looked him in the eye.

"I know this has been hard. But you've got to try not to think about the past. It's not easy, I know. But we've got Samara, and believe me, son, after all we've both been through, she's the right person in the world for both of us right now."

A motor hummed as Samara's van pulled up to the house.

"Hi, guys," she called, smiling. "What's up?"

"Nothing," Logan said. "Can you make tacos?"

"Sure." Samara looked at Jake then back at Logan. "Think you might give me a hand with some groceries in the van?"

That night, they ate a quiet dinner together.

Logan's dad turned in early because he had to leave early in the morning for a job that would take him to Spokane, Salt Lake City, then Great Falls before he got back.

That evening after the dishes, Samara and Logan went outside to the chairs under the big tree. Under the brilliant stars, and to the sound of crickets, she helped him with his music. In the light that spilled from the kitchen window Logan saw concern on her face, as if something major was heavy on her mind.

"Logan," she said. "I want you to know that no matter what you think about me, and no matter what anyone says, you and your dad are the two most important people in the world to me."

Logan said nothing as she gazed up at the Milky Way. She seemed sad.

"Soon," she said, "you're going to be part of history. Soon, everything will be as it should be."

The tear tracks running down her cheeks glistened in the starlight.

"The joy we crave will return for all of us, I promise you."

20

Missoula, Montana

Jake drove west, hauling scrap metal and a load of grief about Logan.

The sudden move to Montana had been hard on his son. Seeing him struggling after all these months tore Jake up and he started asking himself if leaving everything behind in California had been the right thing to do.

His hands tensed on the wheel.

Another headache was erupting, a real pile driver. He downed two pills then searched the plains and the Bitterroot Range, telling himself that moving here with Samara was not a mistake.

She had saved his life.

It was that simple.

But Maggie was his wife. They'd had Logan together. They'd had a life together.

How did they lose control of it all?

Jake blinked at the road markers and the memories flowing by: How he'd met Maggie in high school. Dancing together in the gym. How they'd drive to the beach in his old Ford pickup. How they'd talk for hours. Two lonely people who belonged together. She actually got him interested in books. He liked Joseph Conrad's dark stuff. And he taught her how to drive a standard, at the price of a whiplash or two.

They'd shared dreams.

They got married.

Man, he was so happy. Then Logan came and life got even better. Jake felt lucky, took a calculated risk and got a loan on a bigger rig to earn more. Then on a run to Taos, New Mexico, his transmission blew at the worst time—when he was overextended. It cost him jobs and huge repairs. Gas prices soared. Bills piled up. Loan and mortgage payments became overdue.

It was desperation time.

The only way out was a contract job driving convoys in Iraq. It was risky. People got killed. But they needed the money. So he'd put his life on the line.

Then everything went to hell.

It started with the attack.

He never talked about it. Never told Maggie what happened. Dammit, even mentioning it to Logan was hard.

The attack.

Don't think about it. Stop it.

His head began throbbing like a jackhammer drilling into his brain.

Stop.

All right. Be cool. Hang in there.

The trouble started after he got back from Iraq, with that day in the supermarket when they'd bumped into Ullman, Logan's soccer coach. He was a good-looking guy. College grad. Smart. Smooth. Jake had heard the other moms talk about him.

It was the way Maggie smiled at Ullman.

He'd never seen her smile like that before.

Jake just knew.

She'd cheated on him with Ullman.

Maggie denied it. But he was convinced. He just knew.

But did he really know?

Now, as he looked at the serrated peaks, he asked himself if he could've been wrong about Maggie and Ullman; asked himself if he was the problem, if he was all messed up because of the attack.

Pop-pop!

Jake's heart leaped, jolting him in his seat. A passing group of motorcycles backfired.

Pop-pop!

Like gunfire.

Pop-pop!

His head hurt, like it was being squeezed in a vise.

Pull over. Pull over.

Pop-pop!

The sounds sliced through the air and his skull. He geared down, got to the shoulder. Dust billowed, engulfing him.

He shut his eyes.

Pop-pop!

Jake crushed his head in his hands to keep it from coming apart as dust swirled, choking him. It was futile….

…he was being dragged back…

Please. Just stop. Please…

…dragged back to Iraq…

21

The frontier beyond Tal Afar, Iraq. Near the Syrian border

*T*his is not good....

His rig is slow-rolling through a busy market. They'd been cut off five miles back from the larger convoy and the main armored escort.

His radio crackles.

"Get your Kevlar on!"

Jake has a bad feeling about this. They are in a twenty-truck convoy hauling supplies to support a secret mission at the border. But they got cut off and now there are just six vehicles. A Humvee in lead, a Humvee in back. Jake's Mercedes is the last rig. A guy from Spain, one from Amsterdam, and Mitchell, Jake's pal from Texas whose wife just had a baby, are driving the other rigs.

Jake hates being cut off.

Being cut off is like being plucked from the herd.

They are going too slow. Too damn slow. This is a hot insurgent zone.

A kill zone.

He just wants to get to the damn camp without getting shot. Without getting rocks hurled at his windshield. Just get to the camp. Shower. Eat. Sleep. Count one more day closer to home. Closer to Maggie and Logan.

Now they are crawling.

Damn. Please do not be a checkpoint. Please do not tell me this is an Iraqi police checkpoint. Please.

Insurgents wear fake police uniforms.

"Okay, we gotta stop," the radio bleats. "It's a checkpoint."

Jake curses. All the saliva in his mouth evaporates.

The diesel rigs idle in the broiling sun.

Eyes locked open, heart thumping, mouth dry, do-or-die, trickles of cold sweat down his back, listening to the chatter on the air, scanning the stalls, the beggars pushing carts, the old men hunching over the open fires heating teapots, kids chasing a dog, hitting it with a stick. Stay alert, stay alive, delivering democracy to your door.

Maggie and Logan smile at him from the photo taped to his dash.

Get me through another day. Get me home, is all I pray.

Come on. This is taking way too long.

Scanning the old men, the kids, the dog, the burned-out cars, the idling trucks growl as beggars pass by pushing carts.

Radio chatter. A blur in his periphery.

Pop-pop!

Gunfire. A muzzle flash in the market and Hayes in the lead Humvee is frantic over the radio to the crew in the rear.

"T-Bone! Heads up! Behind you!"

Wham! The Hummer behind Jake is ablaze! A beggar's cart tips.

"Ambush! Ambush!"

Hayes opens fire with his M2 lighting up the target behind Jake. People are scrambling, screaming.

Jake is trapped.

The air splits. The beggars fire an RPG!

Thump! The ground shakes. The rig in front explodes, burning fragments rain on Jake's rig. A large chunk thuds on his hood.

A head.

Mouth agape, Mitchell stares wide-eyed at Jake.

Oh, Christ!

Mitch!

Oh, Jesus!

To his right, smoke puffs from the burned-out car. A grenade rips at the lead Humvee. Vibrations. Shadows in Jake's mirrors; out of nowhere several men are splashing water on his rig. No. The smell. It's gasoline!

They're going to kill him.

The convoy is returning fire. The guys from the lead Humvee are on the road burning. A soldier shooting is on fire, shrieking.

"Grease the mothers!"

Ghost figures swarm all sides of Jake, climbing onto his rig.

They're all over him.

Pop-pop!

The American soldier's trying to pick them off. Rounds whiz-clang off his truck.

Jake reaches for his sidearm. The mob is pulling at

his doors. Coming through his windows, smashing the windshield.

He's going to die.

Someone slams the sidearm from his grip. He claws for his knife, grabbing it in time to slice across an attacker's throat—his blood spraying. Jake meets his eyes, meets his hate, smells his breath.

Mitchell's head watches from his hood.

Jake's door rips open.

They have his arm, someone has his ankle. Jesus. He glimpses a smoke cloud, a grenade sizzling toward his cab.

No. No. No.

The searing inferno concussion ejects Jake, propelling him skyward, arching clear as the ground rises, slam-pounding his breath from his chest.

In the brilliant sun the last thing he sees is Maggie smiling on the beach and Logan running to him with open arms.

22

Cold Butte, Montana

After Samara finished the breakfast dishes, she made tea and turned on her laptop.

Jake was on the road. Logan had left for school.

She had two hours alone before she had to leave for the clinic.

Using an array of IDs and passwords, she clicked along a complex network of Web sites to check a number of Internet accounts.

The e-mail she was expecting had not arrived yet.

Samara clicked to her hidden folder to visit the joy in her life: her husband, her son, her mother and father. She smiled at their faces in the photos as her heart filled with love. For each day brought all of them closer to eternal happiness.

As it had been destined.

Samara shut off her computer and gazed at the boundless Montana sky. Soon the world would know the pure, unassailable truth of her action. Soon her name would be spoken by every human being on earth.

Samara Anne Ingram.

Her father, John Ingram, was a British archeology student who had been completing his Ph.D. on a dig near Mosul when he'd met Amina, a nursing student working at the site. They fell in love and Amina returned to London with him.

After they'd finished their studies, John and Amina were married in London, where Samara was born. Her parents settled in the city's East End, where her father taught at a small college and her mother worked in a hospital.

Samara's life with her parents was a happy one.

Until she lost them.

She thought of them every day, recalling her mother's sweet smile and the way she filled their house with the aroma of samoon or khubz, delicious breads Samara loved to eat with jam and honey.

Her father would sit in his study for hours, smoking his pipe, pondering artifacts of Assyrian ivory, or fragments of ancient pottery. Often, they'd all go to a local teahouse to talk about art, history or Samara's goal to become a nurse like her mother.

She wanted to help people.

Samara dedicated herself to studying and was accepted into university, where she met and fell in love with Muhammad, a medical student from Iraq. He was the intelligent, handsome son of a doctor in Baghdad. Muhammad got along well with Samara's father and, of course, charmed her mother, who loved to cook for him.

After Muhammad received his degree in medicine and Samara graduated into nursing, they were married in a small ceremony in London. Then they moved to

Baghdad, for Muhammad believed with all his heart that their purpose in life was to alleviate suffering.

"Together we will help a great many people who need it, Samara."

But he'd cautioned her. Life would not be easy in Iraq. They would have to grapple with the devastation of the Gulf War and the sanctions.

Nearly a year after they arrived, Samara faced her greatest challenge—but it had nothing to do with any hardships in Baghdad.

Samara was working a night shift when her supervisor called her to the phone. It was a British diplomat who'd located her through her British passport. He told her that her mother and father had been on vacation in Greece when their rental car left the road and struck a cliff side.

They were killed instantly.

Samara collapsed.

Only last week she'd learned that she was pregnant and had planned to call her parents in a few days. Overwhelmed, Samara feared for her baby. Muhammad rushed to her side. She could not have survived without him. They traveled to London together. He helped her bury her parents, then helped her mourn them while ensuring she channeled love and healthy energy to their baby.

"It's just the three of us now. We must work together to get through this," Muhammad told her on the return flight to Iraq.

It was a difficult time but Samara drew upon Muhammad's unyielding love and resolve and gave birth to a healthy baby boy.

Ahmed John.

Their miracle.

Her little son helped mend the hole in her heart. Day by day she was able to move forward with life which, in Iraq, was getting worse.

In the years after Ahmed was born, the sanctions continued exacting a heavy toll on the country. Vital medicine was in short supply and not getting through to the people whose lives depended on it.

Muhammad and Samara didn't care about Saddam, didn't care about politics. They wanted the suffering to stop. They wanted to help the children, women and men dying needlessly in their crowded hospitals. Each day they struggled under a regime that seemed to be hated by much of the world.

And each day Samara wondered how much longer things could continue.

Then came the day the world stood still.

The day the planes crashed in New York, Pennsylvania and Washington, D.C. "What madness," Muhammad whispered as they watched news reports. "Now more people will suffer, Samara."

Their sadness was compounded when they learned that two student friends they'd met in London, stock traders, had died in the towers. In the time that followed, the people of Iraq grew uneasy as the United States focused its anger on Saddam.

The attack unleashed a global storm of accusations and debate over Iraq.

Some eighteen months after the hijackings, fears intensified as foreign jets screamed over the city. Huge lineups formed at passport offices, people scrambled to leave Iraq, others hid valuables and moved to the countryside.

Muhammad and Samara knew that the majority of poor people who could not afford to leave the city would need help most if things got worse.

They were determined to stay.

Everywhere in the city, Iraqi soldiers had set up heavily armed checkpoints. The streets became deserted as the United States and other nations marshaled forces in Kuwait while Washington issued ultimatums to Saddam.

Saddam ignored the deadlines.

The bombings began in the night.

Shock and Awe.

Sirens sounded, tracer fire lit up the sky which boomed with a distant thunder that grew louder as it pounded them, explosions shaking the very earth under them. The noise became so loud Samara's clenched teeth banged together and her rib cage vibrated.

As Muhammad shielded her, she held Ahmed in her arms and prayed.

In the aftermath of the bombings, dark clouds rose over the capital.

The smoke and smells of a burning city under siege filled the streets with funereal, apocalyptic haze.

Large sections of Baghdad had been destroyed.

One morning, while going to help at a hospital overrun with wounded, Samara was waiting at a traffic checkpoint in front of a building that had been razed. She spotted a tiny object amid the rubble on the street and went to investigate.

A small human foot.

It appeared to be a little boy's foot because it was still in a sandal that had a little blue football on it.

The foot was about the same size as her son's.

Samara covered her mouth with her hand.

What are we doing to each other?

It was not the first body part she would see on the streets of her city.

Within weeks U.S. forces had taken Baghdad; and in the months and years that followed, life changed. Many people were jubilant over the demise of Saddam and the promise of a better Iraq, but extremists called upon Iraqis to kill the foreign soldiers who'd invaded their homeland.

The country struggled to recover and rebuild against never-ending violence. Factions fought factions, insurgents continued to wage war against occupying troops. The stream of car bombings, suicide bombings, sniper attacks, hostage takings, mines, booby traps and gun battles ensured that blood gushed through Baghdad's streets.

Much of it innocent.

The nightmare worsened when several foreign soldiers were killed after insurgents ambushed them near the edge of Samara's neighborhood. Muhammad and Samara were part of the civilian medical response team that rushed to the scene to offer aid.

Later, word spread that the anguished troops had vowed revenge. That a massive retaliatory operation was coming.

Days passed without activity.

It was deceptively tranquil, and dread gripped the neighborhood before it came.

Unleashed with sudden fury.

Explosions and gunfire began at three-thirty one morning, ripping through the entire neighborhood as if hell had descended upon them.

Everything happened with such terrible swiftness.

Muhammad went outside to assess what his neighbors knew, when a teenager warned him that it was not over. "Revenge squads" were going door-to-door hunting for the ambushers.

After Muhammad had returned to protect Samara and Ahmed, a patrol smashed open their door. In an instant, soldiers seized Muhammad, beat him, then pulled Ahmed from Samara's arms. They dragged them into their living room, bound them to chairs, shouting insults and swearing as they smashed their faces.

Ahmed was crying.

Samara screamed for him in the chaos.

Outside, the night screeched with gunfire. Tracers and explosions lit the sky, while inside, the house was in darkness.

Intense flashlights stung their eyes as the soldiers accused them of being the insurgent ambushers.

When Muhammad begged, explained that the soldiers should recognize them as medical staff, he was beaten.

Samara couldn't see the soldiers' faces under their camouflage, couldn't see their shoulder flags. Most of the interrogation was in Arabic, but she'd detected English speakers, along with the reek of alcohol.

She pleaded for mercy and was punched.

Then all of her clothes were torn from her, leaving her naked in the chair.

Muhammad protested. He was kicked, forced to watch as soldiers pinned Samara to the floor. A soldier lifted her exposed buttocks, opened his pants and raped her.

Samara screamed.

In the strobe of tracer fire, she saw Muhammad, helpless, while the soldiers forced him to watch. Then Samara saw the horrible confusion in her son's small eyes. Ahmed was crying as she prayed that none of it was real.

Ahmed looked so tiny in the soldier's grip.

Like a toy about to be broken.

Then a second soldier took his turn with her.

Then a third.

Ahmed screamed.

Outside, the explosions and gunfire became more intense. Suddenly the walls of the living room disintegrated as rounds stitched across them.

"The shit's getting too close," one soldier said.

American? British? Australian? Contractors?

"Shoot them! They died in the crossfire! Let's go!"

A soldier seized Muhammad, dragged him to Samara and pressed his gun to the back of his head.

She looked into her husband's eyes.

His face exploded, splashing warm cranial matter on her skin.

Ahmed wailed.

"Shut the fucker up! Let's go!"

Gunfire popped.

Then a brilliant light flashed in the house and it was as if the earth split open.

It was the last thing Samara remembered before everything went black.

23

Cold Butte, Montana

In Montana, Samara brushed tears from the corners of her eyes and cupped her hands around her tea.

A chill had penetrated her.

Images from the night her world ended still burned.

In the morning, dust and smoke had arisen from the ashes of Samara's house. A gentle wind carried wisps of cloud across the smoldering neighborhood.

The soldiers had vanished.

Samara was in shock, uncertain she was alive.

Her ability to feel, to form a thought, to speak, had shut down as scenes unfolded around her in a staccato slide show of horror.

Ahmed! Muhammad!

Someone called their names over and over.

Medical relief workers helped Samara into the rear of an ambulance. They treated her until she shook them off to watch rescuers extract two bodies—one large, one small—from the ruins of her home.

Ahmed! Muhammad!

Samara could not, did not, accept that they were dead.

It was an evil dream.

Wake! Wake!

When would she awake?

Old women in black robes came to her with solace and prayers, supporting her as she knelt before the corpses set side by side on the ground. The sheets that covered them glowed white against the scorched earth. A hood had been tied around Muhammad's head.

His face was gone.

She took his hand and held it to her cheek, her tears webbed along the dust that encased his skin.

She felt the warmth of his smile on the day they'd met at the university in London.

Muhammad.

She felt his goodness, his spirit, leave this earth.

Muhammad.

Then the women pried Samara from him and she watched the workers, faces covered with surgical masks, load him into the truck to take him to the morgue.

Muhammad!

She fell upon the smaller corpse.

Ahmed.

She pulled back the sheet.

To see his face in death.

Her son.

Her child.

Her life.

All who were near were jolted by Samara's banshee wail that reached a degree of sorrow beyond this earth. Then, like an exaltation of angels, the robed women gathered over her to share the burden of her pain.

Samara raised her hands to heaven to ask why.

A black combat helicopter patrolling the aftermath thudded above slowly. She saw the dark visors of the crew.

Watching the scene.

In that instant, her answer had been delivered, although it would not be revealed to her until later.

Samara looked upon Ahmed.

Tenderly she slid her hands under the sheet.

Lovingly she collected her son.

The old women admonished the relief workers who tried to take him from her and pushed them back.

Ahmed was weightless in her arms as Samara began walking through her devastated city to the morgue.

The old women followed, beating their chests with clenched fists, shouting prayers as others joined them to form a death procession.

As they passed from neighborhood to neighborhood, weary soldiers, fingers on triggers, eyed them, scanning them for signs of an insurgent ruse.

They glimpsed Ahmed's small hand that had escaped his death shroud, as if to reach for reason in a time and place where it did not exist.

Helicopter gunships continued to hover directly above Samara as her tears fell upon her dead son.

In the time after, people from the hospital, neighbors and kind strangers from relief agencies helped her.

Samara had a vague and mixed memory of what followed.

She'd been taken to a room in the local mosque.

Muhammad and Ahmed were naked, side by side on tables where the old women guided her in washing them for their journey to paradise.

The women prayed as the bodies were cleansed.

Then they were wrapped in cloths and placed in coffins.

The next day the coffins were secured to the roofs of cars, draped with flowers and driven slowly in a procession to a cemetery on the bank of the Tigris River, one of four rivers said to flow from Eden.

The coffins were lowered into a single plot to rest together, father by son. Samara's friends struggled to keep her from throwing herself into the grave.

Depleted of life, Samara refused to leave the cemetery.

Hours passed, day turned to twilight, which turned to night and prayers. The old women understood and watched over her. Covering her with blankets and shawls.

When a new day approached, they made her tea and brought her bread. They sat with her in silence, contemplating the Tigris, a river as old as time.

A river that knew great sorrows and great joys.

A river that held the answers.

And as the sun broke, the old women answered the call to prayer, leaving Samara to gaze upon the Tigris.

Statue-still, she was a portrait of pain.

Numb, alone, disconnected from the world, Samara was being transformed.

Every passing second, every tear, every beat of her broken heart, brought her closer to an awful knowledge.

The chant of the old women completing the morning prayers ended. Without invitation, one of the oldest among the mourners took her place next to Samara and took her hand.

Gnarled fingers wrapped in leathery, sunbaked smooth skin traced the lines of Samara's palm. The old woman studied it in silence for a long moment.

Then she spoke to Samara in an ancient dialect.

She had known Samara's mother and her grandmother, she said, knew her people, that Samara's tribe was descended from Bedouins, near the disputed region.

Samara will soon go there.

She will return to her people and the desert because the next stage of her life is there.

It is already foretold, here. The old woman gave Samara's hand a gentle squeeze.

In the weeks that followed, Samara journeyed to the cemetery every day to contemplate her loss, the river and the old woman's prophecy.

A few months later, she made inquiries to international relief agencies.

Samara asked favors of influential doctors who knew diplomats, who could expedite matters as she prepared to go to the desert, to find whatever awaited her there.

24

The Rub al Kahli, Empty Quarter, Arabian Peninsula

The battered Land Rover and Mercedes trucks, each bearing the star symbol and lettering for a global relief agency, lumbered over the great dunes.

Occasionally they vanished in the sandstorm as they pushed deeper into the no-man's-land straddling Yemen and Saudi Arabia's Ash Sharqiyah, in the Eastern Province.

The two-truck convoy was on a rescue mission that had begun two days earlier. A twin-engine plane ferrying rig workers to the Gulf of Oman for a Dutch oil company spotted the remains of an attack on a Bedouin encampment some three hundred kilometers southeast of Abaila near the Yemeni border.

Nowadays, camel caravans were rare and Bedouin tribes seldom wandered this deep into the Empty Quarter. The desert in this isolated part of the world was among the most forbidding on earth, covering some half a million square kilometers with fine, soft sand and sand sheets. The region was largely waterless, uninhabited and, until the 1950s, was unexplored. Now, it was early summer, season of the *shamal,* the severe northwesterly winds which produce the most blinding and suffocating sandstorms ever known.

The Empty Quarter was a lawless zone ruled by terrorist gunrunners and extremist rebels. Local gangs routinely kidnapped tourists, foreign oil workers or travelers and held them for ransom.

Failure to pay resulted in beheading.

After traveling a day and a night and aided by a temperamental GPS, the small search party had reached the reported location. It was not likely they would find survivors, the flight crew had warned.

It was dangerous proceeding as the winds hurled wall after wall of sand at the trucks, rattling windshields and hampering visibility. The relief workers were led by an Egyptian doctor from Cairo. Then there was a Brazilian, who'd left his job as a Sao Paulo banker, a young female American death-penalty lawyer from Texas, and an Italian soldier from Venice.

Out of the hot swirling sand-laden winds, which had blotted the sun, a large piece of fabric, a remnant of a tent, suddenly enshrouded the Rover's grill, flapping madly on it like a traumatized victim as the party came upon the carcass of an animal, its stiffened limbs pointing skyward.

"Looks like a goat," said the soldier, stopping the Rover. Pulling his head scarf around his face and stepping into the storm, he leaned over the carcass and saw it was not a goat but the corpse of an old man. He had been disemboweled. The soldier said nothing as the wind slammed against him. He knew the work of the group behind the crime. They would find no survivors here. When the soldier returned to the truck, he said to the others, "Let's keep moving."

From Ethiopia to Algeria, Kurdistan and Sudan, each of the relief workers knew the horrors visited upon the dispossessed. The stare of a dead child's eyes, the stench of a corpse, the colors and textures of human organs, torn limbs, the feast of maggots on a decapitated human head, all were common experiences for them.

They were acquainted with evil.

As expected, they'd found no survivors among the several dozen victims of what was an attack by a fundamentalist extremist group of bandits. Many of the victims had been beheaded after they were tortured. "That is their signature," the soldier said as they searched for documents and identifying items that would be recorded in a regional data bank at Riyadh. Even the camels, sheep and goats had been killed.

The toll was four men, six women and eight children aged two months to thirteen, according to the doctor's estimates.

Bedouins were camel and goat herders, a vanishing people who, for centuries, had been nomadic from Afghanistan to Sudan. Although some tribal vendettas carried for generations, this attack exceeded any perversion of tribal law, sect or creed.

It was an unfathomable outrage, the American wrote in her journal.

By nightfall they had assembled the corpses and built a huge funeral pyre from the remnants of tents, bedding, handwoven blankets and camel saddlebags. The night was clear. Tranquil. The winds slept. Constellations wheeled overhead as the flames and smoke ascended into the eternal desert sky. The bodies burned with the putrid smell one never forgets as the Egyptian doctor recited a passage from memory.

"We only have the life of this world. We die and we live, and nothing destroys us but time."

That night as the fire crackled and the group settled into their tents, the workers did not speak, or even attempt to comfort each other. The Egyptian searched for answers in the worn copies of his holy books. The Brazilian and the soldier played chess. The American wept in private until sleep took her.

In the morning, they rose with the sun as the winds resumed. Exhausted, the foursome said little to each other as they departed. They had driven for nearly three hours when the Brazilian squinted from behind the wheel of the Mercedes into the sandstorm. "It looks like something ahead. An animal."

"A goat from the camp. A survivor," the doctor said. "Let's pick it up."

"I'm not certain what it is." The Brazilian radioed ahead to the soldier in the Rover.

The soldier reached for binoculars, trying to discern the small form ahead.

"That's not an animal! It's a woman!"

He shifted gears.

Oblivious to the trucks, the woman walked determinedly, even as the trucks overtook her and braked in front of her. All four workers climbed out and stood in her path, staring at her. Only when she reached them did she halt.

She appeared to be in her thirties. From the quality and fabric of her tattered garments, she at first appeared to have been a shepherd's wife. But the Egyptian doctor saw something more, saw the vestiges of an educated woman, a middle-class woman of standing, perhaps.

A woman who did not belong here.

Under her head scarf, they saw her face was bruised and scarred with dried blood. Her parched lips mute. Her blank eyes did not regard the workers. They did not regard anything.

"What is your name?" the doctor asked first in Arabic, then several other languages, including English and French.

No response.

"She is in shock and dehydrated," he said, then to the woman, "You are safe. You are now with friends."

At that, the woman collapsed. The soldier caught her.

"Let's get her onto a stretcher," the doctor said.

Wind-driven sand hissed and pelted the canvas of the Mercedes as the doctor and the American aided her, checking the woman's vital signs, setting up an IV drip. Examining her, the doctor found she had cuts and contusions from severe beating.

When they resumed their journey, the doctor watched over the woman in the rear, swaying with the truck's rhythmic rocking.

She was semiconscious. Her vital signs were good. They had been traveling for nearly an hour; all the while the doctor wondered, Who was this sole survivor?

She was not a tribeswoman. She seemed misplaced in the region. She had smooth skin, almond-shaped eyes. She was beautiful. He tried to comprehend what she had witnessed and fathom reasons for her being here. Running a soothing hand over her forehead, he noticed an unusual protrusion within her clothing.

He discovered a hidden, zippered pocket cleverly sewn along a seam. He opened it, extracted its contents. Documents. He studied them carefully, absorbing her identification.

Samara Anne Ingram.

Her photograph. A nice smile. Dual citizenship. An Iraqi from Baghdad. A British subject. A certified nurse. Small photographs of a man and a little boy. Her husband and child? But they were not among the dead.

Why was she here?

An aid worker, perhaps?

An idea landed on the doctor.

"Change our course now!" he yelled to the front. "We must go to Yemen!"

"Yemen?" the Brazilian responded over the engine's roar. "Why?"

"I know medical people there. Good ones. It's better we take her there. Tell the others on the radio! We must change course now! Turn around!"

"But the guards at the border will make things difficult."

"I can take care of that."

"You're the boss."

Few people alive knew the Egyptian's true identity and his role as senior recruiter for one of the deadliest networks in the world. The doctor touched his waist and his concealed money belt. It was thick with cash, bribe money that would ensure entry into Yemen with no questions asked.

If that failed, he only had to put his lips to an ear, whisper a name, and all doors would open for him.

All doors.

He was oblivious to the radio's chatter—the Italian cursing the GPS again—and the swish of petrol in the trucks' many exterior storage containers as transmissions ground and the trucks turned and headed off for the lethal zone of Yemen's northern border with Saudi Arabia.

The Egyptian was oblivious to it all.

For he was no longer a doctor with the relief agency. Now, he was performing his other duty—one the others knew nothing of.

No one saw him slide Samara's identity papers inside his boot.

His old friend would be pleased.

He had found a potentially powerful soldier.

A perfect soldier.

25

I am dead.

Samara was lying in the bed of a darkened room and discerned two figures watching her. Seated in chairs, they were silhouetted against the brilliant sun that bled through the huge wooden shutters.

Was this the next stage of death?

The torment of the tomb?

The old women had told her the stories—how after a believer's death, after the mourners had left, two angels would appear and question the dead, to judge their entry into paradise.

"Where am I?"

"With friends, who wish to help you."

"Help me?"

"Into the next life."

Nausea surged through her and she vomited into the pan at her bedside.

Her head throbbed with pain. She was disoriented, groggy from sedation.

But alive.

An IV drip was taped to her arm, her body sore as fragments of memory strobed.

The bandits attacking the camp.

She'd hid for days under the corpses; how they twitched as the vultures fed on them.

Then the horror of Baghdad.

The blinding thunder flashes, the earth splitting open.

Carrying her son in her arms.

As she recovered, she saw vials for drugs at her bedside.

A cup of water was handed to her.

"Samara, we've learned much about you in the few days you've been here after we found you in the desert." The man's voice was soft, sympathetic, as he looked over her papers. "Through our contacts, we know of the injustices that have been inflicted upon you. We know of the tragedies of Baghdad months ago, that forced you back to your people, your distant Bedouin relatives, to aid them."

"Who are you?"

"Your brothers."

"My brothers?"

"We will help you."

"What of the others? Did any of the others in the camp survive, the children? The mothers? There was an old man, he tried to help me."

"There is only you."

"Oh!"

"Pray with us and you will understand."

Samara wept.

"How can I pray? My faith has been destroyed."

"This will change, you have been called to your destiny."

My destiny?

Something was taking shape.

It had been five months since the deaths of Ahmed and Muhammad. Five months since Samara began her search and now, here, the answers Samara had sought were emerging. As if rising from a shimmering mirage, something illusory was coming into view, as foretold by the old woman.

Although hesitant and unsure at the outset, Samara soon found herself echoing the men in prayer, like so many others who prayed at the appointed times of the day throughout Shibam.

The city, with its red and orange clay buildings towering over each other from the narrow terraced streets, was the city where frankincense traders had gathered for the great camel caravans that had journeyed along the ancient spice route.

It was the city where her ancestors had prayed and honored the old ways.

In the weeks that followed, as Samara's injuries healed, the shadow men emerged as patient teachers. Day after day, they filled her with the knowledge she needed to devote herself to that which they said was preordained.

During that time, pieces of the woman Samara had been broke away from her, turned to dust and disappeared into the desert.

Samara was reborn.

Transformed in the consuming drug-hazed winds of prayer and fanaticism.

The teachers enlightened her to *their* truths.

That her bloodline reached back for generations to an ancient Bedouin tribe. That according to ancient Bedouin belief, a person in Samara's circumstance was required to adhere to a somber custom. That the family of those who have been murdered must exact vengeance on those responsible.

In an act of blood revenge.

"Deep within you, Samara, your heart thirsts for vengeance. *Embrace it.*"

Over several days of more medication and prayer, she came to accept that her anger was the fuel for the action she must take, until one day she said aloud, "I hate them. I hate them for what they've done."

Then her teachers enlightened her to a metaphysical nightmare as they placed her cherished photographs of her family in her hands. Samara's broken heart warmed as she touched her fingertips to their faces.

"When the unbelievers murdered Muhammad, Ahmed, your husband and your son did not go to paradise as your heart believed."

Samara looked toward the speaker.

"Where are they?"

"They are at the door to eternal hellfire."

"No."

"The same is true for your mother and father, who died in Greece. The same is true for your relatives who were slaughtered in the camp."

Samara wept for the beautiful children, their kind mothers, their gentle fathers.

"They remain in agony because you have not yet acted. You are the sole survivor. Only you can deliver them. When you complete your transition and become a willing warrior and carry out the action, Samara, you will join them in eternal paradise."

If you become a willing warrior.

After weeks of medicated recovery and indoctrination, Samara accepted their teachings.

"What is my action?"

"It is simplistic to say you must exchange pain for pain, but for you, Samara, a greater role, one of monumental significance, awaits. Are you prepared to accept the greatest sacrifice?"

The old woman's prophecy had come true. Samara had found her answer in the desert—she must rescue her family and join them in paradise.

Even if it meant the greatest sacrifice.

"Yes. I accept."

26

Karachi, Pakistan

Lights of the megalopolis glittered against the Arabian Sea as Samara's jet from Yemen landed at Jinnah International Airport.

A forger from Istanbul had been well-paid by Samara's sponsors to produce the required travel documents. The caliber of his work allowed her to pass easily through immigration as a British nurse with a global relief agency.

The next morning, before dawn, two men from the agency arrived at Samara's hotel-room door. They were Egyptian chemistry engineers who'd studied in Germany. They loaded her bags into their four-by-four, saying little as they began their long drive without revealing the destination to her.

After leaving Karachi's sprawl, Samara noted the cities they passed—Uthal, Bela, and Khuzdar.

As the road descended into the plains to Surab, Samara scanned the vistas that stretched for miles, as if searching for herself. The vastness underscored her sense of emptiness. She confirmed her vow to accept whatever they set before her.

Samara knew from maps she'd studied on the flight that their northern route paralleled the porous border with Afghanistan to the west. Its rugged terrain was threaded with hidden roads used by smugglers, drug dealers and refugees.

By sundown they had arrived at a camp of outbuildings hidden in the hills close to the Urak Valley overlooking Quetta.

The city twinkled at her feet.

She was taken to her private quarters in a small clay house, to a room no bigger than a cell consisting of a sleeping mat, gas lamp and footlocker. Exhausted, Samara slept for a few hours before she was called to predawn prayers.

Apart from armed guards and instructors, a dozen people were in her group, including three other women. One from Oman, one from Syria, another from the Philippines. While Samara's face bore her loss, the faces of the women burned with righteous devotion. However, it would not be long before Samara's face was indistinguishable from the others.

After prayers, they were led in training exercises. "For your protection as relief workers in dangerous zones." An instructor smiled.

They learned self-defense, how to kill an attacker using a knife or a pencil. A loaded automatic rifle was placed in her hands. She was taught to shoot by firing at a dummy. The gun was surprisingly light but the recoil nearly knocked her down.

Later on, during classroom sessions in a small mess hall, theoretical operations and procedures were discussed, such as how to ID a U.S. Air Marshal.

Weeks passed with the same routine.

Then a rumor floated through the camp.

Someone important had arrived.

That evening, Samara was taken to a secret site, deeper and higher in the hills, where they were escorted by heavily armed guards to a small encampment.

She was introduced to a handful of older men, sitting at a campfire drinking tea. As the flames lit their faces and embers swirled into the sky, they talked quietly for several moments until one stood and embraced Samara.

"Welcome, sister." His garments smelled of jasmine. Then he held her in his sad, tired eyes. "We know of your suffering. We know of the violations. You honor your family by fulfilling your destiny. Come, share our tea and we'll tell you something of your purpose."

He explained how through religious groups and international relief agencies, Samara had been recommended for a nursing job in a remote American community that faced chronic shortages of medical staff. Soon, she would be dispatched to the U.S. to be interviewed for working and living there.

The man encouraged Samara to blend in with Americans, find an American boyfriend, he shrugged, even marry, while she awaited instructions for her mission.

"Where am I going?"

"Montana."

"Why there?"

The man looked to a colleague who held several files. One contained a printout from the Web site of Father Stone's newsletter. The one that had given Washington concern because it had prematurely announced the pope's upcoming visit to Lone Tree County.

"It is with great joy that we can confirm the Holy Father will visit Cold Butte."

But the man didn't offer Samara many details about what she was destined for in Montana.

"It will become obvious to you when you arrive."

It would take several weeks, months in fact, before all was finalized. Until then, Samara would work with a relief group in Iraq, building credibility for her job in the United States.

"So, we will work and we will wait," he told her. "Your American operation, like many others we have designed, is being reviewed. The instrument you require will be delivered to you in the U.S. at the appointed time. Others will be there to help you. Still others will watch over and protect the operation, unseen at every stage unless it is compromised and must be aborted.

"Your mission, above all else, will change history. It will mark the end to centuries of oppression and humiliation inflicted by the nonbelievers."

His eyes bore into hers.

"For you, this sacrifice will guarantee you and your family eternal happiness in paradise. Sister, now, with all that has been thrust upon you, do you accept that it has been preordained?"

Samara fought her tears and nodded.

Again, he embraced her.

In darkness, guided by flashlights, she was taken through the hills, back to the camp and her room.

Lying on her mat, by the pale light of her lantern,

Samara stared at photographs of Ahmed, Muhammad, her mother and father.

Tears rolled down her face.

Soon they would be together again.

27

The frontier beyond Tal Afar, Iraq. Near the Syrian border

Days later, at the convergence of the Syrian and Turkish borders, Samara's small group stole into northwestern Iraq.

Supplied with counterfeit documents, they joined members of their network's relief agency.

A week later, they'd learned that a battle had broken out with a U.S. convoy near Tal Afar. They were close. The carnage was still burning in the market when they arrived. Samara had learned that one wounded American truck driver had been captured, that the insurgents intended to hold him hostage and make demands.

Ultimately, they would behead him.

Samara's group intervened and won his release in exchange for cash. They would return him to U.S. authorities as a sign of goodwill.

But after studying his ID, Samara had an ulterior plan.

Jake was lost.
Disoriented.

On his back, in tranquil light, cool water was sponged on his skin and the smell of flowers perfumed the air. He woke to the dark eyes of the woman tending to him.

His skull throbbed with flashes of Mitchell's severed head.

Someone was shouting.

The woman calmed Jake, her touch comforting. Her soft voice carried a British accent and soothed him as she explained that he'd been wounded in an ambush but needed rest to survive.

Her name was Samara.

She was a nurse with the relief agency that had negotiated his release from the insurgents who'd attacked his convoy.

He was safe now, she said.

They were in an isolated remote reach, near the Syrian border. Messengers had been dispatched to get word through trusted channels to the nearest U.S. camp.

So soldiers could get Jake home to America.

In the days that followed, while Samara helped him, they'd learned something of each other.

Samara was born in London. Her father was a British professor, her mother an Iraqi nurse. Samara had married an Iraqi medical student she'd met at university in London. They moved to Iraq, where they had a son. Both her husband and son were killed in the insanity that had plagued the country, leaving Samara to devote herself to frontline aid agencies.

Now, she was preparing to go to America to start a new life.

Jake thanked her for saving his.

"If you're ever in California, contact me." Jake gave her his e-mail address and phone numbers.

He showed her pictures of Maggie and Logan, told her about America, about his love for the open road, football, hot dogs and country music.

Samara never smiled.

She just looked at the photo of Maggie and Logan.

Then she looked at Jake.

She never revealed her thoughts to him.

Samara was amazed by Jake's resemblance to her husband. He shared his good looks. He also had a young son.

Reflecting on it, as she treated Jake, Samara cautioned herself not to become distracted. But as Jake recovered, as they talked, grew familiar with each other, something happened. Conflicting emotions overwhelmed her, something that had died inside her had stirred.

One clear night when the sky was a sea of diamonds, after the others had gone to the nearest village for food, Samara and Jake found themselves alone.

In his tent, Samara checked on Jake's condition and vital signs. Her face was beautiful under the dim lamplight. Her touch was soft. Jake searched her face, her eyes flickered like falling stars. Her shirt had slipped, exposing a patch of her bare shoulder. He put his arm around her and she didn't resist.

He drew her near.

Samara looked into his eyes.

She didn't resist when he kissed her.

A long, deep kiss.

Which she returned.

She sighed as she grew aroused and began to unbutton his shirt, her hands exploring his hard chest, sending a shock wave burning through him, until he forced himself to break away.

It was wrong.

He thought of Maggie and Logan.

This was wrong.

No words were needed.

Samara left the tent.

They never spoke of it the next day, or the next when two Hummers arrived.

"Sergeant Kyle Cash," said the U.S. soldier whose grin preceded him out of the truck. "Mr. Conlin, sir, we done thought y'all was dead. Some folks back in Blue Rose Creek, California, are going to be mighty happy. Mighty happy, sir."

"Thank you for coming for me, Sergeant."

It was that sudden.

Jake thanked Samara and the relief workers then climbed into the Hummer. She stood there watching him as they pulled away. Not smiling, not waving, just watching him pull out.

Jake looked back at her.

The woman who'd saved his life. He looked at her until she'd vanished in the dust, leaving him to doubt whether he would ever see her again.

"You know, sir, it's a miracle any way you cut it," Cash shouted to Jake, who nodded. "When word got to us that a relief agency was ensconced up here and had saved an American, well, no one believed it."

"Why?"

"Intelligence says this zone is rife with death squads."

28

At that time, their kiss meant nothing, Samara remembered now, as she got ready to leave the bungalow for the clinic.

Samara had sworn to heaven it meant nothing.

In the moment after it had happened, she'd begged her husband's memory for forgiveness and her heart hardened toward Jake Conlin, the American, who'd beguiled and tempted her. Afterward they never spoke of the kiss.

But Samara kept Jake's contact information along with his offer to help her when she arrived in the U.S.

He could become an asset.

Unexpectedly, the U.S. military brass in Baghdad gave Samara's group an official letter of appreciation from the U.S. government for helping a U.S. citizen to safety.

That letter, along with Samara's British passport, and other documents, helped her gain entry into the U.S. to work temporarily.

In Montana, Father Stone, the local priest who'd

chaired Lone Tree County's hiring committee, was impressed with Samara's application, which was received in response to the county's online employment notice.

"You come highly recommended and highly qualified," he'd said. "You're like an answered prayer. Cold Butte is always desperate for doctors and nurses."

Stone said Samara's duties would include a backup role with the tricounty on-site medical response team that would support the papal visit to Lone Tree County.

The pope was coming to Montana.

Samara now knew her target.

At the outset of their papal security checks, federal agents were guarded about Samara because she was a foreign national who'd spent time in Iraq. But her references, doctors with aid agencies, confirmed that Samara was a British subject who'd helped injured American personnel and should not be deemed a security risk.

Samara's name, or fingerprints, did not appear in any classified databases, or indices searched by U.S. intelligence and security agencies. No red flags, black notices, no attention at all, when they checked her background. Just a letter of appreciation from the U.S. government for aiding a U.S. citizen in Iraq.

In the beginning, Samara's life in Montana was a solitary one. While she'd been instructed to blend in, she was not one to socialize by visiting the local bar.

Many nights were spent alone with her laptop, watching for updates on her operation. At times she would risk a call routed through secured channels to an old friend from the camp.

Samara missed Muhammad and Ahmed. Although

she kept to herself, she started to yearn for company. For the sake of her operation, she needed to work harder at trusting people if she was going to blend in.

When the county sent her to Los Angeles to take a three-week course on event planning and emergency response for the papal visit medical teams, she e-mailed Jake Conlin, using his secret Internet account.

He'd been thinking of her.

"Your timing is good," he said.

They met privately for dinner and by dessert he'd confided to her that he'd been deeply confused and hurt since his return from Iraq.

"I am convinced my wife has been unfaithful."

Sitting across from him, Samara was again overcome by how much Jake reminded her of Muhammad, his eyes, his voice. His presence was strikingly similar.

During her three weeks in California, she met Jake several times. They'd had long conversations about life, with Jake appreciative of how Samara had saved his.

"Maybe it's some kind of sign for us," he said.

On the last visit before she left, they hardly spoke.

Samara left him a key to her room.

Their night started with a long, deep kiss.

In the morning, Samara studied Jake as he slept beside her in bed, enjoying his skin next to hers. When he woke, she invited him into the shower.

"Come live with me in Montana," she said. "Bring your son. We can start new lives there."

Jake searched her eyes for a long moment.

"All right."

He needed time to make arrangements.

That's how it happened.

That's how Samara had succeeded in blending in.

Samara shifted her thoughts, glanced out her window at the wide-open prairie and checked the time.

She had to go.

As she finished her tea, she moved to shut down her computer, when it beeped.

Using an array of passwords, she clicked along a complex network of Web sites to check one of her Internet accounts.

The e-mail she'd been expecting had arrived in Arabic.

Grandmother sends her love. Her gift has arrived. Cousin will call with details about picking it up and the next stage of planning for the big day. All love and kisses —Uncle.

Samara's stomach lifted.

She'd been activated.

Her operation was now in motion.

She looked at Ahmed and Muhammad, her mother and father.

Nothing would stop her now.

29

Addis Ababa, Ethiopia, Africa

At dawn a muezzin climbed to the minaret of a central mosque and issued the day's first call to prayer.

It echoed over the schools, the government buildings, the monuments and the high stone walls surrounding the luxury hotels.

It mingled with the haze of the pungent cooking fires rising from the tin-roofed shanties, jammed into the slums that nearly engulfed the capital.

His cry carried to Addis Ababa's Mercato and its vast grid of streets overflowing with kiosks, stalls and shops, the largest market between Cairo and Johannesburg.

As his call died over Mercato, roosters crowed at the rising sun while caged chickens awaited slaughter. The smells of goats and spices blended with coffee, tea and baked bread as merchants opened stalls and shops to sell products such as vegetables, fruit, furniture, clothing, handicrafts, jewelry, DVDs and coffins.

The streets teemed with sellers, shoppers, pickpockets, prostitutes and would-be guides hustling the *faranji* tourists in English, Italian, French, Arabic, Amharic and other languages as local folk, reggae and hip-hop music throbbed from radios.

African fabrics were abundant in Mercato.

Block after block of tables, stalls and shops brimmed with handwoven cloths in a spectrum of traditional and modern colors. They cascaded in sheets from stall walls, spilled from shelves or teetered in towers of bolts on tables where women in burkas, or men in long robes, beards trimmed, heads covered with small caps, beckoned to shoppers.

Deep in the labyrinths of the fabric district, Amir, a soft-spoken middle-aged merchant, reflected on the market and the world.

His heart broke a bit more each day at the common cruelties he'd seen. Ragged crippled beggars slept in the street amid animal feces. Alongside them were tiny children orphaned by AIDS, flies flecking their faces, death looming like a vulture.

Yesterday, he had discovered a live newborn wrapped in bloodied newspaper. The infant girl had been abandoned in an alley next to a sewage trough crawling with rats. Two dogs stood over her, their ribs pressed against their mange, saliva dripping from their yawning jaws before Amir chased them off and urged the local women to take the child to a hospital.

As he came to his shop, Amir shifted his thoughts, for he had much on his mind.

His store was a lush jungle of colored tapestries and handmade fabrics, all of which were presided over by his sales manager, Meseret, a hardworking mother of three boys from Kechene.

"Good morning, Mr. Amir."

His sad, tired eyes lifted into a rare smile for her.

"Teferi has your tea, sir."

He patted her shoulder and moved toward the soft clacking at the back. In the next room, a man in his thirties sat on a portion of the floor that had been recessed so he could put his legs under the pit treadle loom he was operating.

Teferi was a Doko weaver from the highlands, one of the best in Africa, a master at making every type of cloth, from simple patterns to sophisticated inlays.

The two men shared tea and quiet conversation about the new types of fabric Teferi had made according to specifications for Amir's clients.

After tea, Amir went to the back to his small office crowded by his desk, computer, phone, filing cabinet with invoices and boxes stuffed with fabric. He pushed back heavy curtains that hid a small door.

He unlocked it and entered, locking the door behind him.

A naked bulb lit the room which, like the previous room, was choking with stock. He moved some of the clutter to uncover a massive mahogany travel chest with ornate carving. He unlocked it and lifted its lid to reveal an electronic security mechanism.

A small computer with a blinking yellow light indicated readiness.

Amir pressed his face against a small lens on the computerized box. It beeped as it scanned his iris. He then entered an alphanumeric code on the keypad. It caused a metal shelf inside the chest to slide open, revealing the top of a narrow stairway. Turning his shoulders, Amir descended to the bottom, where he flipped a switch, closing the door above his head as he entered another world.

Soft green fluorescent light illuminated a clean, dry, low-ceilinged bunker, measuring three meters by four meters. Several computers, big-screen monitors and satellite phones sat on the worktable in the room's center.

The systems were powered through hookups expertly hived off the nearby luxury hotel, government buildings and foreign embassies.

Addis Ababa's elevation made it the world's third-highest capital above sea level. Amir's satellite and cellular links used microdishes and relays aligned through air vents. They had encrypters and scramblers. They were safe and strong.

He turned on his computers.

No intruder would ever see this room and live to tell about it.

Meseret and Teferi had silent panic alarms to alert Amir. They also had Glock-17 pistols under their garments. The room had a series of propane tanks that Amir could detonate remotely after he'd fled through one of three escape tunnels that surfaced elsewhere in the market.

The room was secure.

Like Meseret and Teferi, the few people Amir trusted were devoted to his philosophy and his protection.

This room is where secrets remained secret.

For few people alive knew anything of Amir's life.

It had remained a mystery.

To the market gossips, Amir was one of hundreds of fabric merchants; a quiet, private man, rumored to be wealthy with a farm on the banks of the Blue Nile River, although no one had seen such a farm.

Then there were the stories that Amir was a Yemeni prince who had rejected his family's wealth because of his extreme beliefs. Others said his family was from Oman, that he was an engineering student educated around the world and fluent in several languages, but that his passion for a woman had brought him to Addis.

One rumor had Amir being a former senior officer with the Saudi al-Mabahith al-Amma who was an expert at conducting covert operations without leaving a trace of evidence.

Perhaps that's why U.S. and European intelligence agencies did not believe Amir was anything more than a myth. They were unable to confirm his location, let alone secure a photo of him. Frustrated, the Germans had nicknamed him "Desert Ghost," the Italians called him "the Wind," while the Americans doubted his existence.

But Amir was real.

In body and in the hearts of his followers. His small organization reached around the globe. Yet few of his disciples had met the man known as "the Believer."

His wisdom and faith ran deeper than the others who came before him, such as "the Samaritan," who'd become enamored with his fame through his televised videos and declarations.

Yes, the Samaritan and his martyrs had, in one day

and in one operation, surpassed the words of a million speeches calling for action.

But the fire they had ignited was not the decisive blow.

Amir thought of the abandoned baby dying in a gutter.

No, to end the centuries of oppression and humiliation inflicted by the godless nonbelievers, the snake that had led the crusade that stole the holy lands needed beheading.

And Amir had been preparing for that great day.

Like a patient gardener, Amir had nurtured his web of worldwide support. His funding networks, donations, blood diamonds, narcotic sales, money laundering and Internet lottery schemes ensured infinite sums of cash. His intelligence networks were impenetrable. His planning network drew upon the best minds of believers, physicists, chemists, nuclear researchers and engineers.

All of them followed Amir, worshipping him as a visionary and architect.

All of them worked on refining technological advances to defeat the enemy. Dozens of operations had been in development. Some for years. Plane operations, naval operations, event operations, assassination plans, hostage operations, hits on pipelines, subways, cities, skyscrapers, malls or famous symbols to the narcissistic greed of the debauched nonbelievers.

In all cases, the agents were unaware of the full scope of their mission. Cell groups responsible for certain stages were unaware of others. Different aspects were guided by lieutenants who reported to commanders who, at times, disguised as merchants, would report directly to Amir.

A few days ago he'd gone to a secret location to see the people behind a major operation that was showing promise.

The meeting was arranged north of the capital among the remote mud-road villages on the mountain hillsides where Amir had contracted a group of expert weavers. No one troubled them, for they had long been banished over fears that they held the power to issue curses.

Amir recalled how the smoke from their charcoal fires wafted over the villages where the goats wandered freely, except in the chief's hut. It was there where Amir had met a small group of foreign brothers who'd come a great distance to brief him on their impressive new weapon.

In the cool shade of the hut, bolts of common cotton fabric sat on the thatched mat in an array of colors and patterns. Laptop computers glowed with displays of chemical and mathematic tables, formulas and calculations. Some of the men talked softly into secure satellite phones.

The delegation had been led by Ali Bakarat, a specialist in chemical engineering from Libya, and Omar Kareem, an engineer in molecular nanotechnology from Kuwait. Amir had been dealing with them for the past year. Amid the gentle click-clack of the weavers' looms in the hut nearby, Bakarat had placed his hands on the bolts and explained the engineering of the new material.

In some ways, Bakarat said, the engineering was

similar to the advanced technology the military was using in combat wear for camouflage, thermal or nerve-agent detecting capabilities.

The fabric looked, felt, smelled and responded like any common cotton weave.

But interwoven into this material was microscopic tubing that was hollow and transparent. The tubing was filled with a volatile liquid developed through a complex process. The liquid was injected with millions of nano-radio receptors which floated within the tubing and were programmed to receive a coded ultra-low-frequency signal.

Once received, the signal first activated the liquid in a process that took sixty seconds, after which the new material would become an extremely powerful explosive in proportion to its volume.

A bomb.

Detonation could happen at any point—within the next half second, or next month. But it could only be triggered from a second radio signal which could be transmitted from an encrypted code programmed into any device that could send a wireless signal, such as a cell or satellite phone, or camera with laser auto-focus, or a wireless laptop.

The critical quality of the new material was the fact it was undetectable by sniffer dogs, swabbing, analysis, scoping—any type of bomb detection method known.

It was an invisible bomb.

To achieve this state, the fabric must be steeped for a few hours in a special clear solution before it is tailored into any type of apparel or common item. That clear solution was en route to the U.S. west coast by ship, while bolts of the fabric had arrived in New York City's garment district, where they awaited shipment to anywhere in the U.S.

Bakarat and Kareem would soon depart to enter the U.S., where they would oversee the final stages of the operation.

After watching their demonstration video, Amir smiled and embraced the men.

"Well done, my brothers, well done."

Now, as Amir worked in his bunker, he glanced at his printout of the newsletter that had been posted online many months ago by the boastful priest who could not refrain from sharing advance news of a papal visit to Montana.

"It is with great joy that we can confirm the Holy Father will visit Cold Butte."

Amir almost smiled.

The Montana project was emerging as his jewel, as the time for execution was nearly upon them. The operation would be carried out by the widow of Baghdad.

"The Tigress."

Her determination was profound.

A few gentle keystrokes and she appeared before him on his laptop's screen in video recordings.

Samara.

Amir studied her ferocity as she swore her vengeance during her interview. Then he clicked to her training in the mountains along the Afghan border with Pakistan. Then he saw her in the United States.

Preparing.

Her instructions were to assimilate into American society and to get a job in her profession in the target zone.

That is all she was to know until further instructions.

Other agents in local religious and professional associations played roles in helping her succeed at every step of the way, sponsoring her, acting as references, exercising influence when needed.

All of it so subtle as to be invisible.

The security cell was headed by a young group. Its agents had been outstanding, protecting the operation at every step, eliminating vulnerabilities.

"All is well," one reported in an encrypted dispatch. "Our brothers are watching over our sister."

Amir nodded.

Then he clicked on to other video recordings. One was a family vacationing in the wilderness. Amir watched the camera take him along a river cutting through a magnificent mountain range.

A scream rises above the river's rush.

The video cut to a city street and news box displaying headlines about a tragic accident and the deaths of an American family. Then a cut to the surveillance images of a woman who appeared to be working in a large American bookstore.

Amir nodded, then touched one of the laptops on his table.

One not in use.

It belonged to Ray Tarver.

Amir watched another video recording.

It showed a boy eating a hamburger at a picnic table.

Logan Conlin.

He looks into the camera, refusing to smile for the person behind it.

Amir was pleased. Yes, all was well.

Soon the course of history would be forever changed. Amir sent an e-mail to Samara.

Grandmother sends her love. Her gift has arrived. Cousin will call with details....

Book Three:
Breaking Point

30

Blue Rose Creek, California

Maggie pushed the green button and the dispenser spit out a parking ticket.

The barrier arm lifted and she parked at Mercy General Memorial Hospital. This was where Madame Fatima's friend had told her to come for information on Logan.

As Maggie walked to the hospital doors, she looked at the clouds swirling overhead, recalling that a storm warning had been issued.

She'd forgotten her umbrella.

She didn't care.

In the wake of all she'd been through these past few days, getting wet was not a concern. She wasn't sleeping. She wasn't eating. Bit by bit she seemed to be slipping from reality into a dream that took her from disappointment to disappointment along an ever-darkening road.

But she was not defeated.

One goal, one crystalline purpose, kept her going.

She would never give up searching for her son and her husband.

As Maggie approached reception, the woman at the desk eyed her coldly.

"I'm here to visit Fatima Soleil."

"Spell it, please."

Maggie did and the woman's keyboard clicked.

"Your name?"

"Maggie Conlin."

"Family or friend?"

"Friend. I was called here by her friend Helga Kimmel."

The keyboard clicked and the woman found Maggie's name listed.

"I'm going to need a photo ID."

"Is my driver's license okay?"

The woman nodded then traded Maggie's license for a visitor's badge and her signature on the visitor's log attached to a clipboard.

"She's on the ninth floor. When you get off the elevator, go right, to the nurses' station."

"Thank you. Can you tell me her condition?"

"Ask the nurses on the ninth floor."

As the elevator ascended, Maggie tried to keep her hope in check.

In her heart she believed Fatima had detected something during her session. Maggie had, too. She swore she could feel Logan nearby. Now, she tried not to guess at the information Fatima had for her.

Did it matter?

Maggie would pursue any possibility.

The chime sounded for the ninth floor.

The air was heavy with antiseptic smells. Down the hall a short, thickset woman in faded jeans and an oversize flowered shirt was talking to a nurse. It was Helga.

"Excuse us, Nancy," Helga said to the nurse. "I need to talk with Maggie."

"Hi," Maggie said.

"Come this way, there's a lounge around the corner."

The bright-colored walls could not mask the gloom that resided here in the brownish-gray vinyl couches and the outdated copies of long-forgotten magazines.

Helga sat down, rubbed her bloodshot eyes and exhaled.

"They do not expect Madame to live through the night."

"Oh, my God." Maggie touched Helga's knee. "I'm so sorry."

Helga nodded.

"The cancer is eating her up. She has no time left. She's not in pain. She's heavily sedated and is in and out of consciousness."

Maggie took quick stock. No other people were in the lounge or down the hall.

"Has she no family?"

"I am her only family," Helga said. "Madame told me to summon you. She wants to give you information."

"Did she say what it is?"

"It can only be about the session concerning your son. Are you ready to see her?"

Maggie nodded and Helga led her to a private room.

"I'm going to leave you alone with her until you are done. The nurses are monitoring her from their station. You will have privacy. Do not be alarmed that she passes in and out of consciousness. She knows if people are in the room."

Maggie slowly pushed the door and entered.

The room was dimly lit and fragrant from the floral

arrangements. The gentle hum of the equipment monitoring Fatima's breathing, blood pressure and heart rate was calming.

Maggie was not prepared for what she saw next.

She actually took a step back to fetch the nurse believing that Fatima had vanished as evidenced by the empty crumpled sheets of her hospital bed. It took a second to register that Fatima *was there*—under the sheets—her body so ravaged as to be nothing more than a living skeleton.

An oxygen tube ran under her nose. An IV dripped morphine. She was unconscious.

Death's work was nearly complete.

Maggie sat in the cushioned chair next to her bed.

Fatima turned her bare head to Maggie and opened her eyes to acknowledge her presence.

"I've come as you have requested."

Fatima blinked then resubmerged into unconsciousness.

Maggie sat with her for an hour. She stood to leave the room for a short break and almost screamed.

Fatima's ice-cold fingers had seized Maggie's wrist.

Maggie didn't move.

Fatima's grip was strong. Her eyes opened but revealed only white orbs. She moaned and her skeletal jaw began to work.

"I lied to you, Maggie. I did see something."

The pressure of Fatima's grip increased.

"Do you wish to know?"

"Yes."

"It is not good. Do you wish to know?"

Maggie's chin crumpled and she fought to push the word out of her mouth.

"Yes."

"I am seeing it now. Your son is alive."

"Where is he?"

"But he is in danger."

Fatima's grip was hurting Maggie. She fell to her knees at the side of the bed.

"Where is he?"

"He does not know he is in danger."

"Please, I'm begging you, where is he?"

"There is a woman. I see a woman. There is fire, explosions, destruction. She is carrying something."

"Who is the woman?"

"The woman is carrying a child."

"Is it Logan?"

"The child is dead."

"No! Nooo!"

Fatima released her grip.

Her body convulsed. Her jaw locked open and she was still. The monitor began ponging with alarm.

"Help!" Maggie called. "Somebody!"

A nurse hurried into the room, uncollared her stethoscope. Listened, then pressed a button on the intercom system above the bed. "We've got an expired DNR in 921."

Maggie covered her face with her hands, stepped back into a far corner out of the way. What followed unfolded in snatches.

Helga entered and sobbed.

The nurses consoled her, Maggie consoled her, for how long, she couldn't be certain. Maggie was not sure how long she stayed with Helga, or how she made it back to reception to retrieve her license. She remembered it was raining.

She remembered thunder, lightning, her skin prickling the entire time she walked to her car. She remembered the words of a dying psychic warning her that Logan was in danger.

"The woman is carrying a child."

31

Washington, D.C.

The plot to kill the pope played out in grainy photos on the computer monitor of Special Agent Blake Walker of the U.S. Secret Service.

The gun rose from the crowd in St. Peter's Square.

A Browning 9-mm semiautomatic pistol.

In the right hand of Mehmet Ali Agca who fired five shots at Pope John Paul II.

The first round penetrated the pope's stomach, the second hit his hand, the third his arm. The fourth and fifth shots wounded spectators.

The Holy Father fell back into the arms of his secretary.

May 13, 1981.

A day most of the world would not forget, Walker thought. He was lead advance agent with security for the pope's upcoming U.S. visit. For Walker, a stickler for research, this was the umpteenth time he'd studied papal assassination attempts.

Next.

The Philippines. 1995.

During a papal visit, firefighters in Manila were called to an apartment fire near the Embassy for the Holy See, where the pope was to sleep. Among the ruins they discovered: bomb-making material, the route of the papal tour marked on maps and two sets of priests' cassocks.

Suspects were tied to the first attack on the World Trade Center.

That one was chilling; so was the next.

During the pope's recent visit to South America, a violent group of Marxist extremists cut power to the airport as the pope's plane was making a night landing. Every single light went black on the ground. The pilots couldn't see. At the last moment they aborted the landing and flew to another site. Later, airport police rushed to investigate an abandoned truck in a forest road near a runway. Inside they found a shoulder-launched surface-to-air missile that had malfunctioned.

Walker studied the database index.

So many *confirmed* attempts. Now, as time ticked down on the pope's U.S. visit, intelligence agencies were picking up more chatter and more threads of new potential threats every day. As Walker loosened his tie, there was a knock on his door and his assistant appeared.

"Fran's calling again."

His face tensed at his ex-wife's name but he stayed focused on his work.

"I can't take it. Tell her I've got back-to-back meetings."

"She *demanded* I tell you that it's about support."

"Annette, I can't talk to her now."

"Sure thing, boss."

The door closed and Walker exhaled. He'd never wanted the divorce.

For a shining moment he remembered sweeter times as a rookie with the NYPD. On the beat and at night school at John Jay. Then the move to D.C. to join the FBI where he met Fran, a paralegal. Then came the births of their daughters, his commendations, secondments to counterterrorism at the CIA, then the Secret Service, Presidential Protective Division, then Intelligence.

Always on call. Always on the road. Always on edge.

Then Fran started accusing him of loving his job more than her and the girls. Then she'd found a new boyfriend at their church: Miller Higby, a nine-to-five accountant to help her nag for support payments, which Walker had never missed.

Never.

That would be an error.

Walker couldn't afford errors. Not in his line of work. He'd come close to a career-killer once.

Thanks to an asshole reporter named Ray Tarver.

Walker had met him briefly at an event. Shot the breeze, traded cards. Months later Tarver called cold saying he was going to run a story alleging Russian mobsters had compromised members of the White House security detail. The story was that the mobsters had blackmailed agents over gambling debts. Tarver claimed he had it documented on a classified CIA report; Blake Walker was one of the extorted agents.

Walker nearly lost his mind.

The story could not be true.

But instead of informing his superiors, Walker actually started suspecting agents who might have been behind the damning story. It drove him crazy. He started his own secret investigation of his colleagues. At the same time, after days of intense work, Walker persuaded Tarver to share the document, which was key to his story.

Walker had the document analyzed. The experts questioned its authenticity.

Just like the entire story.

Tarver refused to tell Walker how he got his document. Walker couldn't rule out that maybe Tarver was set up. Or had *fabricated it*. Tarver killed his story. Walker killed his investigation.

Tarver did have sources everywhere. But they played him. Walker figured him for a flake, so infatuated with conspiracies that he couldn't distinguish between fact and fantasy. Someone would feed him a line and off he'd go. When Walker thought of the harm the case could have inflicted on the detail, his blood bubbled.

But it didn't stop Tarver.

Tipped to other conspiracies, the guy kept popping up. Exaggerating a grain of truth or trying to parlay rumor or innuendo into fact. Walker kicked himself for his knee-jerk reaction to Tarver's first story. Kicked himself for ever suspecting his colleagues. It taught him to be very suspect of reporters like Ray Tarver.

Word had traveled fast about what happened to Tarver up in Canada. And it was in the *Post*. His wife, his kids. All of them. A real shame.

It made Walker wonder if the poor bastard had ever landed a true story.

Walker had to get ready for the next conference call.

As he collected his files, his computer beeped with an intel bulletin from the Department of Homeland Security.

Something about a ship with hostile cargo.

The threats and risks just kept coming.

Like the one with that priest out in Montana. Father Andrew Stone. Months in advance he posts online, for the entire world to see, details of the pope's visit to tiny Cold Butte. It posed a risk as a gift for long-range plotters. Shaking his head, he glanced at his printout of the newsletter. He couldn't do much about it and sought some relief in the fact that Cold Butte was the smallest venue of the tour.

In the middle of nowhere. We shouldn't have to worry too much about Montana.

As Walker closed his computer files, he glanced again at the photos of John Paul II from that May in 1981.

Aga's hit pulled Walker back to his own heart-stopping day with the president.

Summer.

Shaker Heights, Ohio. Mall parking lot. The president's moving along a good crowd, shaking hands. Walker spots the guy. Alone. White, late twenties. Stone-cold face and something in his hand. Instinct and training kick in. Walker has him on the ground. The team gets the president in the car and out of there. The gun is real. It is loaded. The kid had been dumped by his girl and thought that killing the president would win her back. "It would show her just how much I loved her."

The kid was that close.

Just like all the others.

32

Washington, D.C.

The jetliner's wing dipped to show Graham the Potomac, the Jefferson Memorial and the Washington Monument before landing at Reagan National.

In the terminal, Graham noticed a pregnant woman, hesitated and thought of Nora. The woman was holding a little girl's hand. As they walked by him at the luggage carousels, he was pulled back to images of that night.

Then back to the river.

And Emily Tarver.

Holding her as she took her dying breaths.

Don't hurt my daddy.

What happened to the Tarvers?

Were they murdered? Or was he crazy to think so?

That's why he was here. To find answers.

Or was it to hide from ghosts?

He'd lost Nora. He couldn't save Emily Tarver.

Admit it, his boss was right. That's what this was all about.

Redemption for his failures.

No. He was trying to clear a case and had to focus on it.

Graham tightened his grip on his bag, looked for his ride and left his doubts at the terminal.

Sergeant Luc Cleroux, the RCMP's liaison officer at the embassy, enjoying the chance to speak French with Graham, had set things up for him.

To assist Graham, the FBI provided Chuck "two weeks to go before retirement" Carson, who picked him up at Reagan.

"Between us, you don't want me to babysit you on this, what is it, an insurance thing?" Carson said as they headed downtown.

Graham considered Carson's suggestion.

As a foreign cop in the U.S., Graham did not carry his gun and had limited powers of arrest. He was in Washington on various business matters, including confirming background on the Tarvers as it related to their Canadian travel insurance policy. If he betrayed the fact he was there to rule out homicide, he'd be on the next plane home. That was Stotter's direct order and his promise.

"I think I can take care of myself."

"Good. Here's my card. Keep me posted and call me if you need anything."

Graham's hotel was a few blocks from the White House and The Mall. Graham checked in, showered, then followed up on inquiries. First call: Cleroux at the Canadian Embassy.

"Yeah, I got nothing from my Interpol contacts," Cleroux said in French. "Anyway, I've passed your other requests to Reg Novak, a good guy with MPD. He's expecting your call."

When Graham reached Novak, the D.C. detective invited him to the Metropolitan Police Headquarters on Indiana Avenue. The Henry J. Daly Building was named to honor the homicide detective shot by an intruder in 1994.

Novak, a craggy-faced veteran, signed Graham in with the usual firm handshake and "Have a good flight?" small talk.

After Graham cleared the electronic security, Novak led him to his office and put a cup of coffee for him on his desk. Novak groaned as he settled in his chair and flipped through his tattered notebook.

"Read about them in the *Post*. Just terrible what happened up there. Here we go. I ran those checks you'd wanted."

Graham's pen was poised over his notebook.

"And I got zilch. Sorry. Wish I could help you with more but Raymond Tarver is not in our system. The same for Anita. No complaint history at their house, either. They live in the district side of Takoma Park."

"Nothing?"

"Not a thing. I did some asking around for you and what I *can* tell you is that Ray was a reporter, but he wrote more about national politics, international scandals and whatnot."

"I've heard that."

"He was a real character, looked for big doomsday conspiracy stuff. Then he sorta faded, or something." Novak shrugged before sipping from his Washington Capitals mug. "You might want to check with the feds, FBI, Secret Service, Homeland and the like. I heard Ray traveled in those circles."

"I have an appointment later."

"Good they could squeeze you in. Most of those all-stars should be busy with the pope's visit. I know some of our guys are helping. Not me personally, thank God. Got enough on my plate. But checking those watch lists can be a headache. These things tend to excite every nut job in the country." He closed his book. "Think the Flames have a shot this year?"

"As good as the Caps."

"So you still haven't found Tarver's body, have you?"

"No. Sometimes we never find them in mountain deaths."

"I gotta ask you." Novak's gaze fixed on Graham's, letting a detective-to-detective understanding pass between them. "It's your case and all, but you didn't really come all this way to look into insurance crap, did you?"

"I did. Among other things."

"*Among other things.* Care for some advice from a jaded old flatfoot?"

"Go ahead."

"The primary activities in this town are ass covering and finger pointing."

"It's a government town."

"It is. And from what I understand, Ray Tarver pissed off a few government people in security circles."

"What're you telling me?"

"Truth is often a fugitive in D.C. and searching for it can be damaging to your career. Be careful, my friend."

Graham returned to his hotel with time to eat a club sandwich before heading to the United States Secret Service headquarters on H Street.

A number of days before his meeting he'd faxed his date of birth, passport number and RCMP regimental number, as security required.

"Special Agent Blake Walker," Graham told the woman at reception when she'd asked who he was there to see.

She typed on her keyboard, spoke softly into her headset, then said, "Corporal Graham, Agent Walker apologizes. He has conflicting meetings and would like to reschedule, if you agree?"

"I'd prefer that we did this now, I'd only need about twenty minutes."

"Stand by, sir."

She spoke into the headset, listened, then nodded.

"Agent Walker will try to give you time now. Someone will be down to get you." She exchanged Graham's driver's license for a visitor's badge. "Please wear this at all times and return it to me when you leave."

A man barely out of his teens, who was about six foot seven and wearing a loose-fitting dark suit, white shirt, tie and ID badge that said T. Simms, came for him. Graham figured him for an intern. Simms smiled at Graham in the elevator as the car ascended several floors before it stopped.

They stepped into a carpeted corridor dividing high-walled cubicles from closed offices. Tension was evident in the sober faces of people working at terminals and talking on phones in muted tones.

Graham's escort delivered him to Walker's office then left.

The door was open.

Walker was in mid-phone conversation, standing at his desk, kneading the back of his neck. He seemed to fill the room as he waved Graham in, held up two fingers, mouthing two minutes, then indicated the guest chair.

A good-size office window offered a slice of downtown Washington. On the far wall, Walker was everywhere in framed photographs with several presidents, even the new one. And there was Walker with the CIA director, the FBI director, the UN secretary. There he was again with colleagues standing before Buckingham Palace, in Red Square, in front of the Eiffel Tower, the Vatican and other capitals.

Two young girls grinned from the gold-framed photograph beside his monitor.

Walker finished his call.

"Sorry for that. Blake Walker."

Graham shook his hand.

"Dan Graham."

"I was dealing with my ex. You married?"

His personal question came without warning.

"No. I was. But, no, not anymore."

"Good. Stay single. Enjoy life the way God had originally intended. Paradise before Eve came along." Walker smiled, pointed to the mug on his desk. "Coffee?"

"I'm good, thanks."

"Okay, let's get to it. You're here on the deaths of Ray Tarver's family."

"Yes. Just checking background, regarding the insurance and trying to clear it."

"No, no. Stop right there. First, why come to me?" Walker said. "How did my name come up in this?"

Graham passed a sheet of paper to Walker, who glanced at his watch before reading the document.

"I photocopied this from Tarver's notebook," Graham said. "It's from a series of cryptic notations. This was one of his last entries. A handwritten note that says, *See S.A. Blake Walker at SS on H again.*"

Walker took a deep breath then cursed under it.

"What is it?" Graham asked.

"This was not in the summary you'd sent me in your meeting request. Matter of fact, your summary was a tad short on details. Let me get my head around this. You still insist on me believing that you're here solely to snoop around on Tarver for insurance purposes?"

"Checking his background, so I can clear it. Tying up loose ends for the file, yes."

"Bull. Shit."

"Pardon me?"

Walker threw Graham's paper down on his desk.

"What the hell's going on with you guys up there?"

"I don't follow you."

"What happened to the Tarver family is tragic. Sure, Ray Tarver was a bit of a wild-card reporter, but the family's drowning was not suspicious."

"And how would you know that?"

"Everyone knows it. Don't you guys talk to each other up there?"

"You've lost me. Who's everyone?"

"You're familiar with your Canadian Security Intelligence Service?"

Graham's pulse quickened at Walker's condescension.

"Of course."

"I'm sure you're aware that our security agencies talk to your security agencies."

Walker continued but Graham didn't like where he was going.

"Four American citizens from the district die on foreign soil, one of them being a former D.C. wire service reporter known to write about U.S. geopolitics and security issues. It's a given we'd make a routine check into anything remotely untoward. You with me so far, buddy?"

Graham held his tongue as Walker went on.

"We've been advised that the deaths have been classified as accidental and the case is cleared. I don't think we've got much to discuss."

"Really?"

Walker put his files down. His dark eyes drilled into Graham.

"Over the years Ray Tarver would come to me," Walker said. "He went to a lot of people in the intelligence community. He'd call, he'd want to meet in some dive. He'd claim he had sources who'd fed him intel on grand conspiracies.

"He'd say, I think this is going to happen or that will take place. But when it came to providing a shred of corroboration he had nothing. I would then attempt to confirm his so-called leads, which turned out to be 'jackass theories.'

"In Washington, there's no shortage of people like Ray Tarver. People who take a slender thread of hearsay and twist it into a full-blown conspiracy. You understand what I'm saying?"

Graham said nothing.

"Now, I am sorry for what happened to the family. It's a tragedy. But in life, Ray Tarver lived in a fantasy world with other conspiracy nuts. The fact you're here, convinced you're onto something because of some note, is not only sad but a further waste of my time.

"Don't get me wrong, it's part of my job to investigate crackpots like Ray Tarver, so why don't you leave it to the experts and head back home. In case you missed it, the pope's arriving soon, and I'm kind of preoccupied. Now, I'm sure you've got better things to do up there. Okay?"

Walker looked at his watch, then other files.

Maybe it was jet lag, or his grief, his self-doubt, or the fact Walker's arrogance pissed him off, but Graham decided he'd swallowed enough.

"Agent Walker. *Special Agent* Walker, I don't know where you're getting your information about my case being cleared, but to use your term, it's bullshit."

Walker's jaw pulsed.

"That a fact?"

"It is a fact," Graham said. "It's true, the deaths of Anita Tarver and her two children are believed to have been accidental. The fact is, and it is a fact, their deaths remain unclassified. How you, sir, are able to conclude the cause of Ray Tarver's death as accidental right here in this very office, when we've yet to locate his body, is miraculous. I applaud your supernatural skill." Graham nodded to Walker's wall of glory. "Must be why you're special and all these important people want to shake your hand.

"You must be aware then that Ray Tarver's laptop appears to be the only item missing from his family's inventory. And you must also be aware that in the hours before his family's deaths were discovered, Tarver was seen in a local restaurant showing data on a laptop to an unidentified stranger.

"Now what amazes me, is the fact that it is about

twenty-four, twenty-five hundred miles from the chair where your special ass is parked and the Faust River where I held Emily Tarver as she took her last breaths, where I felt her heart beating against mine. Yet you, sir, have all the answers. All of them. But what disturbs me, about this uncleared, unclassified case concerning the deaths of three U.S. citizens, possibly four, is that your name is among the last entries Ray Tarver made in his notebook. That would make you a person of interest, wouldn't it?"

Walker's eyes burned into Graham's in a mounting standoff that was interrupted by Walker's phone. He hit a button, activating the speaker.

"Blake, they're waiting for you on the call with Seattle and Vatican security. Are you joining them in the big room or do you want the call code?"

Graham left.

"Tell them I'll be there in two minutes."

Graham was at the elevator when Walker caught up to him.

"Dan." Walker ensured they were alone and lowered his voice. "I was a jerk back there. The stress of the papal visit, and we've got to advance a presidential visit to Canada next month, and my ex. You took the brunt of it. I was out of line. You know how things can get to you."

Graham knew.

He considered Walker's hand, then shook it.

"Dan, I'll do what I can to help you, but I'm really jammed, and I'm late. What do you need?"

Graham considered the offer. "There's one thing."

"Shoot."

"I'm not sure what this means. It's one of the last entries in Tarver's notebook."

Walker looked at it. "Blue Rose Creek." He shook his head. "That's it?"

"That's it."

"Off the top, it means nothing. I'll check it out—give me your contact numbers. I'll get back to you."

33

Kate Morrow knew things about Ray Tarver.

And she wanted to tell Graham but was uneasy about it.

Afraid, almost.

He'd sensed it as they talked at the Washington Bureau of the World Press Alliance wire service where Tarver had worked. Graham was there to see Tarver's reporter friends, like Morrow, a lifestyles writer, who'd sat beside him.

"Ray loved Anita and those kids," she said. "They were his world."

"I understand."

"Under his tough-guy skin, he was actually a teddy bear." She smiled. "He used to give me gum every day."

"Gum?"

"Bubble gum. He'd give it to me around deadline. Used to say chewing gum kept you focused. Ray was a gum-chewer."

Morrow's gaze shifted beyond their small glass-walled meeting room to the newsroom and the people working before computer terminals at desks heaped with outdated newspapers, reports, press releases and takeout coffee cups.

"The guys here had written Ray off as a conspiracy junkie, a kook," she said.

"Is that what you think, too?"

"He was a good reporter." She let a moment pass. "When I heard what happened in the mountains, when the story moved on the wire, I was shattered. It was so sad because Ray had just slipped away from us. It left me with a lot of questions."

"Such as?"

Morrow searched in vain for the answer. Something was eating her up. It was in her body language, how she avoided meeting Graham's eyes, kept twisting her bracelet chain, adjusting her glasses and clearing her throat.

"Ms. Morrow, is there something about Ray that you think I should know?"

She didn't answer.

"Ms. Morrow—" Graham dropped his voice "—do you think someone may have wanted to harm Ray because of the stories he pursued?"

She looked at him.

"It was a boating accident, right?" she asked. "That's what the Canadian reporters who called us for comments had said."

"It looks like a boating accident, but the cause of death is unclassified. What do you think, given what you know of Ray?"

"Me?" She blinked back tears. "What do I know? I write about embassy parties, diplomats, diets, decor."

"You said he was a good reporter. What happened to make him leave?"

"He was always chasing leads, protecting sources. Always guarded about his secret work on big stories. Some people thought he was odd and teased him about aliens, grand doomsday plots, Hoffa, Elvis. It was cruel, but by the end so many of the stories he'd promised had fallen through. He was under a lot of pressure from the editors to produce something until finally he quit to freelance."

"And that was the last time you had contact with him?"

A long silence passed before Morrow slowly shook her head.

"Tell me about your last contact with him after he'd quit."

"Ray wanted help."

"What kind of help?"

"Freelancing means you don't get a regular paycheck and you do expensive research on your own dime. Ray wanted me to use my access to our databases, to run searches of names for him through our story archives, information databases, voter lists, property, addresses, like that."

"When was this?"

"Four, maybe five months ago. I'm not sure."

"Did you help him?"

"You've got to keep this confidential."

"I will."

"Yes, but I got scared. My searches were flagged. Editors questioned the costs, suggested my research was off my beat. Then they issued a bureau-wide memo about costs, hinting at budget cuts, staff layoffs. Our company is losing money. My husband's a local TV producer who just got laid off. My mother lives with us. She's very ill and I'm not covered for all her treatment. I could not risk my job, so I told Ray I couldn't help him anymore."

"How did he react?"

"He begged me to help him just a bit longer, started telling me about the story he was working on, swore me to secrecy."

"What was the story?"

"Something about some new secret weapon being developed by some Middle East extremists, or something."

"Did he have any details?"

"None really. It made no sense at all. It started to sound like another one of his cloak-and-dagger escapades, then—" Morrow twisted her ring. "He asked if he could borrow money. It was terrible. I thought he was losing it and told him to go to the *Post* or the *Times*. I told him to get a job and take care of his family. That's the last thing I said to him."

Morrow cupped her hands to her face.

"And now, I think of those sweet kids, Anita and him." Morrow glanced toward the empty desk where Tarver used to sit. "I'm sorry. This is hard for me. I've got a lot on my plate right now and I can't do this anymore, please."

Graham left her with his thanks and his card.

Morrow was the last reporter he needed to see. While leaving, he was stopped by a tall man in a tailored suit and bow tie.

"You must be the mounted police officer from Canada."

"Yes."

"Will Blair. I saw you talking to the others about Tarver. I'm sorry I missed you but I had to step out. I'd be happy to help you."

"Great, you want to go somewhere?"

"Now's not good for me. I'm meeting a senator. I suggest you come to the Wandering Eye tonight around seven. I'll get you an address."

"The Wandering Eye?"

"It's the church we attend religiously for spiritual renewal. To others, it's a bar."

Graham spent the afternoon in his hotel room making calls and writing up interview notes. Then he checked with Calgary for any developments. Tarver's body had still not been located and the search operation was winding down.

In the cab to the bar, he considered the case as he looked out at Washington's landmarks. Was he crazy to think the Tarver tragedy was anything more than a wilderness accident involving the family of an oddball reporter who believed in conspiracies?

Was he compensating for losing Nora?

Glancing up at the Washington Monument, he set his doubts next to the facts: Ray's missing laptop, the stranger, the notation of Blue Rose Creek and Emily Tarver's last words.

Don't hurt my daddy.

Should he ignore those circumstances?

Graham wasn't sure. He wasn't sure about anything

as he stepped from the cab. The bar was northwest of Dupont Circle at the edge of Georgetown. Richard Nixon greeted him from the poster on the wall of the bar's entrance.

Looked like a news shot from his resignation address.

Watergate.

Started out as a far-fetched story no one believed, Graham thought before he heard his rank followed by his name.

"Corporal Graham, please join us."

Three of the reporters he'd met earlier—Al Sallard, Michael Finch and Will Blair, his bow tie undone— were ensconced in a large cushioned, high-backed booth.

"Where's Kate Morrow?" Graham settled in.

"Working late. Couldn't make it." Finch, who covered the White House, sat up. "So tell us, sir, why aren't you wearing red and a Stetson?"

"And where's your horse?" Sallard winked. "You're supposed to be mounted. I bet women like that phrase."

Graham smiled at the forest of empty glasses on the table and explained that the red serge and Stetson were largely ceremonial. For the most part, Mounties patrolled in cars and wore daily uniforms, or detectives wore plain clothes, like most major forces.

"But you always get your man, that's your motto?" Finch asked.

"No, that's Hollywood's motto. Just ginger ale for me," Graham told the waitress. "Our company line is, 'Maintain the Right.'"

"So you learn enough about the sad case of our friend Ray?" Sallard said.

"I think I'm getting a picture."

As the evening progressed, the reporters colored that picture.

They told Graham that Tarver was a loner obsessed with phantom conspiracy stories culled from tips, rumors and wild theories gathered from other like-minded reporters—"they must have a club"—and discredited intelligence officers around the world. Trouble was, Ray's work consisted of more theories than facts. It reached a head when editors suspected he was exaggerating his claims to the point of near fabrication so that he could secure a book deal.

A publisher's fact-checker had called the bureau after Ray submitted an outline and a few chapters, proposing some blockbuster on harvesting human organs. That led to a review of some of Ray's previous news stories and more questions. That led to trouble.

Ray was forced to quit. That was the real story.

"It's so damn tragic," Finch said, "because Ray Tarver used to be a great reporter, a helluva digger before he lost it and became a newsroom joke."

"What do you mean, he'd become a joke?"

"We called him, 'What's-The-Frequency-Ray?'" Blair said. "You know, it comes from what the nut job in New York had asked Dan Rather. Something like, 'Kenneth, what's the frequency?' just before he attacked him."

The evening evolved into a eulogy of sorts as they toasted and traded Tarver stories, like the one where he was convinced the Russian Mafia controlled the White House.

Or, how about the time Tarver was trying to infiltrate

a cult and had the bureau install a special secret phone line so he could pose as a lost soul. "Yes, brother, like the Good Book says, I believe in the power and the glory," Sallard bellowed.

Then there was the one about blood-drinking Satanists who were burying sacrifice victims under fresh graves and how Tarver drove all over half a dozen states chasing hillbilly sources who were playing him for free beer, burgers and cigarettes as he helped them dig holes in cemeteries looking for evidence.

That's how much of the night went with Graham assessing their regard for Tarver and its significance to his case until his cell phone went off around 11:30 p.m.

The number was blocked.

He excused himself and took it privately.

"Corporal, this is Kate Morrow. I need to talk to you some more about Ray."

"Okay, want to set up a time for the morning?"

"No, I'd prefer to meet you tonight. Privately. No one must know. It's about the last story he was working on."

"What about it?"

"I didn't tell you everything."

34

Washington, D.C.

Twenty minutes later Graham sat alone in a corner of The Stargazers Club, a sleepy bar two blocks from his hotel.

Morrow had given him directions to it for their clandestine meeting.

He got there just ahead of the rain and wondered if the shower would delay her. While waiting, he checked his hotel for any messages. He had one from Tarver's father confirming the time he would meet Graham the next morning.

Good.

A moment later, Morrow arrived in a navy trench coat with her collapsed umbrella dripping. She placed her shoulder bag on the bench seat and caught her breath as she pushed aside her hair and dabbed her damp face with a tissue.

They ordered coffee.

Morrow waited for the server to leave then said, "This is crazy. I don't do this sort of thing."

"I understand. It's all right."

"This has gnawed at me since it happened. It got worse after I'd talked to you."

"I sensed you had more on your mind. This is about Ray's last story, about some kind of weapon?"

"Yes, there's more, but you have to swear that what I'm going to tell you doesn't come from me. You have to give me your word no one knows it came from me."

"We protect our sources just like you guys do."

"I've never told anyone this. No one at the news bureau, not even my husband."

"May I take notes?"

Morrow hesitated then nodded.

"Ray wasn't like the other reporters who are spoon-fed their stories by people with a political agenda. He dug and he had many sources."

She stopped when their coffee came and resumed when the server left.

"This may mean absolutely nothing, but Ray told me he had a source who was a former CIA counterintelligence officer who became a contractor and trusted Ray because they'd cooked up a deal to do a book together on the guy's life story.

"This guy worked at arm's length for the CIA, FBI, DIA. Everybody. He was plugged in to foreign intelligence networks and contractors from Britain, Germany, France, Israel, India, Africa, everywhere.

"He used the name of Cliff Grady. Ray said it wasn't his real name. Anyway, Grady was supposedly a specialist at extracting information from captured hostile operatives. One night he called Ray to tell him that he'd just returned from Africa."

"What was he doing there?"

"He'd been dispatched to Nigeria to help interview a terror suspect who, it was believed, had information on a large-scale attack being planned on a major target. Ray said the suspect was from Ethiopia and was being held in a secret prison on the outskirts of Abuja, the Nigerian capital. Grady wanted to tell Ray about it right away, before he reported to his clients so as 'to protect the integrity of the true information,' as Ray put it."

"Which is?"

"I don't think we'll ever know. Grady told Ray that the suspect was very determined not to reveal any information and that local security, in trying to impress him, went too far. They tortured him and he died in custody.

"Ray had no other details. Grady told him the thinking was that the target was London, Washington, Berlin or Rome."

"Which means they really don't know?"

"I guess."

"So how did Ray come by this information specifically?"

"Ray got it from Cliff after meeting him late in a bar near Langley."

"Where the CIA has its headquarters."

"That's right."

"Then what?"

"Ray said Cliff never made his report to any U.S. intelligence agency."

"How did Ray know that?"

"Because Cliff was killed that night driving from the bar."

"What?"

"I know, this is how a lot of Ray's stories go. He comes up with something earth-shattering that's impossible to confirm. I checked every way I could for any report of a fatal car wreck, even called police. There is absolutely no record of a fatal crash in the area in the time that Ray insists it happened."

"So it's like it never happened?"

"That's right."

"And Cliff Grady never existed?"

"You've got it."

Graham peered into his coffee, unsure of what to make of this.

"It sounds like some kind of spy novel," he said.

"I know."

"Hold on. Does the name Blue Rose Creek figure into this or mean anything?"

"No." Morrow reached for her bag. "But you can search Ray's files."

"You have his files on this?"

"I made you copies of all the stuff he passed to me. He was working on a Pentagon source trying to obtain the names of every civilian driver involved in the secret convoy attacked in Iraq so he could interview them. That's where I was helping him by running expensive data searches."

Morrow passed a tattered legal-size file folder to Graham.

"Corporal Graham. I know this is all crazy. Ray was an eccentric. A lot of the stories he chased were over the top and I know he'd stretched the truth before they forced him out. Tragically, that's all true.

"For that reason, I didn't take this to anyone in our

newsroom, or, for that matter, anyone inside the Beltway. They'd laugh it off because it was Ray. And I didn't want people knowing that I'd been helping him with bureau resources. Because of my personal situation, I just can't afford to get caught up in Ray's world, you know?"

"I understand."

"I know it's all nuts and it may not mean much. But Ray was my friend and I figured I owed his memory something, that I'd never forgive myself if I didn't pass it to somebody. I believe Ray would want that. I hope you understand."

"I do."

"Thank you. And good luck."

After Morrow left, Graham ordered another coffee and flipped through Ray Tarver's file.

He stopped when he saw one handwritten note.

Blue Rose Creek—possibly in California—keep checking.

35

"Again."

The prisoner's head was thrust into a steel tub of ice water and held there.

He was naked, on his knees on the cold hard floor.

At eight seconds without oxygen he struggled against his bindings, leather straps used to restrain the criminally insane.

At twelve seconds he bucked.

His interrogator was seated comfortably nearby, waiting. She was known only as "the Colonel." A woman in her forties, who spoke six languages and was expert in interrogation techniques used by the Stasi, the CIA, Mossad and the SS.

Was her background Israeli, or German? Some guessed her as a Pole.

At sixteen seconds, she nodded to the handlers, who were contractors, and the prisoner's head was pulled from the bucket. He gorged on air, his limp body trembling. He had not been allowed sleep in four days. He'd been forced to stand naked in a cell while being drenched periodically with frigid water.

His condition was failing fast. He could not stand without being supported. As a military doctor checked his vital signs, the Colonel stood and drew her face near to the prisoner's.

"Is there an operation underway?"

He was known as Issa al-Issa, a key operative, invisible in the world. Issa was an alias he had employed for longer than he should have. He may have been a former police official from the U.A.E. It was never determined. Months of intelligence work led to his clandestine midnight abduction from an apartment for immigrant workers in Kuwait City. He'd been handcuffed, and a sack was tied over his head before he was deposited into a private Gulfstream jet.

He was first flown to Jordan, then Nicosia.

Then he was flown to a region established by Byzantines where the Danube flowed in the Black Sea. Then he was driven in the trunk of a car to Building #S-9846.

A building once used by the KGB to harvest information.

A building that did not exist.

In fact, for official purposes, neither did Issa al-Issa.

He was a ghost prisoner.

"Is there an operation underway, Issa?"

The doctor turned to the Colonel and shook his head. Issa's condition had deteriorated, reaching a critical point. The Colonel nodded to the handlers to release him.

He crumbled to the floor, able to rest for the first time in one hundred hours.

As he lay there trembling, she bent over him.

"What more can you tell me before you die, Issa?"

She waited with the full knowledge she would not receive an answer.

With an animallike groan the prisoner expelled a massive breath.

Then he was still.

The doctor knelt beside him and checked his heart, his eyes, waiting, listening, rechecking before pronouncing the man deceased.

"Take care of it," she told the handlers.

Swiftly and efficiently they moved Issa al-Issa's corpse into a body bag. Then they carried it outside the building and deep into the dense forest, to the grave the prisoner had been forced to dig on the first day of his arrival.

As the handlers buried Issa al-Issa, the Colonel remained in Building #S-9846 and flipped through her logged notes. Issa had been one of the hardest interviews she'd ever conducted. She'd failed to extract as much as she'd hoped from him.

But what she had was vital.

She reached for her satellite phone.

She dialed the number for her contact at the embassy.

Issa's information could prove valuable to some governments, perhaps enough to warrant a significant amount of cash.

36

Vatican City

In the moments before sunrise, the pope stood alone at the window of the papal apartment in the top floor of the Apostolic Palace.

He watched twilight paint the Basilica, Bernini's colonnade and St. Peter's Square in pale blues and purple as a few police officers strolled the empty, silent piazza.

Weariness settled more heavily than usual on him because of his troubled sleep. Again, he had struggled to determine the meaning of his distraction.

It was the dream.

First light dawned.

He left the window for his private chapel and a session of private prayer. He prayed for the world's troubles and for the personal requests sent to him. The ten-year-old boy from El Salvador who had lost his family in the recent earthquake; the grief-stricken widow in Belfast afraid of losing her faith after the death of her husband; even for the little Swiss girl who had lost her kitten and included a photo and a little map, "so God will know where to look."

He smiled at that one.

After prayers, he celebrated Mass with a small group then ate breakfast with a few invited guests, a delegation of nuns from Brazil. Then he went to his private office to study his draft texts for his upcoming visit to the U.S. They concerned the environment, human reproduction, abortion, the sanctity of family, the erosion of the numbers of priests and the role of women in the church.

But in a far corner of his mind he thought of the dream.

At midmorning he held a series of scheduled audiences in the public part of the papal apartment. They were followed by lunch with a number of newly arrived diplomats posted to Rome and the Holy See, from the Netherlands, France, Japan, India and Chile.

Later, he returned to his office and opened the locked pouch that had arrived from the Secretariat of State. It contained secret correspondence with world leaders and other important documents, such as a highly classified note pertaining to security for the U.S. visit.

The note was written by the U.S. Secret Service, with an attached analysis by the chief of papal security for the trip. It outlined a number of ongoing threats, suspected sources, analysis, probability of success and ongoing counteraction.

Such analysis was done for all foreign trips.

The pope stroked his chin at the underlined portions, requesting that he wear "specially designed body armor" during all public events of his seven-city visit.

"Intelligence indicates the strong likelihood that

an attack will be attempted to gain instant and world-wide impact."

Such threats were common and some were carried out.

The pope considered the recent and past history of attempted papal assassinations, including the shooting of John Paul II in St. Peter's Square.

The prospect of assassination lived in a pope's shadow. He was not foolish about this aspect of his office. Since the days of Peter, it was part of the job.

He accepted the risks.

A familiar two-beat knock sounded at the door.

The deputy chief of the Secretariat of State appeared.

"Apologies, Holiness. It is time to meet with the cardinals and others on the final preparations for the American trip."

The pope took in a long breath, let it out slowly, then accompanied his trusted secretary, never tiring of the splendor of the Apostolic Palace as they walked along floors of sixteenth-century marble, lined by walls with ornate tapestries, gilding and Raphael frescoes.

The others, some two dozen in all, had been briefed by the deputy chief on the most pressing matter. The pope immediately raised his hand, the one with the Fisherman's Ring, inviting those present to begin speaking freely.

"Your Eminence," the first cardinal began, "the Americans are responsible for papal safety during the visit. They have provided us with intelligence suggesting an assassination attempt is probable. But there's nothing specific. And some U.S. church groups are growing vocal, openly urging the Vatican to abbreviate the visit. The U.S. Secret Service is asking us to make a decision on the visit's final agenda."

The pope acknowledged this as the cardinal continued.

"Eminence, to curtail matters now diminishes the importance of the papacy. It is out of the question."

"It is simply too late," another said.

And so it went from chair to chair to chair while the pope's thoughts left the room for the photographs on his nightstand of the Buffalo Breaks in Montana. They were beautiful in conveying the vastness of what was known as "Big Sky Country." Last week, he had requested the Vatican library also fetch him the private journals kept by the Jesuits who first arrived there in advance of white settlers in the early 1800s.

He enjoyed reading the poetry of their descriptions at night before he fell asleep.

"This is a place like no other," one had written, "where the earth meets heaven, where your relationship with God, your sense of self-importance, is either heightened, or diminished. I fear it is a place of reckoning."

A place of reckoning.

Then there was the pope's recurring dream.

He'd told no one.

It was more like a vision.

Sister Beatrice, incandescent, ascending above the prairie, telling him he must come, that his destiny was here.

Someone was speaking to him.

"Excellency?"

"Yes."

"As the date of your visit to America draws near, we are requested to give a prompt response to Washington."

The pope nodded thoughtfully.

In his own private assessment, he looked to the history of the church. In carrying out their work, priests and nuns had been murdered and had faced every threat and danger imaginable.

In many parts of the world, this remained true today.

And in many parts of the world it held true for the congregation as well.

The pope, above all, was a priest.

If God had decided these would be his final days, then he embraced the decision.

He was not afraid to die.

Your destiny is here. A place of reckoning.

"Your Excellency?"

The pope sighed.

"We need to examine this a bit more," he said. "Meanwhile, original preparations should continue. We'll provide our response to Washington by the end of the day."

37

Daniel Graham worked at his hotel-room desk mining Tarver's files for a lead.

Anything.

He'd been up since dawn.

His hair was tousled. He wore a faded T-shirt, sweat-pants, and downed stale coffee as he scoured the articles and reports Tarver had collected on immigration policies, terrorist sleeper cells and technology for building dirty bombs.

The file also had government records on civilian contract truckers in Iraq that Tarver had obtained through the Freedom of Information Act. Consequently, under national security and privacy legislation, most portions had been blacked out.

Whatever Tarver had been looking for, he'd been looking hard.

But Graham couldn't find a link to Tarver's last story and the tragedy in the Rockies.

The facts Graham knew firsthand gnawed at him: The stranger. The missing laptop, Emily Tarver's last words. Again, he reviewed the notebook he'd found at the Tarver campsite and Ray's final handwritten entry on Blue Rose Creek.

Possibly in California.

What is Blue Rose Creek? He scratched his whiskers. What does it mean?

Is there a connection?

He hadn't heard back from Walker. He asked Reg Novak and Carson, the FBI agent, to run the term through their systems. They'd found nothing. Graham had searched for it on the Internet but found nothing he could use, some obscure blogs, some poetry. Some results showed a suburb near Riverside County, California.

Maybe Ray's father had found something. Graham glanced at the time, thinking that he needed to get cleaned up before their meeting, when the hotel phone rang.

"Nice work on keeping things low-key," Inspector Mike Stotter said from Calgary. "Tell me why I shouldn't haul your ass back here on the next plane?"

"I'll explain what happened."

"No, I'll explain. The Secret Service called RCMP Headquarters in Ottawa. Ottawa called Edmonton, who called my boss, who had me spend much of yesterday defending you."

"I can explain."

"Tell me something, Dan. Why in the hell did you tell a senior Secret Service agent on the papal security detail that he's a suspect in the Tarver case?"

"How is it that this agent is informed that the case, *my case,* has been officially cleared and closed?"

"That's not the issue here."

"It damn well is, sir. It's not only a breach. I was betrayed by somebody feeding him BS."

"Likely came from Ottawa bureaucrats, making an assumption and making nice."

"Making nice? What're you talking about?"

"Look, right now, every U.S. security agency is strained by the pope's visit because they have to check every single burp by every nut job who makes a potential threat. Add to that the fact the president is scheduled to visit Canada in one month. Throw in the fact U.S.-Canada relations are chilly right now, means everybody's tightly wound."

"So? What's that got to do with me looking into Ray Tarver's background?"

"Ottawa does not want any tension with U.S. security people right now. Especially with the president coming to Canada and especially over this sort of thing."

"I'm dealing with multiple deaths and you're talking politics."

"What happened to this family was terrible. But they died tragically while camping. You've followed your hunch. There's nothing criminal or sinister here. Nothing concrete. It's got the hallmark of a tragic accident."

"What?"

The long-distance line hissed before Stotter resumed.

"Dan, you know I'm right. And I'm sorry but I'm going to cut your trip short. We've got other cases and I need you back here."

"Don't do this, Mike. Let me have the time you gave me."

"Dan, listen, I let you go down there because I

thought it might help you. You're one of our best investigators. You've been through a lot. I need you at full strength and I thought you needed to do this."

"What're you saying, Mike? That this was a pity assignment?"

"Dan."

"I don't believe this. Tell me, Mike, have we found Tarver's body yet?"

"No."

"Did we find his laptop yet?"

"No."

"So why is everybody but me convinced this was an accident?"

In the awkward silence Graham sensed an uneasy answer being formed.

"You're the one who heard voices, Dan."

"That little girl spoke to me, Mike. Before she died, she spoke to me."

"Dan, are you sure it was the little girl you heard?"

Graham's stomach quaked and he squeezed the phone.

"Sir, I request permission to complete my assignment in the time you'd allotted."

Graham knew he couldn't justify staying in the U.S. but in some small corner of his heart, someone, or something, was screaming for him to keep investigating.

"You're there at my discretion."

"I know, sir."

"You've got a few more days. That's it. Do I make myself clear?"

"Yes, sir."

38

Some ten miles south of downtown Washington, D.C., in a secured Central Intelligence Agency conference room overlooking the Potomac Valley, experts from nearly twenty intelligence branches met to discuss papal and national security.

Special Agent Blake Walker was among the contingent from the Secret Service.

Top of the agenda was a briefing by a high-ranking CIA officer who pointed to the man whose face stared at the group from the room's large monitor.

"This is Issa al-Issa. Last week he was captured in Kuwait."

Murmured reaction went round the table.

"As a result, what we've learned gives us reason to believe a major strike is planned during the pope's visit to the U.S., and that the operation is well advanced."

The agency had fragments of information indicating several key, but as yet unidentified, operatives linked to Issa's network were in the United States. Those operatives were said to be scientists or engineers in the fields of chemical, biological and atomic weaponry. These cells may be operating with other support cells who may provide access to money or resources.

"So what are we talking here?" asked a Homeland Security official. "Assassination by way of a nuke or dirty bomb?"

"Those are worst-case scenarios. The venues would provide an MCI and global exposure. The strike would be a grand slam in terms of symbolic meaning of a papal assassination on U.S. soil."

A top military advisor to the Joint Chiefs of Staff pressed to know how the agency could ensure the veracity of the information.

"We've been down this road before," the military advisor said. "Our understanding is that Issa was captured by mercenaries hired by a private international company contracted by the agency. The contractor was paid for its information in spite of a bad ending to Issa's questioning under severe duress."

The CIA officer studied his pen for a moment then said, "Unfortunately during his interview Issa passed away owing to a preexisting heart condition."

"Look," the military advisor said, "if Issa was tortured in any way, it taints his information. He'd have told you any bull he thought you'd want to hear."

A supervisor with the National Security Agency interjected.

"All that aside, the threat of a strike is consistent with some of the chatter we've intercepted that suggests something is underway."

"Such as?"

"A number of ships steaming to U.S. ports reportedly with hostile cargo."

"That kind of intelligence is a matter of routine," the military advisor said. "And from what we understand, most of those reports have already been investigated and cleared." The military advisor put his next question to those around the table: "Has anyone been able to link the information *we think we have* from Issa and the chatter?"

"What about this case of four Americans killed in Canada?" the man with the National Security Agency asked. "An investigative reporter from Washington, D.C., who'd reported on national security. Anything to this case that we should be concerned with?"

Blake Walker shook his head and took the question.

"We're working with the Canadian Security Intelligence Service in Ottawa and the Royal Canadian Mounted Police in Alberta. At this point there's no link. It appears to be an accidental wilderness case. They drowned in the mountains when their canoe capsized. It seems the RCMP has dispatched a member to Washington to follow up on Tarver's background. I believe we're covered."

Walker's colleague nodded for him to continue with other reports. Working with Egyptian and Italian security agents the Secret Service had uncovered a plot by the KTK, a fanatical group out of Cairo, to kidnap the pope in the U.S. "The group had planned to televise their members holding a sword over the pontiff's head while demanding the release of KTK members held in Israeli jails," Walker said.

And working with German intelligence, the Secret

Service and CIA had identified a small group of elite ex-mercenaries, veterans of brutal wars in Rwanda and Congo, who had been hired by an ideological group of disillusioned young aid workers. "They had conspired to kidnap the pope during his U.S. tour to draw world attention and aid to Africa. All conspirators had been arrested in Europe," Walker said.

"It seems to me—" the military advisor looked at his watch "—that at this stage all we have are potential pieces of a jigsaw puzzle. And we're not certain a puzzle exists. And looking at the files, we've got a growing number of threats that we're still processing for analysis. We haven't connected any dots here."

No one challenged the advisor so he continued.

"We know the public grows threat weary, that we can't always cry wolf."

A few heads nodded.

"We're seeing more church organizations who are concerned with security, urging the Vatican to shorten the visit. This is unprecedented."

"Any word on the Vatican's response?"

"We expect to hear soon."

"Look, this presents all kinds of problems." The State Department official launched into a discourse on Washington-Vatican relations and geopolitics.

The tension was growing. Blake was familiar with it; the time before a major event that robs agents of sleep, tightens stomachs and causes ulcers.

As the officers debated security, Walker glanced at his files and his calendar.

Time was ticking down on the pope's arrival.

First, Boston, where the president would receive

him, then New York, Miami, Houston, Los Angeles before moving into Walker's zone, the northwest, then concluding the tour in Chicago.

Walker had already joined advance teams, inspected sites three times, worked with field offices and briefed local and state police and emergency personnel. Soon his group would fly to Seattle and pick up the visit there, joining the main teams who'd be with the pope the entire trip.

Walker's group was responsible for the pope's security on his visit to Seattle, Washington, then a smaller event in Lone Tree County, Montana.

He flipped by Father Stone's newsletter prematurely announcing the visit.

It renewed Walker's thoughts about the Montana leg. Now, with the visit upon them, amid the intensifying rush of threats, Walker prayed Father Stone's premature boasting to the World Wide Web would not be a factor.

Any further thought about it was pushed aside by the soft lowing of his vibrating phone. Walker had received an encrypted message from his supervisor.

VATICAN SAYS NO CUTS TO AGENDA. FULL-BORE VISIT AHEAD.

Walker absorbed the update then swallowed hard.

39

Takoma, D.C.

Would he find answers here?

The Tarvers had a modest Victorian home.

It was where they'd lived, where they'd dreamed and where Ray, a reporter who'd lost the respect of his colleagues, had continued his pursuit of his conspiracy theories.

The house sat back from the street, inviting visitors to a veranda edged with an ornate spindled railing and sheltered by overhanging gables. It was walking distance from the Takoma Metro station, the last stop on the red line in D.C. before Silver Spring, Maryland. When Graham arrived, Jackson Tarver was on his knees digging among the roses that lined the front walk.

"You're right on time." Tarver stood.

"It's a beautiful house."

"Anita took care of most things." Tarver's gaunt face was bereft of light when he greeted him. "Any word on if the searchers located Ray?"

"No, sir. I'm sorry."

Tarver turned to the house, gazing at it as if his son,

his daughter-in-law and grandchildren were inside waiting. His Adam's apple rose and fell.

"Let's get started. I'll show you around, like you wanted, whatever you need."

They began with the back.

It was typical with a barbecue and a patio set with an umbrella table arranged on a deck that stepped down into the well-kept fenced yard. There were dells of rhododendrons and ferns shaded by sugar maples, and a tall beech tree with a tire swing for the kids. Tarver gave the tire a gentle push.

"They loved it here," Jackson Tarver said.

As the old rope squeaked, Graham imagined the children playing in the yard, Anita gardening, Ray and his father at the grill sharing beers, talking sports or politics.

Living their lives like most families.

"Excuse me, are you related to Ray and Anita Tarver?" Both men turned to a woman in her early thirties standing at the side of the house.

"I'm Ray's father, Jackson Tarver."

"I'm Melody Sloane. I live down the street. My twins played with Emily and Tommy."

"Come in, Melody."

"I don't mean to barge in on you. I saw you out front."

"It's all right."

"My condolences, Mr. Tarver." She cupped a hand over her mouth, then embraced him. "I read about it in the *Post*." Her voice weakened. "It's so awful. I'm so sorry."

"Thank you."

"Some of the neighborhood moms were wondering about a service. The two detectives who were here the other day didn't know if arrangements had been made."

"No, nothing's been decided yet. Anita and the children were cremated. We'll have a memorial service when we have Ray, when they're all together."

"Of course, please, let me know if there's anything you need." She turned to leave.

"Ms. Sloane, if I may?" Graham gave her his card. "Corporal Daniel Graham with Royal Canadian Mounted Police."

She looked at the card and its stylized bison head seal.

"I'm handling matters in Canada. Could you tell me a bit more about these two detectives?"

"Goodness. Well, it was at the time when the story had been in the *Post*. I'd come to the house to leave a card in the mailbox. The two men got here just before me. I think they'd tried the door, no one was here and they were looking around the side."

"Did they show you any ID?" Graham asked. "Were they D.C. police? FBI? Secret Service?"

"No, no identification."

"Did they tell you what they wanted?"

"They wanted to know who was looking after the house. I said that I didn't know."

Graham turned to Tarver. "Were you ever contacted by detectives?"

"We got a lot of calls from people. Some from police and you, but I haven't been thinking too clearly."

"Have you shown police through the house?"

"No."

"So we really can't confirm who they were."

"What's the concern?" Tarver asked.

"Just curious."

"Could've been reporters, or Ray's friends, sources, you know," Tarver said.

"Could've been." *Could have be someone else who's investigating, too,* Graham thought. He made a note, then asked Melody to call him if she remembered anything more.

After she left, Tarver took Graham to the garage. He took stock of the family car, a Toyota Corolla, the workbench, tools, extension ladder hooked on one wall above the mower, the kids' bikes and toys. In one corner, cardboard boxes were stacked and labelled, *Clothes For Charity* printed in clear letters with a fine-point marker. Done by Anita, Graham thought as Tarver led him through the breezeway and into the house.

"I haven't touched a thing," Tarver said. "Look through anything you like, search what you need. I'm going to brew some coffee."

The living room had hardwood floors and an L-shaped sofa with fat cushions, facing a large TV next to a wood-burning redbrick fireplace. It was framed by bookshelves with DVDs like *Titanic, Sophie's Choice, The Searchers, The Paper,* CDs by Springsteen, the Beatles and Van Morrison, hardcover books by F. Scott Fitzgerald, Steinbeck and Faulkner, a small gallery of framed photos, mostly of Tommy and Emily, and a family trip. Orlando, judging by the Mickey Mouse hats.

The room flowed into the dining room with a ranch-style table and six chairs, and a glass-fronted hutch. A chandelier hung in the center of the room.

The dining room led to the hall and the bed-room area.

The first bedroom had soft-colored wallpaper with tiny unicorns and rainbows and a small bed with a frilly bedspread. Above it, a multicolored crayon drawing of a castle that said *Princess Emily's House,* was taped to one wall. Stuffed toys crowded the top of the dresser and shelves. Graham traced his fingers over the flowers printed on the pillowcase, detecting a child's sweet scent.

She took her last breaths in his arms.

A small, clean bathroom connected the room to the next bedroom.

In that room, a model of a space shuttle was hanging by a thread from the ceiling. A large map of the solar system covered one wall, while the others were papered with the U.S. flag, posters of the Wizards and Batman. All faced a loft bed with a desk and a collection of picture books. Hanging on his closet door was a T-shirt emblazoned with *Tommy the Conqueror.*

Princess Emily and Tommy the Conqueror next to their mother in the Medical Examiner's Office.

Next, Graham came to the Tarvers' master bedroom at the end of the hall.

It had a large window that overlooked the backyard, a walk-in closet and an en suite bathroom. Nicely decorated. Graham noticed a pleasant soapy hint of perfume and cologne. The bedroom walls were cream, a framed Rembrandt print hung over the queen-size bed, which had a quilted spread and throw pillows. A hard copy of a romance—*Knights With Lonely Maidens*—was on one nightstand, on the other, an alarm clock and a textbook: *Revealed: One Hundred Terrorist Plots.*

Sadness rolled over Graham as he flipped through it.

The world had ended for this family. Graham was standing in a crypt, trying to make sense of what had happened.

Maybe their deaths were accidental?

Then what the hell am I doing here?

40

Takoma, D.C.

"Be careful."

Graham looked at the steaming mug of coffee Jackson Tarver held out for him.

"It's hot."

They stood in Ray and Anita's bedroom letting a moment of respectful silence pass.

"What exactly are you looking for?"

"To tell you the truth, I'm not sure. I hope I'll recognize it when I see it."

"You know, I'm up most nights convincing myself that Ray's alive, hurt and waiting down along the river. That he'll come back and we'll help him through this."

"You said that he'd quit the wire service, but from the people I've talked to I get the sense that that's not quite what happened."

"Ray would never talk about it. But I always feared that he'd been forced to leave. Or was fired and it put him in a desperate situation. We only wanted to help him out, so I gave him money from time to time, like when he said he needed to take Anita and the kids on a vacation to the mountains."

"Do you think Ray was in danger because of his work?"

"Corporal, is there something you're not telling me?"

"I just need to be satisfied that it was an accident. We still haven't found his laptop. Did he ever talk about the last story he was working on?"

"The only thing he told me was that it was big and that he was certain he'd get a book deal out of it."

"Anything to do with terrorists? He seemed to be researching the subject."

"I don't know. Maybe."

"Do you think he may have exaggerated his story?"

The suggestion landed on a nerve.

"Not every lead he chased resulted in a story. That's the nature of the news business."

"Did he have enemies?"

"I wouldn't know. Are you trying to tell me that someone killed my son and his family because of a goddamn story?"

You have to protect key facts of the case, Graham warned himself.

"No. That's not what I'm saying. The fact is, I don't know. I'm sorry. I'm just trying to rule out anything criminal, so we can be sure. Ray's missing laptop concerns me. It could've been a robbery gone wrong, or someone took it after Ray and everyone left their campsite. That sort of thing."

Tarver stared at Graham.

"All I can tell you is that my son was a good reporter. He questioned everything. He dug deep. I know he was a loner, even ostracized. Anita told me. But Ray wasn't like most reporters in Washington who swallow whatever they're told."

"I understand."

"Now, Ray's office is in the basement. This way."

The basement smelled of laundry detergent and was divided into a series of small, low-ceilinged rooms finished with paneling that had survived the '70s. The area contained a small bedroom, a two-piece bathroom with an outdated linoleum floor, a combination laundry and furnace room, then an office.

Graham estimated the office was eight feet square. It was crammed with floor-to-ceiling bookshelves, two three-drawer file cabinets and a large desk with a computer and monitor.

"Nothing in this room's been touched since the day they left for Canada. The file cabinet's unlocked. Do what you need to do on his computer. Take all the time you need. I'll be upstairs."

Newspapers rose in a tower in one corner against the bookshelves. At one end, laminated press tags hung in clusters from chains. A number of framed news awards for breaking news and investigative reporting were piled on one shelf.

Tacked to one frame was a paper target, a silhouette of a man's upper torso in a scoring ring punctured with holes. A handful of empty shell casings stood next to it.

Yellowing front pages of big city newspapers for San Francisco, Dallas, Miami, Boston, Minneapolis, Philadelphia and Denver, with Ray Tarver's bylines hung on one wall. Snapshots of Ray with other reporters in Europe, the Middle East, Kuwait, Iraq, Japan, Africa. Here's Ray with President Bush. Here he is with President Clinton.

Is that Springsteen with Ray?

The guy got around.

Graham set his mug on the desk, sat down and switched on the computer. As it fired up, he looked at his watch. The time was 10:20 a.m. He began reading every file he could access off the desktop, then searched the hard drive.

Much of it was in the same vein as the file Kate Morrow had given him—articles, reports, notes that made no sense to Graham. Then he looked at the history of Tarver's online travels and the sites he'd visited, starting with the most recent.

As expected, airlines, car rentals, hotels, tourism sites, U.S. and Canadian travel requirements, passports, borders, online banking, credit-card use. Graham was surprised the passwords had been saved.

Credit-card and banking records offered nothing unusual. All travel and household related. Wait. What was this charge for *Investigative Search Services?* Graham noted that one before returning to Tarver's online history.

Further along he'd seen that Ray had visited sites for finding people, located work histories, unions, associations, driving records, voting records, property records for various states. A lot of work on California.

He was searching public records for counties in Southern California.

Then the history ended. That was it.

Next Graham flipped through every hard-copy file

of news reports, studies, notes, photocopies from text-books. Nothing jumped out at him, nothing that connected anything to anything.

It was nearly 5:00 p.m. when he finished.

He rubbed his eyes and neck and got up to leave when he glanced at the bunches of press tags.

Something among them, almost hidden, was beckoning from a chain.

A USB flash drive.

People used them to back up computer files. This one had a tiny handwritten label.

LAPTOP.

Graham held his breath as he held the drive in his hand.

Do you believe this?

He inserted it into the computer port and as it loaded he wondered—no, hoped—that whatever files Ray had put on his missing laptop, he'd backed them up here before the trip.

And, here we go.

Files appeared.

Graham's hopes wilted. They duplicated what he'd already seen. Before quitting, he ran a search for the term *Blue Rose Creek,* as he'd done before, expecting it to be futile. As the program searched he rubbed his eyes.

He'd buried his tired face in his hands and had begun considering returning to Alberta, when the computer chimed with the message.

One file located.

This was new.

He opened it. Tarver had made notes, a few weeks before the trip.

The FOIA records indicate one American driver among those in the convoy attacked in Iraq with links to the new weapon operation. Details on the driver were censored to respect privacy laws. A Pentagon source put the driver's location in California, near Riverside County. Further investigation with trucking associations and transportation sources confirm the driver's address.

10428 Suncanyon Rise, Blue Rose Creek, California.

Homeowners: Jake & Maggie Conlin.

Bingo.

Graham steepled his fingers to think for a moment.

Then he went online to check out flights to Los Angeles.

41

Blue Rose Creek, California

Across the country, Maggie Conlin was losing hope.

She felt it slip from her as Fatima Soleil was lowered into the ground of the Whisper Wood Cemetery, buried in a plot that overlooked an orange grove at the county's edge where a small group had gathered for her funeral.

One by one they dropped roses on her oak coffin.

After the service Maggie went to the reception in the community hall of Fatima's mobile-home park. Maggie didn't know the mourners; most were older women, Fatima's neighbors.

But she felt obligated to be there.

Maybe because she'd been with Fatima at the end of her life.

Maybe because she needed to understand Fatima's last words.

"Your son is alive...but he is in danger."

Whatever Maggie was seeking, she didn't find it at the grave site, or among the mobile-home widows wearing overapplied makeup, too much perfume and chewing sadly on egg salad sandwiches.

She couldn't stay.

Maggie hugged Helga then left.

She drove fast but couldn't escape her mounting fear, or the darkness that had engulfed her since Jake had taken Logan.

What did Fatima's death gasp mean?

"There is a woman…fire, explosions, destruction…she is carrying a child…the child is dead."

Maybe it meant nothing?

Was it real? Maybe Fatima had hallucinated her vision? She had been sedated. An IV was delivering drugs into her system at the time.

Maggie knew about drugs.

On her passenger seat her open purse revealed the tip of the bottle of sedatives her doctor had prescribed in the weeks after Jake and Logan had vanished. Maggie didn't take them often but when she did they numbed her pain.

Helped her rest.

Let her be with Logan and Jake in her dreams.

A horn blasted. Maggie jumped. She had veered into the next traffic lane. She steered back safely and exhaled. Pay attention, she told herself as she came to the freeway exit for Blue Rose Creek.

She dreaded returning to her empty house, where the only thing awaiting her was despair. She still couldn't escape her paranoia that something was gaining on her, couldn't escape the raw, sick feeling that her hope of ever seeing Logan and Jake again had somehow been lost.

Buried with Fatima's casket.

What if they're dead?

Stop thinking like that.

She had to go somewhere. To clear her mind.

Maggie brushed away her tears as she pulled into a large family restaurant with a gigantic U.S. flag waving in the breeze. She went inside to a table near the window, touched the corners of her eyes and searched the freeway traffic.

"Are you okay, dear?" the waitress asked.

"Yes, I'm fine."

"What can I get you?"

"Just tea, please. Whatever you have is fine."

"Coming up."

Maggie struggled to think of something positive but it was futile. She'd heard nothing from police. The last contact she'd had from the private investigator was an invoice. No word from the courts. Nothing from the lawyer. Nothing from Logan's school, his doctor. Reporters remained indifferent to her case. Her online searching had led nowhere. Support groups were sympathetic and had worked hard to help but nothing had surfaced that would lead her to Logan and Jake.

What more could she do?

Her body sagged.

What more could she do? Nothing. She had nothing. She was alone.

Maggie swallowed, fighting not to lose it right there at her table.

A teacup, saucer and spoon rattled.

"Here you are. Some nice tea. If you want anything else, just wave."

After the waitress left, Maggie spotted several women at the far end of the restaurant.

Soccer moms from Logan's team.

They were subtly nodding as scraps of whispered conversations spilled her way.

"…yes, that's her…Logan's mom…should go over there…"

No, please. Today of all days. Leave me alone, please.

She couldn't face them.

She fled to the restroom, thankful it was empty apart from the stranger in the mirror with worry etched in her face. Her ordeal was exacting such a toll she was barely recognizable to herself.

"Maggie?"

Dawn Sullivan had entered. She and her mechanic husband, Mac, had moved to California from Dallas a few years ago and their boy, Arlo, played on Logan's team.

"Hello, Dawn."

"So it *is* you." Dawn joined her in the mirror. "My Lord, it has been ages, hasn't it?"

"Quite a while, yes."

"So how you all holding up?"

"To be honest, not so good, today."

"You just hang in there."

"Thanks, I'll do my best."

"You know, my sister's divorce from the jerk she married nearly killed her. Custody can get ugly, but she survived and was stronger for it."

"Jake's not a jerk. And we aren't divorcing."

"Sorry. It just seemed so obvious things were headed there after his blowup on the field that day—then him leaving you and all."

"That's not right, Dawn."

"Damn straight it's not right, what with Jake seeing another woman and all."

"What?"

Maggie turned to Dawn.

"I'm sorry, but it took some kind of nerve for him to accuse you of—"

"What did you say?"

Dawn turned to assess Maggie from her head to her shoes.

"My Lord, you really didn't know?" Dawn touched her shoulder. "Sweetheart, we thought you knew. Everyone knows."

"What are you talking about?"

"Some of Mac's trucker buddies saw Jake at a bar with a woman a long time back, then again a couple months before he left you."

"What's that supposed to mean?"

"Your husband was stepping out on you, that's what it means."

"No, there's got to be a mistake. Where did they see him?"

"No mistake. Those guys knew Jake. I think it was Bakersfield first."

"What?"

"Then it could've been a truck stop outside of Las Vegas. Or both in Bakersfield. No matter. They *definitely* saw your husband with another woman."

"Dawn, tell me *exactly* what you know?"

"They said they saw Jake with a woman and they were together."

"No, no. That can't be. Jake had problems after Iraq, but nothing like that."

"Honey, he's a trucker. And some men live other lives on the road."

Maggie felt the earth shifting under her feet, felt the room spin.

"No, this can't be right. Who is this woman? What's her name?"

"Lord if I know. Mac's friends said she was dark-haired. Pretty. Does it matter? The point is, we all heard about what happened to you and now it's going round that you're talking to *psychics*. Good Lord."

"Dawn, please."

"Now, Maggie, listen to me. I'm telling you, woman to woman, you have to let this crap with Jake go. It's gone on way too long."

"You don't understand a single thing about me."

"Sugar, I understand way more than you think. See, before I met Mac, I went down the same road you're on, only my asshole was named— Oh, forget it. Most men are born assholes. They should all have it for a first name."

"Dawn, stop. Please."

Maggie seized her purse to leave. Dawn held her arm gently.

"You've got to take charge, girl. Talk to a lawyer, go for custody of your boy, start proceedings."

"Let go of me, I've heard enough."

"I am trying to help you with the benefit of my experience."

Maggie's fingers clenched her purse. She invaded Dawn's space and dropped her voice. "Let go of me or I'll break your fucking arm."

Dawn's jaw dropped as Maggie shook her off.

Maggie stormed out of the restaurant then left three feet of burning rubber as she exited the parking lot. She drove home in a swimming fog, her ears pounding with rage and fear.

Another woman.

In her heart she couldn't believe Jake would cheat on her. In spite of everything after Iraq she had never even considered the possibility.

Had he really taken Logan and left her for another woman?

It couldn't be true.

Why didn't anyone tell her? Why didn't the private investigator know? Why didn't police know? Why didn't the support groups looking into her case know?

Why didn't SHE know?

Maggie's self-recrimination intensified as she unlocked her house. Her knees were buckling. She slammed the door shut, her back thudding against it, her dress bunching up behind her as she slid to the floor.

Defeated.

Her fears encircled her, edged toward her, snarling, growling, *another woman, a casket descending, a dying psychic's visions of a woman carrying a dead child, and a video of the wrong boy.*

A great banshee wail erupted from Maggie as she surrendered to the darkness, remaining as still as death on the floor with her back to the door.

Until night came for her.

She didn't know how many hours had passed by the time she finally got to her feet. Something was in her hand. She gripped it hard as she floated from room to room, images swirling in a tear-streaked fog.

In Logan's room she ran her fingers along his small desk, the books lining his bookshelves, his scale models of racing cars, warships, the posters of his heroes, and Jake smiling by his rig in Iraq. She opened his closet to T-shirts, khakis and jeans, touching a Dodgers jersey to her face, inhaling Logan's scent.

I love you so much.

She went to the master bedroom and stood in it, feeling herself floating in the cool darkness before she went to their closet. She touched one of Jake's flannel plaid shirts to her cheek. She could sense his cologne, feel him.

Hear him.

She reached to the top shelf. She knew it well, knew where everything was because she'd put most of it there. She searched the odds and ends, old files, old books, old purses and photos before locking on to the thing she needed.

Tears slid down her face as she went to the kitchen for a candle and bottle of wine, her arms cradling everything as she moved to the couch in the gloom of the unlit house.

She lit the candle and inserted a DVD into the player.

Maggie steeled herself for the remembrance of happier times as images of her wedding to Jake played before her, images of buying the house, painting the walls and each other. Memories of being aglow with pregnancy, her belly swollen. Logan's birth, his first birthday, his first steps, family vacations to the beach, Disneyland. Jake with a new rig, Jake with Logan on his shoulders. Her own last birthday, a cake glimmering with candles. Logan and Jake serenading her with "Happy Birthday."

"I love you, Mom."

Maggie froze the frame and knelt before the screen, traced her fingers over Logan's face.

Where are you? I want to be with you. We can be together again. Where are you?

Something rattled in her hand.

Her sedatives. Over three-dozen powerful pills.

She stared at the bottle. She wanted to end her pain. She wanted her life back.

Logan.

Book Four:
The Perfect Weapon

42

Blue Rose Creek, California

The hydraulic flaps of Graham's jet groaned as Southern California's suburbs streamed below as far as he could see.

The landing gear grumbled down and locked for a smooth landing.

As the plane rolled to the terminal, Graham resumed questioning his decision to fly here. He now had a California link to Blue Rose Creek, which was the final entry in the notebook he'd found in Tarver's tent in the Rockies. Something was emerging. But what? He could be dead wrong about all of it.

What if Blue Rose Creek was nothing but useless data from an oddball reporter who chased wacky conspiracies and probably died accidentally with his family in the mountains?

What if it was nothing more than that?

What if it wasn't?

Where's Tarver's laptop? Who was that stranger with him?

Don't hurt my daddy.

There had to be something to this. Graham rubbed his eyes and the back of his neck as he waited at the luggage carousel. After grabbing his bag he climbed into the car rental shuttle. If he was going to clear this case, he needed to talk to the Conlins.

As the shuttle wheeled from LAX, he checked his cell phone for messages.

Before leaving Washington, he'd made a number of calls. The first was to his boss in Calgary, where he left a brief message about a good lead that could break the case. "I have to leave Washington. I'll keep you posted."

Then he called the cell phone of Secret Service Agent Walker and left a message. Graham hoped to clarify matters and seek any help on the California lead. Walker hadn't responded.

Graham had also called ahead to the county sheriff's office and gave a youthful-sounding deputy named Tillman his regimental number and a summary of his business, including the Conlins' address, which Tillman checked.

"Oh, you should talk to Detective Vic Thompson."

"Why? Is there an investigation?"

"I don't know all the details. A custody thing, or something, Vic's out right now. I'll put you through to his voice mail."

"Wait, could I get a complaint history on the address?"

"Sure, I'll get back to you, Corporal Graham."

That was some five hours ago and not a word from Thompson or Tillman.

After getting into his rented car, Graham called again and left messages with Thompson and Tillman. Nothing. Screw it. Graham decided to proceed. He'd come this far and didn't have time to wait around. He consulted his map, selected the best freeway to Blue Rose Creek and navigated through L.A.'s traffic.

Sure, he was going way out on a limb.

He hadn't heard back from his boss in Alberta; maybe his vague message had bought him some time. Graham had not requested permission to follow information to California. Why give them the chance to say no? Besides, he didn't recall any travel restrictions being placed on him. A weak defense but he needed to see this case through and the clock was ticking on him.

About an hour later he came to the exit for Blue Rose Creek and made his way through the serpentine streets of the Conlins' neighborhood. It appeared to be a middle-class suburb of well-kept homes with trim lawns and palm trees.

Graham hadn't called ahead.

He didn't want to give the Conlins advance notice that he was coming. He found that he got a better read off people when he surprised them.

The Conlins lived at 10428 Suncanyon Rise in a stucco bungalow set back from the street. It had two palms, neat shrubs and a red tile roof. A small Ford was parked in the carport. Next to it, a vacant parking pad, large enough to accommodate an RV. Nice-looking place, Graham thought. He drove by, down the street and well out of sight before he parked and got out of his car.

In the distance he heard children's laughter and the splash of a pool as he walked to the house. Breezes carried birdsong and something sweet-smelling as he approached the front door and rang the bell.

The house was silent.

A pair of swallows blurred by.

Graham glanced at the newspaper sticking out of the mailbox, at the snippet of headline about the pope's U.S. visit, which was underway.

Neglected paper and no sound coming from the house.

Not good.

A sign that no one was home.

He knocked hard on the door.

Nothing.

Graham stepped to the side of the door, shaded his eyes from the glare and peered through the window but saw nothing.

Clank.

What the—? Metal against metal. Came from the side of the house. Graham set off to investigate, walking along the paved driveway and under the carport, spotting the iron gate to the back. It was unfastened and clanging against the latch.

The house was emitting a soft low hum.

What was that?

Beyond the gateway Graham saw a small backyard and the walk to the rear door.

"Hello!"

Nothing. No dog. Nothing.

He called again, giving it a long moment before going to the back door. He rang the bell and called out again.

"Hello!"

Nothing.

Again, he pressed his face to a window, cupped his hands near his eyes and looked into the house.

He saw the hardwood floor of the kitchen, had a partial view of chairs, a table, a dishwasher, countertop. Something was droning. Farther along he saw a hallway, a living room, then he glimpsed a hand.

A hand?

On the floor. Attached to an arm that reached into the hallway.

Someone was on the floor. Someone unconscious.

"Hello!"

Should he kick the door? He had limited jurisdiction. He reached for his cell phone, pressed the Conlins' number, banging on the glass while it rang. He could hear it ringing in the house and hung up when a recorded message answered.

Graham went to the door and knocked hard, then tried the handle.

It opened.

Odd.

Graham considered his next move, then stepped inside.

"Hello!"

Bracing for a possible intruder, he made his way to the person on the floor, scanning hidden areas, wishing he had his gun.

It was clear.

A woman in her early thirties was on the floor. Unconscious.

Graham knelt down and checked for a pulse. Nothing. He had trouble hearing over the deep hum. It was the television. He pressed his ear to her chest again. This time he was certain.

She was breathing.

A prescription bottle was on the floor next to her.
Empty.
Graham grabbed her phone, called 911.

43

Blue Rose Creek, California

The paramedics took Maggie to Inland Center Hospital, where the emergency staff worked on her.

Afterward they put her in a private room with a large window and through her tears she counted the clouds sailing by. Her stomach and throat hurt from the gastric lavage but her deepest pain was her ache for Logan. To say she was sorry. For in desperation, she had done what she had vowed never to do.

Abandoned her search.

She had not intended to kill herself, according to the psychiatrist who'd left her room a little while ago after assessing her. Maggie had reacted to a deluge of "stressors": the abduction of her son by her husband, prophetic visions, a funeral, painful gossip.

"Accidental overdose," the psychiatrist called it.

Maggie wiped her eyes and took stock of her hospital wristband, the IV tube in her arm.

Her life.

How had it come to this? She and Jake used to be so happy.

Crazy in love, he called it.

Dancing in the gym under the crystal ball.

"Hey, Jude."

Tears in Jake's eyes on their wedding day.

His chest swelling with pride when Logan was born.

Crazy in love.

Iraq had damaged him.

What really happened over there? He came home a changed man. Did he find someone else? Was it true? Why was this happening?

She wanted her life back.

For better or for worse, because it was the only life she had.

She would fight for it.

She would go home and pick up the pieces. She'd demand more information from Dawn Sullivan's husband and somehow she would find Jake, find Logan.

Find the truth.

And somehow she would live with it.

Maggie lost count of the clouds and reached for her hospital cup.

It was empty.

"May I have some more water please? And more tissues?"

The young woman sitting with her set aside her textbook.

"How are you doing, Maggie? Still a wee bit sore, I bet?"

Her name tag said, Hayley, Student Social Worker.

"Yes. Thank you." She accepted the cup and tissues. "Can I ask you a question?"

"You sure can."

"How did I get here? I don't have any friends or relatives."

"You mean who found you?"

"Yes."

"You're very lucky. A police officer just happened to come to your house. When he found you on the floor, he called 911 and gave you CPR. Our emerg people said that if it wasn't for him—well—he's the one who saved you. See, God sent your guardian angel into the game."

"What officer just 'happened' to come by my house?"

"The Mountie from Canada."

"A Mountie?"

"I think his name is Graham."

"Where is he now?"

"Uhm." Hayley bit her bottom lip, looked to the door and flushed from the sudden fear that she may have revealed more than she should have.

"I want to talk to him. He's here, isn't he?"

"I'm not sure if the doctor wanted me to say."

"Hayley, where is he?"

"He's been here all this time. Waiting to make sure you're all right."

"Find him. Bring him in. I want to see him."

"I'd better find the doctor first. I'm not sure if you're supposed to have any visitors before they discharge you. I think—"

"Hayley. Find the Mountie and bring him in here. I *need* to talk to him now."

44

Graham was running out of time.

As he flipped through his umpteenth tattered *Newsweek,* an emergency intern carrying a clipboard approached him in the waiting room.

"You're the officer here with Maggie Conlin?"

"That's right. Will she be okay?"

"She should be fine, but we're trying to locate a relative."

"Did you try her husband, Jake Conlin?"

"We're not having much luck, any suggestions?"

"Sorry, I don't know the family," Graham said. "But I'd like to talk to Maggie as soon as it's possible."

"The psychiatrist is assessing her. We'll have to see if she advises visitors. Can you hang in for a bit longer?"

"Sure."

"Good job with the CPR, by the way."

The intern left Graham to return to the magazines and his dilemma.

All Graham had wanted was to follow up Tarver's Blue Rose Creek notes by talking to Jake and Maggie

Conlin. See what came out of it. Finding Maggie Conlin on the floor of her home near death was unexpected. As he considered his next steps, his cell phone vibrated and he went outside to take the call.

"Graham."

"Corporal Graham, Vic Thompson, county sheriff's department. Sorry we had trouble hooking up."

"You're swamped, I understand."

"We've caught a triple homicide and I'm about to get on a plane to San Francisco to interview a witness. You're at the hospital with Maggie Conlin?"

"Yes. What can you tell me about the Conlins?"

"For starters, you shouldn't have gone to Maggie's door without talking to me face-to-face. I don't think you would like me doing that in your backyard."

"I called in with my regimental and stated my business. They said you were too busy to meet me."

"I confirmed your particulars. Aren't you a tad out of your jurisdiction?"

"Look, if you want an apology, you've got it."

"Just so we're clear. It's good you found her. I would have alerted you to her instability. Now, we've got a deputy at the Conlin house in Blue Rose and he'll be heading to the hospital for your statement."

"No problem."

"He said there's no sign of forced entry. Did you kick the door?"

"The back door was unlocked," Graham said. "I understand the Conlins were in a domestic situation?"

"It's a parental abduction."

"A parental abduction?"

"About five, six months ago, Jake took off with their nine-year-old son."

"Where?"

"We don't know. We've got a warrant out for him. He never notified anyone with an address, never initiated divorce action, nothing from the school, the doctor, phone or financial records."

"He's gone underground with his son?"

Graham's phone beeped with a call-waiting tone. He ignored it.

"Looks that way. Jake's a long-haul trucker. They could be anywhere. And he's likely changed their names. We've alerted the FBI, got them in NCIC, and such. We don't think Jake's violent or will harm his son. But anything's possible. Like most of these cases, this one's a mess. Maggie took it hard but at first she didn't want to press things. Didn't want to make it worse. She thought that if we could find Jake she could talk sense into him, be a happy family again."

"What happened?"

"They had their troubles. Jake had publicly accused Maggie of cheating on him with Logan's soccer coach. Some of the other parents told me that Jake seemed paranoid ever since he got home from a contract truck-driving job overseas. Could be a post-traumatic stress thing happening."

"Where was his contract job?"

"Iraq."

Iraq.

That stopped Graham cold.

Iraq.

Would that have anything to do with Tarver's story?

"So tell me again why you're here," Thompson said. "Your message said it was some kind of accidental death insurance thing. Are you pulling my leg?"

"It's complicated."

"Uncomplicate it fast, we're starting to board."

"I've got a family from Washington, D.C., whose members appear to have been killed recently in a wilderness accident in a river in the Rockies near Banff. Got three confirmed dead, a mom and her two children, a boy and a girl. We haven't located the dad yet. Ray Tarver. Heard of him?"

"Doesn't ring any bells. What's the insurance part?"

"The death benefit is large, so I'm checking background."

"Right, like maybe the dad did it? Or had help, since you haven't found him. Maybe he'll stumble out of the woods to collect?"

"Or maybe someone killed them."

"What's your evidence?"

"A lot of circumstance and a gut feeling."

"Not the best ammunition for court. Is that what brought you here?"

"The dad was a reporter, a bit of an oddball who chased wild conspiracy theories. The Conlins' name and address in Blue Rose Creek came up in his files. The reporter may have been onto a big plot story at the time his family died in the mountains. This Iraq thing is new to me. What do you know about Jake Conlin's time there?"

"Not much. It was dangerous. He drove in supply convoys that often came under fire. What was the reporter's plot story?"

"It was vague about a terror group developing a new weapon."

"Really. Like what? A dirty bomb or something? We're boarding now, I gotta hang up."

"I don't know. Could've been a fantasy he was chasing."

"Did you pass what you have to the security people in D.C, Homeland, the FBI, let them connect the dots and figure it out?"

"There's a Secret Service agent the reporter was in touch with. I've been talking to him."

"Look, Graham, you give me your word that if you find anything you keep me in the loop."

"I will."

"I'll do the same. I'm not sure what we can do, but I'll help where I can, just call. I gotta go."

The line went dead.

When Graham turned to go back into the hospital, a pock-faced girl with braces, wearing a white lab coat with a name tag that said, Hayley, Student Social Worker, was waiting for him.

"Excuse me, Corporal Graham?"

"Yes."

"The officer who brought Maggie Conlin in?"

"That's right."

"She's awake and wants to talk to you."

45

Blue Rose Creek, California

As Hayley led Graham to Maggie's room, his cell phone vibrated.

Caller ID indicated it was his boss.

"Hold up, Hayley, I have to take a call."

He stepped back outside and answered.

"What're you doing in California, Corporal?"

"Following the case."

"I never authorized you to travel there."

"I got a strong lead on the last thing Tarver wrote in his journal. Let me give you a case status report."

"No. I'll update you. First, you piss off the Secret Service in Washington telling an agent he's a suspect."

"We cleared that up."

"Don't interrupt. Then you fly to California without my knowledge or authorization. Imagine my delight to be surprised with a call from a Captain Emillio Sanchez of the county sheriff's department. It seems a Detective Vic Thompson complained that you'd exceeded your jurisdiction and broke into a house to question someone."

"That's wrong. I arrived to find my subject had overdosed. I'm at the hospital about to interview her. And I spoke with Thompson. We straightened it out."

"Well, your assignment down there is over."

"Over? Why?"

"We've found Tarver."

"What?"

"A couple of boys at a Bible camp way downriver found him this morning washed up against the rocks. The body was in bad shape. Found his wallet on him. So get yourself home, do the paperwork and clear this thing."

"Wait. We're going to autopsy Tarver, right?"

"Just as soon as we can. We've got other cases. Got to autopsy a woman and her baby killed in a ranch fire outside Pincher Creek. We suspect her husband shot them before torching the place. After them, the M.E. will process Tarver, confirm his ID. This Tarver thing is looking like what we suspected. The D.C. reporter and his family died in a mountain accident. End of story."

"That's it?"

"Look, you had a good hunch and I let you follow up on it. Turns out it was a goose chase. Now, we need you back here."

A few seconds of silence passed between them without Graham's response.

"Dan?"

"Give me a day or so to wrap some things up, all right?"

"Wrap it up and get back here, ASAP. That's an order. No more surprises."

The call ended.

That was it.

Graham ran his hand over his face.

Was he right to pursue this the way he did? To the point that he'd stepped into a domestic whirlwind with a parental abduction and a near suicide. Had he let emotion and speculation serve as substitutes for evidence? In reality, a lot of threads never made sense in a case.

In life, we never get all of our questions answered.

But he was convinced the facts in this case just didn't add up.

It didn't matter now. It was over.

Graham noticed Hayley waiting a respectful distance away. He gave her a little smile. Might as well wrap things up. Check in on Maggie. Say hello and goodbye. Reaching into the back pocket of his jeans for his leather-bound notebook, he joined Hayley and she escorted him to Maggie's room.

A nurse was standing at Maggie's bed, reviewing a chart. Graham introduced himself, showed his ID. The doctors had already cleared him to visit.

"I'd like to talk to Officer Graham alone, please," Maggie said.

After the nurse and Hayley left, Graham sat in the chair next to Maggie. Her skin was pale, raw. Her reddened eyes reflected her anguish. Her knuckles whitened as she clenched and unclenched a tissue she held in her fist.

"They said that I would've died if you hadn't found me." A fragile smile flashed. "Thank you for saving my life."

He nodded.

"I guess they told you a bit about my situation," she said.

"A bit."

Graham summarized what he'd learned from Detective Thompson, then Maggie told him the rest, ending with questions.

"Why did you come all this way to my house? Does it have something to do with my husband and son?"

"I'm not sure. Do you know of a reporter from Washington, D.C., named Ray Tarver?"

"A reporter in Washington? No. Has this got something to do with Jake?"

"I don't know."

Graham told her only what he could about the Tarvers, starting with the tragedy in the mountains. Maggie brushed away more tears. Then Graham explained how his discovery of Jake and Maggie's name and address in Tarver's notes led him to California.

"I needed to talk to you, to Jake, to see what the connection might be. What do you know about your husband's time in Iraq?"

Maggie thought for a moment.

"Sometimes his convoys came under fire. Something happened to him over there, but he refused to talk about it. He had nightmares, he brooded and there was the outburst."

"What do you know about the types of missions he drove on?"

"Nothing. He never talked about it the whole time he was back. And, as far as I know, nothing got in the press. He was damaged when he came home, he was withdrawn, mistrustful. Not the same man. It took a toll on me and Logan."

Maggie stared at the ceiling looking for the rest of the words.

"We tried hard to work things out. Now he's gone. He took Logan and now I have no one. *I have nothing.* It's like they died."

Maggie's whispered voice cracked.

"I just want to find them. I need to find them."

"I know."

"Help me, please."

"Help you?"

"Help me find my son and husband."

"Me? But I can't get involved. I'm sorry. I wouldn't know what to do."

"*You found me.* You came all the way from that river in the mountains and you *found me.* Please."

"I'm sorry."

"*Please help me!*"

Maggie released a heartbreaking shriek. Graham glanced at the door.

"I have no one, please!"

He shifted awkwardly in his chair.

"Will you help me? Please help me!"

He tried to calm her, to stem her rising hysteria. He took her hand.

Like Emily Tarver in the Faust River, this woman was drowning.

Graham had to make a decision.

And he had to make it now.

46

Blue Rose Creek, California

While Graham was in the hospital helping Maggie Conlin, his parked car was being studied by two men who'd followed him from her neighborhood to the hospital.

No one noticed the strangers loitering around his sedan parked in a shaded corner of Inland Center Hospital's large, north lot, which was nearly filled to capacity.

The men were in their late twenties, clean-cut, dressed casually and wearing dark glasses. Visitors passing by saw nothing unusual as the pair leaned against the van next to Graham's car.

They appeared interested in the front page of the *Los Angeles Times*.

But occasionally they spoke in low tones as they ignored the paper to scan the interior of Graham's rental, looking for anything to answer their questions.

Who was he? Why did he visit Maggie Conlin? Why was she taken to hospital?

The taller man, Faker, was a doctoral student at UCLA visiting from Amsterdam. He was studying religious philosophy. Faker, a U.S. citizen, had lived largely in Dubai, Bahrain and Doha with his father, an oil executive from Houston. When Faker rejected his family, he wandered the world in search of answers to life.

He found them in the extreme anti-West movements of European campuses.

His friend, Sid, was raised in Brooklyn, New York. A deeply introverted young man, Sid had been abandoned as a young boy and raised in foster homes where he'd been abused. As a teen, he sought solace in a number of storefront religious groups before he ultimately left for Afghanistan, where he joined the Taliban.

Faker and Sid were believers.

They were also security agents for the network's most important project. Their job was to ensure nothing threatened its success.

"Sid, there. See?"

On the passenger seat, under a corner of an open map, luggage tags from Graham's carry-on bag peeked out, offering them his name and address. Quickly, they made notes, including the letters RCMP—GRC, which framed one of the tags.

The men then vanished into their vehicle some distance away but within sight of Graham's car.

Behind the darkened windows of their vehicle they worked very fast on laptop computers, using search engines, news databases and Web sites.

Within minutes they learned the stranger who had visited Maggie Conlin was Daniel Graham, a corporal with the Royal Canadian Mounted Police in Canada.

Graham was from Alberta and, according to news reports, part of the investigation into the sudden deaths of Ray Tarver, the reporter from Washington, D.C., and his family.

"They're getting close," Faker said. "We should alert our uncle."

Faker reached for their satellite phone and in seconds his call bounced off satellites orbiting miles above the earth to a secured series of relays in Istanbul, Vienna, Prague, Casablanca, Lagos then to Addis Ababa.

The scrambled signal remained beyond the immediate reach of the NSA security net. When the call was answered in Africa, it was followed by a cryptic conversation in an ancient language.

"Hello, uncle, this is your nephew in California."

"Yes, and how is the family?"

"They're fine for now, but we have some news. We may not be able to go forward with the event. A stain has been found on Grandmother's carpet."

A few moments of silence passed before Faker continued.

"Uncle, we're getting close to the event, Grandmother would be disappointed if something went wrong. We suggest we attempt removal of the stain."

Several beats of silence passed.

"Uncle, do you agree?"

47

Riverside, California

Graham wheeled into the Chrome Coast Truck Center near the edge of the interstate with his duty and instincts at war.

He was torn.

Maggie's pain had got to him.

It obliterated the distance that should be kept between a cop and a victim and led to his promise to help her. Graham put in a call to Novak with the D.C. police, asked him for a favor with a check through NCIC. Novak came through for him.

Now, as Graham sized up the truck center, he wondered if his sympathy for Maggie had blinded him. Was he sticking his neck out, becoming entangled in a domestic case because he felt sorry for Maggie Conlin? Or was he here because he couldn't leave the Tarver case with so many questions unanswered?

Either way, he'd defied orders.

The center's service office door opened onto repair bays with air smelling of rubber and diesel, and echoing with the clank of steel tools and compressors. Some-where a radio was playing "On The Road Again."

A tanned, bald man wearing a smock with Bruno Krall, Manager, embroidered over his heart, ended a call when Graham stepped to the counter.

"Can I help you?"

"I'm looking for Mac Sullivan."

"Mac, Mac," the manager said, squinting at his computer screen. "He's on a job. Can I help you with anything?"

"A buddy told me Mac had a line on a truck I was interested in. I'm only in town for today. Just needed a minute or two with him."

"Charlie!" the manager called through the doorway to the repair floor.

"Yo!"

"Tell Mac to clock out and come to the counter."

The radio had started another song, "Wichita Line-man," by the time a man with a Vandyke, red bandana and wearing grease-stained coveralls arrived.

"This guy's looking for you."

Intense blue eyes carried a question to Graham.

"Hey, Mac. Dan Graham. A friend told me you might have a line on a rig I'm interested in." Graham nodded to the lot. "Can I show you some information I have on my laptop in my car?"

Sullivan looked at his manager.

"Ten minutes, Mac. Go."

In the car, Graham showed Sullivan his badge and photo ID.

"What's this? You're a cop? A Mountie?"

"That's right. Your boss doesn't know. Yet. You help me and I'm gone and he never needs to know."

"Help you with what? You're from Canada, right? I don't know nobody in Canada."

"You know Jake Conlin."

"What about him?"

"Four Americans were killed in my jurisdiction. In my review of the case, Jake Conlin's name came up."

"You think Jake killed people in Canada?"

"I didn't say that. But I'm pretty sure you know where he is."

"What makes you think that?"

"Let's shift gears for a bit." Graham opened his notebook. "I did some checking and I understand you've got a stolen truck parts beef in Texas?"

"That was put on me and that was ten years ago."

"Mac, I need you to understand that I don't have time to waste. I have four deaths. I've come to you for help. Are you going to obstruct me in my duty?"

"I don't know what you're talking about."

"Conlin's name came up. I need to locate him. Now, you can help me the easy way, point me anonymously and truthfully in the right direction. Or I can ask the county sheriff and the FBI to help me with warrants for your personal phone records, computer records, including work here, the whole deal. Say we find you're involved in extracurricular action. We get another warrant. Gets kinda unpleasant."

"You can't do that, you've got no jurisdiction for that."

"I just call the locals, make a request through the D.A. Countries have these things called international treaties and agreements."

Sullivan began stroking his beard, taking inventory of the rigs on the lot, seeing nothing but his own desperate thoughts. Graham prodded him a bit.

"As I understand it, Mac, you know people who saw Conlin and a woman in Bakersfield, or Las Vegas."

"Guys come in the shop and bullshit all the time."

"This is how you want to play things? I'm running out of time."

Sullivan looked hard at Graham then swallowed.

"I don't know nothing about what he's been doing since he left, you got that?"

"We're clear on that. I'm sure that if I need to seize your phone and computer records, that will be confirmed."

"Hold on, I'm cooperating."

"Keep going."

"Before he left, Jake came to me, swore me to secrecy, said his old lady had cheated on him when he was driving in Iraq and he was going to split with his boy and start over. He asked about selling or trading his rig and keeping it off the books."

"Keeping it off the books?"

Sullivan shrugged. "Guess he didn't want her chasing him for support. Maybe he had another woman he was seeing, I don't know."

"Let me enlighten you. What Jake did was a parental abduction. He committed a crime. Now, you could be considered as a person who aided him in his offense. Does that help you remember anything else?"

"Son of a— What do you want from me?"

"Did Jake Conlin sell or trade his truck?"

"I believe he did a deal with Desert Truck Land."

"Where's that?"

"Las Vegas."

"With who? I need a name there."

Sullivan rubbed his chin.

"This doesn't come from me?"

"A name."

"Dixon. Spelled with an X, I think, I'm not sure."

"That a last name?"

"Yes."

"And Dixon's first?"

"Karl, I think."

"Karl with a K?"

"I think so."

"Karl with a K, Dixon with an X. Thank you."

"Tell me how in hell did you find out?"

"I don't give up sources. Now, if Karl Dixon doesn't exist, or if he should learn of my interest in advance, in any way, I'll automatically request those warrants and note your role."

"And if you get what you need?"

"You'll never hear from me again."

"Good."

"Of course, I don't speak for local law enforcement."

"Are you shittin' me? I cooperated with you."

"Just a little something to keep in mind, if I need more help, Mac."

48

Samara's concentration bounced from her printed Internet map, to the van's GPS, then down the street.

"There it is."

She pointed for Jake, who was driving.

"I'm not blind."

"I wasn't implying you were." She folded her papers. "You've been so reticent. What's troubling you?"

"I've got a headache coming on," he lied.

And she knew it.

The strip mall came into view.

It was a plain, single-story square, sheltered by two tall madronas. It offered half a dozen glass storefronts: a nail salon, a pet shop, a check-cashing outlet, a restaurant, a chiropractor's office and Samara's objective: Top Line Men's & Women's Alterations.

Earlier that week, Samara said she needed a break and wanted to get away. At the same time she'd concluded that she didn't have anything appropriate to wear for the papal visit and she pressed Jake to take her to

Seattle. Top Line was known for designing and making the best handcrafted suits on the west coast.

Rush orders were their specialty.

Given that he drove all over the country for a living, the prospect of a long jaunt from Cold Butte through the Rockies to Seattle and back on his time off didn't appeal to Jake. But the trip to Seattle was not the real problem. His doubts about Samara, about what he'd done, were slowly eating away at him.

Samara was intent on going to Seattle and had offered to share the driving. She suggested they make a holiday weekend of it, see some sights, take in a ball game.

Logan jumped on that.

Anything to escape his boring prairie prison.

Jake was outvoted.

Samara made an appointment and they set off to journey through a time zone so she could get a tailor-made suit.

Was the fuss about clothes a British thing?

What the hell, Jake shrugged it off. We're talking about meeting the pope. And the school had sent out a notice requiring children, families and staff to wear their "Sunday best" for the pope's event in the school. They'd stayed at a motel last night. Got up early, and now, here they were.

"I'm just going in to be measured. You two wait at the restaurant. If I'm not out in forty-five minutes, come for me. Then we'll spend the day seeing the sights. Go to Pike's, then the game."

"Sure," Jake said.

Samara looked at him for a moment then left.

"Dad." Logan's attention was on the pet shop window. "Before we go to the restaurant, can we go to the pet store and look at the parrots?"

"Okay, pal."

After the pet store, which reeked, Jake and Logan sat in a booth in the diner, where Logan drank chocolate milk and read the comics in the *Seattle Times*. Jake had coffee while pretending to read the sports pages.

The truth was he was wrestling with discontent that verged on resentment. The fire between Samara and him had cooled. She'd grown distant, preoccupied with work, her online correspondence courses, her late-night calls to her friends all over the world. Even on this trip, she'd devoted much of her time to her laptop, as if he and Logan weren't there.

Peering into his coffee, he again questioned his decision to leave Maggie. Had he thought this deal through? What sort of future did they have with Samara?

He didn't know.

"Dad, is it time for us to go get her?"

"Not yet, son, we just got here."

Bells chimed over the transom when Samara entered the shop.

A man in his forties was on the phone, behind the counter. A U.S. flag was pinned to the wall above the counter. The man was wearing a navy vest and a white shirt with rolled sleeves; a measuring tape was collared around his neck. He interrupted his call for his customer.

"I'm Samara," she said. "I have an appointment."

"Oh, yes. Please look around, I'll be with you shortly. My daughter will help you. Jasim!"

A pretty young girl emerged from the back to guide her through the shop's offerings. It was crammed, floor to ceiling with bolts of fabric, Egyptian cotton, Italian and British wools, cashmeres, silk charmeuse, chantilly lace. Samara flipped through sample books until the man ended his call.

"Apologies, Samara, I'm Benny."

He was a master tailor, originally from London, where his father had created suits on Savile Row.

"I understand you were also born in London. I believe we have mutual friends."

"That's true. Our uncles know each other."

As they shook hands, she noticed his sharp, brown eyes.

"You'd like us to create a suit for a very big occasion."

"Yes."

"A rush job, you said?"

"Unfortunately, yes."

"Not a problem. It's my pleasure to help. Allow me to show you what I've started since your call."

Benny opened a well-used notebook to show her sketches of a three-piece suit—a jacket, skirt and camisole ensemble.

"Simple understated elegance," he said.

The jacket would have princess seams, and ribbon-trimmed faux-flap pockets. The skirt would be cut below the knee, fully lined, with side zipper and ribbon detail. The camisole would be satin.

"All in taupe." He held up a sample. "Yes, it works for you. Come to the mirrors and I'll get some measurements."

During Benny's measuring, note taking and small talk about life in Montana, their eyes found each other in the reflection.

"This is a monumental event, Samara." He'd lowered his voice. "Are you nervous?"

"No. Are you?"

"No. I'm honored to be part of it."

"What fabric are you suggesting?"

"A new import I just got in via New York from Africa. It'll be excellent."

The transom bells chimed as Jake and Logan arrived.

"Be right with you, gentlemen."

"They're here for me," Samara said. "That's Jake and his son, Logan."

Benny greeted them.

"Welcome, welcome."

Jake appraised Benny, then the large U.S. flag and framed photos of U.S. troops in desert combat dress above the counter caught his attention.

"You know people overseas?" Jake said.

"Friends. Clients for graduations and weddings. Got to support the guys," Benny said. "As you and Samara know, it's difficult for the people still over there."

Jake nodded.

"So, Logan, Samara tells us you're going to meet the pope. You must be thrilled beyond measure?"

"It's cool, I guess."

"Very cool. Jake, you must be so proud."

"It's a once-in-a-lifetime deal, for sure."

"Would you like us to make you a suit for the occasion, Dad?"

"Me? No, I mean I couldn't afford—"

"I'll give you a very deep discount, out of respect for your contribution overseas."

"How did you know about that?"

"Samara and I were chatting."

Jake nodded, glanced round the shop.

"That's kind of you. But I'm good in that department. Got a suit that does the job. I'm not inclined to wear one much."

"I see, but a hand-cut suit would fit like a dream. Are you certain you wouldn't like one?"

"I'm sure."

"How about young Logan? How would you like to be the sharpest dressed kid to meet the pope in Montana?"

"I don't know." He looked to his dad. "I got a shirt and a tie. I don't like to get all dressed up."

"Permit me. Let's try something." Benny assessed Logan, then selected a small blazer from a rack and held it open so Logan could slip it on.

"Now that fits nicely," Benny said, then positioned Logan for some quick expert measurements. "Tell you what. I'll make Logan a suit at no charge."

"Free?" Jake asked.

"Free."

"Why?"

"To have my work be part of history would be payment enough," Benny said, smiling.

Jake looked to Logan.

"Would you like a free suit made just for you, son?"

Logan shrugged. "Guess that would be okay."

"Terrific." Benny got more measurements. "I'll start work on your outfits immediately. We're very fast here."

Samara hugged Benny.

* * *

They spent the rest of the morning downtown at Pike Place, Pioneer Square, then they went up into the Space Needle. It was about six when they made it to Safeco and got tickets behind home plate, above the press box, for the Mariners' home night game against Cleveland.

Nine innings and several hot dogs later they returned to the motel. They were exhausted from a long day of fun and were just settling in when Samara's cell phone rang.

It was Benny. The suits were done.

Within thirty minutes he'd delivered them personally to the motel, apologizing for the late hour.

Logan was exhausted but Jake helped him try the suit on. It was perfect. Then, in the awkward moments Samara was in the bathroom trying hers on, Logan fell asleep watching *Jaws* on TV and Jake thanked Benny for going out of his way to save them driving time in the morning.

Samara's suit also fit perfectly.

It looked good, in fact. Samara grabbed her purse before she stepped outside to see Benny off.

Jake could hear them outside the door.

As they talked in low, serious tones in Arabic, a tiny wave of suspicion rippled through him.

Something felt wrong.

Was he jealous at the way she smiled at Benny? Was it something he thought he'd detected in their body language? Or was it his imagination?

He didn't know.

The next day during the long drive through the mountains back to Cold Butte, Jake ruminated on Samara and Benny.

Samara spent much of the return trip on her laptop, coping with an erratic wireless connection as she worked between taking her turn at the wheel.

As the miles rolled by, Logan sensed the unspoken tension mounting from his dad's dark mood.

It scared him.

He knew that something was getting wound tighter and tighter. Sooner or later something was going to happen.

Now, more than ever, Logan needed to call his mom.

As they ascended and descended through mountain passes, he saw Samara's purse.

It had opened a crack.

Logan saw her cell phone and returned to an idea that he had been forming.

If he was going to act on it, he'd better do it soon.

Time was running out.

49

Blue Rose Creek, California

Daniel Graham was Maggie's savior.

Standing alone in her kitchen making coffee, she studied his business card then glanced at her kitchen calendar, circled with dates for her psych sessions.

She didn't think she needed therapy.

All she needed was to find Logan and hold him. Find Jake and talk to him.

Her overdose was an accident. She'd wanted to kill a moment, not herself. Graham had revived her will to fight, to keep her promise to find her family.

As the coffeepot filled, Maggie stole a glimpse of him.

He was on the sofa in her living room. He'd arrived saying he'd talked to Dawn Sullivan's husband, that he had new information.

Graham checked his watch.

This was a mistake and he knew it, yet something kept him here. The first thing he should've done was alert Vic Thompson at the county sheriff's department, and the FBI, to his Vegas lead. He could still do it and have time to make his flight to Calgary today.

Do it, then. Take care of business, then get the hell home.

So what was stopping him?

He looked toward the kitchen where Maggie was.

The aroma of fresh-brewed coffee floated into the living room and he resumed looking at the album Maggie showed him. Logan blowing out birthday candles. Good-looking kid. Logan at the wheel of Jake's rig. The Conlins at Disneyland. The Conlins at the beach. Jake smiling. A happy family man. Maggie glowed. No question, she was pretty in these portraits of family bliss.

Graham had killed his chances for that kind of life.

He closed the album.

"Here you go. Cream and sugar on the side." Maggie set a tray down. "What did Dawn's husband tell you?"

Graham explained that it appeared that Jake had sold or traded his rig at Desert Truck Land in Las Vegas.

"Oh, my God!" Maggie said. "That's the first solid information I've had."

"Now I'll pass this to the county and the FBI who can work with people in Las Vegas to follow this up."

"No, wait," Maggie said, writing in a small notebook. "I want to go there first."

"Excuse me?"

"I want to go to Desert Truck Land in Las Vegas. Now! With you, to follow this up. Together."

"I can't. I have to fly back today."

"Please. This is the only real hope I've had. And it's

because of you. Please. We can drive to Las Vegas in three or four hours. Then maybe the people there will tell me more about where Jake went. What if he's living there? I'm so close to Logan now, I can feel it! Please."

Graham weighed the idea.

Everything about the Tarver case gnawed at him.

If he talked to Jake Conlin about Ray Tarver's conspiracy story, he might find answers. *Or more questions.* But then there were the optics. Taking a civilian along on a case and into another jurisdiction beyond yours was not smart.

Neither was jumping into a raging river.

But Graham did it because he knew it was right.

And if it hadn't been for the little girl, he wouldn't be alive today.

He had to keep trusting his gut on this. Something was emerging, he knew it.

The logistics of Maggie's idea were not difficult.

Graham could change his airline ticket, drop his rental car in Las Vegas, fly from there to Calgary on a later plane, maybe by tonight.

"I have to check out of my hotel, make some calls, then I'll be back to get you in about an hour. We'll go in my rental. I'll fly home from there."

Tears glistened in Maggie's eyes. She hugged Graham and smiled.

Her first real smile since the day Logan vanished.

50

Pysht, on the Juan De Fuca Strait, Washington

Fog cloaked the north shore of Olympic Peninsula as Kip Drucker eased his SUV along the old trail road to the small cove.

He keyed his radio microphone and gave his dispatcher his location.

"Vanessa, Stan wanted me to follow up that CPB call first thing this morning."

U.S. Customs and Border Protection had alerted the Clallam County Sheriff's Department that a small craft may have illegally unloaded contraband from a larger foreign vessel in the Strait, which forms the border with Canada.

The report originated from a Chinese cargo ship. Chinese crew members had noted the larger ship was out of Yemen and was navigating suspiciously. The captain took a few days to mull over the incident before reporting it to U.S. authorities.

The Chinese crew witnessed the smaller craft landing on U.S. soil some five to seven miles southwest of

Clallam Bay, near Pysht. Wind-driven swells and fog had hampered an effective search.

"I'm going to investigate this zone," Drucker told his dispatcher.

"Ten-four. And, Kip, I've stacked your other calls. First one is Chester Green. Wants you to go to his place for more on his stolen boat from the weekend."

"Ten-four. Seventy-one out."

Drucker had two years in as a deputy with the patrol division. He and his wife planned to start a family once he made detective. He still had a lot of course work before he could take the exam. His wife wanted to get going on the baby thing.

Pay attention, he told himself as he walked the desolate shoreline.

Drucker's sergeant had instructed him to look for anything out of the ordinary. Should be easy as nobody lived out here. Nothing around for a mile or so in either direction. Pysht was beautiful. The name came from an old Indian word. Something about the wind, Drucker couldn't remember.

The fog cast everything in gray and silver-white. It was surreal the way it blotted out the forest and the Olympic Mountains. Water lapped against the beach and gulls shrieked. Drucker contended with the smells of dead fish and seaweed, while welcoming the occasional trace of spruce and cedar.

He'd gone nearly a mile, and had come to a large piece of driftwood where he'd decided to turn back. That's when he heard the chink of glass.

A beached wooden shipping crate jostled gently in the surf. It contained two-dozen brown bottles of liquid. Beer. Made in Nigeria, according to the faded red lettering.

Drucker looked at it, as he tugged on his latex gloves and pulled out a bottle to check the labels. The water had loosened most of them. *Big Mountain Taste. Nigerian Blended Ale.* Drucker tried to twist a cap. Not a twist cap. His keys jingled as he reached for his jack-knife, flipped to the opener and popped the cap. He held his nose over the contents.

It was beer. No question.

He dripped some on the rocks, watching it foam, wondering how it would go down chilled on a Sunday during a Seahawks game. He glanced at the other bottles in the crate, noticing one had split along the seam.

Drucker plucked it.

Leaking, droplets hissed on the rocks. Not like beer foam.

Plumes of smoke rose; smoke with an odd smell. Kind of like medicine, but different. Drucker set the bottle down on the rocks. A tiny thick cloud of smoke rose as the liquid seeped from the bottle.

"What the hell. That's not beer."

Drucker reached for his shoulder microphone and called his dispatcher.

Within minutes of Drucker's dispatch, his call reached the highest levels of national security.

His report pinballed among local, state and federal agencies to Washington, D.C., where intelligence analysts captured it. They red-flagged it as evidence supporting earlier foreign intel concerning a Yemini ship bound for the U.S. with hostile cargo from Africa.

Connecting dots.

Was it a potential puzzle piece of an impending attack during the papal visit?

But few in the security chain possessed the clearance needed to access that analysis. It was shared on a need-to-know basis.

On the ground at Pysht, Drucker had been advised to treat the mysterious substance as a potential explosive, or biohazard.

Offshore, vessels from the U.S. Coast Guard, Washington's Department of Fish and Wildlife, and Clallam County, kept watercraft from nearing the site.

No residents lived within a one-and-a-half-mile radius of the area. Drucker was told that immediate evacuation was not necessary. A public announcement was not necessary. Backed up by Washington Highway Patrol and local firefighters, Drucker sealed the scene, as state emergency biohazard experts arrived to make a preliminary assessment.

The Bureau of Alcohol, Tobacco, Firearms and Explosives dispatched a team from the Seattle Field Division to study the substance. The FBI dispatched an evidence response team from the Seattle Field Office to pursue foot and tire impressions leading from the site, treating it as if it were a crime scene.

At the same time across the country a mechanism had been triggered.

An elite new unit drawn from several federal agencies and the Chemical Biological Incident Response Force had been deployed.

The team of ten personnel, and some seven hundred pounds of state-of-the-art equipment, lifted off in a small, unmarked twin-engine jet from its military base at Indian Head, Maryland.

Dr. Tony Takayasu headed the unit. Like the CBIRF, its mission was rapid response to help local officials in threats involving chemical, biological, nuclear or radiological incidents.

Takayasu had been seconded from the Livermore Lab in California. He'd headed secret military research on the creation and detection of unknown substances. He was one of the world's authorities on molecular structures.

Next in command was Karen Dyer, a Harvard professor of advanced chemistry. She also held degrees in physics and DNA research from Berkeley.

Other members included a leading field doctor from the Center for Disease Control, a veteran technician from the FBI's Explosives Unit who'd worked on the Unabomber case, the World Trade Center bombing and the Oklahoma City bombing. There was also a nuclear physicist from Los Alamos, and several military personnel expert in explosives and biological, nuclear and chemical warfare. As their jet crossed the country, Takayasu and his team studied updates sent to them from investigators on-site.

Some three hours later, their plane landed at an airfield near Clallam Bay normally used to transport convicts from the state prison nearby. They were met by a convoy of waiting emergency vehicles which ferried them and their equipment to the site.

Upon arrival, they waited for county and state public safety officials to complete the decontamination process before they were debriefed.

"We're not sure what it is. We haven't been able to identify it," a state official said, as members of the new unit pulled on camouflaged hazardous-material suits and gas masks. "We don't think it's a germ or nerve agent. What we can tell you is that the case labelled beer held twenty-two bottles containing beer. Two contained an unknown substance. We need to identify it. Our concern is how many bottles, or cases, have penetrated the border. Somebody's up to something."

Takayasu's team muscled their equipment to the site. It was protected by yellow police tape and a huge canvas canopy. They set to work to collect a sample of the liquid, analyze and identify it in order to determine whether it was lethal.

Each team member conducted examinations and undertook various component testing using advanced equipment, such as micro UV laser fluorescence bio-sensors. They ran a number of protocols and formulas. They swabbed, chilled, burned and baked on-site, analyzing residue, processing it through secure laptops with links to databases across the country.

"I don't get it, Tony," Dyer said. "This liquid substance defies our on-site testing. What the heck is it?"

Takayasu was stumped, shook his head and kept working. At sunset he walked from the site and removed his mask, enjoying the cool refreshing air. He gazed out at the water.

The fog had lifted in the twilight and he recalled himself as a seven-year-old boy walking into the bedroom of his newborn sister. She was so still. He'd alerted his mother, whose screams he still heard. His sister had died. Later, when he was a high-school student, Takayasu went to the county office and obtained her death records. The cause was sudden infant death, a syndrome that still perplexes many. It drove him to devote his life to science, to unravel that which is unknown.

Takayasu shifted his attention back to his current challenge and considered calling his wife in the east. He was going to miss his daughter's violin recital in Georgetown. He'd reached for his cell phone, when some of the others approached him.

"What do you think?" one of them asked.

Takayasu showed them his notes where he'd circled *C3H5(NO3)3?*

"Nitro?"

"No, not nitro," he said, "in some ways it exhibits similar characteristics but it's not nitroglycerin." Takayasu gazed at the water.

"You look troubled, Tony. You got any thoughts on this?" Dyer asked.

"We're going to have to do more work in the lab."

"Sure, but what is your gut telling you?"

"I suspect this is a component that is to be applied to another. It could also be a substance not yet fully processed. At a conference in New Zealand I recall learning about a wild theory or research going on in China. Something involving nanotechnology and radio transmissions. All of it undetectable. What I've seen here strikes me as being remotely similar to one of the theoretical components."

"We're talking about some kind of explosive?" the FBI bomb expert asked.

"It's just one component, but I have no clue about the form of delivery."

"So it could be anything, then?"

"Anything."

51

Near Seattle's southern edge at the fringe of a neglected urban nightmare, an unmarked government sedan stopped at an aging apartment complex.

Two well-dressed federal agents entered, scanned the tenant list of the apartment's lobby panel, then buzzed E. R. Glaxor.

"Yes," the tin-sounding response came through the intercom.

"Mr. Edwin Glaxor?"

"Yes."

"Special Agents Blake Walker and Melody Krover of the Secret Service. We'd called in response to your concerns, sir."

"Yes. Come in. Unit 615."

The door lock buzz-clicked, allowing them to enter.

They stepped into the elevator. Krover, a new agent with the Seattle Field Office, had pulled Glaxor's name from the list. Seattle agents had visited him twice. Her valise contained his file, which Walker had read a third time on the ride over. He'd read it before on his previous two flights to Seattle. The field people took pride in their work, and resented Walker's micromanaging of their files.

Walker didn't care.

Edwin Richard Glaxor, age thirty-six, was a night watchman who'd bombarded the Vatican with letters demanding "the pope resign and confess his crimes as the *anti-pope*" in an address to the United Nations, or Glaxor would "eliminate" him during his visit to Seattle.

"I have been authorized to prosecute the act," he wrote.

Glaxor's file, which included notes from his employer, indicated he talked to inanimate objects. He had no criminal record, no history of violence. Did not own, or have access to, firearms, or explosives. Other than "showing up at the rope" at various presidential visits along the west coast over the years and glaring at the president, Glaxor had not acted on his threats.

A pungent mixture of muscle ointment and cat litter greeted the agents when Glaxor opened his apartment door for them.

The black-framed glasses he wore were held together by white tape. He was overweight with stringy hair and greasy skin. His apartment was dimly lit.

"I am averse to light, that's why I work nights," Glaxor said as he sat in a large, somewhat elevated chair, while the agents stood.

"I am glad you're here. Time is of the essence." Glaxor spoke articulately and rapidly. "I've recently been in contact with the GHD, and he demands the pope end his tyrannical reign and resign before fate— that being me—intervenes."

Krover opened the file. "The GHD would be the 'Great-Horned Demon' you converse with?"

"Yes, the GHD's manifested as a gargoyle in the park downtown as a conduit for communication."

"Could we please let in a little light, Edwin? Just a bit?"

Walker opened the curtains slightly. Glaxor's chair was a throne constructed entirely of Bibles. After listening to Glaxor's nonsensical theories for nearly twenty minutes, Walker interrupted.

"Edwin, we believe your concerns warrant more research. We've talked to your family about a facility where you can discuss your situation with the appropriate medical experts."

Glaxor steepled his fingers, touched them to his chin and nodded.

"May I bring the data I've collected?"

"I'll discuss that with the doctors, but it shouldn't be a problem."

"All right, I'll do it."

"Good, son. Under the circumstances, this is the right thing to do."

Walker reached for his cell phone to advise Glaxor's parents and psychiatrist.

Glaxor was a letter writer, like hundreds of other people on the Secret Service watch list. Part of the job was to be up to speed on the list, a file of several hundred people who had ever threatened the president, or a visiting head of state, even with an e-mail, a letter or a comment overheard in public.

People like Glaxor who weren't in facilities were visited by agents in advance of VIP visits to update their threat status, chiefly to determine if they had the ability and opportunity to carry out their threat.

Glaxor's family had agreed that he would undergo assessment in a psychiatric ward during the pope's visit. Like the Secret Service and the FBI, King County and Seattle PD put him on their watch list.

This threat had been neutralized.

Back in the car, Walker reviewed his files.

They had several more cases to double-check as part of continuing advance work to assess threats and identify risks. They worked on everything, from potential lone assassins to terrorist groups. As Krover drove them to the next case, Walker inventoried his files to ensure he hadn't overlooked anything.

They were in order, yet something niggled at him.

Something that had arisen from one of the roundtable calls at Langley. As hard as he tried, Walker couldn't identify it. And now, as the time for the northwest leg of the papal visit ticked down, it continued to irritate him.

Walker scanned the latest bulletin on activity and chatter concerning FTOs.

Nothing there.

At that moment, his BlackBerry vibrated with an alert from Homeland Security.

U.S. Customs and Border Protection investigating unconfirmed report of border penetration by unauthorized vessels suspected of at-sea transfer of hostile contraband. Location: U.S.-Canada border. Washington State. Strait of Juan de Fuca. Primary vessel registered under Panamanian flag. Vessel origin: Yemen. Secondary vessel origin: unknown.

52

East of Great Falls, Montana

Distant reddish-brown figures emerged in the field glasses slowly coming into focus.

White-tailed deer.

Some two hundred yards off.

A doe and two spotted fawns stepping from the forb and dogwood.

Snouts to the ground, they browsed around the lone U.S. flag affixed to a pole of pine dowelling. Quite a sight against the grand sky. Nothing out there but the deer and the flag, flapping in the open range at a height of precisely five feet.

The flag had been erected by the deer watcher, Ali Bakarat, a specialist in chemical engineering.

Using an alias, Bakarat was identified as a professor from England. He was visiting the U.S. to attend an international symposium in Portland, Oregon. It had ended a week ago. He'd told American authorities that he was taking a holiday and driving across America to New York, before his return to London.

Previously, he'd flown from Addis Ababa, to Algiers,

to Cairo, to Istanbul, Paris then London. None of which was known because he'd used counterfeit documents.

His fingerprints and eye scan did not raise any red flags. He didn't exist on any no-fly or Interpol watch lists. But here he was, east of Great Falls, Montana, at the fringe of Malmstrom Air Force Base, finalizing his part of the operation.

He'd broken a salt lick, spread chokecherries and snowberries, and set a water bucket around the flagpole. It was like a candy stand for the deer. They would graze for hours. Bakarat looked at his watch when he saw his partner's Jeep approaching, raising dust.

Bakarat's associate, Omar, an expert in molecular nanotechnology, had arrived with the operative.

The nurse.

Samara.

She wore jeans and a Seattle Mariners T-shirt, which enhanced her figure. Even under her ball cap and dark glasses, her beauty exceeded the description given Bakarat by the old men in Africa.

The Tigress had blended in nicely, Bakarat thought.

Omar shouldered Samara's computer bag then set up her computer alongside their equipment on the folding table where Bakarat was working under the shade of a beach canopy.

To anyone who'd happened upon them, they were researchers for a European wildlife magazine.

"Sister," Bakarat greeted Samara. "This is a great honor. Uncle sends his prayers."

She nodded then took stock of the hardware on the table. The laptops, cameras, field glasses, satellite phones. Well-thumbed notebooks with codes, tables, calculations.

"Is everything ready?"

"All is ready," Bakarat said. "Conditions are good. Our subjects are well positioned." He passed Samara a set of binoculars to use to see the deer.

Omar was making calculations in his notebook, then entered them on one of the laptops. Then he set the co-ordinates into one of the satellite phones.

"Are we ready, Omar?" Bakarat asked.

"Ready."

"Sister, this is what you need to know."

The scientists explained to Samara the basics behind the new weapon. Then they showed her an animated program which simplified the science that had gone into developing the system. They'd produced a new synthetic fabric that was highly explosive, undetectable and detonated through radio frequencies.

It worked like this:

A radio signal was sent to activate the new material, which was equipped with nanoreceivers. After the signal was received, it took about sixty seconds for the process to "warm up" to the stage of detonation readiness. At that point, the controller could detonate it at will.

Samara studied the animated demonstration on Bakarat's laptop.

"You send a radio message to the material. Upon receipt it takes sixty seconds to warm up," Bakarat said.

"Then it's a bomb," Samara said.

"A bomb waiting for a second command to detonate."

"And how do you explode it?"

"You send a second signal. It can be sent from

anywhere in the world via a laptop, wireless through the Internet, as long as it is programmed with the proper codes, see?"

Bakarat's animation showed it bouncing from satellite phones via wireless connection to a laptop.

"Or, through your camera," Omar said. "Many digital cameras have a focus assist beam. When pressed, it emits an infrared light beam from the front of the camera to the subject to measure distance. We've programmed your camera with the codes to send a signal to your laptop."

Omar, who was very soft-spoken, repeated the process.

"You activate the fabric, wait sixty seconds, and a green light will flash indicating you may detonate the bomb at any time. The next second, or the next day."

"The kill zone is tight," Bakarat said. "Everything within eight to ten feet."

Samara looked at him.

"If you use the camera, you can be at any distance, as long as nothing obstructs your focus beam. On the laptop, you can set a timer to start a countdown to the process, or use the camera. We've programmed the codes, set you up with everything."

Samara studied her laptop with the step-by-step instructions Omar had installed.

"Are you clear?" Bakarat asked.

"I think so."

"Ready to test it?" Omar handed her a camera.

Samara studied it.

"Go ahead, photograph the flag down there."

Samara focused and pressed the button.

"See."

They watched her laptop count down sixty seconds.

As they waited, Bakarat chuckled.

"The irony is rich, don't you think?"

"What do you mean?" Samara asked as the seconds ticked down.

"We're at the edge of Malmstrom, part of the strategic command for the American Minuteman III intercontinental ballistic missile," Bakarat said. "There are some five hundred nuclear warheads buried in silos across North Dakota, Wyoming and right here in Montana."

Samara nodded.

"And did you also know that U.S. forces bound for Iraq once trained here before deployment."

The seconds ticked.

"And here, in the realm of America's might, we prepare to plunge a sword of sorrow into the heart of the entire nonbelieving world."

A light flashed green and beeped.

"You're good to go," Omar said.

"You now have a bomb. Point your camera at the flag and take a picture."

Samara found the flag and deer in her viewfinder.

She pressed the button.

Her brain registered the blinding white flash before she heard the whip-crack of the blast and saw the bloodied-dust plume in the distance.

When it cleared the flag and deer were gone.

53

East of Great Falls, Montana

A sudden burst of distant light near the ground flashed in Jim Yancy's periphery.

What the hell?

Must be a lightning strike, the rancher thought before the firecracker *pop* rolled across the plain to him.

No, couldn't be lightning. Not with this clear blue sky.

Yancy shrugged it off, edged his ATV forward and went back to repairing fencing along his property near Malmstrom Air Force Base. Likely military people doing some live fire exercise, or detonating old shells. But he hadn't seen them do any of that for years.

The more Yancy thought about it, the more it made him curious. He squinted under his ball cap toward the flash and watched an SUV driving from it, kicking up dust clouds.

After it vanished, Yancy left his fence and headed to the site. It was odd. Nothing out there but a whole lot of nothing. Yancy had lived in these parts most of his life and that SUV was no military vehicle.

He had a bad feeling about this.

He came upon a tattered rag the size of a washcloth. Red, white and blue, like Old Glory. He saw a salt lick, a fragment of a tin bucket, blood-soaked shortgrass crowned with the head of a white-tailed deer.

Its dead eye locked in open horror on Yancy.

"Gee-Zuss-H!"

Yancy called the Cascade County Sheriff.

The deputy and Malmstrom military personnel arrived first. Then came the Air National Guard fire-fighters, Malmstrom's EOD technicians, Montana Highway Patrol and the FBI.

It was clear that something had exploded, but after investigating they were puzzled as to just what it was. The components remained a mystery. More calls were made through the chain of command to Washington, D.C., and by that afternoon Tony Takayasu's team had arrived from Maryland.

They'd barely had time to recover from their call to Pysht and had only begun further analysis of the sub-stance in the Nigerian beer bottles, when they were deployed to Malmstrom in Montana.

During the flight, Takayasu, Karen Dyer and the others studied all the e-mailed Montana reports and photos. With the fragments of a salt lick, a bucket, the incident seemed premeditated, planned.

Like a test.

Takayasu's unit also kept in mind Montana's history of domestic acts, such as the Unabomber and the armed antigovernment extremists who forced a standoff with the FBI near Jordan.

After their jet landed at Malmstrom they were taken to the site in a school bus. On the way, they were briefed by FBI Special Agent David Groller, an intense man who let it be known he'd lost friends in the towers.

"We know this can't be attributed to kids from the university playing a prank," Groller said. "And we don't think the animals stepped on any unexploded devices, or that someone local is testing a new method for culling a herd."

Groller underscored the fact Malmstrom controlled missiles with nuclear warheads.

"And," he continued, "the pope is due to arrive in Montana within some seventy-two hours, so the heat's on us to identify the substance ASAP, assess whether or not it is a threat, who's the target, who's behind it, then hunt the mothers down."

Takayasu's elite team suited up and worked flat out.

As they did in Pysht, they collected samples, analyzed residue, tested the air, the soil, measured and took readings and photographs.

Analysis showed that recovered pieces of fabric seemed to originate from a U.S. flag. The material seemed to be a cotton weave common in East Africa. So maybe a Third World sweatshop had manufactured the flag.

Nothing unusual.

However, the residue taken from the parts of the dismembered deer exhibited troubling characteristics as the team conducted a number of examinations.

Karen Dyer applied an advance test involving a microscopic silica film treated with nitrogen-containing macrocyclic molecules known as porphyrins. Then she scoped it with fluorescent light. Sensors picked up minute traces of triacetone triperoxide that seemed to have been mixed with pentaerythritol tetranitrate. All invisible to the naked eye.

"What do you think, Tony?"

"I don't know how this was done." Takayasu pointed to his laptop screen. "Look at these animal parts. Appears to have been an adult and two young deer. Look at the average weight for the species common here."

"I know."

"Whatever exploded was something vastly more powerful in proportion to its volume. Thirty, forty times, maybe more. I've never seen anything like it."

"But what's the vehicle for delivery? We've found no components."

"I don't know. It's like it doesn't exist."

Takayasu conducted one last analysis before packing up—the early results unnerved him.

"Karen, once again, we've got to get back to the lab for more testing, to break this down."

"I'll alert our pilots."

54

Cold Butte, Montana

Watching from the window, Jake placed his beer on the TV, then went to the driveway to meet Samara.

He was at her van door before she could get out.

"What's wrong?" she asked.

"Where were you?"

"Great Falls. It was a meeting for medical staff for the visit. Why?"

"No one at the school or clinic knew about it."

"Few people did. It was about security. Why did you call them? I left you a note."

"Tell me what's going on, Samara."

"What're you talking about?"

"You're always working on that damn computer. Or whispering to someone on your cell phone. You force us to go to Seattle, then you disappear to Great Falls. What's going on?"

Any warmth in Samara's face evaporated.

"Get away from the door," she said.

Jake took half a step back.

"What the hell's going on, Samara?"

"Lower your voice."

She collected her things, tried to go around him but he grabbed her arm.

"Let me go."

"I asked you a question. Why are you sneaking around?"

"Have you been drinking?"

"Did you hook up with that guy from Seattle? That it?"

"What? I don't believe this!"

"Dammit, Samara! We left everything for you! Gave up everything! And you act like we're not even here!"

Her eyes burned with icy fury as they pulled Jake's attention to Logan standing at the doorway behind him.

"Release me now and get hold of yourself."

A tense moment passed before Jake surrendered her arm.

"I've told you," she said. "I am taking advanced correspondence nursing courses online. I also talk to my friends in London and Baghdad. I had a life before we met. You know all this, Jake. And, I went to Great Falls today to prepare for the visit."

Staring at her, he realized that they were strangers to each other. He dragged the back of his hand across his mouth then walked off down their lane.

"Dad!"

Logan started after him but Samara held up her hand to stop him.

"Let him go. He needs to cool off."

"Dad!"

Jake cut a lonely figure as he walked off to the end of their long lane. He stood there searching the empty land. As the afternoon faded he made his way back to the house but remained outside, perched on the picnic table, contemplating the setting sun.

Samara watched him from the kitchen window while she prepared dinner.

She and Logan ate without him.

Afterward, she came out and set a plate next to him: a big chicken sandwich, baked beans and coleslaw. She also brought him a black coffee in a large ceramic Mariners mug.

Jake had to leave soon for a job that would take him away for a couple of days.

"Are you good to drive?" she asked.

"I barely touched that beer."

Jake said nothing more and Samara returned to the house.

After he ate, he sat there wrestling with his situation until darkness fell. Iraq had messed him up, no question about it. And Samara had saved his life. That was a fact. But he'd lost himself over there.

Maggie had been right all along. His experience over there, all the crap he faced, had changed him.

Jake covered his face with his hands then peered over his fingertips, feeling a fog lifting from his mind as he realized that he might have made a huge mistake.

"Dad?"

Logan was standing beside him.

"Hey, son."

"Dad, what's happening with everything?"

"I'm just doing some thinking."

"Dad, I need to ask you something but promise you won't get mad, okay?"

"Go ahead."

"I want to have Mom here, you know, for the big day. Everybody says, like, it's historic and stuff, and it just doesn't feel right without her."

Jake closed his eyes to find patience, then smiled.

"Logan. I know you want her here but we've talked about this. It's just not going to happen. I'm sorry."

Logan started to cry.

"But I miss her so much it hurts."

"I miss her, too."

"Really?"

Jake pulled him closer and held his shoulders. "So much it hurts."

Logan looked into his father's face, surprised by what he found. His dad, his real dad was back. Logan heard it in his voice, saw it in his eyes. His dad was telling him the truth, that he still loved Mom.

A lot.

"I thought you were going to stay mad at her forever."

"You know I saw some terrible things in Iraq. Terrible things."

Logan knew it was bad there.

"I don't talk about it much but I got banged up pretty good. I still get headaches, real whoppers."

"I know."

"The whole deal shook me up, crossed my wires. I got confused about things. Like that time with your soccer coach."

"It's okay, Dad."

"Well, there are a couple of things I am clear on. One is I love you and, in spite of what I may have said when we left, I know your mom loves you, too."

Logan cried again.

"She never stopped loving you and she never will. She's a good mother."

Logan nodded.

"Samara's a good person, too. She risked her life in Iraq to help people, including me. If it wasn't for her, I wouldn't be here, son. It's that simple. I've just got a lot of thinking to do these days, okay?"

"Okay."

"The pope's visit is going to be a once-in-a-lifetime thing, son. You're going to do a good job. Samara's going to take lots of pictures. I'll be there. I've got to leave now for a couple of days, but I'll be back in time. I won't miss it. After it's all over we can talk some more."

Logan nodded and brushed away his tears.

"I love you, Dad."

"I love you, too, pal. And so does your mom. Always remember that."

It was a little before midnight when Jake pulled out.

Logan watched from his bedroom window, watched his running lights glow against the immense night sky.

Logan watched until they vanished.

Not long after, he heard the familiar soft tapping coming from the living room.

He left his bed and cracked open his bedroom door. Samara was there, working on her laptop. As he watched her, he spotted her purse.

Logan had a secret plan.

He was sure it would work.

It had to.

55

Maggie and Graham left the Los Angeles area for Las Vegas on Interstate 15, each mile taking Graham further out on a limb.

Edging him closer to insubordination.

But he'd taken steps to reduce the risk.

He'd called his boss again but had timed it when he knew he'd be in a meeting, and then left another vague voice mail about a lead in Las Vegas. Then he called Vic Thompson's voice mail and updated him with general information on Nevada. Then Graham advised Las Vegas Metro, and the FBI, he was coming to town.

He'd played loosely by the rules.

But soon he'd either have to give up, or make his own rules because deep down he didn't care. Deep down he wasn't ready to let go. There were too many unanswered questions and it was eating him up.

As the road rushed under them, Graham went back to that day, back to the riverbank, staring at the boy's body with Liz DeYoung, the medical investigator.

"Mother Nature's your suspect," Liz had said.

Graham considered her words as he watched L.A.'s urban sprawl melt into the Mojave desert. Maggie had fallen asleep beside him. Her window was open, breezes played with her hair. She wore sunglasses, white Dockers, a lavender T-shirt that complemented her figure.

A cell phone was strapped to her wrist. A manifestation of her faith that she'd talk to her son. She'd forwarded her home number to her cell. She'd brought her laptop, she'd booked time off work, again. She'd nearly maxed out her credit cards.

Nearly took her own life.

Who was this anguished mother?

Graham knew one true thing about her. She'd put everything on the line just like him. He felt the stirrings of a partnership just as a rig roared by, its air horn sounding a blast that woke her.

Maggie massaged her temples, then checked her phone for messages.

They were strangers yet comfortable with each other, letting silence pass in long stretches along with the miles. Maggie asked Graham about the Mounties and he handed her his badge. She ran her fingers over the gold crown, the wreath of maple leaves, the words *Royal Canadian Mounted Police,* the bison's head encircled with the scroll bearing the motto.

"I thought your motto was that you always get your man?"

"No, it's there, in French, see: 'Maintiens le Droit,' means 'Maintain the Right.'"

"Why the buffalo head?"

"Bison kept the guys alive when they marched west, half-starved in the 1800s, for a buck a day pay."

"How come you're not wearing a red serge and Stetson?" She smiled.

"That's pretty much ceremonial."

"Do they still make you eat buffalo meat?"

"No, you can be a vegan Mountie if you like."

"They pay you more than a buck a day?"

"Depends what day."

Maggie laughed, the first time she'd laughed since Jake took Logan from her. She wanted to thank Graham for that; instead she turned to the desert, watching it flow by. Graham asked her how she'd met Jake and she told him about high school. Then she asked Graham if he had a family.

"My parents are still living. That's it."

"Wife and kids?"

"No kids. I was married. My wife died."

"I'm so sorry. What happened?"

He adjusted his grip on the wheel, looked down the road ahead.

"I'd prefer not to talk about that, if that's okay."

"No, sure. Sorry."

Graham's phone rang.

"Danny, Len Bowman in Banff. You heard we found Tarver?"

"I heard. Is the autopsy done yet?"

"No. You'd best get back here, Stotter's not in a pleasant frame of mind."

"I'm working on it. Is that why you called?"

"The wardens want the Tarvers' campsite released. So, seeing that we've found him, do I have your verbal? We've been sitting on this thing for a long time, Dan."

Mother Nature's your suspect.

At that instant Graham was struck with an idea—an overlooked aspect finally revealed itself.

"Wait! Len. Did Arnie process it with you?"

"For blood splatter?"

"Yes."

"I think he looked in the tent, the SUV, scoped them and stuff."

"Tell him to do the whole area leading to the river."

"What? You want him to scope the woods?"

"Remind him about the Icelandic study about outdoor application. Arnie will know. He's the one who told me about it. After he processes the area, call me."

"I'll do it, but it's your head in the chopper when Stotter gets word. Because as far as he's concerned this one's been cleared."

"Tell him, it's all me. That should make things easy for you and Arnie."

After the call, Graham lost his thoughts in the traffic. Maggie suspected that he had been discussing the Tarver case but didn't ask him about it. Nor did she ask him when they pulled into a service center for gas and burgers.

Later, when they'd returned to the freeway, they didn't notice the car following them. A blue Impala with tinted windows and a front bumper that was scraped on the driver's side.

The same Impala that had followed Maggie a few nights ago.

This time one of the two men in the car had affixed a small transmitter to Graham's rental. The signal was strong on the laptop computer they were using to monitor Maggie and Graham's movements.

56

Two dogs surfaced from the skeleton of a rusted rig.

Big animals with spike collars linked to long chains that dragged over the dirt yard and dog shit as they cautiously advanced toward their owner.

Karl Dixon.

The dogs inched forward, ears down, growling, coats stitched with permanent scars. Half-starved and mean. Just the way Dixon needed 'em. The ones not mean enough were buried by the grease pit in the back.

Dixon shifted the fat cigar in his mouth, set down the bowl of raw pig meat. In his other hand, he gripped a steel rod encased in barbed wire dotted with tufts of hair and flesh.

As the hungry dogs moved nervously to the food, Dixon bit down on his cigar, exposing brown teeth, then raised the rod over his head.

The dogs flinched and yelped.

Satisfied, Dixon held off striking them.

"Not today, boys. You still have a job."

He chuckled, tossed the rod, removed his cigar, spit and took stock of his kingdom.

Desert Truck Land.

Some sixty tractors and trailers encircled by a ten-foot chain-link fence topped with coiled razor wire. His dealership sat on an old auction yard where the train tracks severed West Hacienda, west of Las Vegas Boulevard and I-15.

Dixon loved having power over everything in his world. His dogs, his ex-wives and his crooked deals. Walking back to his office, he tallied up last week's sales to buyers from Montreal, Portland and Tulsa. They'd brought in some one hundred and fifty thousand, thanks to some creativity with the paperwork, the odometers and whatnot.

Leave gambling for the rollers.

Dixon never lost on a deal. And he never would. That's how he ran his show.

He was careful. No complications.

He'd only gone a few steps before he stopped.

"Now what's this?" he asked no one.

He squinted to the far end of the yard and the office, a no-frills wooden-framed rectangle with a noisy air conditioner atop a foundation of cinder blocks. A man and woman in a sedan went inside and had started talking to Wanda, the ex-showgirl who was Dixon's secretary and girlfriend.

Dixon was a long way off but saw them all through the large window that opened to the yard. His skill at reading situations arose from his days as a polygraph examiner for the military.

Back in those days he'd lied about results in exchange for ten thousand dollars.

As Dixon neared the office, he got a bad feeling about these strangers. The way they were showing records to Wanda, their body language.

They weren't truck people.

They looked like cops.

And Wanda was not the brightest light on the Strip.

Dixon picked up his pace.

The woman at the small, worn counter offered a sincere smile.

"Hi, how can I help you?"

She seemed happy to have visitors, but Graham was not optimistic.

Before he and Maggie had arrived they'd gotten rooms at a clean, reasonable motel off the Strip next to a wedding chapel. Graham made calls, then visited Las Vegas Metropolitan Police where he met Sergeant Lou Casta, with LVMP's multiagency vehicle theft task force.

After confirming Graham's credentials and his Tarver tragedy slash insurance story, Casta said his detail had Desert Truck Land down for some complaints, alleged odometer tampering. "Nothing strong enough to support a charge." The local command and the humane society had DTL on file for ill treatment of dogs. Nevada Highway Patrol had a couple of records complaints, and the FBI was looking into an interstate complaint on some rigs purchased at DTL.

"Other than that, you're clear," Casta said.

Now, at Desert Truck Land's counter, Maggie Conlin took the initiative and Graham figured a mother's nonthreatening appeal might work with the friendly receptionist, so he let her go.

"Hi. Well, I'm hoping you can help me find my son."

"Your son?"

"Logan Conlin. My name's Maggie Conlin, I'm from Blue Rose Creek, near Los Angeles."

Maggie pulled a file folder from her bag, opened to pictures and documents.

"Oh, what a good-looking boy," Wanda said. "How old is he?"

"Nine. His father, Jake Conlin, my husband, is a trucker. He took Logan with him on a trip and I haven't seen them since. It's been almost six months."

Maggie touched her hand to her mouth and blinked several times.

"That's terrible," Wanda said. "What happened?"

"Jake was a contract driver in Iraq and came home a little traumatized. Things got strained at home, you know."

"I know. My sister's son, Kyle, was over there with the marines. Still has nightmares."

"I'm trying to find Logan and Jake. It's possible they passed through Las Vegas and Jake may have sold, or traded, his rig. A Kenworth. Here's a picture of him with it and here are copies of all the records."

Wanda looked and started to nod, each nod getting bigger as she looked again at Logan's picture, then at Jake and the rig again.

"This is all familiar. You know, I think we did do business with him. I think we did a trade for an older rig and some cash." Wanda took one of the pages from the file and turned to the tall steel file cabinet behind her and opened the second drawer.

At that moment, the office door opened.

"Hello, folks, Karl Dixon. Owner operator. How can I help you?"

He quickly eyed Graham and Maggie.

As Maggie repeated her story, Dixon went behind the counter, placing himself between Wanda and the file cabinet, subtly bumping the door closed.

"I see, well, can you folks help me with some ID? Wanda must've told you we get all kinds of people telling all kinds of stories so they can get some kinda deal."

He nodded at Maggie's California driver's license, but his head recoiled from Graham's ID.

"A Canadian cop?" His feigned warmth dropped a degree. "Now I'm confused. Is there some reason for police from another country to be here?"

Graham casually explained the Tarver deaths, the insurance matter and the thread of the Conlins and how he and Maggie needed to talk to Jake.

"Just a matter of getting pointed in the right direction."

Dixon took a second, then shot out his hand.

"We'd better help you out. May I have your file?"

Maggie handed it to him, but he did not turn to the file cabinet. Instead, he sat before a computer keyboard and screen.

"All of our records are accessed through here, including vehicle databases. I'm sure if there's something we can find it."

"Thank you," Maggie said.

Dixon was very smooth, Graham thought.

After ten full minutes of clicking and searching,

Dixon shook his head and handed the file back to Maggie.

"I'm sorry, Mrs. Conlin, but we've got nothing matching your information here. Did you try the department of motor vehicles?"

"Wait, a sec. I don't understand." Maggie looked at Wanda. "You said they looked familiar. That you'd probably traded with my husband."

"She was wrong," Karl said.

"You didn't look in the file cabinet," Maggie said.

"Everything's in the computer. We get a lot of people with a lot of trucks. They tend to look the same."

"No, please. I have to find my son. Look some more. Please."

"Maggie," Graham said. "It was an obvious mistake."

"I'm sorry, ma'am," Dixon said. "I wish we could help you. Fine-looking boy you got there, don't you think, Wanda, honey?"

"He sure is."

In the instant Wanda's eyes met Maggie's, something passed between the two women.

An ache. A plea. Fear.

Maggie didn't understand and collected her file.

"You folks have yourselves a nice day." Dixon showed them his brown teeth in what he meant to be a smile.

After Graham and Maggie drove off, he turned to Wanda.

"You disappoint me. I saw you going to the cabinet."

"Karl, she's looking for her kid."

"She was with a cop!"

"I didn't know that at the time."

Dixon grumbled something that sounded like "dumb bitch" before extracting the keys to his Cadillac from his pants.

"I have to go to the bank, then I have to go to Frank's. Don't know how long I'll be. Think you can find your brain while I'm gone?"

The whole time Wanda watched him leave she kept turning a small card in her hand. The one Maggie Conlin had left from her motel.

Maggie had penned her cell-phone number on it, too.

Wanda kept turning it over and over, running her finger along the edge, wishing it were a knife as Karl finally vanished.

57

From their booth in the family restaurant, Maggie bit back on her anger as she watched the sun set on the Las Vegas Strip traffic.

"I just know they were lying at Truck Land about Jake."

"Dixon's got a lot to hide," Graham said.

"So how can you just give up?"

"Maggie, I explained all of this before we left Los Angeles."

"No, tell me. After coming this far, getting this close, how can you quit."

Graham set his coffee down, glanced at their plane tickets for the morning. Hers for California. His for Calgary.

"I am not quitting. I am out of my jurisdiction. Since we left Dixon's place my boss has called me twice ordering me home. I'm not sure I still have a job."

"Make him understand how our cases are linked."

"It's complicated. Listen, no one's stepping back from your lead on Jake. I told you, I spent an hour with

Casta at Las Vegas Metro, then I spoke to the FBI and I reached Vic Thompson. They can press for warrants to seize all of Dixon's records. It's only the beginning with him."

"That could take weeks. It's not a priority for them. Besides, I bet Dixon's good at hiding things."

Graham didn't respond.

Frustration and fatigue had settled upon them like a losing streak. They left the restaurant and drove to their motel. Maggie watched the colossal hotels down the Strip, gleaming in the twilight.

"Can I ask you something personal?" she said.

"Sure."

"Even if you don't want to talk about it?"

"You can ask."

"How did your wife die?"

Graham took a few moments and he looked straight ahead.

"A car accident."

Their rooms were separated by a few others on the motel's upper level.

They overlooked the pool and offered a view of the Spring Mountains.

In his room, Graham had his TV turned low on CNN as he worked on his laptop. The pope's visit to the United States dominated the news.

Graham read over his case notes. He was not ready to walk away from Tarver.

That was the truth.

But Stotter had given him an explicit order to return.

Graham checked e-mails. The autopsy on Tarver was still pending. Arnie Danton, the blood expert, had also sent an update.

Dan, given this case is supposed to be done with, I'm having a hard time getting a green light from my boss, but I'm working on it. Maybe tomorrow, or the next day.

Graham shut things down, closed his laptop, set his alarm to allow for enough time in the morning to drop off the rental and make their flights. He fell asleep as CNN featured an expert discussion on papal security against terrorist threats.

"You know, Brent, there was that chilling plot against John Paul II in Manila that narrowly...."

A few doors down, Maggie stepped into a hot bubble bath, stared at her cell phone on the tub's lip and wept.

She was so tired, her muscles tremored in the water.

This must be what hell was like. She must have died and been damned to eternal torment by getting so close to Logan, Jake and the truth, only to find it was a lie.

All a lie.

She would never see them again.

She closed her eyes and for a moment she was with Logan and Jake on a warm beach until the cold bathwater woke her.

Maggie didn't know how long she'd slept.

Later, her body heavy, as she got ready for bed, she decided to update her file. She'd put it in the nightstand to the right of the bed, under the Gideon's Bible, before they went to Desert Truck Land.

But when she opened the drawer, the file wasn't there.

Odd. She specifically remembered placing it under the Bible when she'd checked in earlier.

Maggie looked in the nightstand to the left of the bed. Her file was there.

Strange. How did it get moved? This was not where she'd left it. Maybe housekeeping came in. Maggie picked up the phone and called down to the desk.

"No, ma'am. No one was in your room today. They're not scheduled to clean until you check out."

Maggie was puzzled. Weird. Maybe she'd moved it herself and didn't remember.

She checked her door, the lock, the dead bolt, the bar and the chain, then got into bed.

As she fell asleep she tried to resurrect her beach dream.

A block away, an Impala with darkened windows was invisible among the hundreds of cars in a public lot that offered a clear line of sight on the motel through high-powered military binoculars. While one man snored in the back, the second was alert, watching the doors to Maggie's and Graham's rooms.

Every hour he would type an updated report on his laptop and e-mail it to his uncle in Addis Ababa.

58

Las Vegas, Nevada

Most Las Vegas dreams started, or ended, at McCarran International Airport.

The transit point for winners and losers.

Here, the consequences of first and last gambles played out with the perpetual chime and clack of slot action.

After returning the rental car, Graham and Maggie found a soft-lit lounge where they waited under a cloud of defeat to check in for their flights. Maggie had tea and glumly poked at the bag while it steeped. Graham had orange juice and a muffin.

News clips of the pope greeting ecstatic Americans jammed into a stadium flashed on the TV monitors suspended over the bar as Graham took a call on his phone from Casta, who had follow-up questions on Dixon.

To take her mind off things, Maggie changed a dollar into four quarters and went to the slot machine in the corner. Lemons, oranges, bells and bars clattered from left to right, with the first coin she played. No win. It was the same for the second.

And the same for the third quarter.

Typical.

She played her last one and the first reel left a cherry at the payline; so did the second, and the third. Then the fourth. Lights flashed, pongs sounded during the rollup as the machine tallied Maggie's win, releasing a torrent of coins into the tray.

At that moment Maggie's cell phone rang. As she answered, she hurried outside the lounge to get away from the noise.

"Maggie Conlin?" the female caller said.

"Yes."

"This is Wanda."

A tense moment passed between the two women.

"I'm sorry about what happened yesterday at the office."

"Will you help me?"

Seconds passed with Maggie pressing her phone to her ear. She looked at the happy families, the excited couples, the tour groups with snippets of German, French and Japanese conversations, all streaming by in rivers of smiles.

She squeezed her phone hard.

"Wanda? You didn't call just to apologize. Will you help me?"

"Karl is who he is. He cuts corners and is afraid you were cops and—"

"I don't give a damn about him, I need to find my son. Please."

"I'll help you."

Maggie waved frantically at Graham until he saw her. Then to Wanda she said, "We're on our way to your office now! Soon as we get a taxi."

"No! Don't come. That's a bad idea. I'll tell you over the phone."

"Okay, give me a second." Graham joined Maggie. She pointed to a table, pulled out a notebook and scrawled, *WANDA. WILL HELP.* He gestured to his ear. "Okay, Wanda, it's noisy here, I have to turn up the sound. Speak up, speak clearly, please!"

Maggie adjusted the sound to its maximum level then turned it so Graham could hear. Their heads touched as they listened.

Graham pulled out his notebook.

"Your husband, Jake, traded his rig with us. He looked familiar in the pictures and I checked our other files. Karl keeps a second set of books."

"What did Jake trade for? Where did he go?"

"It was an International, but the records were changed. You won't find it. It's what Karl does to make money under the table. He alters serial numbers and vehicle identification numbers, then he pays guys to help him authenticate records. I'm telling you because I'm leaving him because he— I think you know what men like Karl do to women." Wanda made a swallowing sound like she was drinking. "And you seemed so nice."

"Life can be hard, Wanda, I know. Is that all you can tell me about Jake?" Maggie's voice broke. "Can't you tell me anything else? Please."

"Jake and Karl talked in Karl's office for a long time. Karl made me bring them coffee. They were loud. I heard Jake say that he had a line on work and some property in Montana. That he was going to start new there, put the past and his ex behind him."

"Ex? I'm not his ex. That's not— Wanda, where in Montana?" Maggie made notes.

"I don't know."

"Nothing?"

"A couple weeks after the deal, Karl had me send Jake some paperwork he needed to make the truck 'legal,' so I have an address that might help you."

"In Montana?"

"Yes, a P.O. box address care of the Sky Road Truck Mall, Grizzly Tooth Freeway, Great Falls, Montana."

"Thank you, Wanda. Oh, thank you."

"I saw your boy. Recognized him in your pictures, too."

Maggie's heart nearly burst.

"You saw him!"

"He was here with your husband. Came in to use the bathroom."

"How was he?"

"A little sad-looking, little stressed. As I recall, he was with this woman, Jake's girlfriend, I think."

"What do you know about the woman? Do you have her name, a description?" Graham was jotting something, Maggie read it into the phone. "Did she touch anything that no one else has touched?"

"Don't know. But she was pretty. Kind of dark, in an exotic way. She didn't say much, barely smiled. Oh— I have to go, sorry. Good luck. I hope you find your son."

"Thank you. Thank you so much."

Maggie ended the call and looked at Graham.

"I'm taking the next plane to Great Falls," she said. "Are you coming?"

Book Five:
"Forgive me for what I've done…"

59

Seattle, Washington

A King County sheriff's helicopter thudded above the city in the clear morning sky.

People filled Pioneer Square and several surrounding blocks for a glimpse of the pope. Thirty-five thousand, according to estimates coming through Blake Walker's earpiece.

He scanned the faces at barricades and windows overlooking the square.

This was it.

His team's turn to protect the pope.

Everyone on the Secret Service's advance team had been pulling nineteen-hour days for this leg of the papal visit. Drawing from the watch list and working with local police, they'd studied the Service's Trip File and The Album, they'd interviewed all the people who had ever uttered a threat against the pope, or the president.

No major security breaches had happened in Boston, New York, Miami, Houston or Los Angeles, the previous cities on the papal visit.

In New York, a seventy-six-year-old grandmother

wrapped her arms around his neck and refused to release him as she broke down with emotion. In Los Angeles, a poor construction worker, whose wife had been diagnosed with terminal cancer, broke through the barricade and tugged at the Holy Father's vestments before security escorted him back. Later, the pope met privately with the man and prayed with him.

Investigation and analysis of the marine border penetration up the coast at the Strait of Juan de Fuca was ongoing. Preliminary reports had yielded nothing conclusive to constitute a threat.

Walker and senior agents continued working with all intelligence agencies. Nothing had emerged to corroborate the information from the capture of terror suspect Issa al-Issa obtained by secret operatives in the U.S.

U.S. and foreign intelligence desks continued to scour all chatter, reports and known activities of foreign terrorist organizations.

Walker knew that not every threat could be anticipated.

Not every action could be stopped.

But with hard work and vigilance, risks could be reduced. Unknown to the public, the traffic of threats against the pope was increasing.

Security in Seattle was overwhelming.

Uniformed officers were everywhere, along with armed officers and federal agents in plain clothes who blended with the crowd. Secret Service agents in suits formed a protective box that moved with the pope.

Sharpshooters and spotters from Seattle, King County, Washington State Patrol and the FBI and ATF lined the rooftops. Heavily armed officers patrolled the streets.

High and unseen overhead, jet fighters provided top cover to guard against any aircraft attempting to penetrate restricted airspace in a suicide attack on the pope's stage. Such a plan was outlined in computer records found two years ago with captured Algerian terror suspects.

Walker took another deep breath and reviewed the major events on the day's agenda.

The pope would bless a shelter in Pioneer Square run by an order of nuns. His blessing would honor a devoted sister who'd recently been murdered while performing religious duties at the shelter.

Afterward, he would meet the public at the barricades outside the shelter as he made his way to the popemobile for the half-mile parade down 1st Avenue to Qwest Field, home of the Seahawks. Use of the infield expanded the stadium's capacity to allow him to celebrate Mass with some one hundred thousand people.

That evening the Holy Father would have a private dinner at the residence of the archbishop for the Archdiocese of Seattle, where he'd spend the night. The next morning, he would fly to Montana for events there before going on to Chicago to conclude the tour.

Walker checked his earpiece.

The pope had just finished inside the shelter and would exit.

Agents outside the shelter stiffened.

Walker was on "the shoulder" as he scanned faces at the barricade. He assessed a tall, thin, long-haired man. Next to him, an elderly man in a ball cap, eye clenched behind a camera that had been inspected. Then a small woman wearing a kerchief and white gloves. Next to her, a young man, but Walker couldn't see his eyes. The guy had dark glasses, blond hair and was smiling. Maybe a little too much. Where were his hands? Walker watched him as some in the crowd began to sing and cheer.

"Is he coming? Do you see him?" asked a woman wearing gold-framed glasses and clutching a tiny U.S. flag.

Walker's stomach tightened.

Secret Service radio transmissions crackled softly in his ear.

"Halo advancing to Chariot—"

Halo was Secret Service code for the pope. Chariot was the popemobile. The alert rippled along the perimeter. Agents braced. Walker swallowed. His pulse quickened.

"There he is! I see him!" a woman in the crowd shouted, triggering deafening cheering that rose like a shock wave.

The pope emerged from the building, smiling and waving as agents escorted him along the barricades toward the waiting motorcade.

Walker studied faces. The woman with the glasses, the long-haired man, the old man with the camera. People waved, shouted. Necks stretched, they elbowed for a glimpse. Where was the young, blond-haired man? Walker had lost him. He'd moved.

The blond-haired man had moved closer to the barricade's closest point. But something wasn't right. This guy was close but Walker couldn't see the guy's eyes behind those dark glasses. His unease grew with the crowd's cheering.

Walker's heart was racing. The pope was shaking hands, reaching for people, touching people, heads, faces, cheeks, smiling, allowing himself to be touched, taking his time.

The agents wanted him to move faster to the protective bubble of the popemobile.

The young blond-haired man looked all wrong in his military jacket. His smile was not right and, dammit, why couldn't Walker see the guy's right hand tucked in his jacket pocket? The guy's shoulder muscles started moving and his mouth opened as he called to the pope.

"Holy Father! Over here, Holy Father, please!"

His hidden hand sprung from his pocket.

Walker's heart stopped.

Gun?

Was he leveling a gun at the pope? It looked like a barrel and fingers were positioning on the grip and trigger.

Walker's training took over; he alerted the sniper commander, pulled at the pope's shoulder to shield him just as two plain-clothed officers materialized, seized the suspect's hand and took him to the ground amid shouting, screaming and chaos in the immediate area.

Walker and the other agents rushed the pope toward the popemobile, glancing back to see an agent hold up the weapon.

A wooden cross.

Likely wanted the pope to bless it.

False alarm.

Walker exhaled.

As they moved the pope to the popemobile, Walker's earpiece crackled with a report from a spotter.

"...glint of a scope between the curtains of a window due south overlooking the square..."

Cursing, Walker glanced at some of the nearest high buildings—the Smith Tower and Columbia Center.

Both were in sniper range.

Agents encircled the pope and, in a calm orderly manner, moved him back inside the shelter. "An unexpected delay, Holy Father."

The pope nodded.

It was done so smoothly no one in the crowd was aware. The spotter locked on the building on 1st Avenue South overlooking the route, then the precise location, twenty-fifth floor, northeast window.

Security moved with lightning speed, those on the ground and those on the roof.

While Walker and the other agents moved the pope out of the line of fire and back into the shelter, SWAT members stormed the suspect building, seized the elevators and ascended to the twenty-fifth floor.

Helicopters thundered over the buildings. Much of the action was lost on the public. However, some news crews detected the sudden activity and cameras were trained on the building, and reporters began making their way to it.

Something was happening.

Sharpshooters locked on the window's exterior. Inside, SWAT members rushed from the elevator to the room. Heavily armed agents kicked the door, rushed inside to find a boy and his grandfather, watching the pope with a telescope.

The old man cursed.

His traumatized grandson stood frozen with his hands in the air and his eyes wide open.

"I'm sorry. Please don't kill me. I'm sorry."

Then the boy started to cry.

The old man was a retired architect.

Walker's team had argued strenuously for the windows and curtains in all buildings overlooking the procession route be shut or closed. But local anger forced Seattle city officials to push back.

Later, at Qwest Field, the pope's open-air Mass for one hundred thousand people took place without any security incidents. As did the evening's events at the Archdiocese.

Long after the pope had retired, Walker and the other agents continued working with updates, debriefs and briefings on the Montana site.

It was well past midnight when they'd finished.

But Walker couldn't sleep. Adrenaline from the day's drama pumped through his system.

He soothed himself, anticipating that the next day's events in Lone Tree, Montana—the middle of nowhere—would be easier than Seattle. Just as his eyes began to flutter, Walker's BlackBerry vibrated with a bulletin.

A rancher had reported a mysterious flash explosion at the northeast edge of Malmstrom Air Force Base. Cascade County Sheriff's Office and the base military were investigating.

The specialized unit from Indian Head had been dispatched.

Walker's heart rate wouldn't be normal again until the pope's jet lifted off for Rome.

60

In-flight to Montana

Within four hours of Wanda's call, Maggie and Graham had canceled their flights and had located and boarded a departing charter that served Great Falls, Montana.

"You're in luck," the ticket agent had said, smiling. "A number of seats just opened up and we want to fill them."

Maggie had paid for her ticket out of the six hundred thirty-one dollars she'd won on the slot machine. Graham paid out of his own pocket, deciding to take care of the expense claim when he got back to Calgary.

Because he had accepted the truth.

He could not walk away from the Tarver case.

Even though he'd been ordered to return, he couldn't. Not yet. There were too many questions. Now, as the plane skirted the Great Salt Lake Desert and neared Yellowstone, and as Maggie drifted off, he searched the clouds for answers.

Emily Tarver's dying words troubled him. And he swore he'd heard Nora's voice when he was in the water. If he didn't pursue the family's deaths, he'd be haunted by the ghosts of his failures for the rest of his life because this went beyond the case.

This was about Nora.

Maybe he could live with what went wrong if he could make something right for someone else.

Maybe.

By the time the plane passed over the Bitterroot Mountains, Graham had resolved to request immediate personal leave, freeing him to investigate the case on his own and on his own dime.

And if that was denied?

He'd resign.

Would he?

If that's what it took.

Because he'd be finished.

Because he was hanging on by a thread.

Great Falls was about a seven-hour drive from Calgary, or a short flight. Funny, he thought, looking at the snowcapped peaks reaching up to him, reaching all the way north to the Faust River where he'd stood not so long ago, drowning in guilt as he held Nora's ashes.

He'd pretty much come full circle.

When the captain announced their descent into Great Falls, Maggie woke, left her seat and took her place in line for the restroom at the rear.

Upon returning, she met the intense eyes of another passenger, a man squeezing by her. Her polite little smile was received with stone-cold indifference, sending a shiver coiling up her spine as he brushed by.

It couldn't be.

He looked familiar. Like that creep from her bookstore.

Maggie glanced back at him, but other passengers blocked her view. She took her seat thinking, no, it couldn't be him. It was her imagination, given all she'd been through.

Nearly overdosing. Graham saving her. Getting her to Las Vegas, which got her to Montana. Closer to Logan. Closer to Jake.

Closer to what awaited her.

Maggie buckled up. The landing gear lowered. As the jet neared the runway, she prayed she would finally find the truth.

Whatever it was.

61

Great Falls, Montana

The Sky Road Truck Mall was situated on a thirty-acre site off the interstate, where it curled a few miles southwest of Great Falls International Airport.

It was an expansive twenty-four-hour operation offering fueling, two restaurants, a chapel, a massage therapist, a medical clinic, laundry, shower facilities and more. The complex was landscaped with clipped shrubs; its neo-deco facade had glazed windows. Huge Montana state and U.S. flags waved on gold-tipped poles high above the entrance.

Maggie and Graham parked their rented sedan as dozens of rigs eased in and out of the mall, their diesel engines growling, air brakes hissing.

Before they'd left Las Vegas, Graham again notified local law enforcement. Strangely, one of his calls was bounced to an FBI Special Agent in Billings.

"Thanks for the courtesy call," the agent said. "Not sure to what extent we can assist. Most of our resources are going to supporting security for the pope's visit."

Graham also called upon Novak, the D.C. detective,

to help him query Montana Highway Patrol to run Jake Conlin's name through state motor vehicle records, for an address, for anything.

Nothing came up.

Novak had also run it through NCIC, the FBI's National Crime Information Center. Apart from the Conlin parental abduction file, nothing showed for Montana.

Now, inside the administrative office of the Sky Road Truck Mall, Cheyenne Mills, the duty manager, rotated her wedding ring as she listened to Graham and Maggie's situation. Then she made a few calls. Confirmed a Jake "Conlynn" had rented a postal box at the mall for two months. Paid cash. No other useful details were on his rental form. Then she nodded to the glass wall of her second-level office overlooking the busy mall.

"Three, maybe even four thousand people pass through here weekly. Our customers are the salt of the earth. They'll help you if they can. Anyone gives you trouble, tell them I said it was okay for you to show them pictures."

For the next few hours, Maggie and Graham talked to men and women in plaid shirts, ball caps and jeans in the restaurants, the lounges, the arcades and the stores while TVs tuned to news networks showed the latest on the papal visit *"…the pope visits Seattle today then it's on to Montana and Chicago…"*

They showed pictures of Jake and Logan and asked for help locating them.

But after scores of inquiries, nothing promising had emerged.

Frustrated but not defeated, Maggie stood in the

lobby before the huge map of Montana, Idaho, North Dakota, British Columbia, Alberta and Saskatchewan. Below it was the usual truck stop message board, papered with ads for driving jobs, rigs, trailers and parts. The faces of missing children, women and fugitives also stared at her from old posters.

"Excuse me, are you the lady looking for a trucker and his son?"

Maggie nodded at a slim woman in her sixties, hoop earrings, bright eyes behind bifocals, snapping gum.

"Betty Pilcher. My husband, Leo, and I run the B and L Barbershop, the other side of the mall. The guys were telling us about you showing pictures. I have to run up to admin but drop by our shop in a few minutes, hon. Leo's good at remembering faces."

Fifteen minutes later, Leo Pilcher, a retired U.S. Army barber, stepped from the customer in his chair to stare long and hard at the photos of Jake Conlin, as Maggie and Graham awaited his assessment.

Leo nodded and went back to cutting hair.

"He was here. Only he doesn't look like that since I worked on him."

Graham and Maggie exchanged glances.

"You're sure?" Maggie asked.

Leo stepped away again. The needle point of his scissors touched the corner of Jake's right eye.

"Got a little scar right here?"

"Yes," Maggie said.

"It was him. I'm sure. He stands out because of the scar and the changes."

"Changes?"

Graham pulled out his notebook and asked for details.

"He walked in here, oh, about four, five months back. He had a beard, few weeks' growth. Good head of thick, healthy hair. He wanted all the hair shaved off and wanted the beard shaved into a Vandyke, some call it a goatee. A beard without the sides. I'll show you. Can I draw on this?"

Maggie gave Leo a pen from her bag and he sketched a Vandyke on Jake, then put his thick fingers over Jake's hair.

"See? Like a different guy. I asked him, 'Hey, you hiding from somebody?' And he sort of laughed and said, 'Something like that.'"

"Any chance he said where he was living or who he was driving for?"

Leo shook his head.

"He was the silent type. Kept to himself. I've seen him since in the mall, probably couple times a month. He could be local."

Graham and Maggie went directly to the mall's business office where Graham scanned the altered photo into his laptop computer. He e-mailed it to the Forensic Identification Section in Alberta with an urgent request for FIS to give him a clean photo of Jake Conlin with a shaved head and a Vandyke.

Less than four minutes after he sent the file, Graham's cell phone rang.

"Corporal Graham, Simon Teale with FIS. Got your request. We're swamped, got plenty of priority cases we're processing now and I've got cases out of Red Deer and Medicine Hat in the queue ahead of you. How soon do you need this?"

"We needed it yesterday."

"And by the case number, this is the Tarver matter. The family in Banff."

"Yes, is there a problem, Simon?"

"No, just confirming. I'll do my best to expedite things. Maybe later today or tomorrow."

"It's just an updated photo."

"I know we could do it quickly, but we're short-staffed and you know I need sign-off. Bear with us."

"Call me the moment you have it."

Muttering about bureaucracy, Graham told Maggie that they needed to find a motel.

62

Great Falls, Montana

The pope's visit to Montana—the first in the state's history—was a day away, according to the *Great Falls Tribune*.

It ran large photos and a huge headline that stretched across the front page.

The paper sat unread on the bed in Graham's motel room.

He was in the shower and would read it when he finished, then meet Maggie for dinner, to figure out their next steps.

She was in the lobby using the motel's complimentary high-speed guest computer, trying to contact school officials, hoping they could search Logan's birth date to determine if he was in their system.

It was late afternoon and she wasn't making any headway. Time was working against both of them because Graham didn't think Teale would get back to him today.

The pulsating hot water had nearly worked all of the tension from Graham's neck and shoulders when his cell phone rang. He stopped the shower, wrapped a towel around himself, grabbed the phone from the towel rack hoping it was Teale.

It wasn't.

"Let me get this straight," Graham's boss said. "You're in Great Falls?"

"That's right."

"What're you doing? Taking a bus home?"

"Mike, I'm making progress on the link to Tarver."

"Link? There's no link."

"Listen."

"Dan, you have to stop this. From what I understand, you're now traveling with the California woman and you're entangled in her case, a parental abduction?"

"Maggie Conlin. It's all linked to Tarver. The Conlin name and address were the last things Ray Tarver was checking."

"You're sinking deeper into trouble. It's over. We've just got the autopsy on Raymond Tarver."

"And?"

"And nothing. His death was just like his wife and kids. Head trauma consistent with a wilderness accident. Nothing suspicious. Case cleared."

"No, that's not right. I told you Emily Tarver spoke to me."

"Dan, it was in the minutes before she died. The little girl was in shock."

"It's *what* she said, Mike. She spoke to me, and *Nora spoke to me.*"

"Nora?"

"I know it's weird, but I swear when I was in the water, I heard her."

"Dan."

Several long moments passed as Stotter absorbed the fact that one of his best investigators had just revealed that his dead wife was speaking to him on the case. In the silence, Stotter groped for a response before he exhaled slowly.

"Dan, at the outset I respected your suspicions on Tarver. They were valid. I thought letting you go after them would help the case. And I thought it would help you. You've been through hell and maybe it was too soon to throw you back in the mix. Maybe the California woman is some form of psychological compensation for what you've been through."

"Mike, you've got to listen to me."

"Dan, you're a good detective, but you've still got some things to work through. It's going to take time."

"I'm not coming back until I'm done."

"Dan, I'm giving you an order. If you're not back here in twenty-four hours, I'm sending somebody to get you. Is that clear?"

Graham hung up then met himself in the mirror.

He'd just refused a direct order.

Everything was on the line now.

63

Montana

Time was going to be tight for Jake.

Around midnight, he was rolling northeast out of Helena bound for Great Falls to take a load of groceries to Shelby. At Shelby, he'd haul lumber back to Lewistown.

He'd be heavy both ways. He made good time with the jobs in Butte and Missoula. He'd make money.

And, if he was lucky with traffic, even allowing for buildup for the pope's visit, he'd be back in time to catch some sleep before Logan's big event.

Logan.

Jake ran his hand over his face.

He tightened his grip on the wheel because something powerful was pulling at him. He saw it, a few hours ago, in the moment he rolled away from the house.

He saw it in Logan's tiny silhouette in the window as he watched him pull away.

In that moment, Jake saw the truth.

In that moment, Jake realized that for the past five or six months since they left Blue Rose Creek he had been a fool. He'd made the biggest mistake of his life.

So what was he going to do about it?

Jake was about ten miles south of Great Falls when his cell phone rang.

"Hey, it's Crocker at dispatch. Great Falls, Shelby and Lewistown been scrubbed."

"No way. All three?"

"Yup. Sorry, amigo, it happens."

"Man, I was counting my money."

"Head home. You'll be paid for the trips you did up to this point. I've got you for Atlanta this Sunday. That's a lock."

Frustrated, Jake wheeled east through Great Falls to head to Cold Butte and his predicament.

The facts were inescapable now.

The horror of what he'd seen in Iraq had turned him into a monster. Take that day in the supermarket, which led to the embarrassment on the soccer field. Consumed with paranoia, he'd been convinced Maggie had cheated with Ullman.

But he was dead wrong.

It had never happened.

He was the one who'd cheated with Samara. And he was the one who'd ruined everything by running off with her, taking Logan with him and lying to him.

How could he have done that?

Tear the boy from his life and tell him that his mother no longer loved him.

It was unforgivable.

Overcome with shame, Jake steadied his grip on the wheel as the truth continued hammering at him.

Samara had saved his life.

She was a good person who'd suffered her own tragedies. She was good to him and Logan but she was distant, aloof, as if she were still in mourning.

Jake didn't belong with Samara.

He belonged with Maggie.

His wife. The only woman he'd ever loved. Dancing with her in the gym.

"Hey, Jude."

Iraq had taken something from all of them.

Jake gazed up at the stars, wondering if it was too late to go back to Blue Rose Creek and Maggie.

Traffic had slowed ahead at a security checkpoint.

Checkpoint.

Jake fought off a flashback.

He knew about the advisory to drivers concerning all big rigs heading into Lone Tree County. Standard procedure around VIP events. He was going to be hung up for an inspection.

No problem, he was empty.

Some forty minutes after the inspectors cleared him, the Montana Highway Patrol waved Jake through.

It was after 3:00 a.m. when he got to Cold Butte, got down Crystal Road, then turned into their lane. He took care to crawl to a near-silent stop next to the house, without waking Logan and Samara.

Hungry, Jake helped himself to a slice of apple pie. As he ate, his problem gnawed at him until he was interrupted by a soft ping in the living room.

Samara's laptop was on.

That never happened. She never left her computer open like that. Guess she didn't expect him home. The screen bathed the room in soft blue.

Jake had an idea.

After he'd finished his pie, he went to their bedroom and checked on Samara. She was asleep. In the room's dim light he saw the outline of her tailored suit hanging on the closet door.

Jake went to Logan's room.

The little guy was sawing logs.

A small Bible and rosary that he wanted the pope to bless waited on his nightstand. Logan's new suit was on the doorknob in anticipation of the visit.

Then it hit Jake full force. It really sunk in.

His son was going to sing for the pope!

Jake swelled with pride and he blinked several times then closed Logan's door.

Jake turned to the living room.

He'd reached a decision and pulled out his wallet, thumbing through a collection of IDs and business cards, until he found a worn one for:

Stobel and Chadwick

It was Maggie's card; it had her business e-mail, and her home e-mail was penned on the back. He sat before Samara's laptop and logged in to his Internet e-mail account. Waiting for the connection, he noticed her screen saver. Big photos of Samara's husband and son stared at Jake, until the screen filled with his e-mail site.

Maggie, Jake started, I don't know where to begin. I don't dare expect you to ever forgive me for what I've done. All I can hope for is that maybe you'll understand. First, I'm going to bring Logan home to you...

For the next half hour, the sound of a tapping keyboard broke the silence as Jake emptied his heart into his letter. When he finished, he read it over. Satisfied, he pressed Send.

The account's completion bar showed the e-mail going through, until it reached ninety-nine percent, then the machine suddenly shut down.

Some kind of glitch?

Jake considered what he might do, when the machine restarted itself. A symphony of bleating and whirring as images blurred by.

What the heck? What kind of computer was this? It was unlike anything he'd seen. A lot of Arabic, then something just plain weird.

A video popped up, accompanied by a series of timers, some Arabic writing next to it. Then a series of pop-ups, ongoing chat in Arabic. The computer was doing strange things.

A video started.

Jake froze.

Samara was in it.

"What the hell?"

She was wearing a white hijab, sitting with clasped hands before her on a plain wooden table. A framed photograph of her son and husband came into view.

"I am Samara. I am not a jihadist."

Jake's jaw dropped. Ice shot up his spine. His gut convulsed with the collision of disbelief and knowing.

As the video played, the pieces locked together.

Jake knew.

Iraq.

The papal visit.

All her time on this computer, her long-distance calls and private conversations.

"And it is for these crimes that I deliver my widow-mother's wrath. For these crimes you will taste death in your country..."

This was Samara's suicide video.

She was security cleared as medical staff for the visit. She would get close to the pope.

God, what have I done! I've got to get Logan out of here! Call the FBI! We have to stop—

A flash, movement of light; a shadow blurred on the screen and Jake felt a soft punch to his throat.

What?

It hurt.

He couldn't swallow.

He pressed his hands to his throat and something warm and wet cascaded through his fingers. The computer and the room began to spin. Jake's hands were coated with blood. He turned, fell to the floor.

He saw Samara standing over him.

She held a large serrated knife and watched in silence as Jake's life slipped away.

Calmly she slid her arms under his, locked them in front and dragged him into their bedroom. Straining, she lifted his corpse onto his side of their bed and covered him with sheets.

Taking pains not to wake Logan, she got cold water, dish soap, a plastic pail and washed away the blood.

She glanced at the faces of Muhammad and Ahmed on her computer before shutting it off.

Nothing would stop her from keeping her vow.

It was down to hours now.

64

Faust's Fork. Near Banff, Alberta, Canada

Campsite #131.

The Tarver family site.

Still cordoned by yellow tape.

Stepping from his truck to stretch, Royal Canadian Mounted Police Corporal Arnie Danton took in the scent of pine forests, the view of the majestic Nine Bear Range and the rushing Faust River before he began his preparations.

He used the remaining daylight to set up, going to the back of his truck, pulling out his lamps, his coveralls, his gloves, and arranging his solutions, his cameras.

Then he sat on the tailgate and ate his dinner, a sub sandwich, potato chips with a bottle of water and a peanut butter cookie, chewing contentedly as he waited for night.

He needed the darkness.

Sitting alone with the rush of the river for company, he thought of Graham. He felt sorry for the guy and for what had happened to his wife. That's why Danton was here on his own time doing him a favor. A lot of guys had been doing Graham favors lately.

Night came quickly in the mountains.

Danton crumpled his food wrappings, placed them neatly in his recycle bag, then set out to determine if blood was spilled anywhere in or around the Tarvers' campsite by applying luminol.

A fifteen-year veteran who'd trained at the RCMP Academy, several universities, and crime labs in Germany, Sweden, Japan and the U.S., Danton was recognized by courts in Canada and the U.S. as an expert in analyzing bloodstain patterns at crime scenes. He had a keen interest in the process of chemical luminescence.

The process detected the presence of blood that is otherwise invisible to the naked eye by applying a solution of water, sodium perborate, sodium carbonate and luminol to a given area. Once the solution contacts blood, even minute traces, it reacts by turning bright blue under ultraviolet light.

Danton pulled on hooded coveralls, a face mask, latex gloves. On his head, he then slipped on an expensive lightweight surgeon's headlight offering LED illumination and magnification. He prepared a large batch of the solution, then poured it into a cylinder resembling a diver's air tank. He connected it to a hose and sprayer applicator, then slipped the tank on his back.

In the black, moonless night, Danton began working on the scene.

Section by section.

Spraying then scoping with the ultraviolet lamp.

Spraying. Scoping.

He'd devoured every study on outdoor application of luminol.

The Russian, Swedish and Icelandic studies showed that months, even years of rain and snow, did not entirely eliminate the presence of human blood. Of particular interest was the study that indicated human blood was present on a centuries-old stone the Vikings had used for ritual ceremonies.

Anyone coming upon Danton would have witnessed a surreal ballet as he worked the scene like an artist.

First, the immediate campsite. Then the ground, the picnic table, the trees.

All remained as dark as the sky.

All negative.

Danton followed the short path to the riverbank and worked his way back slowly.

Spraying. Scoping.

A couple of paces from the water he froze.

Two small circles glowed blue.

"And thy brother's blood crieth unto me from the ground."

Danton, like most blood-pattern experts, knew the passage from Genesis.

He continued, moving forward from the riverbank toward the campsite.

Spraying. Scoping.

More blue droplets glowed until they formed a virtual Milky Way of blood.

For the next half hour, Danton painstakingly worked in a pattern that radiated from the site.

Spraying. Scoping.

He was running low on solution and about to pack it in when something in the bush glowed.

Like a distant star.

A grapefruit-size rock with bluish smears.
Danton examined it.
Now, this would be your murder weapon.

65

Great Falls, Montana

That night, beyond the pool, across the motel's manicured courtyard, the crack splitting the drawn curtains of the silent room moved ever so slightly.

Binoculars were trained on the units used by Graham and Maggie. The tranquility was deceptive. The watcher's breathing had quickened.

Stay calm, Sid told himself.

Crickets chirped as he rolled the focus wheel.

Sid and Faker had taken shifts in their intense surveillance, for they'd reached a critical point in the operation; one underscored by the headlines of the newspapers neatly arrayed on the desk.

The pope would arrive in Montana in the morning. The network's operation was advanced and proceeding. However, since Graham, the Alberta RCMP officer, had emerged in the U.S., Sid and Faker had been urging termination action. They knew there had been operational activity in Canada.

They could not permit anything to put the greater mission at risk.

A few days ago, after Sid and Faker had urged termination, they were ordered not to take any action, other than to observe and report.

But now, the stakes were higher. The threat was closer and gaining. They were running out of time and continued to press for termination action.

Faker was talking softly on the satellite phone. His voice was so low, Sid had to struggle to hear. At times, Faker would pull the phone away to whisper updates.

"Some of them are getting nervous," he told Sid, "because the threat is getting close to the messenger."

Of course, Sid nodded, the risk of the mission being shut down was huge.

"Some want us to remove the threat now. Others say it would jeopardize the operation, draw attention and lead to a cancellation, or more tougher security, or possible exposure of the network."

Sid couldn't bear the debate.

All of his life, from the day his teenaged mother had abandoned him in the pew of a Brooklyn church, he'd yearned to be part of something greater than himself. Ached to make his mark in history.

As Faker returned to the phone, Sid's thoughts rolled back to all the work that had gone into this operation. Risks had been eliminated to get them to this stage. The termination operations in Virginia and Canada proved that threats to its success could be eliminated with efficiency.

"That's it." Faker finished the call. "Our orders are to take no action. We are to observe and report."

Sid shook his head.

"Don't they realize how close the Canadian cop is," he said. "They are making a grave error."

"I agree." Faker joined Sid at the window with his own binoculars. "I've told the clerk at the desk that we're investigating an infidelity case. I've bribed him to alert us to any movement."

"Good, then contrary to orders, we'll take action."

"We will do whatever it takes to ensure success, my brother."

Sid did not pull his eyes from his binoculars.

66

Nearly two hours before dawn, the motel phone next to Graham's bed rang.

Half awake, he grabbed it on the first ring.

"Corporal Graham, it's Teale in FIS. I've just e-mailed your photos to you."

"Okay, hang on." Graham got on to his computer, went into his e-mail, found the attachment and opened it. Jake Conlin stared back at him, bald, with a Vandyke beard, along with photos showing his left and right profiles. "Got it. Great. Thanks, Simon. Gotta go."

Graham called Maggie's room.

Some forty minutes later, they were back at the Sky Road Truck Mall.

Graham printed off copies of the photos in the twenty-four-hour business office. They started in the big restaurant. The strains of country music, the smells of strong coffee, frying bacon and the clink of cutlery filled the air as they showed people Jake's updated mug shot and asked for their help.

They approached bleary-eyed drivers coming off all-night runs and early risers fixing to hit the road. They went from table to table, receiving head shakes, shrugs, a "looks familiar," a "maybe, I don't remember," an "I'm not sure," a "naw," a "good luck" and "I'll say a prayer for you."

Maggie was growing anxious as they left the restaurant for the store.

At the checkout, the first person they went to was a tall man in a battered cowboy hat paying for toothpaste and shampoo. Maggie asked for his help.

"Sure, darlin'." His smile faded as he realized Graham was with her. "Just got in from Denver, I'm beat, but go ahead, show me your pictures."

The cowboy looked at the updated photos and scratched his whiskers.

"Now, tell me again. Who's asking and what's this about?"

"I'm his wife and he's with our son. I need to talk to him."

"Whoa. I don't want to get involved in no family spat, you understand."

"Sir," Graham said, "no one's asking for that. Please, have you seen him?"

"And you would be?"

Graham told him.

"Police?" The man handed the picture back. "I'm not so sure."

"Sir, this lady's just trying to find her little boy."

"I've seen that man in your picture," another voice said.

Maggie, Graham and the cowboy turned to the clerk,

a girl in her twenties with a small diamond stud in her pierced right nostril.

"Sorry," she said, "I overheard you and peeked."

"You saw Jake Conlin?" Maggie was hopeful.

"His name's not Jake. It's Burt Russell."

"How do you know that?" Graham wrote it down.

"That's him in your picture. I held truck magazines for him a couple of times. He said his name was Burt Russell. He comes in every couple of weeks."

"You have anything with his name on it, a credit-card receipt, check, an order, anything with proper spelling or an address?"

"No, he's a cash customer."

"Any idea where he lives?"

The girl shook her head.

Encouraged by the lead, Graham used a public landline phone to call Reg Novak, his friend in D.C., to query Montana Highway Patrol and the FBI's National Crime Information Center.

"Can you run the name Burt Russell, and variations on the spelling, through state motor vehicle records. He might be the RO of a large truck."

"Give me some time to make a request," Novak said. "You're running up a big tab with me. Going to cost you Flames tickets if I ever get out your way."

"You've got a deal, Reg."

Graham and Maggie found a booth in the restaurant.

After they ordered breakfast, Maggie went to the restroom. Waiting alone, Graham glimpsed morning headlines about that day's papal visit to Montana.

As the sun rose, a new concern dawned on him.

What if Ray Tarver's conspiracy story was remotely valid?

What if Jake Conlin and the pope's visit to Montana were linked?

Graham paged through his notes from his interview in Washington with Tarver's reporter friend, Kate Morrow. Before he died, Tarver's ex-CIA source had told him about intelligence out of Africa on plans for a *"large-scale attack being planned for a major target."*

But the information was vague, like countless other threats.

Walker, the Secret Service agent protecting the pope, knew all about Tarver's theories. Graham kept turning pages. Walker said Tarver *"lived in a fantasy world with other conspiracy nuts."* Walker had chased Tarver's leads, which in the end, *"turned out to be jackass theories."*

Yes, but given today's events, shouldn't he pass his info to Walker? Walker's card was in Graham's notebook. He tapped it, wondering if Arnie Danton had applied luminol to Tarver's campsite yet. Graham needed to know the result.

If the Tarver deaths were truly an accident, then his boss, Stotter, was right.

He'd been traveling the U.S. on a wild-goose chase.

Graham ran his hand over his face, then called Walker's cell phone.

He got his voice mail and left a message.

Leaving the restroom, Maggie was stopped by something she hadn't noticed before. Outside Barney's, the second restaurant, the painter's drop sheet that had covered the entrance wall yesterday was gone, revealing a gallery of people.

Photographs of men, women and children were tacked to a corkboard headed, Birthday Blasts At Barney's. Maggie was drawn to scores of glowing faces and searched them until she came to a pair of eyes that pierced her.

Logan.

She gasped and touched his face.

He was smiling, but something was not right.

In the same picture, she saw Jake. So different. Bald head. Goatee. A half smile. On the table before them, a cake with the words, *Happy Birthday, Samara.*

Who was that?

A woman was also in the picture, seated with Jake and Logan. Midthirties, dark hair, beautiful. Maggie caught her breath.

The other woman.

Maggie studied her, looked hard into her eyes. They were deep, intelligent, giving off a fierce light of defiance.

Maggie leaned closer, almost squaring off with her.

67

Great Falls, Montana

Graham was concerned when Maggie returned to their booth.

"You look pale," he said. "What is it?"

"We're so close."

Maggie handed him the birthday snapshot. He studied it just as the waitress brought their food. They had nearly finished eating when Graham's cell phone rang.

"It's Novak with your info. You got my hockey tickets?"

"Man. I owe you."

Montana's DMV records showed Burt Russell's residence as 10230 Crystal Creek Road, Cold Butte, Montana. Graham unfolded his state map, and drew an X on the spot east of Great Falls, between Petroleum and Garfield counties.

"A two-and-a-half-hour drive, give or take. Let's check out of the motel and get moving."

In the parking lot, a stranger was ducking down

between their rental and another car, a white sedan. It looked like the man had been tinkering with Graham's car.

"Excuse me. Can I help you?" Graham squinted in the morning sun.

The man stood. His attention bounced from Graham to Maggie and back. He gripped a steel tire iron in his right hand, rotated it slowly. He was Graham's height, but thinner. Clean-shaven with short dark hair, dark eyes and an angular face that bordered on menacing, until he smiled.

"No. Thank you. I'm almost finished. Flat tire." His accent suggested he was British, or European. As Maggie and Graham got in, Graham noticed the man's open trunk had four plastic fuel cans. Odd, he thought.

As they pulled away, Graham turned to Maggie.

"Write this down." He recited the stranger's Montana plate, make, color of his car and a description of the man, time and location.

"Why?"

"A cop habit."

"Good thing. I think I saw that guy on our plane. Small world, huh?"

Graham saw her nervous smile but did not return it.

"Too small, maybe."

There were no messages at the motel, which puzzled Graham. Nothing from Arnie, or Stotter even. Before leaving, Graham went online and extended his wireless access service for his laptop. Maggie used the motel computer to print off all she could on Cold Butte in Lone Tree County. After paying for their rooms, they asked the manager for directions out of Great Falls.

"Cold Butte? You going to see the pope like everybody else?"

Maggie shot Graham a look. Neither of them had gotten around to reading details of the papal visit to Montana.

"I thought he was visiting Great Falls?" Graham said.

"Lands here, then goes to bless a shrine out near Cold Butte. Good luck getting out there. I expect traffic will be bad and security's tight as a rusted nut."

Unspoken tension mounted in the car as they crossed the 10th Avenue Bridge over the Missouri River and headed east out of the city. Traffic flowed well on U.S. Highway 87. Maggie studied the *Tribune*'s reports on the papal visit.

"Are you going to tell me what's going on, Graham? Because I'm getting scared."

"We only learned of Jake's link to Montana about twenty-four hours ago."

"You lied to me. Tarver was chasing a story about a plot, or attack, wasn't he?"

"I did not lie to you, I can't discuss every aspect of a case."

"I have a right to know. Jake drove in Iraq. Something happened to him there. Now he's living in Cold Butte, *where the pope's going to be.* I know that big rigs, tankers, trailers, can be used as weapons. If someone wanted to hijack, or trick him, he's— *Please, no, my God, he's got Logan with him!*"

"Maggie! Stop imagining the worst and listen to me."

"I know my husband's unstab—not been himself— since he returned."

"Maggie, stop this."

"Can you discuss this aspect of *your case*." She held up the birthday snapshot. "Who is she?"

"I don't know. Listen, Maggie, Ray Tarver dealt with theories based on fragments of truth. He never had all the facts and he was always wrong. Some people believe he may have fabricated things."

"Then why are you here?"

She'd stopped him cold.

"You lied. This isn't about *insurance,*" she said. "You think Tarver was murdered, don't you?"

Graham turned to the sky and the plains.

"All I know is that we both need to see this through."

About twenty minutes east of Lewistown, traffic slowed to a crawl. Maggie consulted her pages for the school number in Cold Butte. It was large and served the tricounty area. It was a good bet Logan would be enrolled there. According to the *Tribune,* the school was involved in the pope's visit.

The paper had published an agenda for the event.

Maggie called the school.

Static hissed on the line as it rang four times before it was answered. Maggie spoke quickly, pleading for help to locate Logan. The annoyed school assistant on the phone had trouble comprehending her above the din of people talking, shouting and public announcements. The line crackled, the connection was tenuous.

"I said he might be listed as Logan Russell. Here's his birthdate."

"I'm sorry, I can hardly hear you."

"Please, if I could just talk to a teacher and explain.

I may lose you, take my number, please. Can you find a teacher, please?"

"Sorry, it's impossible to help you today because of the pope. Maybe tomorr—"

"No, wait!"

The line died. Tears stung Maggie's eyes as the traffic ground to a stop.

"Try again," Graham said.

Before she could, her cell phone rang. *The school calling back?*

"Maggie Conlin," she said.

"Mom?"

Maggie's face went white.

"Logan! Is that you!?"

"I miss you, Mom." The line was breaking, his voice was far away, so weak, so distant, clawing at her heart. "Mom, Dad said he misses you, too."

"Oh, Logan, I love you! I love Daddy! He's just confused."

"Mom, I want to come home, I—" Their connection buzzed.

"Where you are? I'm coming as fast as I can! Honey, just tell me!"

The line sizzled. The call was lost.

Maggie groaned to the sky.

68

Cold Butte, Montana

Logan woke with his heart racing.

He was a little scared because of something Billy Canton had said about the entire world watching them today.

The entire world. Man, oh, man.

But meeting the pope wasn't the only reason Logan was nervous. He had to carry out his plan when the time was right. Okay, first things first. He glanced out his window wondering if his dad had...

Yes!

Logan saw his dad's red truck. He'd got back in time like he'd promised.

Logan's anxiety turned to excitement as he hurried to his dad's bedroom door. It was open slightly, offering a sliver view of his arm hanging over the side. Logan was about to enter when he was suddenly pulled away.

"Let him sleep," Samara whispered and shut the door. "He got in late."

"But he's coming, right?" he whispered.

Samara pushed him gently toward the kitchen.

"Absolutely. He's going to join us later at the school."

"Will there be time?"

"Yes. Don't worry. One of the other fathers will pick him up. Come, I've made your favorite, bacon and eggs. When you're done, get washed up and put on your suit. We have to leave very soon. I'm going to get ready."

As he ate, Logan noticed the smell of fried bacon mixed with cleaning soap, like the floor had just been washed. Weird. When he heard the shower start he looked down the hall at the closed bathroom door.

Good.

He glanced at the TV with the sound turned low.

Local stations out of Billings were running live coverage of the visit. They showed live pictures of Logan's school, the crowds, reports of the pope before massive stadium crowds in cities he'd already visited.

On top of the TV Logan saw Samara's purse. Her cell phone was inside.

Now was the time.

If he couldn't reach his mom on their phone here, maybe he could reach her on Samara's cell phone. Just one call. Keeping an eye on the bathroom door, Logan plucked the phone from Samara's purse. He pressed his home area code and number. He waited for the connection, praying that in seconds, he would hear his mom's voice.

He nearly burst, before his heart sank.

His call didn't go through. He tried again. It didn't work. The battery level was good. He tried again. Nothing. What was he doing wrong? Maybe he should wake Dad for help? After their talk he'd let him call, wouldn't he? Things were getting better. Weren't they?

Logan looked at the bedroom door.

Hold it.

He'd forgot to press 1 for long distance.

Logan tried it again. Good. It was working this time. There was lots of noise on the line like a thunderstorm of static but it was ringing and ringing. It clicked and Logan caught his breath.

"Maggie Conlin," she said.

"Mom?"

"Logan! Is that you!?"

"I miss you, Mom." Static filled the silence. "Mom, Dad said he misses you, too."

"Oh, Logan, I love you! I love Daddy! He's just confused."

"Mom, I want to come home, I—" Their connection buzzed.

"Where you are? I'm coming as fast as I can! Honey, just tell me!"

The call went dead.

The shower stopped.

Logan switched off the phone, placed it back in Samara's purse, his entire body tingling.

He'd talked to Mom!

He'd have to figure out a way to try again later, he thought as he brushed his teeth, washed up, then put on his suit. His dad had already knotted the tie for him. Combing his hair at the mirror, Logan wished his dad would wake up.

The suit was comfortable. It looked pretty cool.

"Oh, you look so handsome," Samara said when Logan stepped into the living room, where she'd been working on her computer. "Come, quickly." She stood and grabbed her camera. She looked pretty. Almost like a model in her new suit. "Here. Let me take some pictures to share with my friends." She stood him before a plain wall, studied the camera settings and took several frames. "Everyone will be so proud. Don't move. Wait a few seconds."

They waited.

"Nice," she said. "Now some of us together."

Pleased, Samara then fixed the camera to a tripod, set it, then joined Logan. Not only did she look nice, she smelled good, too. Like flowers, Logan thought, as the camera flashed and automatically fired off several more frames of them together.

She checked them on her laptop, waiting a moment. "Good."

Samara set to work downloading the pictures into her computer.

"What about Dad?"

"What about him? He's still sleeping." Samara was typing rapidly on her keyboard. Her attention was on her computer work.

"Don't we need pictures with him, too?"

"Sorry." She glanced at the live TV coverage of the visit, then back to her computer as if she were rushed. "Sorry. No, we'll take more with him at the school with the pope."

Logan went to her, to see what was so important on the computer. She didn't mind him looking over her shoulder. Samara was checking her copy of the official program for the pope's visit—it looked like a minute-by-minute breakdown. He noticed she'd run a cable from the TV to her laptop, so some coverage was playing live on her screen. Then he saw pictures of Samara under a palm tree in Iraq with her son and husband. Then he saw the photos she just took of himself in his new suit, and her.

"What's all this? What're you doing?"

Samara's eyes widened and she smiled.

"Logan, we're taking part in the honor of a lifetime. I want to share it on the Web with my friends around the world. Almost done."

Samara entered codes and commands.

A small timer emerged and started counting down.

"All right. Done."

Samara left her computer on with all of her programs running, picture, timers, live news coverage.

"Let's go—we have to get over to the community hall for our briefing and checks before they take us to the school."

She got another camera from her bag.

"Is that a new one?" Logan asked.

"Yes, a very special one I want to use at the school." Samara lowered herself to Logan and smiled. "Who could ever have imagined this? Very soon, we are going to be meeting one of the most powerful people on earth. You and I will have a place in history, Logan. Soon everyone in the world will see our faces and speak our names."

"They'll say our names? But why?"

"Because we'll be part of history."

69

"**D**id the number come up? Call back," Graham said.

Maggie checked. No number. She hit the call-back feature, got a busy signal. Graham passed her his notebook with the DMV info for Burt Russell, pointing. "Try this number."

The line rang, then an automated response. The number was not in service. Maggie tried the school. That line was busy.

"Damn, damn, damn!" she said.

The rental's engine roared as Graham wheeled hard into the right shoulder. The line of jammed cars, vans, RVs, charter buses, pickups blurred by them as he raced for nearly a mile before a siren sounded.

A Montana Highway Patrol car appeared in his rearview mirror, light bar flashing. In the distance behind it, Graham saw a white sedan following the police car. Traffic cops hated queue jumpers and the lemming effect they inspired.

At a junction just ahead, several Montana Highway Patrol cars had established a choke point where patrolmen were diverting some traffic to secondary roads. One spoke into his shoulder mike, stepped in Graham's path and leveled a finger at him.

Graham stopped.

Three patrolmen, including the one in pursuit, un-strapped their holsters as they approached, ordering Graham and Maggie to put their hands on the dash. Far behind, the white sedan slipped unnoticed back into the traffic line.

Graham cooperated as they studied his badge and Maggie's California license.

Moe Holman, the most senior patrolman and a chronic gum-chewer who'd worked the border at Coutts and Sweetgrass, recognized Graham from years gone by. He'd handle it, he told the others and waved Graham out, taking him aside.

"Hi, Moe."

The men shook hands.

"Key ripes, Daniel, what the hell're you doing? Your passenger's a long way from home and you've got no authority to drive like a sinner. The pope's not going to save you from my ticket."

Graham explained that he and Maggie just needed to get to an address in Cold Butte to check on her boy; it was a pressing domestic matter related to Graham's multiple death case, and that Graham had alerted the FBI in Billings.

Gum-snapping, Holman nodded between traffic calls on his radio. The last thing his crew needed now was more work. The pope deal had them stretched. He let Graham go ahead with a warning, radioed his okay to troopers down the line.

"Drive safely, Daniel. Got a lot of folks filled with the spirit today."

Traffic moved faster as Graham and Maggie left the junction, continuing east for Lone Tree along the two-lane highway that sliced across Montana's midway point.

Maggie fought tears as she tried to reconnect with Logan and the school. Her fingers shook each time she pressed the numbers. Phone service was sporadic, strained by the heavy call volume related to the visit.

No luck.

She kept trying.

Graham made good time swinging into the oncoming lane, passing when it was clear. At a rare, sweeping curve, he fell into line among several slow-moving rigs when a car blazed by them at high speed.

A white sedan.

"That idiot's going way too fast." Graham shook his head. "We're almost there."

He handed Maggie detailed maps for Cold Butte and began discussing a plan. She touched one finger on the school, one on Crystal Creek Road then jumped in her seat as the rig ahead blasted its air horn.

"Oh, God!"

In an instant the rig's brake lights glowed, its trailer veered to the shoulder, stones peppered the car; the truck bucked, something emerged at terrifying speed through smoking rubber.

Something bearing down directly on Graham and Maggie!

Maggie covered her face for the impact as Graham's training took over; he tapped the brake, swerved to the shoulder. A blinding force whipped by within inches of hitting them and the rig behind them.

Graham glimpsed the white car, a missile in his rearview mirror. It launched cleanly off the highway, airborne for some thirty feet before smashing into the grassy plain, rolling end over end, swallowed by a dust cloud that spat fragmenting metal and glass before emitting a thud then a fireball, and a black column that billowed skyward.

The driver in the rig ahead grabbed his fire extinguisher and ran to the car, followed by Graham and the truck driver from the rig behind them. They got within twenty yards when the air split—thwack-boom thwack-boom thwack-boom—as lightning explosions released concussion waves that forced the men to the ground.

The air reeked of gas and melting plastic. Flames and heat engulfed the overturned car, leaving the men helpless to get closer.

"Christ almighty, there are two people in there!" one of the truckers said. "No way they'll survive!"

As the car burned, sirens sounded. Soon, Montana Highway Patrol cars, a deputy sheriff, two firetrucks and an ambulance had arrived.

Water hissed as firefighters doused the blaze.

Moe Holman shook his head at the carnage. "We're going to need this stretch of road to investigate. People stuck way back there will not see the pope. I'm telling you, today just keeps getting better."

His radio crackling, Holman looked at the traffic as his people tried controlling it.

"You really think he was coming at you?" Holman

said to Graham and the truck drivers as he took notes. "Sounds crazy. Maybe he had a seizure?"

"Seizure, my ass." One trucker spit and nodded to Graham. "Looked to me like he was gunning for you, like some dang fool kamikaze."

Graham noticed Maggie off by herself, kneeling on the grass, and went to her. She was looking at a warped object.

"What is it?"

Without touching it, she pointed at a twisted piece of charred metal, the remains of a Montana license plate and a rental logo framed around it.

"It's the guy we just saw in the truck stop parking lot." She checked her notes. "Maybe the same guy on the plane. And I think I saw him watching us in the restaurant in Las Vegas." She looked at Graham. "What's happening?"

"Get in the car. Keep trying your calls."

Graham got Moe Holman's attention and the two men talked alone.

"Moe, it's possible the fatalities in this car are linked to my case and maybe an unconfirmed, uncorroborated threat."

Holman's gum chewing ceased in mid-chew.

"Here? Against the pope?"

"Could be."

"By who and what means?"

"I don't know."

"We never heard anything about this at the briefings this morning. No lookouts, or anything. Maybe you got it confused with the Seattle business yesterday."

"What Seattle business?"

"All I'd heard is they detected some kind of security breach in Seattle. I heard they took care of it but are keeping a lid on the details. Don't think it even got into the press yet. They don't tell us, we're just traffic control."

Graham considered what Holman said.

"What're you holding back from me on your case, Daniel?"

"My case may be related to some raw intelligence out of Africa."

"Africa? What the hell else do you know?"

"A reporter from Washington, D.C., following the story was recently killed, along with his family, while camping near Banff. Looked accidental but we're not certain."

"What? Do you know these people in the car?"

"No. When you run the plate and get a name, alert the FBI and the people on the pope's security detail. Ask for Secret Service Agent Blake Walker. Give him my cell number."

"Count on it. But I'd bet my left one the feds will call me first for everything we've got on this crash. I'll tell them what you said." Holman nodded toward a military helicopter patrolling above the crash. "They've restricted the airspace for the pope's chopper from Great Falls to Cold Butte. The show's going to start soon."

"I need to go," Graham said. "You have what you need from me."

"Could you hold off so I can send someone with you. Make me feel better."

"How long?"

"Until we get things under control here. We can't spare anyone at the moment."

"I want to go now, Moe."

Holman's radio crackled. A busload of pilgrims from South Dakota had hit an RV near Sand Springs. No serious injuries, just another traffic headache.

"This is what happens when the state's population triples and everyone decides to visit your backyard for the day."

Holman resumed chewing, waved Graham off, then spoke into his radio.

To make up for lost time, Graham drove as fast as the line of traffic would permit.

He used every gap to cut in, waving apologies to drivers he'd cut off. He tried calling Walker but his phone couldn't get through. Maggie studied maps and tried calls in vain.

When Cold Butte lay ahead, Graham's phone rang.

"Dan, it's Stotter. Where are you?" Static filled the line. "Graham? Can you hear me?"

"Still in Montana. At Cold Butte. Before you tear into me—"

"Cold Butte? All right. Listen, something's come up. Arnie Danton did a luminol test at the scene and found blood near the river. I know we should've scoped it before. Arnie said it would've got by us if not for your hunch."

"Did he find a weapon?"

"Maybe a rock. Bang them on the head, put them in the canoe. Would've been consistent with the river. Damn near perfect." Stotter's other line rang. "We've still got some lab work to do, so stay put and stay tuned."

"Wait! Mike, I need help. You've got to reach Special

Agent Blake Walker. He's Secret Service with papal security down here. Advise him on Jake Conlin, aka, Burt Russell. Montana DMV has him. He could be with an unidentified female and a child, male. If Tarver was murdered, it gives credence to his conspiracy story."

"We're on it."

As Graham and Maggie got nearer, the traffic flowing into the small town slowed to a near standstill. People had pulled their cars off the highway to park on the grass. They opened trunks and side doors, emptied rooftop racks, collected lawn chairs, coolers, blankets, banners, placards.

Welcome Holy Father, Montana Loves The Pope.

In some cases, groups of men and teenaged boys were carrying elderly people in wheelchairs.

Approximately every twenty or thirty yards there was a volunteer or a uniformed officer directing everyone in steady, peaceful streams toward the school and Buffalo Breaks, site of the shrine where the pope would celebrate Mass for thousands.

"We've got to split up," Graham said. "You get to the school, ask for Special Agent Blake Walker. I'll find the house on Crystal Creek Road."

Before Maggie got out, she took Graham's hand, squeezed it hard and looked into his eyes. There was so much she wanted to tell him but there was no time.

"Go find your son," he said.

Her chin crumpled. She nodded, then hurried into the crowd as helicopters thundered above them in the eternal prairie sky.

Time was ticking down.

Book Six:
Death Signal

70

Montana

Thirty thousand feet above the snow-tipped Bitterroot Mountains, jet fighters from Montana's Air National Guard met the pope's plane.

Special Agent Walker broke from working on his computer to watch from his starboard window as four F-16s assumed protection from the four aircraft of the ANG's Washington Wing.

The lead Montana fighter tipped his wing as welcome and soon after, the formation began its descent to Great Falls International Airport.

They were less than twenty-five minutes out when Walker and the other agents on board were simultaneously e-mailed with classified updated situation reports.

Walker scrolled through the bulletins. The investigation of the border penetration at the Juan de Fuca Strait indicated involvement of a vessel from Yemen: *Preliminary analysis of suspicious items washed ashore showed them to include a "potentially volatile" but as yet unidentified substance. Nothing conclusive to con-*

stitute a national threat or link to other cases. Urgent investigative analysis was ongoing and led by a specialized new unit working with the Chemical Biological Incident Response Force.

Update on the complaint of a mysterious explosion claiming three white-tailed deer—according to the number of hooves found—near Malmstrom AFB: *The specialized unit had responded. Priority given to the ongoing investigation. Accidental detonation was ruled out. "Substance involved yet to be identified." Investigators with the unit note concern as the area is indicative of a "planned test."*

FTO update: *U.S. and foreign intelligence agencies report that chatter of foreign terrorist organizations continues at an "unusually high level."*

As the pope's plane neared Great Falls, Hank Colby, the Special Agent in charge of the detail, called Walker and the other agents to the back for a private huddle.

"A heads-up. The White House is talking about pulling the plug on the Montana visit, possibly Chicago, too."

"Now? At this stage? Do they know something we don't?"

"They're extremely uncomfortable with the situation and the fact none of the ongoing incidents has been reconciled with the intel obtained from Issa al-Issa. The data concerning hidden cells in the U.S. developing a major strike during the papal visit is making senior staff anxious."

"Has something been corroborated?" Walker asked.

"Not that we know. Could be that the NSA or State picked up something hot," Colby said. "The Secret

Service brass have been summoned to the Oval Office. The White House is leaning on the CIA, Homeland and the Intelligence Division to nail down some answers now so they can press the Vatican to agree. If this is political, it's beyond us."

The pilot came over the public address and requested everyone to return to their seats and buckle up for the landing.

"Until we're told otherwise," Colby said, "the visit continues as planned."

In keeping with presidential or VIP landings, a Temporary Flight Restriction had been issued for the Great Falls International Airport, closing it to all traffic but the papal aircraft.

A Montana Highway Patrol helicopter patrolled the space immediately above the landing field. On the ground, a range of VIP and emergency vehicles waited. All roads to the airport had been sealed and all activity at the facility had been halted.

Two fighters roared over the runway at rooftop level several minutes before the pope's jet landed.

A line of Secret Service, military, state and local emergency vehicles followed it as it taxied to a far ramp.

Walker saw the line of local dignitaries waiting to welcome the Holy Father. Some fifty yards beyond them and behind a cordoned area with a heavy police presence, were several thousand people.

They cheered as history unfolded before them. The pope emerged from his jet, the first pope ever to walk on Montana soil.

The Holy Father smiled and waved as he was greeted by the archbishop, the governor, the mayor and a long line of local officials. After making a short address before the group, the pope was escorted to a large military helicopter.

Within minutes it lifted off, along with four others carrying security, Vatican, international press and support personnel to Lone Tree County. The entourage would meet the advance teams and crews already onsite.

Walker ensured his seat belt was secure.

This was shaping up to be the longest day in his life.

71

Indian Head, Maryland

Some twenty miles south of Washington, D.C., in southern Maryland, Tony Takayasu's team worked against time.

In a redbrick lab, tucked in a wooded corner of the military base that overlooked the Potomac River, they applied Takayasu's suppositions.

What if the mysterious liquid smuggled off the west coast was linked to the explosion in Montana? And what if the substance found in the bottles was a component of the unknown explosive used to kill the deer? The liquid was labelled as Nigerian. The flag's fabric was a weave common to East Africa.

These were the theories Takayasu had put to his colleagues on the flight from Malmstrom and, upon landing at Indian Head, they began working on them.

Employing test after test. It took hours but they learned that the flag was more than just cotton fabric from a weave common to the Ethiopian highlands. It had been engineered with molecular nanotechnology. It was permeated with a new explosive liquid substance that could be detonated through the millions of nano radio receptors.

The process was invisible and undetectable by sniffer dogs, swabs, scopes and scanners. It rendered the fabric a powerful explosive that could be detonated at will through a complex, coded, superlow frequency signal. Theoretically, that signal could be sent from a few feet away, or through wireless transmission from anywhere in the world.

It was a perfect weapon.

To test their work, the team tried to replicate the explosion with the recovered components. They set up in the Naval Ordnance Station in an isolated location. They'd affixed a piece of the fabric over a watermelon suspended in netting from a tree. A happy face had been drawn on the melon.

With laptops displaying mathematical calculations and chemical formulas, the team had programmed a digital camera. Through a small open observation window behind a blast shield, Takayasu used the auto focus and snapped a photo from forty yards away.

Seconds passed without a reaction—twenty, thirty, forty, then a full minute.

Nothing happened.

"Tony, I don't think the fabric's aligned with the focus beam," Karen Dyer said, "I'll move it."

As she left the shield and walked to the watermelon, Ron Addison, one of the team's scientists, held his open hand to Takayasu. "Maybe it's the camera, Tony, let me check."

While Addison inspected the camera, Takayasu verified readings on one of the laptops. As Karen was about to touch the melon, Addison raised the camera to his eye to photograph her just as Takayasu was alarmed by a reading on the computer.

"Ron, no!" Takayasu seized the camera. "Karen! Get away! Don't touch it!"

Karen returned to the shield.

"Look at these readings."

The team huddled around his laptop. "Now, let's try it." With his team safe behind the shield, Takayasu snapped a second picture—*crack!*—the air rippled, the shield shuddered as meaty chunks of the melon splattered against it.

For several long seconds the group stood in stunned silence.

"My Lord." Karen's face went white.

"We need to make a lot of calls. Now!" Takayasu said.

72

Lone Tree County Fairgrounds, Montana

Samara drove some two miles outside of town to the fairgrounds.

Situated on an unbroken stretch of short grass, the grounds consisted of a cluster of pavilions—metal and wooden buildings that were used for horse, cattle, needlework and baking shows. Nearby, the soupy dirt infield of the rodeo park served as the site of bucking horse and demolition derby competitions, crowd-pleasers that filled the grandstands.

Today, the grounds were making history as the marshaling point for the pope's visit.

Scores of police and emergency vehicles were gathered here as radio cross talk filled the air. In minutes, the Holy Father's helicopter would land in the rodeo park.

"Look!"

Logan glimpsed the waiting popemobile amid a perimeter of dark security vans.

"Wow."

After their passes were scrutinized, Samara and

Logan were permitted to park. Then they followed the posted signs and trekked across the grounds to Cowboy Exhibition Hall, where those taking part in the school portion of the visit would be briefed.

A burst of abrupt barking greeted them when they entered the hall.

Three police dogs were at the far end among a dozen armed officers, waiting at walk-through metal detectors and other security equipment set up on tables. The dogs and radios echoed against the building's metal walls.

Samara eyed them carefully and swallowed hard.

"Those dogs are going to sniff our butts," Billy Canton said to Logan.

A few of the other boys in the choir giggled.

Samara nodded to the other parents and teachers who were holding cameras and nervous smiles. She estimated three hundred people were gathered here. On the stage, talking and consulting notes were Father Andrew Stone, the choir director, the principal, a few other priests and men in suits who had to be Secret Service.

"Everyone, if I could have your attention!" Father Stone called above the din. "Pretty exciting, right, guys?"

A cheer went up.

"Right, a blessed day." Father Stone smiled. "With me is Father Rosselli, from the Vatican, who assists the Holy Father. Before I turn it over to him, there are a few things we have to cover quickly. Now, a zone is reserved for all of you for the pope's Mass and blessing in the Buffalo Breaks. We'll walk down after the school event. When we are done here, everyone must pass through security, then on to the school buses that will take us to the school and more security."

He smiled at the groans.

"You can't get to heaven without going through security. Okay. We know the agenda. A few greetings to the pope, we sing two songs. The Holy Father speaks and blesses the school. We sing a closing song. Father Nicco Rosselli will give you some important points requested from the Vatican."

"Thank you, Father Stone." The parents loved his Italian-accented English. "When the choir is assembled, the Holy Father may come to you and say a few words to help you relax before you sing."

A few parents laughed.

"When you are done, he will thank each of you personally and invite you to make a procession to his chair where he will personally give each of you, one by one, a small gift. For the sake of time, please do not open it there. Thank His Holiness and exit. The gift is a very nice blessed rosary. Our staff will help coordinate the procession so it moves quickly. Remember, we have about one hundred and twenty thousand people waiting for him in the Buffalo Breaks to honor Sister Beatrice. From the time you reach the Holy Father's presence until the time you leave with your gift, you will have six seconds. Parents, everyone, for pictures, we stress, six seconds for an opportunity that usually comes once in a lifetime. I trust you will have your cameras ready."

He held up his hands and smiled.

"Thank you very much and God bless you."

The briefing ended, then the security people took over.

They quickly organized everyone into orderly lines

that flowed through the security process, akin to going through an airport. Belts, jackets, shoes, cameras, everything was placed in plastic tubs and passed along the conveyor through the X-ray machine. People stepped through the walk-through metal detector; then they were hand-scanned and their items in the tub were swabbed.

The bomb-sniffing dogs patrolled along either side of the queue.

"Watch your butt," Billy Canton whispered to his friends.

Samara tried not to stare at the dogs as they neared her and Logan. She smiled when one arrived, sniffed her jacket then started sniffing her hand. Samara looked at the handler, the words *Secret Service* emblazoned on his vest, radio squawking. His eyes were cool to her as the dog moved on.

Then came their turn at the detectors.

Samara and Logan removed their jackets, shoes. Her camera went into the tub.

"You first, ma'am." A Secret Service agent waved Samara through.

Nothing beeped. A hand scanner was passed over her. Nothing beeped.

Samara noticed the intense eyes of the X-ray scanner operator as he read the screen with her camera. When it passed through, it was wiped with a swab. As Samara collected her jacket and shoes, she watched as the swab was removed and attached to an instrument on a computer for a chemical reading.

A spectrum of colors flashed on the monitor.

"You're fine," the female officer said.

A series of beeping alarms sounded behind her.

"Hold it right there, son!"

Two men with the letters *FBI* on their vests took Logan aside.

"Raise your arms, please."

Worried, Logan looked at Samara.

"Get on the bus, ma'am."

"But he's with me."

Agents passed a hand scanner over Logan. It sounded around his pants.

"Did you empty your pockets, son?"

Logan nodded.

The scanner sounded at the right pocket of his pants.

"Check again."

Logan reached in and withdrew the rosary his mother had given him.

"That's the culprit," the agent said. "Should've put it in the tub."

Logan exhaled.

"Get your things and get on the bus."

73

Cold Butte, Montana

Maggie forced her way through the crowd toward the school.

She scanned faces and body types, locking on to those resembling Logan or Jake, until they all blurred. For each passing second heightened her fear that something bad was going to happen as images swirled in her mind.

Jake after Iraq; Fatima's terrifying visions; the reporter and his family; Samara; the strangers; the crash; Logan's call.

Something horrible was taking shape.

Something terrible was coming.

Maggie kept moving but it was getting harder.

The air above her shook as another low-flying helicopter thundered by.

Her progress became mired.

The road to the school was cleared of traffic, bordered on both sides with police barriers to hold back crowds in lines four or five people deep and growing. Those farthest back strained for a view of the route.

The pope would pass by only a few feet away.

Electric anticipation was written on the faces of children, teenagers, men and women. Some older people prayed with closed eyes and rosaries entwined in fingers, their faces serene.

A smiling woman with a silver cross around her neck, and a large security tag identifying her as a nun, was moving along the police side of the barricades distributing programs to the crowd.

One was placed in Maggie's hand. She studied the events, times, names, pictures, and was drawn to the group photo of the children's choir that would sing for the pope inside the school.

The boy second from the right in the second row.

Logan.

Listed as Logan Russell.

Maggie stared in disbelief. Tears brimming, she called out.

"Excuse me!" She waved her program frantically, asking others to help her get the nun's attention. "Sister! Excuse me! Please, I have an emergency!"

Word was passed along and in seconds the nun returned, leaned toward Maggie as people shifted in place, allowing the two women to talk.

"Yes, how may I help?"

Finding Logan was Maggie's only thought, eclipsing Graham's instruction to locate Blake Walker, compelling her to lie her way closer to her son.

"My nephew's in the choir." Maggie tapped her finger to the program. "I've just arrived. I can't reach his parents on their phone. Do you know where the children are right now?"

The nun looked down the road to the school, about half a block away.

"See the school parking lot?"

Maggie followed her attention and saw the lot, along with more barricades, scores of police vehicles, officers, police dogs, metal detectors, news trucks and cameras.

"They're bringing them to the lot on a school bus with their parents." She glanced at her watch. "Any minute now. They'll go through the checkpoint, see? Then into the school. But I don't think you'll make it through the crowd in time. Ma'am?"

Maggie was not there.

She'd disappeared into the crowd.

As Maggie headed off, Graham spotted a county sheriff's SUV parked nearby and asked the deputy behind the wheel for directions.

"The fastest way to Crystal Road?" The deputy looked harried. "Hang tough a sec." He finished a call, racked his mike, turned away from the traffic and crowds to a vast empty sea of short grass in the opposite direction of the event.

"That's Pioneer Field. Your vehicle should clear it. Go across it, south, that way—" he pointed "—and you'll come up at a road and an old falling down homestead. Go left there for about a mile, then left again at the T-stop. That's Crystal. The place you want is six or eight miles out. Should be no traffic there."

A low-hanging dust trail followed Graham's car along the soft, wind-dried grass, the gently rolling terrain. He came to the homestead, went left to the

T-stop, then left again at a wooden signpost, blistered by sun and rain that said, Crystal Creek Road.

Graham accelerated, raising a billowing cloud as he roared down the empty stretch, punctuated every quarter mile by lonely postboxes, with names like Smith, Clark or Peterson painted on them, or displayed in crafted arches over gateposts that led to small houses, or faraway ranches.

Gravel popcorned against his undercarriage as he drove two miles, then three, then four. Five. No postbox with Russell, or Conlin. He studied each home he passed for a rig or trailer.

No luck.

On the horizon far behind him he saw the helicopters orbiting the papal site.

The odometer told him he'd gone seven miles, then eight.

Was he wasting time?

What if Maggie needed him at the school? Chances were slim his phone would work out here. Hands sweating on the wheel, he rounded a bend and a valley spread below him. Graham descended into it, sped by a stand of cottonwoods at a stream, then crossed a rail-tie bridge.

He climbed out of the valley to a bluff that overlooked it and the town and thought, one more mile and he'd turn around.

That's when he saw it in the distance.

A bright red rig, parked under the broad branches of a cottonwood tree, next to a small bungalow, the site rising like an island amid the windswept land.

The mailbox crowning the post leaning at the entrance bore a name printed on paper in marker, sun-faded and covered with clear plastic, fastened by duct tape that was surrendering its hold.

B. Russell.

The long grass lane reached some one hundred yards to the house, assuring anyone inside a clear view of anyone approaching. Graham expected that with a world event taking place a few miles away, no one would be home.

But he couldn't be certain unless he checked.

He continued down the lane with every measure of cop wisdom screaming that he was going about this all wrong.

74

Aboard the papal helicopter, over Montana

As the papal squadron of helicopters pounded east over the Great Plains, Walker's stomach roiled with dread.

In the wake of the latest situation reports, he feared he'd missed a key piece of data, something that could link the fragments of intelligence that were causing mounting concern in the White House.

Was a threat emerging?

As the world rushed beneath him in a patchwork of cattle ranches, wheat and barley fields, Walker racked his brain.

But it was futile.

The answer he sought was lost out there in the never-ending grassland.

As they neared Cold Butte, he glanced at the pope and his advisors looking down from their windows.

Mile after mile, traffic was gridlocked.

Walker caught a glimpse of smoke billowing from a fire and the flashing lights of emergency vehicles. Looked like a serious wreck due west of the town, maybe twenty miles.

Walker checked his BlackBerry. Montana Highway Patrol had just sent a preliminary report. Two fatalities. No IDs confirmed. Vehicle a rental. Investigation continues. MHP also reported a noninjury collision between a charter bus and RV. Walker had holstered his BlackBerry when it vibrated with a new message, a supplemental to the double fatal, addressed only to Walker.

The MHP note came with urgency, saying RCMP Corporal Graham needed to speak with Walker.

Graham?

Walker took a second to recall their meeting in his office.

The note said Graham needed to talk about his case.

That would be the Ray Tarver matter, Walker remembered. He'd had the Intelligence Division look into it, albeit grudgingly. They'd found nothing to support Tarver's grand conspiracy.

Walker had given Graham a hard time in D.C., so he'd give him a call. Give him one minute of his time.

Walker reached for his phone and dialed Graham's cell-phone number but couldn't get through.

He'd try again later.

75

Graham drove toward the house not knowing what he would face.

Given that the Tarvers had been murdered, that he and Maggie could've been killed in the suspicious car crash, every instinct told him to hold off.

He had no backup, no complaint history on the residence, no weapon, no radio, no jurisdiction and no choice but to keep going.

Besides, he really didn't care much about his own safety.

As his car came to a stop, he scanned the area for dogs, listening for the telltale jingle of a collar or chain as he got out.

"Hello!"

Nothing. He whistled. Still no sign of a dog.

The grass under his feet was worn to an earthen path to the house, a yellow double-wide with bone-white trim. It had flower boxes under the windows. The red-checked gingham curtains did not stir when he came to the side door and knocked.

No response. Nothing but the wind combing the grasslands.

He knocked again, listening for sounds of movement. Pressing his ear to the door. This time he heard a soft hum coming from inside.

The drone of a conversation.

He continued knocking with no response. It puzzled him because he could hear people inside talking.

"Hello!"

He walked around the outside of the house to the rear, coming to a small deck and patio doors. They were open to what Graham figured was a living room, judging from the view the curtains allowed each time a breeze fluttered.

He heard people talking in the house.

Graham cupped his face against the screen and called inside.

No response.

The prairie winds pushed the faint tapping of the distant helicopters across the plain while he peered into the house. It took a moment for his eyes to adjust to the darkened interior. Looking directly through the immediate room, down a hallway, he saw a door.

It was partly open.

Enough to frame an arm draped from a bed.

"Hello! I'm Corporal Graham of the Royal Canadian Mounted Police. I am checking on the welfare of Logan Conlin, or Logan Russell. Jake, Burt? Can you hear me? Can anyone hear me?"

The arm didn't move.

Someone sleeping? Passed out? Hurt?

A new sound.

Somewhere in the house a telephone began ringing. It rang six times then stopped. The person in the bed didn't move.

Under the circumstances, Graham believed he faced a life-and-death situation and drove his foot through the screen and entered. Knowing he could be taken for an intruder, he identified himself as he proceeded, his senses heightened.

The first room he entered was a living room with no one present.

Adjoining it was the kitchen.

Graham scanned everything quickly; the kitchen table was clear, clean. So was the counter. He glimpsed letters, bills, all addressed to Burt Russell. Graham passed the empty living room, a desk, a laptop, the TV—the source of the voices. Live news coverage of the papal visit. Before moving on to the occupied bedroom, he made a very fast sweep of the other rooms, calling out as he progressed.

The bathroom was empty.

The nearest bedroom was vacant except for cardboard boxes and a mattress against the wall.

The next bedroom was vacant but gave him pause.

Clothes scattered everywhere, small jeans, a T-shirt; next to the bed, a framed photo of Jake and Logan Conlin in front of a rig with the Rockies behind them. Jake was bald with a beard—aka *Burt Russell.*

As Graham moved to the occupied bedroom, the TV droned with a woman's voice. Graham was focused on the bedroom and did not comprehend the faint monologue that began:

"...I am Samara. I am not a jihadist..."

76

Lone Tree County Fairgrounds, Montana

Cold Butte came into view as the papal helicopter descended on the small town.

Below, traffic had swallowed the community. Walker and the others marvelled at the site for the outdoor Mass behind the school in the Buffalo Breaks.

A one-hundred-foot cross had been erected over the stage supporting the altar. The venue was in a valley offering a natural bowl. Walker had advanced the site several times when it was empty, checking vantage points and rises.

Now, over one hundred thousand people were gathered, awaiting the pope. His stomach lifted as the helicopter swooped and banked for landing at the Lone Tree County Fairgrounds.

After touching down in the rodeo park, the pope and Vatican officials were greeted by an assembly of local dignitaries. Afterward, papal security officials gathered behind closed doors in the main pavilion building.

Walker expected that they would first go through a very quick, final rundown of the pope's agenda for the visit, assignments and areas of joint and specific responsibility.

That didn't happen.

Colby was on his cell phone. He'd been receiving a steady stream of calls from Washington, the gravity of the latest developments weighing on his face as he waved Walker over to join him in a tight group of Vatican and security officials.

The heat of their ongoing debate was intense.

Monsignor Paulo Guerelli, one of the most important members of the pope's inner sanctum, was shaking his head.

"What Washington is suggesting is impossible based on the facts, Agent Colby."

"I am conveying White House concerns, Monsignor. Please understand that in light of the intelligence reports, it is regrettably but strongly advised the Vatican consider canceling today's events."

"Is there a clear threat that will result in harm to those around the Holy Father?"

"No, we cannot say that with absolute certainty."

"Have you found physical evidence or confirmation of some sort?"

"No, Monsignor, nothing conclusive yet, but urgent analysis is ongoing, arising from a number of disturbing incidents that have the White House concerned."

"Has the White House no confidence in its Secret Service?"

Colby let that one go. He was in the middle of a political firefight.

"Yes," Guerelli said, "these incidents. You're referring to the strange substances in Washington and here in Montana. And, the alleged plan for a strike extracted from Issa al-Issa."

"Correct."

"Have any of these incidents been linked?"

"No, not yet, but it's felt the risk is extreme."

Guerelli took a few seconds for consideration.

"Agent Colby, every time the Holy Father meets the public he faces risk," Guerelli said. "In Seattle, we had two incidents that appeared deadly but ultimately had no impact on the Holy Father's mission."

"Yes."

"The Holy Father has traveled the world and faced many threats. For some two thousand years the papacy has faced wars, attacks, assassination. It is not a weak institution that is easily frightened."

Colby ran his hand over his face.

"But, Monsignor."

"Your job is to protect the pope. Your team is doing it well. We request that you keep doing it in order for the Holy Father to complete his ecumenical work. Tell the White House we will now proceed. We're running behind and the Holy Father is eager to meet the children of the choir."

Guerelli and the other Vatican officials left to join the pope in a private room where he was reviewing his speech to honor Sister Beatrice.

"I don't like this." Lloyd Taylor, a senior agent, shook his head. "Think back to Dallas and how Kennedy refused the bubble on the car. Can we get a vest on him?"

Colby shook his head.

"We tried. He refuses it."

"To cancel now," Taylor said, "would not only dent the morale of the Secret Service, but it would embarrass the nation."

Colby nodded.

"It's beyond us. This administration is terrified. It would rather send the pope back to Rome pissed off than send him back in a coffin."

Colby called a quick last-minute briefing of all the senior security people. They went through the pope's itinerary and everyone's responsibility.

Then they secured him into the popemobile and marshalled the security vehicles.

Amid several streams of radio cross talk by the Secret Service, FBI, Lone Tree County sheriff's deputies and Montana Highway Patrol, the motorcade left the fairgrounds.

Walker was in the second SUV behind the command vehicle.

As the parade moved through streets lined with cheering crowds, his heart started beating faster.

77

Cold Butte, Montana

Struggling to get to the school, Maggie crunched a foot here, banged a shoulder there as she pinballed forward, refusing to be halted.

She was very near to Logan. She could feel it. Nothing could stop her.

A helicopter thudded by at low level going east to west. Then another. The excitement mounted. Maggie continued moving through the crowd, listening to fragments of reports spilling from radios tuned to live news coverage.

"...we're expecting the papal helicopter to land momentarily at the Lone Tree County Fairgrounds outside of town...the popemobile motorcade will take a three-mile route from the fairgrounds through the town of Cold Butte to the school...after he visits the school the pontiff will go directly behind it to the sweeping valley known as the Buffalo Breaks where he'll celebrate Mass for a crowd estimated at seventy-five thousand, no, an update, that's one hundred thousand....among the activities inside the school a children's choir will perform three songs for the pope...."

Maggie navigated her way to the edge of the school's boundary and as she looked through the crowd toward the parking lot she saw a flash of yellow.

A school bus fully loaded with parents and children had arrived at the barricaded checkpoint. Police and soldiers armed with M16s and wearing combat gear slowly guided it into the parking lot for inspection.

Two teams of sniffer dogs probed the bus while soldiers used extended mirrors to scrutinize the undercarriage, and under the hood. Their serious work contrasted with the ecstatic young faces in the bus windows exchanging joy and returning waves to the happy crowd.

The bus was some twenty yards away across the street from Maggie.

She thrust closer to the barricade, ignoring protests of people who had claimed their spots at sunrise.

She didn't care.

She pushed her concentration full bore from window to window to window.

She gasped.

Maggie screamed Logan's name before the cognitive process was done.

He was on the bus!

Waving and smiling from the window, just as he'd done a lifetime ago on the last day they'd been together at home. Only now, Logan hadn't seen Maggie yet.

"Logan!"

Maggie shoved through the crowd to the barricade.

"Hey, lady!"

"What the—"

"I have to get to my son, please let me through! Logan!"

"Where's she going? Call that officer! She's crazy!"

The passengers were directed to step off the bus for further inspection. They formed a neat line before entering the school. Parents were formally dressed, children wore their Sunday best—boys in blazers, white shirts and ties, girls in white dresses.

Stone-faced soldiers and police officers guided them through metal detectors, boys and girls extended their arms, removed shoes, jackets as security wands passed over them and dog handlers patrolled at close proximity.

Once he was cleared, Logan moved with the line toward a school entrance.

Maggie was going to lose him.

"Logan!"

He turned at the sound of shouts but did not see Maggie as she launched herself over the metal barricade, stumbled onto the cleared road and ran toward him calling his name.

People yelled to police and pointed.

At that moment, officers and soldiers rushed Maggie, reaching for their weapons. Radios crackled with rapid-fire transmissions. *Security breach Sector 27! We have a security breach at 27!* A Montana Highway Patrol helicopter turned and pounded toward the scene. TV news cameras wheeled, focused, capturing a hysterical woman running across the empty road to the school live on network television. A cameraman said calmly into his headset, "Alert New York, we've got something here." On the school roof, FBI sharpshooters advised that they had "the target" in the crosshairs of their scope and could drop it in a heartbeat.

"Standing by for green," one FBI shooter whispered

into his headset, then placed his finger on the trigger of his rifle.

A rookie Montana patrolman, who was a former tackle from Missoula, got to Maggie first. He took her to the ground hard. His six-foot-four-inch body covered hers and in one smooth motion he got one metal cuff on her right wrist.

The chopper whooped above.

Other officers swarmed the scene.

Standing there in his new blazer, Logan had witnessed the incident, but without recognizing that the woman at the center of it was his mother.

Maggie screamed for him, reaching through a forest of legs and boots toward him with her soon-to-be-cuffed left hand. But his eyes never found hers. The prop wash from the chopper was deafening, but Maggie saw a question form on his face just as a hand clamped his shoulder and turned him from her, nudging him into the school.

The hand belonged to the person in the picture in the truck stop restaurant.

Samara.

Across the chaos, the two women met in one intense gaze.

Anguished mothers from different worlds, heartbroken by events not of their making, willing to pay any price for their family. Samara's eyes were fixed with purpose, forged in some hellfire of unwavering love that burned into Maggie's.

"That woman abducted my son!" Maggie shouted. "She could threaten the pope! You have to arrest her! You have to alert Special Agent Blake Walker! Now! Logan!"

None of the deputies, troopers or agents understood Maggie over the chopper, let alone gave a second thought to her words.

To them *she* was the threat.

Maggie offered little resistance as they pulled her to her feet, told her of her rights as they completed hand-cuffing her hands in front of her.

"You have the right to remain silent…"

"Logan!"

As Samara entered the school with Logan, she took a deputy and a Secret Service agent aside and showed them several badges of identification.

"I'm a nurse with the county helping with this event," Samara said, then nodded to Maggie. "That woman is psychologically disturbed. She came to the school last week and indicated that she would 'get rid of the pope' if he ever came here."

The deputy and agent nodded as they copied Samara's ID information, took notes then reached for their microphones.

78

Indian Head, Maryland

Immediately after the test, Takayasu assigned team members to alert specialists in an array of fields with federal security agencies.

Calls from Takayasu's unit were rare, but when they came, they were given priority status. Today, they were deemed an "extremely urgent matter of national security." No effort was spared to contact the experts, who were reached at offices, homes, labs, airports, funerals and vacation resorts.

Encrypted password-coded files containing calculations, formulas and findings of the incidents at Pysht, Malmstrom and the test at Indian Head were instantly e-mailed and a teleconference call was convened from the lab's meeting room.

A quick round of introductions showed that the technical expertise on the line came from the highest levels of national security, such as the National Security Agency, the Central Security Service, Army Intelligence, NASA security, the Naval Security Group, members of the Computer Network Defense Red Team and others from Fleet Information Warfare Center.

Before Takayasu led the call, a question was put to him.

"Is this for real?" a man from the NSA asked.

"This is real and we have to move fast. We need to jam the signal, or hijack it with a disabling protocol. Can it be done?"

"We could do something with SDI technology, or, NSA or NASA satellites," another caller said.

"What's the target zone?"

"We believe the target zone is Lone Tree County, Montana," Takayasu said.

"That's where the pope's just landed. We're watching it live!" said one expert. "Didn't they already arrest some hysterical woman who breached security?"

"We're cutting this close! Just cancel the event," the Army Intelligence chief said.

"We've tried. The Vatican refused," a supervisor from the Secret Service Intelligence Division said. "The threat is not confirmed. And yesterday, in Seattle, we had two incidents we thought involved assassination attempts. Both were false alarms. The Vatican almost never cancels an event, even when a threat emerges. As we speak, the pope's got one hundred thousand people waiting for him in Montana."

"We think this new weapon's in play right now against the pope in Montana?" the CSS caller asked.

"Or his next stop in Chicago," the Secret Service caller said. "We're concerned about all the dots: the intel from Issa al-Issa, the intel about a ship, the material found on the coast and at Malmstrom. We can't risk this. We're down to minutes."

Everyone heard the clicking of a computer keyboard.

"Lone Tree County is two thousand two hundred twenty feet above sea level. Longitudinal and latitudinal position is— Hang on." One of the satellite experts on the line was doing the math. "Our best chance at this stage is to send a pulse. But we have to program the nearest bird."

"How long?" Takayasu said.

"Not sure, twenty minutes at least."

"This is going to be close."

"It might not work. And if it does, there's a huge risk that goes with it," the satellite expert said.

79

Cold Butte, Montana

Sirens yelped and emergency lights wigwagged as the papal motorcade made its way through Cold Butte.

Cardiac time again.

Walker was in the SUV among the lead vehicles preceding the papal car. Along the route he scanned the faces of people at the barricades, relieved the pope was not walking at the rope but waving from the moving popemobile.

It was safer.

After Seattle, security had been heightened.

The entire route had been swept seven times. K-9 teams had conducted building probes. Bridges, vantage points and streets were patrolled by deputies from five counties. Officers from the Great Falls, Lewistown and Billings police departments and the Montana Highway Patrol supported federal agents.

All were advised "to check everything again and jump on anything out of place! Anything!"

Four helicopters circled above. Three were security; one was the press pool for aerial news pictures.

Sharpshooters and spotters with binoculars were positioned on all rooftops overlooking the procession. Walker was grateful no building was taller than three stories. Skyscrapers were an assassin's dream.

Huge banners, along with U.S. and papal flags of all sizes, waved and rippled from the street sides. Cameras were ever-present. People smiled, called out to the pope. Some were enraptured, some prayed while news crews captured it all.

As the parade neared the school, Walker's cell phone vibrated against his chest.

"Blake, it's Jackson." The agent calling was out of breath. "We just had a breach on the street at the school. No weapons of any sort."

"What was it?"

"Lone, hysterical woman jumped the barricade, ran to the school as the choir kids arrived. She was screaming gibberish about an abducted kid. We grabbed her. According to a nurse at the school, our woman was here a few days earlier making verbal threats against the pope."

"You got it under control?"

"Yes, but the stranger thing is, the woman is asking for you. By name."

"Me? How does she know me? You get an ID?"

"Margaret Conlin, early thirties, from Blue Rose Creek, California."

Blue Rose Creek, California.

Something about it was familiar but Walker could not put his finger on it.

"She say why she's asking for me?"

"Don't know, she's a bit incoherent."

"Hold her in the command center truck. I'll take care of it after we get through this."

80

Cold Butte, Montana

Graham entered the bedroom in Jake Conlin's house.

Dim light splintered through shutters, casting the room in shadow.

A man lay on the bed; his face was turned.

"Jake Conlin!"

Graham touched the man's shoulder, his fingers found tacky wetness. Nothing moved. The darker shadows were blood-drenched sheets.

Jake Conlin's throat had been cut.

Graham retreated from the room, found a cordless phone. Carefully, he picked it up by the edge of its frame and used a pen tip to press 911.

"This is Lone Tree emergency, do you require police, fire or paramedics?"

"Police and paramedics to 10230 Crystal Creek Road."

"On their way. What is your emergency?"

"White male approximately thirty-five years of age. Deceased in an apparent homicide."

"Homicide? Out on Crystal Creek Road?"

"Yes. Are they rolling?"

"Sir, it will take a bit of time to reach your location. Stay on the line. I need your identification, sir."

Graham identified himself with his regimental number, then said, "Please listen carefully. I request that you immediately alert the Secret Service detail on papal security. And the FBI. This homicide could be related to the two traffic fatalities on Highway 87 east of Lewistown and a pending attack on the pope at Cold Butte."

"Repeat that, sir."

Graham did, then with his free hand he fished his cell phone from his pocket and tried to reach Blake Walker as he returned to the living room.

He'd glimpsed something here. What was it? Something repeating?

He couldn't reach Walker.

Staying on the phone with the dispatcher and searching the living room, he stared at the TV's live coverage then noticed the laptop on a desk. The computer was wired with a Web cam.

The screen was lit.

The machine was running a number of programs and features.

Walking toward it, he saw pictures of Samara, the same woman in Maggie's restaurant photograph with Jake and Logan.

But these photos were different.

She was with another man and another boy. They were happy, smiling. Joyous. Standing in front of a palm tree, standing in a public square, the entrance to a city.

Middle East? Baghdad, maybe?

Drop by drop, the awful realization fell on Graham as he got closer to the computer.

In one corner of the screen a small video was running, repeating itself in a continuous loop.

It was Samara.

Wearing a white hijab. As she stared back at Graham, her eyes burned.

"...I am not a jihadist..."

In seconds as Samara spoke of her pain and her vengeful plan, Graham recognized what he was viewing.

The "martyr's video" of a suicide bomber.

No!

Graham then noticed several cables wending from the back of the laptop to and through an open window. The cables continued outside to a tripod and a satellite dish. Inside, affixed to the cords just behind the laptop, there was a small box with an antenna. The box had several small blinking red and green lights, and a display window with red flashing numbers.

Graham's knees nearly buckled as the enormity landed on him.

All the spit in his mouth vanished and his stomach quaked.

Something would be activated from this laptop!

The small box was a timer clock.

It was counting down!

81

Cold Butte, Montana

The papal entourage arrived at the school.

The pope entered the foyer, where he first embraced Father Andrew Stone.

"God bless you, my brother." The pontiff smiled.

Brilliant light flashes rained on them as news cameras from around the world photographed the meeting.

"Welcome, Eminence." Stone introduced the pope to the line of local officials and school staff backed by hundreds of wildly happy students.

After small presentations and a brief tour, the pope entered the gym, triggering applause and camera flashes as TV crews jostled for angles.

Having hosted state basketball championships, the gymnasium was the largest in the region. But today it seemed small. Nearly eight hundred people in their Sunday best filled rows of folding chairs and bleachers, and crammed the balcony at the back.

Amid the clapping, Walker pressed on his earpiece while he responded to a radio status check and took stock of the venue.

The children in the choir were in place on the stage.

Uniformed police and newspeople lined the walls. FBI and Secret Service marksmen were concealed in strategic points throughout the gym. Federal agents in plain clothes had been inserted into the audience.

Special closed-circuit security cameras had been installed to watch the crowd. They were monitored from the command post truck parked among the scores of emergency vehicles encircling the building.

Walker and the other Secret Service agents took points at stage right and stage left.

Onstage, the pope stood at his chair, spread his hands and smiled to the audience, telegraphing his love.

Next came welcoming remarks from more local, county and state officials as the agents and security cameras continued scanning the crowd.

They were as ready as they would ever be, Walker thought and offered every cop's prayer.

Lord, please don't let anything happen on my watch.

82

Cold Butte, Montana

As the choir prepared, bits of information buzzed in the back of Walker's mind.

Yesterday's false alarms, the unconfirmed intel from Issa about a planned attack, the explosion at Malmstrom.

Did the pieces go together?

The traffic deaths, the call from Graham, the Mountie, still pursuing Tarver—*why call now?*—the security breach by the distraught woman. Something familiar.

From Blue Rose Creek, California.

She knew Walker's name. How could that be?

Walker began making a mental link. Didn't the Mountie go to California? Blue Rose Creek, California? Didn't Tarver's final wild theory concern a planned attack?

Walker's earpiece crackled.

"Agent Walker, this is Baker in command. Sir, please go to your cell phone now for a call patch from Lone Tree emergency dispatch."

"What? No, I can't take one now, pass it to—"

His response was ignored, his phone vibrated. He cursed then answered.

"Agent Walker, this is Corporal Graham of the RCMP."

Gripping her digital camera, Samara sat in the front row of the gym in her new suit.

Her fingers caressed the camera's buttons as she tried to bring her pulse rate to normal. Any anxiety she betrayed fit with the event.

Her heart was still racing from her encounter with Logan's mother. It was fortunate Samara had recognized her from Jake's photos.

How did she track them down to Cold Butte? It meant she knew something.

Samara looked around.

Did others know?

Thank heaven she was able to turn Logan away before he recognized her. It confirmed that her mission was destined because she was protected.

Soon. Very soon.

Three songs and six seconds. One minute to activate, then she could detonate. She brushed the button and welcomed a kaleidoscope of memories, giving her the sensation that she was floating.

She was a few feet from the pope.

Before anyone could stop her, it would be done.

Once the applause faded, Sobil Mounce-Bazley, the choir director, tapped her baton on her podium.

The shuffle of programs and throat-clearing underscored the nervous tension as the magnitude of the event registered with the children.

The helicopters, the police, TV news lights, camera flashes and all these people.

This was such a huge deal.

The man sitting over there was the pope.

This was a once-in-a-lifetime moment.

Sobil commanded the full attention of her singers but Logan couldn't stop thinking about his mother.

He had to find a way to call her again. And that incident with the crazy lady a few minutes ago was freaking him out. She'd sounded a bit like his mom.

And where was his dad?

Logan searched the audience for his father, even his mother, when Sobil tapped the baton and shot him a look.

Time to begin.

Phone tight to his ear, Walker had stepped aside to take Graham's urgent call.

The children's voices filled the gym with the first song as Graham quickly explained the links: Jake Conlin's homicide; Samara's martyr video; the Tarver murders; the traffic deaths; Maggie.

Everything.

The pieces fit.

"You've got to do something, Walker!"

"Give me her name again! She could be listed."

"Samara. Last name could be Russell or Ingram. I'm watching this thing play on her computer at the house." Graham had rifled through files and bills in the house. He detailed Samara's description as the live network coverage cut from the pope, to the choir, to audience reaction and back to the pope. "Walker, she's got to be there. I'm watching it live—there! That's her! There she is! That's her!"

"Where?"

"Grab her!"

"Where!"

"Front row. Taupe suit, dark hair, getting ready to take a picture."

As Walker responded, a few feet from him his boss, Hank Colby, agent in charge of security, got a call from Tony Takayasu in Indian Head, Maryland.

Other officials, including Colby's supervisor, were patched in to the call.

"Agent Colby, this is an urgent update to the substances found at Malmstrom and Washington State," Takayasu said. "We've identified a potential threat. The substances are components of a complex radio explosive."

"Have you confirmed it here? We've swept and scanned everything."

"No. It's a newly engineered fabric. Undetectable. We can't take risks."

"Fabric?" Fabric was everywhere—curtains, flags, school banners. Clothing, upholstery. "Give us details."

"We've got nothing yet," an NSA official explained, "but we've locked on the item's frequency range. Our satellites will alert us to any radio activity."

"Won't it be too late by then?" Colby's boss said.

"Should we detect a signal, you'll have time to respond," the NSA official said. "And, as a countermeasure we'll use the satellites to release a radio pulse to thwart any trigger signal. But the pulse is a last resort because of the downside."

"The downside?"

"It'll knock out all power and wireless transmission for a minute, or two," the NSA official said. "Meantime, sir, your team should work on removing your protectee as soon as possible."

"Will the Vatican pull the pope out?" Colby's boss asked.

"Not without confirmation," Colby said.

"You have my authority to physically remove the pope at your discretion, Hank," Colby's boss said.

Colby's ulcer burned.

He looked for Walker and found him behind a curtain consulting a floor plan, talking on his radio to agents.

83

Cold Butte, Montana

The choir's first song ended; the pope clasped his hands together in approval.

The audience applauded and Samara raised her camera to her face. Her finger moved over the button.

In one minute she would rewrite history.

In one minute the world would know her pain.

In one minute she would be with her husband and child.

She would activate, wait one minute, rush to the pope with her camera, then detonate. Her finger touched the raised button, caressed its smooth surface during the loud applause as she framed her target one last time before—

Someone bumped her.

A hand clamped over her camera, seizing it from her as someone gripped her arms, lifting her from her chair.

Two big men in suits.

"Medical emergency, Samara. Come with us," one said into her ear over the applause.

People watched as they took Samara away. News

cameras recorded her escort from the gym. Most shrugged as attention turned back to the pope.

The children commenced their second song.

From a steel chair in the command post, her wrists and ankles restrained in plastic handcuffs, Maggie Conlin watched events unfold.

The command post was housed in a customized RV equipped with banks of radios, computers, cameras and TV screens to monitor the papal event. Maggie had seen Samara's arrest.

"Oh, thank God, they've got her!"

Agents in the truck were annoyed that Walker had placed Maggie with them rather than in a patrol car. Some suggested it was to keep her from the press.

"Please, you have to let me talk to Agent Walker!"

"Ma'am—" a frustrated agent turned to her "—you need to be quiet, or we'll remove you to a police vehicle."

In an empty school hall, the agents placed Samara's wrists in plastic handcuffs, leaving her hands in front of her. Walker then joined them to rush her out of the school to a cordoned area shielded with steel Dumpsters. Explosives experts in protective gear immediately examined her.

News teams were kept back. Cameras were trained from a distance on the puzzling events rapidly taking place.

Colby called Walker at the scene, advising him that the weapon may be encased in fabric. Walker advised the bomb unit, but their search of Samara was in vain.

Nothing was detected.

Members of the bomb squad then began walking Samara toward a restricted area, beyond a far corner of the school parking lot, where the FBI and ATF bomb units were situated, along with the Montana Highway Patrol.

A specially built bomb hut, half buried and draped with blast mats, sat in an isolated corner. They would keep her in custody there.

But it was a long way off.

Walker didn't go. He hurried back into the school and called Graham to alert him to search the house for a new fabric purchase.

"A flag, material, anything?"

Returning to the stage, Walker feared that Samara wasn't working alone.

Half a world away, in Addis Ababa's Mercato, in the secret bunker hidden under his fabric shop, Amir and his senior commanders also watched events.

Huddled before a bank of laptops and TV screens displaying an array of images, they studied live news coverage of the pope's visit, a replaying of the grisly flag test, and a geo-display map showing the school.

Other images included Samara's martyr video, which would be sent to news organizations after her mission was completed.

"Something's amiss," one of the commanders said. "She should have activated at this stage. And we can't contact the security cell."

"She's been arrested, look." One of the men touched the TV monitor showing Samara being taken from the gym.

"We must abort," the first commander said. "This jeopardizes everything, the network. It could lead them to us. Do you agree?"

Amir blinked thoughtfully, then tapped his computer keyboard. He'd reviewed Samara's reports and her notes on the agenda for the choir.

They would sing three songs.

Then the pope would thank the children.

Personally.

"Patience. We'll override and detonate from here."

At the house, Graham watched Samara's arrest on television with a sinking feeling.

Where's Logan?

Graham searched the audience, then scanned the choir as it began the final song.

He called Walker.

"Walker, it's Graham, I've got more information."

"We've removed Samara." Walker had returned to the stage. "We've removed the threat."

"She should've had a boy with her, a nine-year-old boy named Logan Conlin, or Logan Russell."

"Logan."

"You should remove him, too."

At that moment, in Addis Ababa, Amir nodded and a code was entered into a laptop.

The weapon's one-minute activation count began.

Seconds raced by.

In Lone Tree County, in Jake Conlin's double-wide trailer, a red light began flashing on Samara's laptop and a digital clock began counting down.

Graham's stomach twisted.

"Walker," he said into his phone, "it's started! There's a countdown!"

Where's Logan?

Maggie!

Graham had forgotten about Maggie! Maybe she'd found Logan?

Graham reached for the other phone.

Walker alerted the command post, requesting an agent enter Logan's name into the event database.

His name came up.

"Logan is in the choir," the agent in the truck said, jerking Maggie's attention to the screen. It was split with Logan's school photo and live pictures of him.

"That's my son! That's Logan!"

As the final song ended with applause, Walker alerted the SWAT commander to Logan's position: third from the right, second row, dark suit, silver and navy tie.

"What are you doing with my son?" Maggie said.

Concealed in the ceiling, in the gym's ventilation system, an FBI sharpshooter radioed that he'd locked "the target" into his scope.

Colby, on his cell, had just been alerted by Takayasu.

"We've got activity, we're sending the pulse!"

Colby and Walker took Monsignor Paulo Guerelli aside.

"Monsignor, we must get the pope out of the building now! We have a serious threat!"

Guerelli's smile at the choir dimmed, his jaw tensed with disappointment.

"A threat? As we did in Seattle?"

Cameras flashed as, one by one, the children approached the pope. He embraced them, gave them each a gift.

Six seconds with each child.

"Monsignor," Colby said. "We must get him out!"

Guerelli nodded, then conferred in Latin with the other Vatican officials before responding. "We will leave when the Holy Father is finished giving gifts to the children."

Walker still had Graham on the line.

"Walker, I found a receipt in the house. Samara and Logan got new tailor-made suits a few days ago in Seattle!"

Logan was approaching the pope.

Walker alerted Colby and the SWAT commander. "It's the kid, Logan! *Logan is the weapon, take him out!*"

Maggie heard the order to shoot her son.

"No!"

Logan filled the sharpshooter's scope, Logan's face brightening into a smile as the pope opened his arms.

The crosshairs met square between Logan's eyes.

"I've got the target," the sharpshooter said.

Maggie screamed.

In Addis Ababa, Amir's detonation code left his bunker at the speed of light, hitting a satellite, then Montana at the same time Takayasu's pulse shot to earth.

"I've got him." The sharpshooter's finger began to squeeze.

Time was up.

Walker and several agents rushed to the pope.

At the house, the clock emptied to 00:00, the red light switched to a flashing green. Graham gripped the laptop and hammered it against the floor.

In the school, Logan's suit suddenly heated and he vanished in white from the scope, disappearing into a papal embrace as the satellite signals struck.

The gym's lights went out.

All radio contact died.

All live news coverage ended.

In the command post agents cursed as screens and monitors went black, radios and cell phones hissed with static.

"Damn!" A Brazilian TV crew outside the school had been following Samara's arrest, walking directly behind her escort when their live feed to Sao Paulo was cut.

The crew member's sudden cursing distracted the two agents who'd been taking Samara away from the school. When the agents turned to look behind them at the TV crew, Samara broke free and started running to the school, getting some ten yards ahead of the agents and crew before Amir's satellite signal detonated Samara's suit.

In the blinding, burning flash, Samara met her son, her husband, her mother, her father and smiled as the roaring moment of death hurtled her to communion in paradise.

The concussion wave sent the agents and Brazilian crew skimming over parked vehicles.

A terrifying thud rocked the gym.

The sharpshooter missed his target.

The gunfire triggered screams.

The death signal had reached Samara but the NSA's pulse had stopped it from reaching Logan. Walker had tackled him, pulling him away from the pope, covering the boy with his body.

Dazed and on the floor, the pope stared at them. Agents, weapons drawn, whisked the pope from the school and into an armor-plated SUV.

Walker tore Logan's suit from him; other agents and officers rushed to help.

Children cried in the chaos as school alarm bells clanged and all the gym's doors were thrust open.

"Get everybody out!" Walker shouted, then pointed to sandbags behind the stage. "Get as many of those as you can!"

They buried Logan's suit under sandbags, then hurried him out with the others, evacuating the building in under a minute.

In the command post, Maggie was hysterical.

"What happened! Somebody tell me!"

Agents tried frantically to restore power, switching on a generator. The console flicked back to life. Ignoring Maggie's pleas, the agents worked on restoring order in the aftermath of the attack.

The papal motorcade was shrouded in dust as it raced down an escape route over vacant fields to the Lone Tree County Fairgrounds. The pope was rushed into a helicopter which lifted off to an undisclosed location under jet fighter escort.

Power returned.

A fire burned at the site of the explosion, giving rise

to a small cloud. Paramedics aided the wounded agents and journalists. Miraculously, their injuries were not life-threatening.

Federal agents scrambled to assess the scope of the attack, while police officers helped get people away from the school area.

Colby ordered a controlled evacuation of the large gathering at Buffalo Breaks.

"Don't let them panic. Do it section by section, beginning with those closest to the large stage!"

News crews spoke to their desks, who had been trying repeatedly to reach them.

Two minutes and forty-seven seconds after the incident, a New York wire service issued the first words: EXPLOSION AT PAPAL VISIT TO U.S.—CASUALTIES

The breaking news alert flashed in newsrooms around the world, to TVs, Web sites, and public crawlers in Times Square, Tokyo, London, Toronto, Hong Kong, Berlin, Shanghai.

Within minutes the world knew of the attack.

Amid the confusion, Walker got Logan into a deputy's jacket and as they headed through the parking lot, Graham called Walker. After they exchanged information, Walker ordered Maggie Conlin released, then took Logan directly to the command post truck.

As Maggie emerged from the RV, her eyes found her son. She dropped to her knees and opened her arms.

Logan ran to her.

Against the spectral cloud of Samara's explosion, Maggie and Logan held each other, as the horror reeled around them.

Epilogue

On the day of the attack, the Vatican was steadfast against kneeling before a terrorist act. Hours after the scale of the incident became evident, the Vatican insisted that all the pilgrims who were sent away from the open-air Mass at the Buffalo Breaks be invited back.

Nearly all returned. Calm prevailed over the traffic gridlock and that evening the pope celebrated the work of Sister Beatrice in a ceremony lit with one hundred thousand candles. He called for peace, tolerance, understanding and love for all people of the world, likening those virtues to the stars that would guide humanity through its night of fear.

The investigation by U.S. and international security agencies led to a mercenary hiding in Algeria. The soldier, whose nationality was never determined, admitted to taking part in the assault on Samara's family. His admission led to other suspects and a trial for their crimes in an Iraqi court.

All were hanged.

Other global investigations resulted in the destruction of much of Amir's network, the arrest of several commanders and agents in the organization's cells in

Ethiopia, Morocco, South Africa, Spain, Italy, Malaysia, India, Pakistan, Afghanistan, Canada, Australia, New Zealand and the United States.

The investigation failed to find and arrest "the Believer," who was thought to have vanished somewhere in The Empty Quarter of Yemen and Saudi Arabia.

In Canada, the Royal Canadian Mounted Police, working with the Canadian Security Intelligence Service, the CIA, the FBI, British, German, French, Italian, Egyptian intelligence and other investigators around the world, concluded that Ray Tarver, his wife and their two children had been murdered by agents of Amir's network.

Interrogations of captured operatives in Berlin, Cairo, Rome and Paris enabled them to piece together what had happened.

When the network had discovered that Tarver, a reporter from Washington, D.C., was going to break the story of the attack, Amir devised the strategy to lure Tarver to the Rockies with the promise of a major story. Ray Tarver and his family were then murdered in what appeared to be a wilderness tragedy.

Kate Morrow, Tarver's former newsroom colleague, began writing a book about the case and the price he and his family paid. Part of the earnings would go to a journalism scholarship Ray's former wire service helped establish in his name.

The book's cover bore the powerful news photograph of the moment Maggie and Logan were reunited after the attack. It was shot that day by Luke Rappel, a teenage journalism student. The image would become known worldwide as the iconic portrait of the tragedy and go on to win many awards.

For his part, Graham needed time alone in the Alberta Rockies, where he'd spent entire days searching the Faust River for answers. Had he not been there at the outset, mourning Nora, he would not have found Emily Tarver, or the thread that led to the Conlins and the plot.

Had it all happened for a reason?

He didn't know.

Had he found a measure of redemption?

He didn't know.

For his action from the Faust River to Cold Butte, Graham was told he would receive the Governor General's Medal of Bravery. There was also talk that Graham, Walker and Takayasu's team were being considered for the President's Medal of Valor. And all of the people involved in thwarting the assassination were invited to the Vatican, where the pope thanked them personally.

Because Maggie's information contributed to the capture of key operatives in Amir's global network, a Manhattan law firm offered to represent her without charge, to ensure she received a fair portion of reward money posted by international security agencies. The amount sought was half a million dollars.

Jake Conlin was buried in a small cemetery in Northern California near a place where his parents had gone on vacation every summer. As a boy, Jake lived for the adventure of the long coastal drive. It nurtured his love for the road.

After the funeral, Maggie took comfort in Jake's

final e-mail message to her. She shared it with Logan during counseling sessions.

"He came back to us in the end, honey, always remember that."

Samara lived in her video.

She became known to the world as it played repeatedly in the postincident analysis of what came to be "The Montana Attack." It gave rise to debates and reviews of foreign policy, security, religion and global terrorism.

In the weeks and months afterward, Maggie studied Samara's video, replaying it countless times at night, hating her as the woman who had destroyed her family. But as Maggie continued analyzing the in-depth news profiles that dissected Samara's life and re-created the horrors leading up to the attack, Maggie's regard for her changed.

Again and again, Maggie's thoughts went back to the instant at the school when her eyes had met Samara's in one intense gaze. Maggie's loathing evolved into acceptance that she and Samara were never enemies. They were women from different worlds. They were mothers united by tragedies beyond their control.

And, late at night, when sleep would not come, Maggie found herself reconciling it all with a question that—although she would never know—was identical to the question Samara had asked when she came upon a child's foot on the street in Baghdad.

It was an ancient question no one could answer.

What are we doing to each other?

And in the time that followed, Graham would call Maggie and Logan to see how they were getting along.

Some six months later, he'd returned to California to take part in a symposium on security.

Maggie invited him to visit.

They went to the beach, where Logan flew a kite Graham had bought for him.

Maggie and Graham watched as it soared and held steady against the wind.

* * * * *

AUTHOR NOTE

Often I am asked where I get my ideas. In the case of this book, my ninth thriller, there is no single source. Only moments plucked from time. I was attending university when Pope John Paul II visited my city. As his papal parade passed by, a brooding international student who stood next to me—on what I swear was a grassy knoll—revealed that he didn't care much for the pope and wished that he'd had a weapon in his school bag. He assured me he was joking.

That afternoon, when I attended the pope's large outdoor Mass, I wondered about that student.

Years later, I was a reporter working with a colleague on an anniversary feature about a loner's "missed-by-a-whisker" plan to assassinate U.S. President Richard Nixon. For that item we talked to a number of people. I talked to former U.S. Secret Service agents who reflected on would-be assassins, the stress of protecting VIPs, and the work that goes on behind the scenes.

Then, several months after September 11, 2001, I was on assignment in Africa when I saw a small boy in a Nigerian village wearing a T-shirt bearing Osama bin Laden's face and words that praised him as a #1 hero. These moments, and so many others, stayed with me— like exploring the labyrinthian bazaars of Rabat, Morocco; talking with an armed palace guard in Dakar, Senegal; or visiting mud-hut villages in Ethiopia; or watching old women weave fabric in the slums of Addis Ababa; or driving over Kuwait's northern desert to the border with Iraq to hear UN peacekeepers at the DMZ talk about the toll land mines were exacting on Iraqi children.

Six Seconds took shape by blending these moments with history, my experiences and my imagination, for a tale that considers ordinary people caught up in extraordinary events.

ACKNOWLEDGMENTS

Producing this book was not an entirely solitary effort. In getting this story to you, I benefited by the hard, professional work and kind help of many people. My thanks to my agent, Amy Moore-Benson; and to Dianne Moggy, Valerie Gray and the superb marketing, sales and PR teams at MIRA Books.

I would also like to thank Shannon Whyte, Donna Riddell, Chris Rapking, Beth Tindall. Thanks to Mike Stotter, Ali Karim and the gang at www.shotsmag.co.uk.

George Easter at Deadly Pleasures; Sandra Ruttan at Spinetingler; the crew at Crime Spree Magazine and Mystery Scene Magazine. And Larry Gandle. As always, I am grateful to Wendy Dudley in Alberta. I am also indebted to my friends in the news business for their help and support—in particular, Sheldon Alberts, Washington Bureau Chief for CanWest News Service; Aileen McCabe, Shanghai, China Bureau, CanWest News Service; Juliet Williams, Associated Press, Sacramento, California; Vinnee Tong, Associated Press, New York; Lou Clancy; Eric Dawson; Jamie Portman; Mike Gillespie; colleagues past and present with the *Calgary Herald,* CanWest News, Canadian Press, Reuters and so many others. You know who you are.

For their help on law enforcement and security aspects of this story, I am grateful to Inspector Eddie J. Erdelatz, San Francisco Homicide Detail (Ret.); Superintendent Rick Taylor, Royal Canadian Mounted Police; Chief Superintendent Lloyd Hickman, Royal Canadian Mounted Police (Ret.). If the story rings true, it is because of their help. If it doesn't, fault me for failing to represent their suggestions properly and forgive me for any inaccuracies due to many, and I mean many, creative liberties I took.

As always, a huge thanks to Barbara, Laura and Michael who allow me to disappear into fictional worlds while they deal with the real one. Without their support, this book would not have been written.

My thanks to relatives and friends everywhere for their encouragement.

Again, I am indebted to sales representatives, booksellers and librarians for putting my work in your hands. I would like to thank reading circles and book clubs who've invited me to participate in person and by phone, for your invaluable support. Which brings me to you, the reader, the most important part of the entire enterprise. Thank you very much for your time, for without you, a book remains an untold tale.

I hope you enjoyed the ride and will check out my earlier books while watching for my next one. I welcome your feedback. Drop by at www.rickmofina.com to subscribe to my newsletter and send me a note.

R.M.